D1807959

Political and Literary essays, 1908-1913

by Earl of Evelyn Baring Cromer

CONTENTS

"THE EDINBURGH REVIEW"

I. The Government of Subject Races

II. Translation and Paraphrase

"THE QUARTERLY REVIEW"

III. Sir Alfred Lyall

"THE NINETEENTH CENTURY AND AFTER"

IV. Army Reform

V. The International Aspects of Free Trade

VI. China

VII. The Capitulations in Egypt

"THE SPECTATOR"

VIII. Disraeli

IX. Russian Romance

X. The Writing of History

XI. The Greek Anthology

XII. Lord Milner and Party

XIII. The French in Algeria

XIV. The Ottoman Empire

XV. Wellingtoniana

XVI. Burma

XVII. A Pseudo-Hero of the Revolution

XVIII. The Future of the Classics

XIX. An Indian Idealist

XX. The Fiscal Question in India

XXI. Rome and Municipal Government

XXII. A Royal Philosopher

XXIII. Ancient Art and Ritual

XXIV. Portuguese Slavery

XXV.   England and Islam

XXVI.   Some Indian Problems

XXVII.   The Napoleon of Taine

XXVIII.   Songs, Patriotic and National

XXIX.   Songs, Naval and Military

Index

I

THE GOVERNMENT OF SUBJECT RACES
"The Edinburgh Review," January 1908

The "courtly Claudian," as Mr. Hodgkin, in his admirable and instructive work, calls the poet of the Roman decadence, concluded some lines which have often been quoted as applicable to the British Empire, with the dogmatic assertion that no limit could be assigned to the duration of Roman sway. *Nec terminus unquam Romanae ditionis erit.* At the time this hazardous prophecy was made, the huge overgrown Roman Empire was tottering to its fall. Does a similar fate await the British Empire? Are we so far self-deceived, and are we so incapable of peering into the future as to be unable to see that many of the steps which now appear calculated to enhance and to stereotype Anglo-Saxon domination, are but the precursors of a period of national decay and senility?

A thorough examination of this vital question would necessarily involve the treatment of a great variety of subjects. The heart of the British Empire is to be found in Great Britain. It is not proposed in this place to deal either with the working of British political institutions, or with the various important social and economic problems which the actual condition of England presents, but only with the extremities of the body politic, and more especially with those where the inhabitants of the countries under British rule are not of Anglo-Saxon origin.

What should be the profession of faith of a sound but reasonable Imperialist? He will not be possessed with any secret desire to see the whole of Africa or of Asia painted red on the maps. He will entertain not only a moral dislike, but also a political mistrust of that excessive earth-hunger, which views with jealous eyes the extension of other and neighbouring European nations. He will have no fear of competition. He will believe that, in the treatment of subject races, the methods of government practised by England, though sometimes open to legitimate criticism, are superior, morally and economically, to those of any other foreign nation; and that, strong in the possession and maintenance of those methods, we shall be able to hold our own against all competitors.

On the other hand, he will have no sympathy with those who, as Lord Cromer said in a recent speech, "are so fearful of Imperial greatness that they are unwilling that we should accomplish our manifest destiny, and who would thus have us sink into political insignificance by refusing the main title which makes us great."

An Imperial policy must, of course, be carried out with reasonable prudence, and the principles of government which guide our relations with whatsoever races are brought under our control must be politically and economically sound and morally defensible. This is, in fact, the keystone of the Imperial arch. The main justification of Imperialism is to be found in the use which is made of the Imperial power. If we make a good use of our power, we may face the future without fear that we shall be overtaken by the Nemesis which attended Roman misrule. If the reverse is the case, the British Empire will deserve to fall, and of a surety it will ultimately fall. There is truth in the saying, of which perhaps we sometimes hear rather too much, that the maintenance of the Empire depends on the sword; but so little does it depend on the sword alone that if once we have to draw the sword, not merely to suppress some local effervescence, but to overcome a general upheaval of subject races goaded to action either by deliberate oppression, which is highly improbable, or by unintentional misgovernment, which is far more conceivable, the sword will assuredly be powerless to defend us for long, and the days of our Imperial rule will be numbered.

To those who believe that when they rest from their earthly labours their works will follow them, and that they must account to a Higher Tribunal for the use or misuse of any powers which may have been entrusted to them in this world, no further defence of the plea that Imperialism should rest on a moral basis is required. Those who entertain no such belief may perhaps be convinced by the argument that, from a national point of view, a policy based on principles of sound morality is wiser, inasmuch as it is likely to be more successful, than one which excludes all considerations save those of cynical self-interest. There was truth in the commonplace remark made by a subject of ancient Rome, himself a slave and presumably of Oriental extraction, that bad government will bring the mightiest empire to ruin.

Some advantage may perhaps be derived from inquiring, however briefly and imperfectly, into the causes which led to the ruin of that political edifice, which in point of grandeur and extent, is alone worthy of comparison with the British Empire. The subject has been treated by many of the most able writers and thinkers whom the world has produced—Gibbon, Guizot, Mommsen, Milman,

5

Seeley, and others. For present purposes the classification given by Mr. Hodgkin of the causes which led to the downfall of the Western Empire has been adopted. They were six in number, viz.:

1. The foundation of Constantinople.
2. Christianity.
3. Slavery.
4. The pauperisation of the Roman proletariat.
5. The destruction of the middle class by the fiscal oppression of the Curiales.
6. Barbarous finance.

1. *The Foundation of Constantinople.*—It is, for obvious reasons, unnecessary to discuss this cause. It was one of special application to the circumstances of the time, notably to the threatening attitude towards Rome assumed by the now decadent State of Persia.

2. *Christianity.*—That the foundation of Christianity exercised a profoundly disintegrating effect on the Roman Empire is unquestionable. Gibbon, although he possibly confounds the tenets of the new creed with the defects of its hierarchy, dwells with characteristic emphasis on this congenial subject. Mr. Hodgkin, speaking of the analogy between the British present and the Roman past, says:

The Christian religion is with us no explosive force threatening the disruption of our most cherished institutions. On the contrary, it has been said, not as a mere figure of speech, that "Christianity is part of the common law of England." And even the bitterest enemies of our religion will scarcely deny that, upon the whole, a nation imbued with the teaching of the New Testament is more easy to govern than one which derived its notions of divine morality from the stories of the dwellers on Olympus.

From the special point of view now under consideration, the case for Christianity admits of being even more strongly stated than this, for no attempt will be made to deal with the principles which should guide the government of a people imbued with the teaching of the New Testament, but rather with the subordinate, but still highly important question of the treatment which a people, presumed to be already imbued with that teaching, should accord to subject races who are ignorant or irreceptive of its precepts. From this point of view it may be said that Christianity, far from being an explosive force, is not merely a powerful ally. It is an ally without whose assistance continued success is unattainable. Although dictates of worldly prudence and opportunism are alone sufficient to ensure the rejection of a policy of official proselytism, it is none the less true that the code of Christian morality is the only sure foundation on which the whole of our vast Imperial fabric can be built if it is to be durable. The stability of our rule depends to a great extent upon whether the forces acting in favour of applying the Christian code of morality to subject races are capable of overcoming those moving in a somewhat opposite direction. We are inclined to think that our Teutonic veracity and gravity, our national conscientiousness, our British spirit of fair play, to use the cant phrase of the day, our free institutions, and our press—which, although it occasionally shows unpleasant symptoms of sinking beneath the yoke of special and not highly reputable interests, is still greatly superior in tone to that of any other nation—are sufficient guarantees against relapse into the morass of political immorality which characterised the relations between nation and nation, and notably between the strong and the weak, even so late as the eighteenth century. It is to be hoped and believed that, for the time being, this contention is well founded, but what assurance is there—if the Book which embodies the code of Christian morality may without irreverence be quoted—that "that which is done is that which shall be done"? That is the crucial question.

There appear to be at present existent in England two different Imperial schools of thought, which, without being absolutely antagonistic, represent very opposite principles. One school, which, for want of a better name, may be styled that of philanthropy, is occasionally tainted with the zeal which outruns discretion, and with the want of accuracy which often characterises those whose emotions predominate over their reason. The violence and want of mental equilibrium at times displayed by the partisans of this school of thought not infrequently give rise to misgivings lest the Duke of Wellington should have prophesied truly when he said, "If you lose India, the House of Commons will lose it for you." These manifest defects should not, however, blind us to the fact that the philanthropists and sentimentalists are deeply imbued with the grave national responsibilities which devolve on England, and with the lofty aspirations which attach themselves to her civilising and moralising mission.

The other is the commercial school. Pitt once said that "British policy is British trade." The general correctness of this aphorism cannot be challenged, but, like most aphorisms, it only conveys a portion of the truth; for the commercial spirit, though eminently beneficent when under some degree of moral control, may become not merely hurtful, but even subversive of Imperial dominion, when it is allowed to run riot. Livingstone said that in five hundred years the only thing the natives of Africa had learnt from the Portuguese was to distil bad spirits with the help of an old gun barrel. This is, without doubt, an extreme case—so extreme, indeed, that even the hardened conscience of diplomatic Europe was eventually shamed into taking some half-hearted action in the direction of preventing a whole continent from being demoralised in order that the distillers and vendors of cheap spirits might realise large profits. But it would not be difficult to cite other analogous, though less striking, instances. Occasions are, indeed, not infrequent when the interests of commerce apparently clash with those of good government. The word "apparently" is used with intent; for though some few individuals may acquire a temporary benefit by sacrificing moral principle on the altar of pecuniary gain, it may confidently be stated that, in respect to the wider and more lasting benefits of trade, no real antagonism exists between commercial self-interest and public morality.

To be more explicit, what is meant when it is said that the commercial spirit should be under some control is this—that in dealing with Indians or Egyptians, or Shilluks, or Zulus, the first question is to consider what course is most conducive to Indian, Egyptian, Shilluk, or Zulu interests. We need not always inquire too closely what these people, who are all, nationally speaking, more or less *in statu pupillari*, themselves think is best in their own interests, although this is a point which deserves serious consideration. But it is essential that each special issue should be decided mainly with reference to what, by the light of Western knowledge and experience tempered by local considerations, we conscientiously think is best for the subject race, without reference to any real or supposed advantage which may accrue to England as a nation, or—as is more frequently the case— to the special interests represented by some one or more influential classes of Englishmen. If the British nation as a whole persistently bears this principle in mind, and insists sternly on its application, though we can never create a patriotism akin to that based on affinity of race or community of language, we may perhaps foster some sort of cosmopolitan allegiance grounded on the respect always accorded to superior talents and unselfish conduct, and on the gratitude derived both from favours conferred and from those to come. There may then at all events be some hope that the Egyptian will hesitate before he throws in his lot with any future Arabi The Berberine dweller on the banks of the Nile may, perhaps, cast no wistful glances back to the time when, albeit he or his progenitors were oppressed, the oppression came from the hand of a co-religionist. Even the Central African savage may eventually learn to chant a hymn in honour of *Astraea Redux*, as represented by the British official who denies him gin but gives him justice. More than this, commerce will gain. It must necessarily follow in the train of civilisation, and, whilst it will speedily droop if that civilisation is spurious, it will, on the other hand, increase in volume in direct proportion to the extent to which the true principles of Western progress are assimilated by the subjects of the British king and the customers of the British trader. This latter must be taught patience at the hands, of the statesman and the moralist. It is a somewhat difficult lesson to learn. The trader not only wishes to acquire wealth; he not infrequently wishes that its acquisition should be rapid, even at the expense of morality and of the permanent interests of his country.

Nam dives qui fieri vult, Et cito vult fieri. Sed quae reverentia legum, Quis metus aut pudor est unquam properantis avari?

This question demands consideration from another point of view. A clever Frenchman, keenly alive to what he thought was the decadence of his own nation, published a remarkable book in 1897. He practically admitted that the Anglophobia so common on the continent of Europe is the outcome of jealousy. He acknowledged the proved superiority of the Anglo-Saxon over the Latin races, and he set himself to examine the causes of that superiority. The general conclusion at which he arrived was that the strength of the Anglo-Saxon race lay in the fact that its society, its government, and its habits of thought were eminently "particularist," as opposed to the "communitarian" principles prevalent on the continent of Europe. He was probably quite right. It has, indeed, become a commonplace of English political thought that for centuries past, from the days of Raleigh to those of Rhodes, the position of England in the world has been due more to the exertions, to the resources, and occasionally, perhaps, to the absence of scruple found in the individual Anglo-Saxon, than to any encouragement or help derived from British Governments, whether of the Elizabethan, Georgian, or Victorian type. The principle of relying largely on individual effort has, in truth, produced marvellous results. It is singularly suited to develop some of the best qualities of the vigorous, self-assertive Anglo-Saxon race. It is to be hoped that self-help may long continue to be our national watchword.

It is now somewhat the fashion to regard as benighted the school of thought which was founded two hundred years ago by Du Quesnay and the French Physiocrates, which reached its zenith in the person of Adam Smith, and whose influence rapidly declined in England after the great battle of Free Trade had been fought and won. But whatever may have been the faults of that school, and however little its philosophy is capable of affording an answer to many of the complex questions which modern government and society present, it laid fast hold of one unquestionably sound principle. It entertained a deep mistrust of Government interference in the social and economic relations of life. Moreover, it saw, long before the fact became apparent to the rest of the world, that, in spite not only of some outward dissimilarities of methods but even of an instinctive mutual repulsion, despotic bureaucracy was the natural ally of those communistic principles which the economists deemed it their main business in life to combat and condemn. Many regard with some disquietude the frequent concessions which have of late years been made in England to demands for State interference. Nevertheless, it is to be hoped that the main principle advocated by the economists still holds the field, that individualism is not being crushed out of existence, and that the majority of our countrymen still believe that State interference—being an evil, although sometimes admittedly a necessary evil—should be jealously watched and restricted to the minimum amount absolutely necessary in each special case.

Attention is drawn to this point in order to show that the observations which follow are in no degree based on any general desire to exalt the power of the State at the expense of the individual.

Our habits of thought, our past history, and our national character all, therefore, point in the direction of allowing individualism as wide a scope as possible in the work of national expansion. Hence the career of the East India Company and the tendency displayed more recently in Africa to govern through the agency of private companies. On the other hand, it is greatly to be doubted whether the principles, which a wise policy would dictate in the treatment of subject races, will receive their application to so full an extent at the hands of private individuals as would be the case at the hands of the State. The guarantee for good government is even less solid where power is entrusted to a corporate body, for, as Turgot once said, "La morale des corps les plus scrupuleux ne vaut jamais celle des particuliers honnêtes." In both cases, public opinion is relatively impotent. In the case of direct Government action, on the other hand, the views of those who wish to uphold a high standard of public morality can find expression in Parliament, and the latter can, if it chooses, oblige the Government to control its agents and call them to account for unjust, unwise, or overbearing conduct. More than this, State officials, having no interests to serve but those of good government, are more likely to pay regard to the welfare of the subject race than commercial agents, who must necessarily be hampered in their action by the pecuniary interests of their employers.

Our national policy must, of course, be what would be called in statics the resultant of the various currents of opinion represented in our national society. Whether Imperialism will continue to rest on a sound basis depends, therefore, to no small extent, on the degree to which the moralising elements in the nation can, without injury to all that is sound and healthy in individualist action, control those defects which may not improbably spring out of the egotism of the commercial spirit, if it be subject to no effective check.

If this problem can be satisfactorily solved, then Christianity, far from being a disruptive force, as was the case with Rome, will prove one of the strongest elements of Imperial cohesion.

3. *Slavery.*—It is not necessary to discuss this question, for there can be no doubt that, in so far as his connexion with subject races is concerned, the Anglo-Saxon in modern times comes, not to enslave, but to liberate from slavery. The fact that he does so is, indeed, one of his best title-deeds to Imperial dominion.

4. *The Pauperisation of the Roman Proletariat.*—This is the *Panem et Circenses* policy. Mr. Hodgkin appears to think that in this direction lies the main danger which threatens the British Empire.

"Of all the forces," he says, "which were at work for the destruction of the prosperity of the Roman world, none is more deserving of the careful study of an English statesman than the grain-largesses to the populace of Rome.... Will the great Democracies of the twentieth century resist the temptation to use political power as a means of material self-enrichment?"

Possibly Mr. Hodgkin is right. The manner in which the leaders of the Paris Commune dealt with the rights of property during their disastrous, but fortunately very brief, period of office in 1871, serves as a warning of what, in an extreme case, may be expected of despotic democracy in its most aggravated form. Moreover, misgovernment, and the fiscal oppression which is the almost necessary accompaniment of militarism dominant over a poverty-stricken population, have latterly developed on the continent of Europe, and more especially in Italy, a school of action—for anarchism can scarcely be dignified by the name of a school of thought—which regards human life as scarcely more sacred than property. It may be that some lower depth has yet to be reached, although it is almost inconceivable that such should be the case. Anarchy takes us past the stage of any defined political or social programme. It would appear, so far as can at present be judged, to embody the last despairing cry of ultra-democracy "Furens."

It is permissible to hope that our national sobriety, coupled with the inherited traditions derived from centuries of free government, will save us from such extreme manifestations of democratic tyranny as those to which allusion has been made above. The special danger in England would appear rather to arise from the probability of gradual dry rot, due to prolonged offence against the infallible and relentless laws of economic science. Both British employers of labour and British workmen are insular in their habits of thought, and insular in the range of their acquired knowledge. They do not appear as yet to be thoroughly alive to the new position created for British trade by foreign competition. It is greatly to be hoped that they will awake to the realities of the situation before any permanent harm is done to British trade, for the loss of trade involves as its ultimate result the pauperisation of the proletariat, the adoption of reckless expedients based on the *Panem et Circenses* policy to fill the mouths and quell the voices of the multitude, and finally the suicide of that Empire which is the offspring of trade, and which can only continue to exist so long as its parent continues to thrive and to flourish.

5. *The Destruction of the Middle Class by the Fiscal Oppression of the Curiales.*—Leaving aside points of detail, which were only of special application to the circumstances of the time, this cause of Roman decay may, for all purposes of comparison and instruction, be stated in the following terms: funds, which should have been spent by the municipalities on local objects, were, from about the close of the third century, diverted to the Imperial Exchequer, by which they were not infrequently squandered in such a manner as to confer no benefit of any kind on the taxpayers, whether local or Imperial. Thus, the system of local self-government, which, Mr. Hodgkin says, was, during the early centuries of the Empire, "both in name and fact Republican," was shattered.

It does not appear probable that an attempt will ever be made to divert the public revenues of the outlying dependencies of Great Britain to the Imperial Exchequer. The lesson taught by the loss of the American Colonies has sunk deeply into the public mind. Moreover, the example of Spain stands as a warning to all the world. The principle that local revenues should be expended locally has become part of the political creed of Englishmen; neither is it at all likely to be infringed, even in respect to those dependencies whose rights and privileges are not safeguarded by self-governing institutions.

There may, however, be some little danger ahead in a sense exactly opposite to that which was incurred by Rome—the danger, that is to say, that, under the pressure of Imperialism, backed by influential class and personal interests, too large an amount of the Imperial revenue may be diverted to the outlying dependencies. If this were done, two evils might not improbably ensue.

In the first place, the British democracy might become restive under taxation imposed for objects the utility of which would not perhaps be fully appreciated, and might therefore be disposed to cast off too hastily the mantle of Imperialism. It is but a short time ago that an influential school of politicians persistently dwelt on the theme that the colonies were a burthen to the Mother Country. Although, for the time being, views of this sort are out of fashion, no assurance can be felt that the swing of the pendulum may not bring round another anti-Imperialist phase of public opinion.

In the second place, if financial aid to any considerable extent were afforded by the British Treasury to the outlying dependencies, a serious risk would be run that this concession would be followed at no distant period by a plea in favour of financial control from England. The establishment of this latter principle would strike a blow at one of the main props on which our Imperial fabric is based. It would tend to substitute a centralised, in the place of our present decentralised system. Those who are immediately responsible for the administration of our outlying dependencies will, therefore, act wisely if they abstain from asking too readily for Imperial pecuniary aid in order to solve local difficulties.

These considerations naturally lead to some reflections on the principles of government adopted in those dependencies of the Empire, the inhabitants of which are not of the Anglo-Saxon race. Colonies whose inhabitants are mainly of British origin stand, of course, on a wholly different footing. They carry their Anglo-Saxon institutions and habits of thought with them to their distant homes.

Englishmen are less imitative than most Europeans in this sense—that they are less disposed to apply the administrative and political systems of their own country to the government of backward populations; but in spite of their relatively high degree of political elasticity, they cannot shake themselves altogether free from political conventionalities. Moreover, the experienced minority is constantly being pressed by the inexperienced majority in the direction of imitation. Knowing the somewhat excessive degree of adulation which some sections of the British public are disposed to pay to their special idol, Lord Dufferin, in 1883, was almost apologetic to his countrymen for abstaining from an act of political folly. He pleaded strenuously for delay in the introduction of parliamentary institutions into Egypt, on the ground that our attempts "to mitigate predominant absolutism" in India had been slow, hesitating, and tentative. He brought poetic metaphor to his aid. He deprecated paying too much attention to the "murmuring leaves," in other words, imagining that the establishment of a Chamber of Notables implied constitutional freedom, and he exhorted his countrymen "to seek for the roots," that is to say, to allow each Egyptian village to elect its own mayor (Sheikh).

It cannot be too clearly understood that whether we deal with the roots, or the trunk, or the branches, or the leaves, free institutions in the full sense of the term must for generations to come be wholly unsuitable to countries such as India and Egypt. If the use of a metaphor, though of a less polished type, be allowed, it may be said that it will probably never be possible to make a Western silk purse out of an Eastern sow's ear; at all events, if the impossibility of the task be called in question, it should be recognised that the process of manufacture will be extremely lengthy and tedious.

But it is often urged that, although no rational person would wish to advocate the premature creation of ultra-liberal institutions in backward countries, at the same time that for several reasons it is desirable to move gradually in this direction. The adoption of this method is, it is said, the only way to remedy the evils attendant on a system of personal government in an extreme form; it enables us to learn the views of the natives of the country, even although we may not accord to the latter full power of deciding whether or not those views should be put in practice; lastly, it constitutes a means of political education, through the agency of which the subject race will gradually acquire the qualities necessary to autonomy.

The force of these arguments cannot be denied, but there should be no delusion as to the weight which should be attached to them. It has been very truly remarked by a writer, who has dealt with the idiosyncrasies of a singularly versatile nation, whose genius presented in every respect a marked contrast to that of Eastern races, that from the dawn of history Eastern politics have been "stricken with a fatal simplicity." Do not let us for one moment imagine that the fatally simple idea of despotic rule will readily give way to the far more complex conception of ordered liberty. The transformation, if it ever takes place at all, will probably be the work, not of generations, but of centuries.

So limited is the stock of political ideas in the world that some modified copy of parliamentary institutions is, without doubt, the only method which has yet been invented for mitigating the evils attendant on the personal system of government. But it is a method which is thoroughly uncongenial to Oriental habits of thought. It may be doubted whether, by the adoption of this exotic system, we gain any real insight into native aspirations and opinions. As to the educational process, the experience of India is not very encouraging. The good government of most Indian towns depends to this day mainly, not on the Municipal Commissioners, who are generally natives, but on the influence of the President, who is usually an Englishman.

A further consideration in connection with this point is also of some importance. It is that British officials in Eastern countries should be encouraged by all possible means to learn the views and the requirements of the native population. The establishment of mock parliaments tends rather in the opposite direction, for the official on the spot sees through the mockery and is not infrequently disposed to abandon any attempt to ascertain real native opinion, through disgust at the unreality, crudity, or folly of the views set forth by the putative representatives of native society.

For these reasons it is important that, in our well-intentioned endeavours to impregnate the Oriental mind with our insular habits of thought, we should proceed with the utmost caution, and that we should remember that our primary duty is, not to introduce a system which, under the specious cloak of free institutions, will enable a small minority of natives to misgovern their countrymen, but to establish one which will enable the mass of the population to be governed according to the code of Christian morality. A freely elected Egyptian Parliament, supposing such a thing to be possible, would not improbably legislate for the protection of the slave-owner, if not the slave-dealer, and no assurance can be felt that the electors of Rajputana, if they had their own way, would not re-establish suttee. Good government has the merit of presenting a more or less attainable ideal. Before Orientals can attain anything approaching to the British ideal of self-government they will have to undergo very numerous transmigrations of political thought.

The question of local self-government may be considered from another, and almost equally important point of view.

When writers such as M. Demolins speak of the "particularist" system of England and of the "communitarian" system prevalent on the continent of Europe, they generally mean to contrast the British plan of acting through the agency of private individuals with the Continental practice of relying almost entirely on the action of the State. This is the primary and perhaps the most important signification of the two phrases, but the principles which these phrases are intended to represent admit of another application.

It is difficult for those Englishmen who have not been brought into business relations with Continental officials to realise the extreme centralisation of their administrative and diplomatic procedures. The tendency of every French central authority is to allow no discretionary power whatever to his subordinate. He wishes, often from a distance, to control every detail of the administration. The tendency of the subordinate, on the other hand, is to lean in everything on superior authority. He does not dare to take any personal responsibility; indeed, it is possible to go further and say that the corroding action of bureaucracy renders those who live under its baneful shadow almost incapable of assuming responsibility. By force of habit and training it has become irksome to them. They fly for refuge to a superior official, who, in his turn, if the case at all admits of the adoption of such a course, hastens to merge his individuality in the voluminous pages of a code or a Government circular.

The British official, on the other hand, whether in England or abroad, is an Englishman first and an official afterwards. He possesses his full share of national characteristics. He is by inheritance an individualist. He lives in a society which, so far from being, as is the case on the Continent, saturated with respect for officialism, is somewhat prone to regard officialism and incompetency as synonymous terms. By such association, any bureaucratic tendency which may exist on the part of the British official is kept in check, whilst his individualism is subjected to a sustained and healthy course of tonic treatment.

Thus, the British system breeds a race of officials who relatively to those holding analogous posts on the Continent, are disposed to exercise their central authority in a manner sympathetic to individualism; who, if they are inclined to err in the sense of over-centralisation, are often held in check by statesmen imbued with the decentralising spirit; and who, under these influences, are inclined to accord to local agents a far wider latitude than those trained in the Continental school of bureaucracy would consider either safe or desirable.

On the other hand, looking to the position and attributes of the local agents themselves, it is singular to observe how the habit of assuming responsibility, coupled with national predispositions acting in the same direction, generates and fosters a capacity for the beneficial exercise of power. This feature is not merely noticeable in comparing British with Continental officials, but also in contrasting various classes of Englishmen *inter se*. The most highly centralised of all our English offices is the War Office. For this reason, and also because a military life necessarily and rightly engenders a habit of implicit obedience to orders, soldiers are generally less disposed than civilians to assume personal responsibility and to act on their own initiative. Nevertheless, whether in military or civil life, it may be said that the spirit of decentralisation pervades the whole British administrative system, and that it has given birth to a class of officials who have both the desire and the capacity to govern, who constitute what Bacon called the *Participes curarum*, namely, "those upon whom Princes doe discharge the greatest weight of their affaires," and who are instruments of incomparable value in the execution of a policy of Imperialism.

The method of exercising the central control under the British system calls for some further remarks. It varies greatly in different localities.

Under the Indian system a council of experts is attached to the Secretary of State in England. A good authority on this subject says that there can be no question of the advantage of this system.

No man, however experienced and laborious, could properly direct and control the various interests of so vast an Empire, unless he were aided by men with knowledge of different parts of the country, and possessing an intimate acquaintance with the different and complicated subjects involved in the government and welfare of so many incongruous races.

On the assumption that India is to be governed from London, there can be no doubt of the validity of this argument. But, as has been frequently pointed out, this system tends inevitably towards over-centralisation, and if the British Government is to continue to exercise a sort of παγκρατορία to use an expressive Greek phrase, over a number of outlying dependencies of very various types, over-centralisation is a danger which should be carefully shunned. It is wiser to obtain local knowledge from those on the spot, rather than from those whose local experience must necessarily diminish in value in direct proportion to the length of the period during which they have been absent from the special locality, and who, moreover, are under a strong temptation, after they leave the dependency, to exercise a detailed control over their successors. It is greatly to be doubted, therefore, whether, should the occasion arise, this portion of the Indian system is deserving of reproduction.

There is, however, another portion of that system which is in every respect admirable, and the creation of which bears the impress of that keen political insight which, according to many Continental authorities, is the birthright of the Anglo-Saxon race. India is governed locally by a council composed mainly of officials who have passed their adult lives in the country; but the Viceroy, and occasionally the legal and financial members of Council, are sent from England and are usually chosen by reason of their general qualifications, rather than on account of any special knowledge of Indian affairs. This system avoids the dangers consequent on over-centralisation, whilst at the same time it associates with the administration of the country some individuals who are personally imbued with the general principles of government which are favoured by the central authority. Its tendency is to correct the defect from which the officials employed in the outlying portions of the Empire are most likely to suffer, namely, that of magnifying the importance of some local event or consideration, and of unduly neglecting arguments based on considerations of wider Imperial import. It enhances the idea of proportion, which is one of the main qualities necessary to any politician or governing body. Long attention to one subject, or group of subjects, is apt to narrow the vision of specialists. The adjunct of an element, which is not Anglo-Indian, to the Indian Government acts as a corrective to this evil. The members of the Government who are sent from England, if they have no local experience, are at all events exempt from local prejudices. They bring to bear on the questions which come before them a wide general knowledge and, in many cases, the liberal spirit and vigorous common sense which are acquired in the course of an English parliamentary career.

It may be added, as a matter of important detail, that it would be desirable, in order to give continuity to Indian policy, to select young men to fill the place of Viceroy, and to extend the period of office from five to seven, or even to ten years.

Although over-centralisation is to be avoided, a certain amount of control from a central authority is not only unavoidable; if properly exercised, it is most beneficial. One danger to which the local agent is exposed is that, being ill-informed of circumstances lying outside his range of political vision, he may lose sight of the general principles which guide the policy of the Empire; he may treat subjects of local interest in a manner calculated to damage, or even to jeopardise, Imperial interests. The central authority is in a position to obviate any danger arising from this cause. To ensure the harmonious working of the different parts of the machine, the central authority should endeavour, so far as is possible, to realise the circumstances attendant on the government of the dependency; whilst the local agent should be constantly on the watch lest he should overrate the importance of some local issue, or fail to appreciate fully the difficulties which beset the action of the central authority.

To sum up all that there is to be said on this branch of the subject, it may be hoped that the fate which befell Rome, in so far as it was due to the special causes of decay now under consideration, may be averted by close adherence to two important principles. The first of these principles is that local revenues should be expended locally. The second is that over-centralisation should above all things be avoided. This may be done either by the creation of self-governing institutions in those dependencies whose civilisation is sufficiently advanced to justify the adoption of this course; or by decentralising the executive Government in cases where self-government, in the ordinary acceptation of the term, is impossible or undesirable.

6. *Barbarous Finance.*—Mr. Hodgkin says that the system of Imperial taxation under the Roman Empire was "wasteful, oppressive, and in a word, barbarous." He gives, as an instance in point, the Roman Indiction. This was the name given to the system under which the taxable value of the land throughout the Empire was reassessed every fifteen years. At each reassessment, Mr. Hodgkin says, "the few who had prospered found themselves assessed on the higher value which their lands had acquired, while the many who were sinking down into poverty obtained, it is to be feared, but little relief from taxation on account of the higher rate which was charged to all."

It is somewhat unpleasant to reflect that the system which Mr. Hodgkin so strongly condemns, and which he even regards as one of the causes of the downfall of the Roman Empire, is—save in respect to the intervals of periodical reassessment—very similar to that which exists everywhere in India, except in the province of Bengal, where the rights conferred on the zemindars under Lord Cornwallis's Permanent Settlement are still respected in spite of occasional unwise suggestions that time and the fall in the value of the rupee have obliterated any moral obligations to maintain them. Nor are the results obtained in India altogether dissimilar from those observable under Roman rule. The knowledge that reassessment was imminent has, it is believed, often discouraged the outlay of private capital on improving the land. More than this, it is notorious that, at one time, some provinces suffered greatly from the mistakes made by the settlement officers. These latter were animated with the best intentions, but, in spite of their marked ability—for they were all specially selected men—they often found the task entrusted to them impossible of execution. Unfortunately political or administrative errors cannot be condoned by reason of good intentions. Like the Greeks of old, the natives of India suffer from the mistakes of their rulers.

The intentions of the British, as compared with the Roman Government are, however, noteworthy from one point of view, inasmuch as from a correct appreciation of those intentions it is possible to evolve a principle perhaps in some degree calculated to avert the consequences which befell Rome, partly by reason of fiscal errors.

In spite of some high-sounding commonplaces which were at times enunciated by Roman lawgivers and statesmen, and in which a ring of utilitarian philosophy is to be recognised, and of the further fact that, as in the case of Verres, a check was sometimes applied to the excesses of local Governors, it is almost certainly true that the rulers of Rome did not habitually act on the recognition of any very strong moral obligation binding on the Imperial Government in its treatment of subject races. The merits of any fiscal system were probably judged mainly from the point of view of the amount of funds which it poured into the Treasury. The fiscal principles on which the Emperors of Rome acted survived long after the fall of the Roman Empire. They deserve the epithet of "barbarous" which Mr. Hodgkin has bestowed upon them.

The point of departure of the British Government is altogether different. Its intentions are admirable. Every farthing which has been spent—and, it may be feared, often wasted—on the numerous military expeditions in which the Government of India has been engaged during the last century would, in the eyes of many, certainly be considered as expenditure incurred on objects which were of paramount interest to the Indian taxpayers. Moreover, a whole category of British legislation connected with fiscal matters has been undertaken, not so much with a view to increase the revenue as with the object of distributing the burthen of taxation equally amongst the different classes of society. Much of this legislation has been perfectly justifiable and even beneficial. Nevertheless, it should never be forgotten that it is generally based on the purely Western principle that abstract justice is in itself a desirable thing to attain, and that a fiscal or administrative system stands condemned if it is wanting in symmetry. It was against any extreme application of this principle that Burke directed some of his most forcible diatribes. It has been already pointed out that the commendable want of intellectual symmetry which is the inherited possession of the Englishman gives him a very great advantage as an Imperialist agent over those trained in the rigid and bureaucratic school of Continental Europe. But the Englishman is a Western, albeit an Anglo-Saxon Western, and, from the point of view of all processes of reasoning, the gulf which separates any one member of the European family from another is infinitely less wide than that which divides all Westerns from all Orientals. Even the Englishman, therefore, is constrained—sometimes much against his will—to bow down in that temple of Logic, the existence of which the Oriental is disposed altogether to ignore. Indeed, sometimes the choice lies between the enforcement on the reluctant Oriental of principles based on logic—occasionally on the very simple science of arithmetic—or abandoning the work of civilisation altogether. From this point of view, the dangers to which the British Empire is exposed by reason of fiscal measures are due not, as was the case with Rome, to barbarous, but rather to ultra-scientific finance. The following is a case in point.

The land-tax has always been the principal source from which Oriental potentates have derived their revenues. For all practical purposes it may be said that the system which they have adopted has generally been to take as much from the cultivators as they could get. Reformers, such as the Emperor Akbar, have at times endeavoured to introduce more enlightened methods of taxation, and to carry into practice the theories upon which the fiscal system in all Moslem countries is based. Those theories are by no means so objectionable as is often supposed. But the reforms which some few capable rulers attempted to introduce have almost always crumbled away under the régime of their successors. In practice, the only limit to the demands of the ruler of an Oriental State has been the ability of the taxpayers to satisfy them. The only defence of the taxpayers has lain in the concealment of their incomes at the risk of being tortured till they divulged their amount.

Nevertheless, even under such a system as this, the wind is tempered to the shorn lamb by the fact that Oriental rulers recognise that they cannot get money from a man who possesses none. If, from drought or other causes, the cultivator raises no crop, he is not required to pay any land-tax. The idea of expropriation for the non-payment of taxes is purely Western and modern. Under Roman law, it was the rule in contracts for rent that a tenant was not bound to pay if any *vis major* prevented him from reaping.

The European system is very different. A far less heavy demand is made on the cultivator, but he is, at all events in principle and sometimes in practice, called upon to meet it in good and bad years alike. He is expected to save in years of plenty in order to make good the deficit in lean years. If he is unable to pay, he is liable to be expropriated, and he often is expropriated. This plan is just, logical, and very Western. It may be questioned whether Oriental cultivators do not sometimes rather prefer the oppression and elasticity of the Eastern to the justice and rigidity of the Western system.

Various palliatives have been adopted in India with a view to giving some elasticity to the working of the Land Revenue system. In Egypt, where the administration is much less Anglicised than in India, and where, for various reasons, the treatment of this subject presents relatively fewer difficulties, it is the practice now, as was the case under purely native rule, to remit the taxes on what is known as *Sharaki* lands, that is to say, land which, owing to a low Nile, has not been irrigated. It is not, however, necessary to dwell on the details of this subject. It will be sufficient to draw attention to the different points of view from which the Eastern and the Western approach the subject of fiscal administration. The latter urges with unanswerable logic that financial equilibrium must be maintained, and that he cannot frame a trustworthy Budget unless he knows the amount he may count on receiving from direct taxes, especially from the land-tax. The Eastern replies that he knows nothing of either financial equilibrium or of budgets, that it has, indeed, from time immemorial been the custom to leave him nought but a bare pittance when he had money, but to refrain from any endeavours to extort money from him when he had none.

Another instance drawn, not from the practices of fiscal administration, but from legislation on a cognate subject, may be cited.

Directly Western civilisation comes in contact with a backward Oriental Society, the relations between debtor and creditor are entirely changed. A social revolution is effected. The Western applies his code with stern and ruthless logic. The child-like Eastern, on the other hand, cannot be made to understand that his house should be sold over his head because he affixed his seal to a document, which, very probably, he had never read, or, at all events, had never fully understood, and which was presented to him by a man at one time apparently animated with benevolent intentions, inasmuch as he wished to lend him money, but who subsequently showed his malevolence by asking to be repaid his loan with interest at an exorbitant rate.

Here, again, many palliatives have been suggested and some have been applied, but many of them sin against the economic law, which provides that legislation intended to protect a man against the consequences of his own folly or improvidence is generally unproductive of result.

In truth, no thoroughly effective remedy can be applied in cases such as those mentioned above, without abandoning all real attempt at progress. Civilisation must, unfortunately, have its victims, amongst whom are to some extent inevitably numbered those who do not recognise the paramount necessities of the Budget system, and those who contract debts with an inadequate appreciation of the *caveat emptor* principle. Nevertheless, the Western financier will act wisely if, casting aside some portion of his Western habit of thought, he recognises the facts with which he has to deal, and if, fully appreciating the intimate connection between finance and politics in an Eastern country, he endeavours, so far as is possible, to temper the clean-cut science of his fiscal measures in such a manner as to suit the customs and intellectual standard of the subject race with which he has to deal.

The question of the amount of taxation levied stands apart from the method of its imposition. It may be laid down as a principle of universal application that high taxation is incompatible with assured stability of Imperial rule.

The financier and the hydraulic engineer, who is a powerful ally of the financier, have probably a greater potentiality of creating an artificial and self-interested loyalty than even the judge. The reasons are obvious. In the first place, the number of criminals, or even of civil litigants, in any society is limited; whereas practically the whole population consists of taxpayers. In the second place, the arbitrary methods of administering justice practised by Oriental rulers do not shock their subjects nearly so much as Europeans are often disposed to think. Custom has made it in them a property of easiness. They often, indeed, fail to appreciate the intentions, and are disposed to resent the methods, of those whose object it is to establish justice in the law-courts. On the other hand, the most ignorant Egyptian fellah or Indian ryot can understand the difference between a Government which takes nine-tenths of his crop in the shape of land-tax, and one which only takes one-third or one-fourth. He can realise that he is better off if the water is allowed to flow periodically on to his fields, than he was when the influential landowner, who possessed a property up-stream on the canal, made a dam and prevented him from getting any water at all.

These principles would probably meet with general acceptance from all who have considered the question of Imperial rule. They are, indeed, almost commonplace. Unfortunately, in practice the necessity of conforming to them is often forgotten. India is the great instance in point. Englishmen are often so convinced that the natives of India ought to be loyal, they hear so much said of their loyalty, they appreciate so little the causes which are at work to produce disloyalty, and, in spite of occasional mistakes due to errors of judgment, they are in reality so earnestly desirous of doing what they consider, sometimes perhaps erroneously, their duty towards the native population, that they are apt to lose sight of the fact that the self-interest of the subject race is the principal basis of the whole Imperial fabric. They forget, whilst they are adding to the upper story of the house, that the foundations may give way.

This is not the place to enter into any lengthy discussion upon Indian affairs. It may be said, however, that the Indian history of the last few years certainly gives cause for some anxiety. Attention was at one time too exclusively paid to frontier policy, which constitutes only one, and that not the most important, element of the complex Indian problem.

That the policy of "masterly inactivity," to use the phrase epigrammatically, but perhaps somewhat incorrectly, applied to the line of action advocated by Lord Lawrence in 1869, required some modifications as the onward movement of Russia in Asia developed, will scarcely be contested by the most devoted of Lawrentian partisans and followers. That those modifications were wisely introduced is a proposition the truth of which it is difficult to admit. The portion of Lord Lawrence's programme which was necessarily temporary, inasmuch as it depended on the circumstances of the time, was rejected without taking sufficient account of the further and far more important portion which was of permanent application. This latter portion was defined in an historic and oft-quoted despatch which he indited on the eve of his departure from India, and which may be regarded as his political testament. In this despatch, Lord Lawrence, speaking with all the authority due to a lifelong acquaintance with Indian affairs, laid down the broad general principle that the strongest security of our rule lay "in the contentment, if not in the attachment, of the masses." The truth of this general principle was at one time too much neglected. Under the influence of a predominant militarism acting on too pliant politicians, vast military expenditure was incurred. Territory lying outside the natural geographical frontier of India was occupied, the acquisition of which was condemned not merely by sound policy, but also by sound strategy. Taxation was increased, and, generally, the material interests of the natives of India were sacrificed and British Imperial rule exposed to subsequent danger, in order to satisfy the exigencies of a school of soldier-politicians who only saw one, and that the most technical, aspect of a very wide and complex question.

Neither, unfortunately, is there any sure guarantee that the mistakes, which it is now almost universally admitted were made, will not recur. Where, indeed, are we to look for any effective check? The rulers of India, whether they sit in Calcutta or London, may again be carried away by the partial views of an influential class, or of a few masterful individuals. It is absurd to speak of creating free institutions in India to control the Indian Government. Experience has shown that parliamentary action in England not infrequently degenerates into acrimonious discussion and recrimination dictated by party passion; in any case, it is generally too late to change the course of events. Still less reliance can be placed on the action of the British Press, which falls a ready victim to the specious arguments advanced by some strategical pseudo-Imperialist in high position, or by some fervent acolyte who has learnt at the feet of his master the fatal and facile lesson of how an Empire, built up by statesmen, may be wrecked by the well-intentioned but mistaken measures recommended by specialists to ensure Imperial salvation. The managers of the London newspapers afford, indeed, be it said to their credit, every facility for the publication of views adverse to those which they themselves advocate. But it is none the less true that, during the years when the unwise frontier policy of a few years ago was being planned and executed, the voices of the opposition, although they were those of Indian statesmen and officials who could speak with the highest authority, failed to obtain an adequate hearing until the evil was irremediable. On the other hand, the views of the strategical specialists went abroad over the land, with the result that ill-informed and careless public opinion followed their advice without having any very precise idea of whither it was being led.

It would appear, therefore, that there is need for great care and watchfulness in the management of Indian affairs. That same inconsistency of character and absence of definite aim, which are such notable Anglo-Saxon qualities and which adapt themselves so admirably to the requirements of Imperial rule, may in some respects constitute an additional danger. If we are not to adopt a policy based on securing the contentment of the subject race by ministering to their material interests, we must of necessity make a distinct approach to the counter-policy of governing by the sword alone. In that case, it would be as well not to allow a free native Press, or to encourage high education. Any repressive or retrograde measures in either of these directions would, without doubt, meet with strong and, to a great extent, reasonable opposition in England. A large section of the public, forgetful of the fact that they had stood passively by whilst measures, such as the imposition of increased taxes, which the natives of India really resent, were adopted, would protest loudly against the adoption of other measures which are, indeed, open to objection, but which nevertheless touch Oriental in a far less degree than they affect Western public feeling. The result of this inconsistency is that our present system rather tends to turn out demagogues from our colleges, to give them every facility for sowing their subversive views broadcast over the land, and at the same time to prepare the ground for the reception of the seed which they sow. Now this is the very reverse of a sound Imperial policy. We cannot, it is true, effectually prevent the manufacture of demagogues without adopting measures which would render us false to our acknowledged principles of government and to our civilising mission. But we may govern in such a manner as to give the demagogue no fulcrum with which to move his credulous and ill-informed countrymen and co-religionists. The leading principle of a government of this nature should be that low taxation is the most potent instrument with which to conjure discontent. This is the policy which will tend more than any other to the stability of Imperial rule. If it is to be adopted, two elements of British society will have to be kept in check at the hands of the statesman acting in concert with the moralist. These are Militarism and Commercial Egotism. The Empire depends in a great degree on the strength and efficiency of its army. It thrives on its commerce. But if the soldier and the trader are not kept under some degree of statesmanlike control, they are capable of becoming the most formidable, though unconscious, enemies of the British Empire.

It will be seen, therefore, that though there are some disquieting circumstances attendant on our Imperial rule, the general result of an examination into the causes which led to the collapse of Roman power, and a comparison of those causes with the principles on which the British Empire is governed, are, on the whole, encouraging. To every danger which threatens there is a safeguard. To every portion of the body politic in which symptoms of disease may occur, it is possible to apply a remedy.

Christianity is our most powerful ally. We are the sworn enemies of the slave-dealer and the slave-owner. The dangers arising from the possible pauperisation of the proletariat may, it is to be hoped, be averted by our national character and by the natural play of our time-honoured institutions. If we adhere steadily to the principle that local revenues are to be expended locally, and if, at the same time, we give all reasonable encouragement to local self-government and shun any tendency towards over-centralisation, we shall steer clear of one of the rocks on which the Roman ship of state was wrecked. Unskilful or unwise finance is our greatest danger, but here again the remedy lies ready to hand if we are wise enough to avail ourselves of it. It consists in adapting our fiscal methods to the requirements of our subject races, and still more in the steadfast rejection of any proposals which, by rendering high taxation inevitable, will infringe the cardinal principle on which a sound Imperial policy should be based. That principle is that, whilst the sword should be always ready for use, it should be kept in reserve for great emergencies, and that we should endeavour to find, in the contentment of the subject race, a more worthy and, it may be hoped, a stronger bond of union between the rulers and the ruled.

If any more sweeping generalisation than this is required, it may be said that the whole, or nearly the whole, of the essential points of a sound Imperial policy admit of being embodied in this one statement, that, whilst steadily avoiding any movement in the direction of official proselytism, our relations with the various races who are subjects of the King of England should be founded on the granite rock of the Christian moral code.

Humanity, as it passes through phase after phase of the historical movement, may advance indefinitely in excellence; but its advance will be an indefinite approximation to the Christian type. A divergence from that type, to whatever extent it may take place, will not be progress, but debasement and corruption. In a moral point of view, in short, the world may abandon Christianity, but can never advance beyond it. This is not a matter of authority, or even of revelation. If it is true, it is a matter of reason as much as anything in the world.

II
TRANSLATION AND PARAPHRASE
"The Edinburgh Review," July 1913
When Emerson said "We like everything to do its office, whether it be a milch-cow or a rattlesnake," he assumed, perhaps somewhat too hastily in the latter case, that all the world understands the functions which a milch-cow or a rattlesnake is called upon to perform. No one can doubt that the office of a translator is to translate, but a wide difference of opinion may exist, and, in fact, has always existed, as to the latitude which he may allow himself in translating. Is he to adhere rigidly to a literal rendering of the original text, or is paraphrase permissible, and, if permissible, within what limits may it be adopted? In deciding which of these courses to pursue, the translator stands between Scylla and Charybdis. If he departs too widely from the precise words of the text, he incurs the blame of the purist, who will accuse him of foisting language on the original author which the latter never employed, with the possible result that even the ideas or sentiments which it had been intended to convey have been disfigured. If, on the other hand, he renders word for word, he will often find, more especially if his translation be in verse, that in a cacophonous attempt to force the genius of one language into an unnatural channel, the whole of the beauty and even, possibly, some of the real meaning of the original have been allowed to evaporate. Dr. Fitzmaurice-Kelly, in an instructive article on Translation contributed to the *Encyclopaedia Britannica* quotes the high authority of Dryden as to the course which should be followed in the execution of an ideal translation.

A translator (Dryden writes) that would write with any force or spirit of an original must never dwell on the words of his author. He ought to possess himself entirely, and perfectly comprehend the genius and sense of his author, the nature of the subject, and the terms of the art or subject treated of; and then he will express himself as justly, and with as much life, as if he wrote an original; whereas he who copies word for word loses all the spirit in the tedious transfusion.

In the application of Dryden's canon a distinction has to be made between prose and verse. The composition of good prose, which Coleridge described as "words in the right order," is, indeed, of the utmost importance for all the purposes of the historian, the writer on philosophy, or the orator. An example of the manner in which fine prose can bring to the mind a vivid conception of a striking event is Jeremy Collier's description of Cranmer's death, which excited the enthusiastic admiration of Mr. Gladstone. He seemed "to repel the force of the fire and to overlook the torture, by strength of thought." Nevertheless, the main object of the prose writer, and still more of the orator, should be to state his facts or to prove his case. Cato laid down the very sound principle "rem tene, verba sequentur," and Quintilian held that "no speaker, when important interests are involved, should be very solicitous about his words." It is true that this principle is one that has been more often honoured in the breach than the observance. Lucian, in his *Lexiphanes*, directs the shafts of his keen satire against the meticulous attention to phraseology practised by his contemporaries. Cardinal Bembo sacrificed substance to form to the extent of advising young men not to read St. Paul for fear that their style should be injured, and Professor Saintsbury mentions the case of a French author, Paul de Saint-Victor, who "used, when sitting down to write, to put words that had struck his fancy at intervals over the sheet, and write his matter in and up to them." These are instances of that word-worship run mad which has not infrequently led to dire results, inasmuch as it has tended to engender the belief that statesmanship is synonymous with fine writing or perfervid oratory. The oratory in which Demosthenes excelled, Professor Bury says, "was one of the curses of Greek politics."

The attention paid by the ancients to what may be termed tricks of style has probably in some degree enhanced the difficulties of prose translation. It may not always be easy in a foreign language to reproduce the subtle linguistic shades of Demosthenic oratory—the Anaphora (repetition of the same word at the beginning of co-ordinate sentences following one another), the Anastrophe (the final word of a sentence repeated at the beginning of one immediately following), the Polysyndeton (the same conjunction repeated), or the Epidiorthosis (the correction of an expression). Nevertheless, in dealing with a prose composition, the weight of the arguments, the lucidity with which the facts are set forth, and the force with which the conclusions are driven home, rank, or should rank, in the mind of the reader higher than any feelings which are derived from the music of the words or the skilful order in which they are arranged. Moreover, in prose more frequently than in verse, it is the beauty of the idea expressed which attracts rather than the language in which it is clothed. Thus, for instance, there can be no difficulty in translating the celebrated metaphor of Pericles that "the loss of the youth of the city was as if the spring was taken out of the year," because the beauty of the idea can in no way suffer by presenting it in English, French, or German rather than in the original Greek. Again, to quote another instance from Latin, the fine epitaph to St. Ovinus in Ely Cathedral: "Lucem tuam Ovino da, Deus, et requiem," loses nothing of its terse pathos by being rendered into English. Occasionally, indeed, the truth is forced upon us that even in prose "a thing may be well said once but cannot be well said twice" (τὸ καλῶς εἰπεῖν ἅπαξ περιγίγνεται, δὶς δὲ οὐκ ἐνδέχεται), but this is generally because the genius of one language lends itself with special ease to some singularly felicitous and often epigrammatic form of expression which is almost or sometimes even quite untranslatable. Who, for instance, would dare to translate into English the following description which the Duchesse de Dino gave of a lady of her acquaintance: "Elle n'a jamais été jolie, mais elle était blanche et fraîche, *avec quelques jolis détails*"? On the whole, however, it may be said that if the prose translator is thoroughly well acquainted with both of the languages which he has to handle, he ought to be able to pay adequate homage to the genius of the one without offering undue violence to that of the other.

The case of the translator of poetry, which Coleridge defined as "the best words in the best order," is manifestly very different. A phrase which is harmonious or pregnant with fire in one language may become discordant, flat, and vapid when translated into another. Shelley spoke of "the vanity of translation." "It were as wise (he said) to cast a violet into a crucible that you might discover the formal principle of its colour and odour, as seek to transfuse from one language into another the creations of a poet."

Longinus has told us that "beautiful words are the very light of thought" (φῶς γὰρ τῷ ὄντι ἴδιον τοῦ νοῦ τὰ καλὰ ὀνόματα), but it will often happen, in reading a fine passage, that on analysing the sentiments evoked, it is difficult to decide whether they are due to the thought or to the beauty of the words. A mere word, as in the case of Edgar Poe's "Nevermore," has at times inspired a poet. When Keats, speaking of Melancholy, says:

She lives with Beauty—Beauty that must die— And Joy, whose hand is ever on his lips, Bidding adieu,

or when Mrs. Browning writes:

... Young As Eve with Nature's daybreak on her face,

the pleasure, both of sense and sentiment, is in each case derived alike from the music of the language and the beauty of the ideas. But in such lines as

Arethusa arose from her couch of snows, etc.,

or Coleridge's description of the river Alph running

Through caverns measureless to man Down to a sunless sea,

it is the language rather than the idea which fascinates. Professor Walker, speaking of the most exquisitely harmonious lyric ever written in English, or perhaps in any other language, says with great truth: "The reader of *Lycidas* rises from it ready to grasp the 'two-handed engine' and smite; though he may be doubtful what the engine is, and what is to be smitten."

It may be observed, moreover, that one of the main difficulties to be encountered in translating some of the masterpieces of ancient literature arises from their exquisite simplicity. Although the indulgence in glaring improprieties of language in the pursuit of novelty of thought was not altogether unknown to the ancients, and was, indeed, stigmatised by Longinus with the epithet of "corybantising," the full development of this pernicious practice has been reserved for the modern world. Dryden made himself indirectly responsible for a good deal of bad poetry when he said that great wits were allied to madness. The late Professor Butcher, as also Lamb in his essay on "The Sanity of True Genius," have both pointed out that genius and high ability are eminently sane.

In some respects it may be said that didactic poetry affords special facilities to the translator, inasmuch as it bears a more close relation to prose than verse of other descriptions. Didactic poets, such as Lucretius and Pope, are almost forced by the inexorable necessities of their subjects to think in prose. However much we may admire their verse, it is impossible not to perceive that, in dealing with subjects that require great precision of thought, they have felt themselves hampered by the necessities of metre and rhythm. They may, indeed, resort to blank verse, which is a sort of half-way house between prose and rhyme, as was done by Mr. Leonard in his excellent translation of Empedocles, of which the following specimen may be given:

οὐκ ἔστιν πελάσασθαι ἐν ὀφθαλμοῖσιν ἐφεκτὸν ἡμετέροις ἢ χερσὶ λαβεῖν, ᾗπερ τε μεγίστη πειθοῦς ἀνθρώποισιν ἁμαξιτὸς εἰς φρένα πίπτει.

We may not bring It near us with our eyes, We may not grasp It with our human hands. With neither hands nor eyes, those highways twain, Whereby Belief drops into the minds of men.

But Dr. Symmons, one of the numerous translators of Virgil, said, with some truth, that the adoption of blank verse only involves "a laborious and doubtful struggle to escape from the fangs of prose."

A good example of what can be done in this branch of literature is furnished by Dryden. Lucretius wrote:

Tu vero dubitabis et indignabere obire? Mortua cui vita est prope iam vivo atque videnti, Qui somno partem maiorem conteris aevi, Et vigilans stertis nec somnia cernere cessas Sollicitamque geris cassa formidine mentem Nec reperire potes tibi quid sit saepe mali, cum Ebrius urgeris multis miser undique curis, Atque animi incerto fluitans errore vagaris.

Dryden's translation departs but slightly from the original text and at the same time presents the ideas of Lucretius in rhythmical and melodious English:

And thou, dost thou disdain to yield thy breath, Whose very life is little more than death? More than one-half by lazy sleep possest, And when awake, thy soul but nods at best, Day-dreams and sickly thoughts revolving in thy breast. Eternal troubles haunt thy anxious mind, Whose cause and case thou never hopest to find, But still uncertain, with thyself at strife, Thou wanderest in the labyrinth of life.

Descriptive poetry also lends itself with comparative ease to translation. Nothing can be better than the translation made by Mr. Gladstone of *Iliad* iv. 422-32. The original Greek runs thus:

ὡς δ' ὅτ' ἐν αἰγιαλῷ πολυηχέι· κῦμα θαλάσσης ὄρνυτ' ἐπασσύτερον Ζεφύρου ὕπο κινήσαντος· πόντῳ μέν τε πρῶτα κορύσσεται, αὐτὰρ ἔπειτα χέρσῳ ῥηγνύμενον μεγάλα βρέμει, ἀμφὶ δέ τ' ἄκρας κυρτὸν ἐὸν κορυφοῦται, ἀποπτύει δ' ἁλὸς ἄχνην· ὣς τότ' ἐπασσύτεραι Δαναῶν κίνυντο φάλαγγες νωλεμέως πόλεμόνδε. κέλευε δὲ οἷσιν ἕκαστος ἡγεμόνων· οἱ δ' ἄλλοι ἀκὴν ἴσαν, οὐδέ κε φαίης τόσσον λαὸν ἕπεσθαι ἔχοντ' ἐν στήθεσιν αὐδήν, σιγῇ, δειδιότες σημάντορας· ἀμφὶ δὲ πᾶσι τεύχεα ποικίλ' ἔλαμπε, τὰ εἱμένοι ἐστιχόωντο.

Mr. Gladstone, who evidently drew his inspiration from the author of "Marmion" and "The Lady of the Lake," translated as follows:

As when the billow gathers fast With slow and sullen roar, Beneath the keen north-western blast, Against the sounding shore. First far at sea it rears its crest, Then bursts upon the beach; Or with proud arch and swelling breast, Where headlands outward reach, It smites their strength, and bellowing flings Its silver foam afar— So stern and thick the Danaan kings And soldiers marched to war. Each leader gave his men the word, Each warrior deep in silence heard, So mute they marched, them couldst not ken They were a mass of speaking men; And as they strode in martial might Their flickering arms shot back the light.

It is, however, in dealing with poetry which is neither didactic nor descriptive that the difficulty— indeed often the impossibility—of reconciling the genius of the two languages becomes most apparent. It may be said with truth that the best way of ascertaining how a fine or luminous idea can be presented in any particular language is to set aside altogether the idea of translation, and to inquire how some master in the particular language has presented the case without reference to the utterances of his predecessors in other languages. A good example of this process may be found in comparing the language in which others have treated Vauvenargues' well-known saying: "Pour exécuter de grandes choses, il faut vivre comme si on ne devait jamais mourir." Bacchylides put the same idea in the following words:

θνατὸν εὖντα χρὴ διδύμους ἀέξειν γνώμας, ὅτι τ' αὔριον ὄψεαι μοῦνον ἁλίου φάος, χὤτι πεντήκοντ' ἔτεα ζωὰν βαθύπλουτον τελεῖς.

And the great Arab poet Abu'l'Ala, whose verse has been admirably translated by Mr. Baerlein, wrote:

If you will do some deed before you die, Remember not this caravan of death, But have belief that every little breath Will stay with you for an eternity.

Another instance of the same kind, which may be cited without in any way wishing to advance what Professor Courthope very justly calls "the mean charge of plagiarism," is Tennyson's line, "His honour rooted in dishonour stood." Euripides expressed the same idea in the following words:

ἐκ τῶν γὰρ αἰσχρῶν ἐσθλὰ μηχανώμεθα.

To cite another case, the following lines of *Paradise Lost* may be compared with the treatment accorded by Euripides to the same subject:

Oh, why did God, Creator wise, that peopled highest Heaven With spirits masculine, create at last This novelty on Earth, this fair defect Of Nature, and not fill the World at once With men as Angels, without feminine; Or find some other way to generate Mankind?

Euripides wrote:

ὦ Ζεῦ, τί δὴ κίβδηλον ἀνθρώποις κακόν, γυναῖκας ἐς φῶς ἡλίου κατῴκισας; εἰ γὰρ βρότειον ἤθελες σπεῖραι γένος, οὐκ ἐκ γυναικῶν χρῆν παρασχέσθαι τόδε.

Apart, however, from the process to which allusion is made above, very many instances may, of course, be cited, of translations properly so called which have reproduced not merely the exact sense but the vigour of the original idea in a foreign language with little or no resort to paraphrase. What can be better than Cowley's translation of Claudian's lines?—

Ingentem meminit parvo qui germine quercum Aequaevumque videt consenuisse nemus.

A neighbouring wood born with himself he sees, And loves his old contemporary trees,

thus, as Gibbon says, improving on the original, inasmuch as, being a good botanist, Cowley "concealed the oaks under a more general expression."

Take also the case of the well-known Latin epigram:

Omne epigramma sit instar apis: sit aculeus illi; Sint sua mella; sit et corporis exigui.

It has frequently been translated, but never more felicitously or accurately than by the late Lord Wensleydale:

Be epigrams like bees; let them have stings; And Honey too, and let them be small things.

On the other hand, the attempt to adhere too closely to the text of the original and to reject paraphrase sometimes leads to results which can scarcely be described as other than the reverse of felicitous. An instance in point is Sappho's lines:

καὶ γὰρ αἰ φεύγει, ταχέως διώξει, αἰ δὲ δῶρα μὴ δέκετ', ἄλλα δώσει, αἰ δὲ μὴ φίλει, ταχέως φιλήσει κωὺκ ἐθέλοισα.

So great a master of verse as Mr. Headlam translated thus:

The pursued shall soon be the pursuer! Gifts, though now refusing, yet shall bring Love the lover yet, and woo the wooer, Though heart it wring!

Many of Mr. Headlam's translations are, however, excellent, more especially those from English into Greek. He says in his preface: "Greek, in my experience, is easier to write than English." He has admirably reproduced the pathetic simplicity of Herrick's lines:

Here a pretty baby lies, Sung to sleep with Lullabies; Pray be silent and not stir The easy earth that covers her.

μήτηρ βαυκαλόωσά μ' ἐκοίμισεν· ἀτρέμα βαῖνε μὴ 'γείρῃς κούφην γῆν μ' ἐπιεσσόμενον.

Many singularly happy attempts to render English into Latin or Greek verse are given in Mr. Kennedy's fascinating little volume *Between Whiles*, of which the following example may be quoted:

Few the words that I have spoken; True love's words are ever few; Yet by many a speechless token Hath my heart discoursed to you.

οἶδα παῦρ' ἔπη λαλήσας· παῦρ' ἔρως λαλεῖν φιλεῖ· ξυμβόλοις δ' ὅμως ἀναύδοις σοὶ τὸ πᾶν ἠνιξάμην.

The extent to which it is necessary to resort to paraphrase will, of course, vary greatly, and will largely depend upon whether the language into which the translation is made happens to furnish epithets and expressions which are rhythmical and at the same time correspond accurately to those of the original. Take, for instance, a case such as the following fragment of Euripides:

τὰ μὲν διδακτὰ μανθάνω, τὰ δ' εὑρετὰ ζητῶ, τὰ δ' εὐκτὰ παρὰ θεῶν ᾐτησάμην.

There is but little difficulty in turning this into English verse with but slight resort to paraphrase:

I learn what may be taught; I seek what may be sought; My other wants I dare To ask from Heaven in prayer,

But in a large majority of cases paraphrase is almost imposed on the translator by the necessities of the case. Mr. William Cory's rendering of the famous verses of Callimachus on his friend Heraclitus, which is too well known to need quotation, has been justly admired as one of the best and most poetic translations ever made from Greek, but it can scarcely be called a translation in the sense in which that term is employed by purists. It is a paraphrase.

It is needless to dwell on the difficulty of finding any suitable words capable of being adapted to the necessities of English metre and rhythm for the numerous and highly poetic adjectives in which the Greek language abounds. It would tax the ingenuity of any translator to weave into his verse expressions corresponding to the ἁλιερκέες ὄχθαι (sea-constraining cliffs) or the Μναμοσύνας λιπαράμπυκος (Mnemosyne of the shining fillet) of Pindar. Neither is the difficulty wholly confined to poetry. A good many epithets have from time to time been applied to the Nile, but none so graphic or so perfectly accurate as that employed by Herodotus, who uses the phrase ὑπὸ τοσούτου τε ποταμοῦ καὶ οὕτω ἐργατικοῦ. The English translation "that vast river, so constantly at work" is a poor equivalent for the original Greek. German possesses to a greater degree than any other modern language the word-coining power which was such a marked characteristic of Greek, with the result that it offers special difficulties to the translator of verse. Mr. Brandes quotes the following lines of the German poet Bücher:

Welche Heldenfreudigkeit der Liebe, Welche Stärke muthigen Entsagens, Welche himmlisch erdentschwungene Triebe, Welche Gottbegeistrung des Ertragens! Welche Sich-Erhebung, Sich-Erwiedrung, Sich-Entäussrung, völl'ge Hin-sich-gebung, Seelenaustausch, Ineinanderlebung!

It is probable that these lines have never been translated into English verse, and it is obvious that no translation, which did not largely consist of paraphrase, would be possible.

Alliteration, which is a powerful literary instrument in the hands of a skilful writer, but which may easily be allowed to degenerate into a mere jingle, is of less common occurrence in Greek than in English, notably early English, literature. It was, however, occasionally employed by both poets and dramatists. Euripides, for instance, in the *Cyclops* (l. 120) makes use of the following expression, which would serve as a good motto for an Anarchist club, ἀκούει δ' οὐδὲν οὐδεὶς οὐδενός. Clytemnestra, also, in speaking of the murder of her husband (*Ag.* 1551-52) says:

πρὸς ἡμῶν κάππεσε, κάτθανε, καὶ καταθάψομεν.

That Greek alliteration is capable of imitation is shown by Pope's translation of the well-known line:

πολλὰ δ' ἄναντα κάταντα πάραντά τε δόχμιά τ' ἦλθον·

O'er hills, o'er dales, o'er crags, o'er rocks, they go.

Pope at times brought alliteration to his aid in cases where no such device had been adopted by Homer, as when, in describing the labours of Sisyphus, he wrote:

With many a weary step, and many a groan, Up the high hill he heaves a huge round stone.

On the whole, although a good deal more than is contained in this article may be said on either side, it would appear that, broadly speaking, Dryden's principle holds good for prose translations, and that experience has shown, in respect to translations in verse, that, save in rare instances, a resort to paraphrase is necessary.

The writer ventures, in conclusion, to give two instances, in one of which there has been comparatively but slight departure from the text of the original Greek, whilst in the other there has been greater indulgence in paraphrase. Both are taken from the Anthology. The first is an epitaph on a shipwrecked sailor by an unknown author:

Ναυτίλε, μὴ πεύθου τίνος ἐνθάδε τύμβος ὅδ' εἰμί, ἀλλ' αὐτὸς πόντου τύγχανε χρηστοτέρου.

No matter who I was; but may the sea To you prove kindlier than it was to me.

The other is by Macedonius:

Αὔριον ἀθρήσω σε· τὸ δ' οὔ ποτε γίνεται ἡμῖν ἠθάδος ἀμβολίης αἰὲν ἀεξομένης· ταῦτά μοι ἱμείροντι χαρίζεαι, ἄλλα δ' ἐς ἄλλους δῶρα φέρεις, ἐμεθέν πίστιν ἀπειπαμένη. ὄψομαι ἑσπερίη σε. τί δ' ἕσπερός ἐστι γυναικῶν; γήρας ἀμετρήτῳ πληθόμενον ῥυτίδι.

Ever "To-morrow" thou dost say; When will to-morrow's sun arise? Thus custom ratifies delay; My faithfulness thou dost despise. Others are welcomed, whilst to me "At even come," thou say'st, "not now." What will life's evening bring to thee? Old age—a many-wrinkled brow.

Dryden's well-known lines in *Aurengzebe* embody the idea of Macedonius in epigrammatic and felicitous verse:

Trust on, and think to-morrow will repay, To-morrow's falser than the former day.

"THE QUARTERLY REVIEW"

III
SIR ALFRED LYALL
"Quarterly Review," July 1913

After reading and admiring Sir Mortimer Durand's life of Alfred Lyall, I am tempted to exclaim in the words of Shenstone's exquisite inscription, which has always seemed to me about the best thing that Shenstone ever wrote, "Heu quanto minus est cum reliquis versari quam tui meminisse!" He was one of my oldest and best of friends. More than this, although our characters differed widely, and although I should never for a moment think of rating my intellectual attainments on a par with his, at the same time I may say that in the course of a long life I do not think that I have ever been brought in contact with any one with whom I found myself in more thorough community of opinion and sentiment upon the sundry and manifold questions which excited our common interest. He was a strong Unionist, a strong Free Trader, and a strong anti-suffragist. I am, for good or evil, all these things. He was a sincere Liberal in the non-party sense of that very elastic word. So was I. That is to say, there was a time when we both thought ourselves good mid-Victorian Liberals—a school of politicians whose ideas have now been swept into the limbo of forgotten things, the only surviving principles of that age being apparently those associated with a faint and somewhat fantastic cult of the primrose. In 1866 he wrote to his sister—and I cannot but smile on reading the letter—"I am more and more Radical every year"; and he expressed regret that circumstances did not permit of his setting up as "a fierce demagogue" in England. I could have conscientiously written in much the same spirit at the same period, but it has not taken me nearly half a century to discover that two persons more unfitted by nature and temperament to be "fierce demagogues" than Alfred Lyall and myself were probably never born. In respect to the Indian political questions which were current during his day—such as the controversy between the Lawrentian and "Forward" schools of frontier policy, the Curzon-Kitchener episode, and the adaptation of Western reforms to meet the growing requirements to which education has given birth—his views, although perhaps rather in my opinion unduly pessimistic and desponding, were generally identical with my own.

Albeit he was an earnest reformer, he was a warm advocate of strong and capable government, and, in writing to our common friend, Lord Morley, in 1882, he anathematised what he considered the weakness shown by the Gladstone Government in dealing with disorder in Ireland. Himself not only the kindest, but also the most just and judicially-minded of men, he feared that a maudlin and misplaced sentimentalism would destroy the more virile elements in the national character. "I should like," he said, in words which must not, of course, be taken too literally, "a little more fierceness and honest brutality in the national temperament." His heart went out, in a manner which is only possible to those who have watched them closely at work, to those Englishmen, whether soldiers or civilians, who, but little known and even at times depreciated by their own countrymen, are carrying the fame, the glory, the justice and humanity of England to the four quarters of the globe.

The roving Englishman (he said) is the salt of English land.... Only those who go out of this civilised country, to see the rough work on the frontiers and in the far lands, properly understand what our men are like and can do.... They cannot manage a steam-engine, but they can drive restive and ill-trained horses over rough roads.

He felt—and as one who has humbly dabbled in literature at the close of an active political life, I can fully sympathise with him—that "when one has once taken a hand in the world's affairs, literature is like rowing in a picturesque reach of the Thames after a bout in the open sea." Yet, in the case of Lyall, literature was not a matter of mere academic interest. "His incessant study was history." He thought, with Lord Acton, that an historical student should be "a politician with his face turned backwards." His mind was eminently objective. He was for ever seeking to know the causes of things; and though far too observant to push to extreme lengths analogies between the past and the present, he nevertheless sought, notably in the history of Imperial Rome, for any facts or commentaries gleaned from ancient times which might be of service to the modern empire of which he was so justly proud, and in the foundation of which the splendid service of which he was an illustrious member had played so conspicuous a part. "I wonder," he wrote in 1901, "how far the Roman Empire profited by high education."

Lyall was by nature a poet. Sir Mortimer Durand says, truly enough, that his volume of verses, "if not great poetry, as some hold, was yet true poetry." Poetic expressions, in fact, bubbled up in his mind almost unconsciously in dealing with every incident of his life. Lord Tennyson tells us in his *Memoir* that one evening, when his father and mother were rowing across the Solent, they saw a heron. His father described this incident in the following language: "One dark heron flew over the sea, backed by a daffodil sky." Similarly, Lyall, writing with the enthusiasm of a young father for his firstborn, said: "The child has eyes like the fish-pools of Heshbon, with wondrous depth of intelligent gaze." But, though a poet, it would be a great error to suppose that Lyall was an idealist, if by that term is meant one who, after a platonic fashion, indulges in ideas which are wholly visionary and unpractical. He had, indeed, ideals. No man of his imagination and mental calibre could be without them. But they were ideals based on a solid foundation of facts. It was here that, in spite of some sympathy based on common literary tastes, he altogether parted company from a brother poet,

Mr. Wilfrid Blunt, who has invariably left his facts to take care of themselves. Though eminently meditative and reflective, Lyall's mind, his biographer says, "seemed always hungry for facts." "Though he had an unusual degree of imagination, he never allowed himself to be tempted too far from the region of the known or the knowable." The reason why he at times appeared to vacillate was that he did not consider he sufficiently understood all the facts to justify his forming an opinion capable of satisfying his somewhat hypercritical judgment. He was, in fact, very difficult to convince of the truth of an opinion, not because of his prejudices, for he had none, but by reason of his constitutional scepticism. He acted throughout life on the principle laid down by the Greek philosopher Epicharmus: "Be sober, and remember to disbelieve. These are the sinews of the mind." I have been informed on unimpeachable authority that when he was a member of the Treasury Committee which sat on the question of providing facilities for the study of Oriental languages in this country, he constantly asked the witnesses whom he examined leading questions from which it might rather be inferred that he held opinions diametrically opposed to those which in reality he entertained. His sole object was to arrive at a sound conclusion. He wished to elicit all possible objections to any views to which he was personally inclined. It is very probable that his Oriental experience led him to adopt this procedure; for, as any one who has lived much in the East will recognise, it is the only possible safeguard against the illusions which may arise from the common Oriental habit of endeavouring to say what is pleasant to the interrogator, especially if he occupies some position of authority.

Only half-reconciled, in the first instance, to Indian exile, and, when once he had taken the final step of departure, constantly brooding over the intellectual attractions rather than the material comforts of European life, Lyall speedily came to the conclusion that, if he was to bear a hand in governing India, the first thing he had to do was to understand Indians. He therefore brought his acutely analytical intellect to the task of comprehending the Indian habit of thought. In the course of his researches he displayed that thoroughness and passionate love of truth which was the distinguishing feature of his character throughout life. That he succeeded in a manner which has been surpassed by none, and only faintly rivalled by a very few, is now generally recognised both by his own countrymen and also—which is far more remarkable—by the inhabitants of the country which formed the subject of his study. So far as it is possible for any Western to achieve that very difficult task, he may be said to have got to the back of the Oriental mind. He embodied the results of his long experience at times in sweeping and profound generalisations, which covered the whole field of Oriental thought and action, and at others in pithy epigrammatic sayings in which the racy humour, sometimes tinged with a shade of cynical irony, never obscured the deep feeling of sympathy he entertained for everything that was worthy of respect and admiration.

Lyall had read history to some purpose. He knew, in the words which Gregorovius applied to the rule of Theodosius in Italy, that "not even the wisest and most humane of princes, if he be an alien in race, in customs and religion, can ever win the hearts of the people." He had read De Tocqueville, and from the pages of an author whose habit of thought must have been most congenial to him, he drew the conclusion that "it was the increased prosperity and enlightenment of the French people which produced the grand crash." He therefore thought that "the wildest, as well as the shallowest notion of all is that universally prevalent belief that education, civilisation and increased material prosperity will reconcile the people of India eventually to our rule." Hence he was prepared to accept—perhaps rather more entirely than it deserved to be accepted—the statement of that very astute Brahmin, Sir Dinkur Rao, himself the minister of an important native State, that "the natives prefer a bad native Government to our best patent institutions." These, and similar oracular statements, have now become the commonplaces of all who deal with questions affecting India. That there is much truth in them cannot be gainsaid, but they are still often too much ignored by one section of the British public, who, carried away by home-made sentiment, forget that of all national virtues gratitude for favours received is the most rare, while by another section they are applied to the advocacy of a degree of autonomous rule which would be disastrous to the interests, not only of India itself, but also to the cause of all real civilised progress.

The point, however, on which in conversation Lyall was wont to insist most strongly was that the West was almost incomprehensible to the East, and, *vice versa*, that the Western could never thoroughly understand the Oriental. In point of fact, when we talk of progress, it is necessary to fix some standard by which progress may be measured. We know our Western standard; we endeavour to enforce it; and we are so convinced that it gives an accurate measure of human moral and material advancement that we experience a shock on hearing that there are large numbers of even highly educated human beings who hold that the standard is altogether false. Yet that, Lyall would argue, is generally the Oriental frame of mind. Fatalism, natural conservatism and ignorance lead the uneducated to reject our ideas, while the highly educated often hold that our standard of progress is too material to be a true measure, and that consequently, far from advancing, we are standing still or even retrograding. Lyall, personifying a Brahmin, said, "Politics I cannot help regarding as the superficial aspect of deeper problems; and for progress, the latest incarnation of European materialism, I have an incurable distrust." These subtle intellectuals, in fact, as Surendranath Banerjee, one of the leaders of the Swadeshi movement, told Dr. Wegener, hold that the English are "stupid and ignorant," and, therefore, wholly unfit to govern India.

I remember Lyall, who, as Sir Mortimer Durand says, had a very keen sense of humour, telling me an anecdote which is what Bacon would have called "luciferous," as an illustration of the views held by the uneducated classes in India on the subject of Western reforms. The officer in charge of a district either in Bengal or the North-West Provinces got up a cattle-show, with a view to improving the breed of cattle. Shortly afterwards, an Englishman, whilst out shooting, entered into conversation with a peasant who happened to be passing by. He asked the man what he thought of the cattle-show, and added that he supposed it had done a great deal of good. "Yes," the native, who was probably a Moslem, replied after some reflection, "last year there was cholera. This year there was Cattle Show. We have to bear these afflictions with what patience we may. Are they not all sent by God?"

But it was naturally the opinions entertained by the intellectual classes which most interested Lyall, and which he endeavoured to interpret to his countrymen. The East is asymmetrical in all things. I remember Lyall saying to me, "Accuracy is abhorrent to the Oriental mind." The West, on the other hand, delights beyond all things in symmetry and accuracy. Moreover, it would almost seem as if in the most trivial incidents in life some unseen influence generally impels the Eastern to do the exact opposite to the Western—a point, I may observe, which Lyall was never tired of illustrating by all kinds of quaint examples. A shepherd in Perthshire will walk behind his sheep and drive them. In the Deccan he will walk in front of his flock. A European will generally place his umbrella point downwards against the wall. An Oriental will, with far greater reason, do exactly the reverse.

But, in respect to the main question of mutual comprehension, there are, at all events in so far as the European is concerned, degrees of difficulty—degrees which depend very largely on religious differences, for in the theocratic East religion covers the whole social and political field to a far greater extent than in the West. Now, the religion of the Moslem is, comparatively speaking, very easy to understand. There are, indeed, a few ritualistic and other minor points as to which a Western may at times have some difficulty in grasping the Oriental point of view. But the foundations of monotheistic Islam are simplicity itself; indeed, it may be said that they are far more simple than those of Christianity. The case of the Hindu religion is very different. Dr. Barth in his *Religions of India* says:

Already in the Veda, Hindu thought is profoundly tainted with the malady, of which it will never be able to get rid, of affecting a greater air of mystery the less there is to conceal, of making a parade of symbols which at bottom signify nothing, and of playing with enigmas which are not worth the trouble of trying to unriddle.... At the present time it is next to impossible to say exactly what Hinduism is, where it begins, and where it ends.

I cannot profess to express any valuable opinion on a subject on which I am very imperfectly informed, and which, save as a matter of political necessity, fails to interest me—for, personally, I think that a book of the *Iliad* or a play of Aristophanes is far more valuable than all the lucubrations that have ever been spun by the subtle minds of learned Hindu Pundits—but, so far as I am able to judge, Dr. Barth's description is quite accurate. None the less, the importance to the Indian politician of gaining some insight into the inner recesses of the Hindu mind cannot for a moment be doubted. Lyall said, "I fancy that the Hindu philosophy, which teaches that everything we see or feel is a vast cosmic illusion, projected into space by that which is the manifestation of the infinite and unconscious spirit, has an unsettling effect on their political beliefs." Lyall, therefore, rendered a very great political service to his countrymen when he took in hand the duty of expounding to them the true nature of Hindu religious belief. He did the work very thoroughly. Passing lightly by the "windy moralities" of Brahmo Somaj teachers of the type of Keshub Chunder Sen, whom he left to "drifting Deans such as Stanley and Alford," he grasped the full significance of true orthodox Brahmanism, and under the pseudonym of Vamadeo Shastri wrote an essay which has "become a classic for the student of comparative religion, and for all who desire to know, in particular, the religious mind of the Hindu." In the course of his enquiries Lyall incidentally performed the useful historical service of showing that Euhemerism is, or very recently was, a living force in India, and that the solar myth theory supported by Max Müller and others had, to say the least, been pushed much too far.

I turn to another point. All who were brought in contact with Lyall speedily recognised his social charm and high intellectual gifts, but was he a man of action? Did he possess the qualifications necessary to those who take part in the government of the outlying dominions of the Empire? I have often been asked that question. It is one to which Sir Mortimer Durand frequently reverts, his general conclusion being that Lyall was "a man of action with literary tastes." I will endeavour briefly to express my own opinion on this subject.

There have been many cases of notable men of action who were also students. Napier said that no example can be shown in history of a great general who was not also a well-read man. But Lyall was more than a mere student. He was a thinker, and a very deep thinker, not merely on political but also on social and religious subjects. There may be some parallel in the history of our own or of other countries to the peculiar combination of thought and action which characterised Lyall's career, but for the moment none which meets all the necessary requirements occurs to me. The case is, I think, almost if not quite unique. That Lyall had a warm admiration for men of action is abundantly clear. His enthusiasm on their behalf comes out in every stanza of his poetry, and, when any suitable occasion offered, in every line of his prose. He eulogised the strong man who ruled and acted, and he reserved a very special note of sympathy for those who sacrificed their lives for their country. Shortly before his own death he spoke in terms of warm admiration of Mr. Newbolt's fine lines:

Qui procul hinc—the legend's writ, The frontier grave is far away— Qui ante diem periit Sed miles, sed pro patriâ.

But he shared these views with many thinkers who, like Carlyle, have formed their opinions in their studies. The fact that he entertained them does not help us to answer the question whether he can or cannot be himself classed in the category of men of action.

As a young man he took a distinguished part in the suppression of the Mutiny, and showed courage and decision of character in all his acts. He was a good, though not perhaps an exceptionally good administrator. His horror of disorder in any form led him to approve without hesitation the adoption of strong measures for its suppression. On the occasion of the punishment administered to those guilty of the Manipur massacres in 1891, he wrote to Sir Mortimer Durand, "I do most heartily admire the justice and firmness of purpose displayed in executing the Senapati. I hope there will be no interference, in my absence, from the India Office." On the whole, the verdict passed by Lord George Hamilton is, I believe, eminently correct, and is entirely in accordance with my own experience. Lord George, who had excellent opportunities for forming a sound opinion on the subject, wrote:

Great as were Lyall's literary attributes and powers of initiation and construction, his critical faculties were even more fully developed. This made him at times somewhat difficult to deal with, for he was very critical and cautious in the tendering of advice as regards any new policy or any suggested change. When once he could see his way through difficulties, or came to the conclusion that those difficulties must be faced, then his caution and critical instincts disappeared, and he was prepared to be as bold in the prosecution of what he advocated as he had previously been reluctant to start.

The mental attitude which Lord George Hamilton thus describes is by no means uncommon in the case of very conscientious and brilliantly intellectual men, such, for instance, as the late Lord Goschen, who possessed many characteristics in common with Lyall. They can cite, in justification of their procedure, the authority of one who was probably the greatest man of action that the world has ever produced. Roederer relates in his journal that on one occasion Napoleon said to him:

Il n'y a pas un homme plus pusillanime que moi quand je fais un plan militaire; je me grossis tous les dangers et tous les maux possibles dans les circonstances; je suis dans une agitation tout à fait pénible; je suis comme une fille qui accouche. Et quand ma résolution est prise, tout est oublié, hors ce qui peut la faire réussir.

Within reasonable limits, caution is, indeed, altogether commendable. On the other hand, it cannot be doubted that, carried to excess, it is at times apt to paralyse all effective and timely action, to disqualify those who exercise it from being pilots possessed of sufficient daring to steer the ship of state in troublous times, and to exclude them from the category of men of action in the sense in which that term is generally used. In spite of my great affection for Alfred Lyall, I am forced to admit that, in his case, caution was, I think, at times carried to excess. He never appeared to me to realise sufficiently that the conduct of public affairs, notably in this democratic age, is at best a very rough unscientific process; that it is occasionally necessary to make a choice of evils or to act on imperfect evidence; and that at times, to quote the words which I remember Lord Northbrook once used to me, it is even better to have a wrong opinion than to have no definite opinion at all. So early as 1868, he wrote to his mother, "There are many topics on which I have not definitely discovered what I do think"; and to the day of his death he very generally maintained in respect to current politics the frame of mind set forth in this very characteristic utterance. Every general has to risk the loss of a battle, and every active politician has at times to run the risk of making a wrong forecast. Before running that risk, Lyall was generally inclined to exhaust the chances of error to an extent which was often impossible, or at all events hurtful.

Sir Mortimer Durand refers to the history of the Ilbert Bill, a measure under which Lord Ripon's Government proposed to give native magistrates jurisdiction over Europeans in certain circumstances. I was at the time (1882-83) Financial Member of the Viceroy's Council. After a lapse of thirty years, there can, I think, be no objection to my stating my recollections of what occurred in connexion with this subject. I should, in the first instance, mention that the association of Mr. (now Sir Courtenay) Ilbert's name with this measure was purely accidental. He had nothing to do with its initiation. The proposals, which were eventually embodied in the Bill, originated with Sir Ashley Eden, who was Lieutenant-Governor of Bengal, and who certainly could not be accused of any wish to neglect European opinion, or of any desire to push forward extreme liberal measures conceived in native interests. The measure had been under the consideration of the Legislative Department in the time of Mr. Ilbert's predecessor in the office of Legal Member of Council, and it was only the accident that he vacated his office before it was introduced into the Legislative Council that associated Mr. Ilbert's name with the Bill.

As was customary in such cases, all the local Governments had been consulted; and they again consulted the Commissioners, Deputy-Commissioners, Collectors, etc., within their respective provinces. The result was that Lord Ripon had before him the opinions of practically the whole Civil Service of India. Divers views were held as to the actual extent to which the law should be altered, but, in the words of a despatch addressed by the Government of India to the Secretary of State on September 9, 1882, the local reports showed "an overwhelming consensus of opinion that the time had come for modifying the existing law and removing the present absolute bar upon the investment of native magistrates in the interior with powers over European British subjects." Not one single official gave anything approaching an indication of the storm of opposition that this ill-fated measure was about to raise. I do not think that this is very surprising, for the opposition came almost exclusively from the unofficial Europeans, who for the most part congregate in a few large commercial centres, with the result that the majority of the civilians, who are scattered throughout the country, are not much brought in contact with them. Nevertheless, the fact that so great a miscalculation of the state of public opinion could be made left a deep impression on my mind. The main lesson which I carried away from the Ilbert Bill controversy was, indeed, that in spite of their great merits, which no one recognises more fully than myself, it is possible at times for the whole body of Indian civilians, taken collectively, to be somewhat unsafe guides in matters of state policy. Curiously enough, the only danger-signal which was raised was hoisted by Sir Henry Maine, who had been in India as Legal Member of Council, but who did not belong to the Indian Civil Service. He was at the time a member of the India Council. When the despatch of the Government of India on the subject reached London, Sir Henry Maine was travelling on the Continent. The papers were sent to him. He called to mind the bitter controversy which arose over what was known as "the Black Act" in Lord William Bentinck's time, and wrote privately a few words of warning to Lord Hartington, who was at the time Secretary of State for India. Lord Hartington put the letter in his great-coat pocket, went to Newmarket, and forgot all about it, with the result that Sir Henry Maine's warning never reached Lord Ripon.

I well remember being present when Mr. Ilbert introduced the measure into the Legislative Council. It attracted but little attention and led to only a very brief discussion, in which I took no part. The papers had been circulated to all Members of Council, including myself. When I received them I saw at a glance that the subject was not one that concerned my own department, or one as to which my opinion could be of any value. I, therefore, merely endorsed the papers with my initials and sent them on, without having given the subject much attention. In common with all my colleagues, I was soon to learn the gravity of the step which had been taken. A furious storm of opposition, which profoundly shook the prestige and authority of the Government of India, and notably of the Viceroy, arose. It was clear that a mistake had been made. The measure was in itself not very important. It was obviously undesirable, as Lyall remarked, to "set fire to an important wing of the house in order to roast a healthy but small pig." The best plan, had it been possible, would have been to admit the mistake and to withdraw the measure; and this would certainly have been done had it not been for the unseemly and extravagant violence of the European unofficial community, notably that of Calcutta. It should, however, in fairness be stated that they were irritated and alarmed, not so much at the acts of Lord Ripon's Government, but at some rather indiscreet language which had at times been used, and which led them, quite erroneously, to suspect that extreme measures were in contemplation, of a nature calculated to shake the foundations of British supremacy in India. This violent attitude naturally led to reprisals and bitter recriminations from the native press, with the result that the total withdrawal of the measure would have been construed as a decisive defeat to the adoption of even the most moderate measures of liberal reform in India. The project of total withdrawal could not, therefore, be entertained.

In these circumstances, the duty of a practical rough-and-ready politician was very clearly indicated. However little he might care for the measure on its own merits, political instinct pointed unmistakably to the absolute necessity of affording strong support to the Viceroy. Lyall failed to realise this fully. He admired Lord Ripon's courage. "We must," he said, "all do our best to pull the Viceroy through." But withal it is clear, by his own admission, that he only gave the Viceroy "rather lukewarm support." "I have intrenched myself," he wrote in a characteristic letter, "behind cautious proposals, and am quoted on both sides." This attitude was not due to any want of moral courage, for a more courageous man, both physically and morally, than Lyall never lived. It was simply the result of what Lord Lytton called "the Lyall habit of seeing both sides of a question," and not being able to decide betimes which side to support. That a man of Lyall's philosophical and reflective turn of mind should see both sides of a question is not only natural but commendable, but this frame of mind is not one that can be adopted without hazard by a man of action at the head of affairs at a time of acute crisis.

There is, however, a reverse side to this picture. The same mental attributes which rendered Lyall somewhat unfit, in my opinion, to deal with an incident such as the Ilbert Bill episode, enabled him to come with credit and distinction out of a situation of extreme difficulty in which the reputation of many another man would have foundered. I have no wish or intention to stir up again the embers of past Afghan controversies. It will be sufficient for my purpose to say that Lord Lytton, immensely to his credit, recognised Lyall's abilities and appointed him Foreign Secretary, in spite of the fact that he was associated with the execution of a policy to which Lord Lytton himself was strongly opposed, and which he had decided to reverse. Lyall did not conceal his opinions, but, as always, he was open to conviction, and saw both sides of a difficult question. In 1878, he was "quite in favour of vigorous action to counteract the Russians"; but two years later, in 1880, after the Cavagnari murder, he records in a characteristic letter that he "was mentally edging back towards old John Lawrence's counsel never to embark on the shoreless sea of Afghan politics." On the whole, it may be said that Lyall passed through this supreme test in a manner which would not have been possible to any man unless endowed not merely with great abilities, but with the highest degree of moral courage and honesty of purpose. He preserved his own self-esteem, and by his unswerving honesty and loyalty gained that of the partisans on both sides of the controversy.

It is pleasant to turn from these episodes to other features in Lyall's career and character, in respect to which unstinted eulogy, without the qualification of a shade of criticism, may be recorded. It was more especially in dealing with the larger and more general aspects of Eastern affairs that Lyall's genius shone most brightly. He had what the French call a *flair* in dealing with the main issues of Oriental politics such as, so far as my experience goes, is possessed by few. It was very similar to the qualities displayed by the late Lord Salisbury in dealing with foreign affairs generally. I give an instance in point.

In 1884, almost every newspaper in England was declaiming loudly about the dangers to be apprehended if the rebellion excited by the Mahdi in the Soudan was not promptly crushed. It was thought that this rebellion was but the precursor of a general and formidable offensive movement throughout the Islamic world. "What," General Gordon, whose opinion at the time carried great weight, had asked, "is to prevent the Mahdi's adherents gaining Mecca? Once at Mecca we may look out for squalls in Turkey," etc. He, as also Lord Wolseley, insisted on the absolute necessity of "smashing the Mahdi." We now know that these fears were exaggerated, and that the Mahdist movement was of purely local importance. Lyall had no special acquaintance with Egyptian or Soudanese affairs, but his general knowledge of the East and of Easterns enabled him at once to gauge correctly the true nature of the danger. Undisturbed by the clamour which prevailed around him, he wrote to Mr. Henry Reeve on March 21, 1884: "The Mahdi's fortunes do not interest India.

The talk in some of the papers about the necessity of smashing him, in order to avert the risk of some general Mahomedan uprising, is futile and imaginative."

I need say no more. I am glad, for the sake of Lyall's own reputation, that the offer of the Viceroyalty was never made to him. Apart from the question of his age, which, in 1894, was somewhat too advanced to admit of his undertaking such onerous duties, I doubt if he possessed sufficient experience of English public life—a qualification which is yearly becoming of greater importance—to enable him to fill the post in a satisfactory manner. In spite, moreover, of his splendid intellectual gifts and moral elevation of thought, it is very questionable whether on the whole he would have been the right man in the right place.

Lyall's name will not, like those of some other Indian notabilities, go down to posterity as having been specially connected with any one episode or event of supreme historical importance; but, when those of the present generation who regarded him with esteem and affection have passed away, he will still deserve an important niche in the Temple of Fame as a thinker who thoroughly understood the East, and who probably did more than any of his contemporaries or predecessors to make his countrymen understand and sympathise with the views held by the many millions in India whose destinies are committed to their charge. His experience and special mental equipment eminently fitted him to perform the task he took in hand. England, albeit a prolific mother of great men in every department of thought and action, has not produced many Lyalls.

"THE NINETEENTH CENTURY AND AFTER"

IV
ARMY REFORM
"The Nineteenth Century and After," February 1904

The autobiography of my old and highly esteemed friend, Lord Wolseley, constitutes an honourable record of a well-spent life. Lord Wolseley may justifiably be proud of the services which he has rendered to his country. The British nation, and its principal executive officials in the past, may also be proud of having quickly discovered Lord Wolseley's talents and merits, and of having advanced him to high position.

Obviously, certain conclusions of public interest may be drawn from the career of this very distinguished soldier. Sir George Arthur, in the December number of the *Fortnightly Review*, has stated what are the special lessons which, in his opinion, are to be derived from a consideration of that career.

Those lessons are, indeed, sufficiently numerous. I propose, however, to deal with only two of them. They are those which, apparently, Lord Wolseley himself wishes to be inculcated. Both involve questions of principle of no little importance.

In the first place, Lord Wolseley, if I understand rightly, considers that the army has suffered greatly from civilian interference. He appears to think that it should be more exclusively than heretofore under military control.

In the second place, he thinks that, in certain cases, the political and diplomatic negotiations, which generally follow on a war, should be conducted, not by a diplomatist or politician, but by the officer who has conducted the previous military operations.

As regards the first point, I am not now dealing with Lord Wolseley's remarks in connection with our general unpreparedness for war, nor with those on the various defects, past or present, of our military organisation. In a great deal that he has said on these subjects, Lord Wolseley carries me heartily with him. I confine myself strictly to the issue as I have defined it above.

Possibly, I have mistaken the significance of Lord Wolseley's words. If so, my error is shared by Sir George Arthur, who, in dealing with the War Office, dwells with emphasis on the occasions when "this great war expert was thwarted in respect of his best considered plans by the civilian element in that citadel of inefficiency," and speaks with approval of Lord Wolseley's "severe strictures on blundering civilian interference with the army," as also of the "censure reserved for the criminal negligence and miserable cowardice of successive Cabinets."

It seems to me that Lord Wolseley is rather hard on civilians in general—those "iconoclastic civilian officials who meddle and muddle in army matters"—on politicians in particular, who, I cannot but think, are not quite so black as he has painted them; and most of all on Secretaries of State, with the single exception of Lord Cardwell, to whom generous and very well deserved praise is accorded.

It is not quite clear, from a perusal of these volumes, what is the precise nature of the change which Lord Wolseley wishes to advocate, although in one passage a specific proposal is made. It is that "a certificate should be annually laid before Parliament by the non-political Commander-in-Chief, that the whole of the military forces of the Empire can be completely and effectively equipped for war in a fortnight." The general tendency of the reform which commends itself to Lord Wolseley may, however, readily be inferred. He complains that the soldiers, "though in office, are never in power." Nevertheless, as he explains with military frankness, "the cunning politician," when anything goes wrong, is able "to turn the wrath of a deceived people upon the military authorities, and those who are exclusively to blame are too often allowed to sneak off unhurt in the turmoil of execration they have raised against the soldiers." I may remark incidentally that exception might perhaps reasonably be taken to the use of the word "exclusively" in this passage; but the main point to which I wish to draw attention is that clearly, in Lord Wolseley's opinion, the soldiers, under the existing system, have not sufficient power, and that it would be advisable that they should, under a reformed system, be invested with more ample power. I dare say Lord Wolseley is quite right, at all events to this extent, that it is desirable that the power, as also the responsibility, of the highest military authorities should be as clearly defined as is possible under our peculiar system of government. But it is essential to ascertain more accurately in what manner Lord Wolseley, speaking with all the high authority which deservedly attaches itself to his name, thinks that effect should be given to the principle which he advocates. In order to obtain this information, I turn to vol. i. p. 92, where I find the following passage: "A man who is not a soldier, and who is entirely ignorant of war, is selected solely for political reasons to be Secretary of State for War. I might with quite as great propriety be selected to be the chief surgeon in a hospital."

I would here digress for a moment to deal with the argument advanced in the latter part of this sentence. It is very plausible, and, at first sight, appears convincing. It is also very commonly used. Over and over again, I have heard the presumed analogy between the surgeon and the soldier advanced as a proof of the absurdity of the English system. I believe that no such analogy exists. Surgery is an exact science. To perform even the most trifling surgical operation requires careful technical training and experience. It is far otherwise with the case of the soldier. I do not suppose that any civilian in his senses would presume, on a purely technical matter, to weigh his own opinion against that of a trained soldier, like Lord Wolseley, who is thoroughly versed in the theory of his profession, and who has been through the school of actual war. But a large number of the most important questions affecting military organisation and the conduct of military affairs, require for their solution little or no technical knowledge. Any man of ordinary common sense can form an opinion on them, and any man of good business habits may readily become a capable agent for giving effect to the opinions which he, or which others have formed.

I may here perhaps give a page from my own personal experience bearing on the point under discussion.

The Soudan campaign of 1896-98 was, in official circles, dubbed a "Foreign Office war." For a variety of reasons, to which it is unnecessary to allude in detail, the Sirdar was, from the commencement of the operations, placed exclusively under my orders in all matters. The War Office assumed no responsibility, and issued no orders. A corresponding position was occupied by the Headquarters Staff of the Army of Occupation in Cairo. The result was that I found myself in the somewhat singular position of a civilian, who had had some little military training in his youth, but who had had no experience of war, whose proper functions were diplomacy and administration, but who, under the stress of circumstances in the Land of Paradox, had to be ultimately responsible for the maintenance, and even, to some extent, for the movements of an army of some 25,000 men in the field.

That good results were obtained under this system cannot be doubted. It will not, therefore, be devoid of interest to explain how it worked in practice, and what were the main reasons which contributed towards success.

I have no wish to disparage the strategical and tactical ability which were displayed in the conduct of the campaign. It is, however, a fact that no occasion arose for the display of any great skill in these branches of military knowledge. When once the British and Egyptian troops were brought face to face with the enemy, there could—unless the conditions under which they fought were altogether extraordinary—be little doubt of the result. The speedy and successful issue of the campaign depended, in fact, almost entirely upon the methods adopted for overcoming the very exceptional difficulties connected with the supply and transport of the troops. The main quality required to meet these difficulties was a good head for business. By one of those fortunate accidents which have been frequent in the history of Anglo-Saxon enterprise, a man was found equal to the occasion. Lord Kitchener of Khartoum won his well-deserved peerage because he was a good man of business; he looked carefully after all important detail, and he enforced economy.

My own merits, such as they were, were of a purely negative character. They may be summed up in a single phrase. I abstained from mischievous activity, and I acted as a check on the interference of others. I had full confidence in the abilities of the commander, whom I had practically myself chosen, and, except when he asked for my assistance, I left him entirely alone. I encouraged him to pay no attention to those vexatious bureaucratic formalities with which, under the slang phrase of "red tape" our military system is overburdened. I exercised some little control over the demands for stores which were sent to the London War Office; and the mere fact that these demands passed through my hands, and that I declined to forward any request unless, besides being in accordance with existing regulations—a point to which I attached but slight importance—it had been authorised by the Sirdar, probably tended to check wastefulness in that quarter where it was most to be feared. Beyond this I did nothing, and I found—somewhat to my own astonishment—that, with my ordinary staff of four diplomatic secretaries, the general direction of a war of no inconsiderable dimensions added but little to my ordinary labours.

I do not say that this system would always work as successfully as was the case during the Khartoum campaign. The facts, as I have already said, were peculiar. The commander, on whom everything practically depended, was a man of marked military and administrative ability. Nevertheless, I feel certain that Lord Kitchener would bear me out in saying that here was a case in which general civilian control, far from exercising any detrimental effect, was on the whole beneficial.

To return to the main thread of my argument. The passage which I have quoted from Lord Wolseley's book would certainly appear to point to the conclusion that, in his opinion, the Secretary of State for War should be a soldier unconnected with politics. Even although Lord Wolseley does not state this conclusion in so many words, it is notorious to any one who is familiar with the views current in army circles that the adoption of this plan is considered by many to be the best, if it be not the only, solution of all our military difficulties.

I am not concerned with the constitutional objections which may be urged against the change of system now under discussion. Neither need I dwell on the difficulty of making it harmonise with our system of party government, for which it is quite possible to entertain a certain feeling of respect and admiration without being in any degree a political partisan. I approach the question exclusively from the point of view of its effects on the army. From that point of view, I venture to think that the change is to be deprecated.

In dealing with Lord Cardwell's attitude in respect to army reform, Lord Wolseley says: "Never was Minister in my time more generally hated by the army." He points out how this hatred was extended to all who supported Lord Cardwell's views. His own conduct was "looked upon as a species of high treason." I was at the time employed in a subordinate position at the War Office. I can testify that this language is by no means exaggerated. Nevertheless, after events showed clearly enough that, in resisting the abolition of purchase, the formation of a reserve, and the other admirable reforms with which Lord Cardwell's name, equally with that of Lord Wolseley, is now honourably associated, the bulk of army opinion was wholly in the wrong. I believe such army opinion as now objects to a civilian being Secretary of State for War to be equally in the wrong.

There would appear, indeed, to be some inconsistency between Lord Wolseley's unstinted praise of Lord Cardwell—that "greatest" of War Ministers, who, "though absolutely ignorant of our army and of war," responded so "readily to the demands made on him by his military advisers," and "gave new life to our old army"—and his depreciation of the system which gave official birth to Lord Cardwell. There would be no contradiction in the two positions if the civilian Minister, in 1871, had been obliged to use his position in Parliament and his influence on public opinion to force on an unwilling nation reforms which were generally advocated by the army. But the very contrary of this was the case. What Lord Cardwell had principally to encounter was "the fierce hatred" of the old school of soldiers, and Lord Wolseley tells us clearly enough what would have happened to the small band of army reformers within the army, if they had been unable to rely on civilian support.

"Had it not been," he says, "for Mr. Cardwell's and Lord Northbrook's constant support and encouragement, those of us who were bold enough to advocate a thorough reorganisation of our military system, would have been 'provided for' in distant quarters of the British world, 'where no mention of us more should be heard.'"

There can be no such thing as finality in army reform. There will be reformers in the future, as there have been in the past. There will, without doubt, be vested interests and conservative instincts to be overcome in the future, as there were at the time when Lord Wolseley so gallantly fought the battle of army reform. What guarantee can Lord Wolseley afford that a soldier at the head of the army will always be a reformer, and that he will not "provide for" those of his subordinates who have the courage to raise their voices in favour of reform, even as Lord Wolseley thinks he would himself have been "provided for" had it not been for the sturdy support he received from his civilian superiors? I greatly doubt the possibility of giving any such guarantee.

But I go further than this. It is now more than thirty years since I served under the War Office. I am, therefore, less intimately acquainted with the present than with the past. But, during those thirty years, I have been constantly brought in contact with the War Office, and I have seen no reason whatever to change the opinion I formed in Lord Cardwell's time, namely, that it will be an evil day for the army when it is laid down, as a system, that no civilian should be Secretary of State for War. My belief is that, if ever the history of our military administration of recent years comes to be impartially written, it will be found that most of the large reforms, which have beneficially affected the army, have been warmly supported, and sometimes initiated, by the superior civilian element in the War Office. Who, indeed, ever heard of a profession being reformed from within? One of the greatest law reformers of the last century was the author of *Bleak House*.

It may, indeed, be urged—perhaps Lord Wolseley would himself urge—that it is no defence of a bad system to say that under one man (Lord Cardwell), whom Lord Wolseley describes as "a clear-headed, logical-minded lawyer," it worked very well. To this I reply that I cannot believe that the race of clear-headed, logical-minded individuals of Cabinet rank, belonging to either great party of the State, is extinct.

I have been induced to make these remarks because, in past years, I was a good deal associated with army reform, and because, since then, I have continued to take an interest in the matter. Also because I am convinced that those officers in the army who, with the best intentions, advocate the particular change now under discussion, are making a mistake in army interests. They may depend upon it that the cause they have at heart will best be furthered by maintaining at the head of the army a civilian of intelligence and of good business habits, who, although, equally with a soldier, he may sometimes make mistakes, will give an impartial hearing to army reformers, and will probably be more alive than any one belonging to their own profession to all that is best in the outside and parliamentary pressure to which he is exposed.

I turn to the second point to which allusion was made at the commencement of this article.

Speaking of the Chinese war in 1860, Lord Wolseley says: "In treating with barbarian nations during a war ... the general to command the army and the ambassador to make peace should be one and the same man. To separate the two functions is, according to my experience, folly gone mad." Lord Wolseley reverts to this subject in describing the Ashantee war of 1873-74. I gather from his allusions to Sir John Moore's campaign in Spain, and to the fact that evil results ensued from allowing Dutch deputies to accompany Marlborough's army, that he is in favour of extending the principle which he advocates to wars other than those waged against "barbarian nations."

The objections to anything in the nature of a division of responsibility, at all events so long as military operations are in actual progress, are, indeed, obvious, and are now very generally recognised. Those who are familiar with the history of the revolutionary war will remember the baneful influence exercised by the Aulic Council over the actions of the Austrian commanders. There can, in fact, be little doubt that circumstances may occur when the principle advocated by Lord Wolseley may most advantageously be adopted; but it is, I venture to think, one which has to be applied with much caution, especially when the question is not whether there should be a temporary cessation of hostilities—a point on which the view of the officer in command of the troops would naturally carry the greatest weight—but also involves the larger issue of the terms on which peace should finally be concluded. I am not at all sure that, in deciding on the issues which, under the latter contingency, must necessarily come under consideration, the employment of a soldier, in preference to a politician or diplomatist, is always a wise proceeding. Soldiers, equally with civilians, are liable to make erroneous forecasts of the future, and to mistake the general situation with which they have to deal. I can give a case in point.

When, in January 1885, Khartoum fell, the question whether the British army should be withdrawn, or should advance and reconquer the Soudan, had to be decided. Gordon, whose influence on public opinion, great before, had been enhanced by his tragic death, had strongly recommended the policy of "smashing the Mahdi." Lord Wolseley adopted Gordon's opinion. "No frontier force," he said, "can keep Mahdiism out of Egypt, and the Mahdi sooner or later must be smashed, or he will smash you." These views were shared by Lord Kitchener, Sir Redvers Buller, Sir Charles Wilson, and by the military authorities generally. Further, the alleged necessity of "smashing the Mahdi," on the ground that his success in the Soudan would be productive of serious results elsewhere, exercised a powerful influence on British public opinion at this period, although the best authorities on Eastern politics were at the time aware that the fears so generally entertained in this connection were either groundless or, at all events, greatly exaggerated. Under these circumstances, it was decided to "smash the Mahdi," and accordingly a proclamation, giving effect to the declared policy of the British Government, was issued. Shortly afterwards, the Penjdeh incident occurred. Public opinion in England somewhat calmed down, having found its natural safety-valve in an acrimonious parliamentary debate, in which the Government narrowly escaped defeat. The voices of politicians and diplomatists, which had been to some degree hushed by the din of arms, began to be heard. The proclamation was cancelled. The project of reconquering the Soudan was postponed to a more convenient period. It was, in fact, accomplished thirteen years later, under circumstances which differed very materially from those which prevailed in 1885. In June 1885, the Government of Lord Salisbury succeeded to that of Mr. Gladstone, and, though strongly urged to undertake the reconquest of the Soudan, confirmed the decision of its predecessors.

Sir George Arthur, writing in the *Fortnightly Review*, strongly condemns this "cynical disavowal" of Lord Wolseley's proclamation. I have nothing to say in favour of the issue of that proclamation. I am very clearly of opinion that, as it was issued, it was wise that it should be cancelled. For, in truth, subsequent events showed that the forecast made by Lord Wolseley and by Gordon was erroneous, in that it credited the Mahdi with a power of offence which he was far from possessing. No serious difficulty arose in defending the frontier of Egypt from Dervish attack. The overthrow of the Mahdi's power, though eminently desirable, was very far from constituting an imperious necessity such as was commonly supposed to exist in 1885. In this instance, therefore, it appears to me that the diplomatists and politicians gauged the true nature of the situation somewhat more accurately than the soldiers.

More than this, I conceive that, in all civilised countries, the theory of government is that a question of peace or war is one to be decided by politicians. The functions of the soldier are supposed to be confined, in the first place, to advising on the purely military aspects of the issue involved; and, in the second place, to giving effect to any decisions at which the Government may arrive. The practice in this matter not infrequently differs somewhat from the theory. The soldier, who is generally prone to advocate vigorous action, is inclined to encroach on the sphere which should properly be reserved for the politician. The former is often masterful, and the latter may be dazzled by the glitter of arms, or too readily lured onwards by the persuasive voice of some strategist to acquire an almost endless succession of what, in technical language, are called "keys" to some position, or—to employ a metaphor of which the late Lord Salisbury once made use in writing to me—"to try and annex the moon in order to prevent its being appropriated by the planet Mars." When this happens, a risk is run that the soldier, who is himself unconsciously influenced by a very laudable desire to obtain personal distinction, may practically dictate the policy of the nation without taking a sufficiently comprehensive view of national interests. Considerations of this nature have more especially been, from time to time, advanced in connection with the numerous frontier wars which have occurred in India. That they contain a certain element of truth can scarcely be doubted.

For these reasons, it appears to me that the application of the principle advocated by Lord Wolseley requires much care and watchfulness. Probably, the wisest plan will be that each case should be decided on its own merits with reference to the special circumstances of the situation, which may sometimes demand the fusion, and sometimes the separation, of military and political functions.

I was talking, a short time ago, to a very intelligent, and also Anglophile, French friend of mine. He knew England well, but, until quite recently, had not visited the country for a few years. He told me that what struck him most was the profound change which had come over British opinion since the occasion of his last visit. We had been invaded, he said, by *le militarisme continental*. In common with the vast majority of my countrymen, I am earnestly desirous of seeing our military organisation and military establishments placed on a thoroughly sound footing, but I have no wish whatever to see any portion of our institutions overwhelmed by a wave of *militarisme continental*. It is because I think that the views advocated by Lord Wolseley tend—although, I do not doubt, unconsciously to their distinguished author—in the direction of a somewhat too pronounced *militarisme*, that I venture in some degree to differ from one for whom I have for many years entertained the highest admiration and the most cordial personal esteem.

V

THE INTERNATIONAL ASPECTS OF FREE TRADE

Paper read at the International Free Trade Congress at Antwerp, August 9-21, 1910

I have been asked to state my opinion on the effect of Free Trade upon the political relations between States. The subject is a very wide one. I am fully aware that the brief remarks which I am about to make fail to do justice to it.

A taunt very frequently levelled at modern Free Traders is that the anticipations of their predecessors in respect to the influence which Free Trade would be likely to exercise on international relations have not been realised. A single extract from Mr. Cobden's writings will suffice to show the nature of those anticipations. In 1842, he described Free Trade "as the best human means for securing universal and permanent peace." Inasmuch as numerous wars have occurred since this opinion was expressed, it is often held that events have falsified Mr. Cobden's prediction.

In dealing with this argument, I have, in the first place, to remark that modern Free Traders are under no sort of obligation to be "Cobdenite" to the extent of adopting or defending the whole of the teaching of the so-called Manchester School. It may readily be admitted that the programme of that school is, in many respects, inadequate to deal with modern problems.

In the second place, I wish to point out that Mr. Cobden and his associates, whilst rightly holding that trade was to some extent the natural foe to war, appear to me to have pushed the consequences to be derived from that argument much too far. They allowed too little for other causes which tend to subvert peace, such as racial and religious differences, dynastic considerations, the wish to acquire national unity, which tends to the agglomeration of small States, and the ambition which excites the desire of hegemony.

In the third place, I have to observe that the world has not as yet had any adequate opportunity for judging of the accuracy or inaccuracy of Mr. Cobden's prediction, for only one great commercial nation has, up to the present time, adopted a policy of Free Trade. It was, indeed, here more than in any other direction that some of the early British Free Traders erred on the side of excessive optimism. They thought, and rightly thought, that Free Trade would confer enormous benefits on their own country; and they held that the object-lesson thus afforded might very probably induce other nations speedily to follow the example of England. They forgot that the special conditions which existed at the time their noble aspirations were conceived were liable to change; that the extraordinary advantages which Free Trade for a time secured were largely due to the fact that seventy years ago England possessed a far larger supply of mechanical aptitude than any other country; that her marked commercial supremacy, which was then practically undisputed, could not be fully maintained in the face of the advance likely to be made by other nations; that if those nations persisted in adhering to Protection, their progress—which has really been achieved, not by reason of, but in spite of Protection—would almost inevitably be mainly attributed to their fiscal policy to the exclusion of other contributory causes, such as education; and that thus a revived demand for protective measures would not improbably arise, even in England itself. These are, in fact, the results which have accrued. Without doubt, it was difficult to foresee them, but it is worthy of note that, in spite of all adverse and possibly ephemeral appearances, symptoms are not wanting which encourage the belief that the prescience of the early Free Traders may, in the end, be tardily vindicated. It is the irony of current politics that at a time when England is meditating a return to Protection—but is as yet, I am glad to say, very far from being persuaded that the adoption of such a policy would be wise—the most advanced thinkers in some Protectionist states are beginning to turn their eyes towards the possibility and desirability of casting aside those swaddling-clothes which were originally assumed in order to foster their budding industries. Many of the most competent German economists, whilst advocating Protection as a temporary measure, have for many years fully recognised that, when once a country has firmly established its industrial and commercial status in the markets of the world, it can best maintain and extend its acquired position by permitting the freest possible trade. Even Friedrich List, though an ardent Protectionist, "always had before him universal Free Trade as the goal of his endeavours." Before long, Germany will have well-nigh completed the transition from agriculture to manufactures in which she has been engaged for the last thirty or forty years; and when that transition is fully accomplished, it may be predicted with some degree of confidence that a nation so highly educated, and endowed with so keen a perception of cause and effect, will begin to move in the direction of Free Trade. Similarly, in the United States of America, the campaign which has recently been waged against the huge Trusts, which are the offspring of Protection, as well as the rising complaints of the dearness of living, are so many indications that arguments, which must eventually lead to the consideration—and probably to the ultimate adoption—if not of Free Trade, at all events of Freer Trade than now prevails, are gradually gaining ground. Much the same may be said of Canada. A Canadian gentleman, who can speak with authority on the subject, recently wrote:

The feeling in favour of Free Trade is growing fast in Western Canada, and I believe I am right in adding the United States.

We have our strong and rapidly growing farmers' organisations, such as the United Farmers of Alberta, and of each Western province, so that farmers are now making themselves heard and felt in politics, and farmers realise that they are being exploited for the benefit of the manufacturer. Excellent articles appear almost weekly in the *Grain Growers' Guide*, published in Winnipeg, showing the curse of Protection.

A Canadian Free Trade Union, affiliated with the International Free Trade League, has just been formed in Winnipeg, and many prominent business and professional men are connected with it.

It ought to be better known among the electors of Great Britain how Free Trade is growing in Canada, that they may be less inclined to commit the fatal mistake of changing England's policy. Canada is often quoted in English politics now, and the real facts should be known.

No experience has, therefore, as yet been acquired which would enable a matured judgment to be formed as to the extent to which Free Trade may be regarded as a preventive to war. The question remains substantially much in the same condition as it was seventy years ago. In forming an opinion upon it, we have still to rely largely on conjecture and on academic considerations. All that has been proved is that numerous wars have taken place during a period of history when Protection was the rule, and Free Trade the exception; though the *post hoc ergo propter hoc* fallacy would, of course, be involved, if on that account it were inferred that the protection of national industries has necessarily been the chief cause of war.

Without indulging in any utopian dreams as to the possibility of inaugurating an era of universal peace, it may, I think, be held that, in spite of the wars which have occurred during the last half century, not merely an ardent desire for peace, but also a dislike—I may almost say a genuine horror—of war has grown apace amongst the civilised nations of the world. The destructiveness of modern weapons of offence, the fearful personal responsibility devolving on the individuals who order the first shot to be fired, the complete uncertainty which prevails as to the naval, military, and political results which will ensue if the huge armaments of modern States are brought into collision, the growth of a benevolent, if at times somewhat eccentric humanitarianism, possibly also the advance of democracy—though it is at times somewhat too readily assumed that democracies must of necessity be peaceful—have all contributed to create a public opinion which holds that to engage in an avoidable war is the worst of political crimes. This feeling has found expression in the more ready recourse which, as compared to former times, is now made to arbitration in order to settle international disputes. Nevertheless, so long as human nature remains unchanged, and more especially so long as the huge armaments at present existing are maintained, it is the imperative duty of every self-respecting nation to provide adequately for its own defence. That duty is more especially imposed on those nations who, for one reason or another, have been driven into adopting that policy of expansion, which is now almost universal. Within the last few years, the United States of America have abandoned what has been aptly termed their former system of "industrial monasticism," whilst in the Far East a new world-power has suddenly sprung into existence. Speaking as one unit belonging to a country whose dominions are more extensive and more widely dispersed than those of any other nation, I entertain a strong opinion that if Great Britain continues to maintain her present policy of Free Trade—as I trust will be the case—her means of defence should, within the limits of human foresight, be such as to render her empire impregnable; and, further, that should that policy unfortunately be reversed, it will be a wise precaution that those means of defence should, if possible, be still further strengthened. But I also entertain an equally strong opinion that an imperial nation should seek to fortify its position and to provide guarantees for the durability of its empire, not merely by rendering itself, so far as is possible, impregnable, but also by using its vast world-power in such a manner as to secure in some degree the moral acquiescence of other nations in its *imperium*, and thus provide an antidote—albeit it may only be a partial antidote—against the jealousy and emulation which its extensive dominions are calculated to incite.

I am aware that an argument of this sort is singularly liable to misrepresentation. Militant patriotism rejects it with scorn. It is said to involve an ignoble degree of truckling to foreign nations. It involves nothing of the kind. I should certainly be the last to recommend anything approaching to pusillanimity in the conduct of the foreign affairs of my country. If I thought that the introduction of a policy of Protection was really demanded in the interests of the inhabitants of the United Kingdom, I should warmly advocate it, whatever might be the effect produced on the public opinion of other countries. British Free Traders do not advocate the cause which they have at heart in order to benefit the countries which send their goods to Great Britain, but because they think it advantageous to their own country to procure certain foreign products without any artificial enhancement of price. If they are right in coming to this conclusion, it is surely an incidental advantage of much importance that a policy of Free Trade, besides being advantageous to the United Kingdom, tends to give an additional element of stability to the British Empire and to preserve the peace of the world.

From the dawn of history, uncontrolled commercialism has been one of the principal causes of misgovernment, and more especially of the misgovernment of subject races. The early history of the Spaniards in South and Central America, as well as the more recent history of other States, testify to the truth of this generalisation. Similarly, Trade—that is to say exclusive trade—far from tending to promote peace, has not infrequently been accompanied by aggression, and has rather tended to promote war. Tariff wars, which are the natural outcome of the protective system, have been of frequent occurrence, and, although I am not at all prepared to admit that under no circumstances is a policy of retaliation justifiable, it is certain that that policy, carried to excess, has at times endangered European peace. There is ample proof that the Tariff war between Russia and Germany in 1893, "was regarded by both responsible parties as likely to lead to a state of things dangerous to the peace of Europe." Professor Dietzel, in his very remarkable and exhaustive work on *Retaliatory Duties*, shows very clearly that the example of Tariff wars is highly contagious. Speaking of the events which occurred in 1902 and subsequent years, he says: "Germany set the bad example.... Russia, Austria-Hungary, Roumania, Switzerland, Portugal, Holland, Servia, followed suit.... An international arming epidemic broke out. Everywhere, indeed, it was said: We are not at all desirous of a Tariff war. We are acting only on the maxim so often proclaimed among us, *Si vis pacem, para bellum.*"

Can it be doubted that there is a distinct connection between these Tariff wars and the huge armaments which are now maintained by every European state? The connection is, in fact, very close. Tariff wars engender the belief that wars carried on by shot and shell may not improbably follow. They thus encourage, and even necessitate, the costly preparations for war which weigh so heavily, not only on the industries, but also on the moral and intellectual progress of the world.

Mr. Oliver, in his interesting biography of Alexander Hamilton, gives a very remarkable instance of the menace to peace arising, even amongst a wholly homogeneous community, from the creation of hostile tariffs. The first step which the thirteen States of America took after they had acquired their independence was "to indulge themselves in the costly luxury of an internecine tariff war.... Pennsylvania attacked Delaware. Connecticut was oppressed by Rhode Island and New York.... It was a dangerous game, ruinous in itself, and, behind the Custom-House officers, men were beginning to furbish up the locks of their muskets.... At one time war between Vermont, New Hampshire, and New York seemed all but inevitable."

To sum up all I have to say on this subject—I do not for a moment suppose that Universal Free Trade—even if the adoption of such a policy were conceivable—would inaugurate an era of universal and permanent peace. Whatever fiscal policy be adopted by the great commercial nations of the world, it is wholly illusory to suppose that the risk of war can be altogether avoided in the future, any more than has been the case in the past. But I am equally certain that, whereas exclusive trade tends to exacerbate international relations, Free Trade, by mutually enlisting a number of influential material interests in the cause of peace, tends to ameliorate those relations and thus, *pro tanto*, to diminish the probability of war. No nation has, of course, the least right to dictate the fiscal policy of its neighbours, neither has it any legitimate cause to complain when its neighbours exercise their unquestionable right to make whatever fiscal arrangements they consider conducive to their own interests. But the real and ostensible causes of war are not always identical. When once irritation begins to rankle, and rival interests clash to an excessive degree, the guns are apt to go off by themselves, and an adroit diplomacy may confidently be trusted to discover some plausible pretext for their explosion.

In a speech which I made in London some three years ago, I gave an example, gathered from facts with which I was intimately acquainted, of the pacifying influence exerted by adopting a policy of

Free Trade in the execution of a policy of expansion. I may as well repeat it now. Some twelve years ago the British flag was hoisted in the Soudan side by side with the Egyptian. Europe tacitly acquiesced. Why did it do so? It was because a clause was introduced into the Anglo-Egyptian Convention of 1899, under which no trade preference was to be accorded to any nation. All were placed on a footing of perfect equality. Indeed, the whole fiscal policy adopted in Egypt since the British occupation in 1883 has been based on distinctly Free Trade principles. Indirect taxes have been, in some instances, reduced. Those that remain in force are imposed, not for protective, but for revenue purposes, whilst in one important instance—that of cotton goods—an excise duty has been imposed, in order to avoid the risk of customs duties acting protectively.

Free Trade mitigates, though it is powerless to remove, international animosities. Exclusive trade stimulates and aggravates those animosities. I do not by any means maintain that this argument is by itself conclusive against the adoption of a policy of Protection, if, on other grounds, the adoption of such a policy is deemed desirable; but it is one aspect of the question which, when the whole issue is under consideration, should not be left out of account.

VI
CHINA
"The Nineteenth Century and After," May 1913

Mr. Bland's book, entitled *Recent Events and Present Policies in China* (1912), is full of instruction not only for those who are specially concerned in the affairs of China, but also for all who are interested in watching the new developments which are constantly arising from the ever-increasing contact between the East and the West.

The Eastern world is at present strewn with the *débris* of paper constitutions, which are, or are probably about to become, derelict. The case of Egypt is somewhat special, and would require separate treatment. But in Turkey, in Persia, and in China, the epidemic, which is of an exotic character, appears to be following its normal course.

Constitutions when first promulgated are received with wild enthusiasm. In Italy, during the most frenzied period of Garibaldian worship, my old friend, Lear the artist, asked a patriotic inn-keeper, who was in a wild state of excitement, to give him breakfast, to which the man replied: "Colazione! Che colazione! Tutto è amore e libertà!" In the Albanian village in which Miss Durham was residing when the Young Turks proclaimed their constitution, the Moslem inhabitants expressed great delight at the news, and forthwith asked when the massacre of the Giaours—without which a constitution would wholly miss its mark—was to begin. Similarly, Mr. Bland says that throughout China, although "the word 'Republic' meant no more to the people at large than the blessed word 'Mesopotamia,' men embraced each other publicly and wept for joy at the coming of Liberty, Equality, and Fraternity."

These ebullitions provoke laughter.

Sed facilis cuivis rigidi censura cachinni.

We Europeans have ourselves passed through much the same phases. Vandal and others have told us of the Utopia which was created in the minds of the French when the old régime crashed to the ground. Sydney Smith caricatured the delusive hopes excited by the passing of the Reform Bill of 1832, when he said that all the unmarried young women thought that they would at once get husbands, and that all the schoolboys expected a heavy fall in the price of jam tarts. A process of disillusionment may confidently be anticipated in Ireland if the Home Rule Bill becomes law, and the fairy prospects held out to the Irish people by Mr. Redmond and the other stage managers of the piece are chilled by the cold shade of reality.

We English are largely responsible for creating the frame of mind which is even now luring Young Turks, Chinamen, and other Easterns into the political wilderness by the display of false signals. We have, indeed, our Blands in China, our Milners in Egypt, our Miss Durhams in the Balkan Peninsula, and our Miss Bells in Mesopotamia, who wander far afield, gleaning valuable facts and laying before their countrymen and countrywomen conclusions based on acquired knowledge and wide experience. But their efforts are only partially successful. They are often shivered on the solid rock of preconceived prejudices, and genuine but ill-informed sentimentalism. A large section of the English public are, in fact, singularly wanting in political imagination. Although they would not, in so many words, admit the truth of the statement, they none the less act and speak as if sound national development in whatsoever quarter of the world must of necessity proceed along their own conventional, insular, and time-honoured lines, and along those lines alone.

There is a whole class of newspaper readers, and also of newspaper writers, who resemble that eminent but now deceased Member of Parliament, who told me that during the four hours' railway journey from Port Said to Cairo he had come to the definite conclusion that Egypt could not be prosperous because he had observed that there were no stacks of corn standing in the fields; neither was this conclusion in any way shaken when it was explained to him that the Egyptians were not in the habit of erecting corn stacks after the English model. All these classes readily lend an ear to quack, though often very well-intentioned politicians, who go about the world preaching that countries can be regenerated by shibboleths, and that the characters of nations can be changed by Acts of Parliament. This frame of mind appeals with irresistible force to the untrained Eastern habit of thought. T'ang—a leading Chinese Republican—Mr. Bland says, "like all educated Chinese, believes in the magic virtue of words and forms of government in making a nation wise and strong by Acts of Parliament." And what poor, self-deluded T'ang is saying and thinking in Canton is said and thought daily by countless Ahmeds, Ibrahims, and Rizas in the bazaars of Constantinople, Cairo, and Teheran.

What has Mr. Bland to tell us of all the welter of loan-mongering, rococo constitution-tinkering, Confucianism, and genuine if at times misdirected philanthropy, which is now seething in the Chinese melting-pot?

In the first place, he has to say that the main obstacle to all real progress in China is one that cannot be removed by any change in the form of government, whether the ruling spirit be a full-fledged Republican of the Sun Yat-Sen type, aided by a number of "imitation foreigners," as they are termed by their countrymen, or a savage, albeit statesmanlike "Old Buddha," who, at the close of a life stained by all manner of blood-guiltiness, at last turned her weary face towards Western reform as the only hope of saving her country and her dynasty. The main disease is not political, and is incapable of being cured by the most approved constitutional formulae. It is economic. Polygamy, aided by excessive philo-progenitiveness, the result of ancestor-worship, has produced a highly congested population. Vast masses of people are living in normal times on the verge of starvation. Hence come famines and savage revolts of the hungry. "Amidst all the specifics of political leaders," Mr. Bland says, "there has been as yet hardly a voice raised against marriages of minors or polygamy, and reckless over-breeding, which are the basic causes of China's chronic unrest."

The same difficulty, though perhaps in a less acute form, exists in India. Not only cannot it be remedied by mere philanthropy, but it is absolutely certain—cruel and paradoxical though it may appear to say so—that philanthropy enhances the evil. In the days of Akhbar or Shah Jehan, cholera, famine, and internal strife kept down the population. Only the fittest survived. Now, internal strife is forbidden, and philanthropy steps in and says that no single life shall be sacrificed if science and Western energy or skill can save it. Hence the growth of a highly congested population, vast numbers of whom are living on a bare margin of subsistence. I need hardly say that I am not condemning philanthropy. On the contrary, I hold strongly that an anti-philanthropic basis of government is not merely degrading and inhuman, but also fortunately nowadays impracticable. None the less, the fact that one of the greatest difficulties of governing the teeming masses in the East is caused by good and humane government should be recognised. It is too often ignored.

A partial remedy to the state of things now existing in China would be to encourage emigration; but a resort to this expedient is impossible, for Europeans and Americans alike, being scared by the prospect of competing with Chinese cheap labour, which is the only real Yellow Peril, as also by the demoralisation consequent on a large influx of Chinamen into their dominions, close their ports to the emigrants. That Young China should feel this as a gross injustice can be no matter for surprise. The Chinaman may, with inexorable logic, state his case thus: "You, Europeans and Americans, insist on my receiving and protecting your missionaries. I do not want them. I have, in Confucianism, a system of philosophy, which, whatever you may think of it, suits all my spiritual requirements, and which has been sufficient to hold Chinese society together for long centuries past. Nevertheless, I bow to your wishes. But then surely you ought in justice to allow free entry into your dominions to my carpenters and bricklayers, of whom I have a large surplus, of which I should be glad to be rid. Is not your boasted philanthropy somewhat vicarious, and does not your public morality savour in some degree of mere opportunist cant?"

To all of which, Europeans and Americans can only reply that the instinct of self-preservation, which is strong within them, points clearly to the absolute necessity of excluding the Chinese carpenters and bricklayers; and, further, as regards the missionaries, that there can be but one answer, and that in a Christian sense, to the question asked by jesting Pilate. In effect they say that circumstances alter cases, and that might is right—a plea which may perhaps suffice to salve the conscience of an opportunist politician, but ought to appeal less forcibly to a stern moralist.

Foreign emigration, even if it were possible, would, however, be a mere palliative. A more thorough and effective remedy would be to facilitate the dispersion of the population in the congested districts over those wide tracts of China itself which are suffering in a less degree from congestion. I conceive that the execution of a policy of this nature would not be altogether impossible. It could be carried into effect by improving the means of locomotion, possibly by the construction of irrigation works on a large scale, and by developing the resources of the country, which are admittedly very great. But there is one condition which is essential to the execution of this programme, and that is that the financial administration of the country should be sufficiently honest to inspire the confidence of those European investors who alone can provide the necessary capital. Now, according to Mr. Bland, this fundamental quality of honesty is not to be found throughout the length and breadth of China, whether in the ranks of the old Mandarins or in those of the young Republicans.

The essential virtue of personal integrity , the capacity to handle public funds with common honesty, has been conspicuously lacking in Young China. The leopard has not changed his spots; the sons and brothers of the classical Mandarin remain, in spite of Western learning, Mandarins by instinct and in practice.

A very close observer of Eastern affairs—Mr. Stanley Lane-Poole—has said that the East has an extraordinary facility for assimilating all the worst features of any new civilisation with which it is brought in contact. This is what has happened in India, in Turkey, in Egypt, and in Persia. Even in Japan it has yet to be seen whether the old national virtues will survive prolonged contact with the West. Hear now what Mr. Bland has to say of China:

Where Young China has cast off the ethical restraints and patriotic morality of Confucianism, it has failed to assimilate, or even to understand, the moral foundations of Europe's civilisation. It has exchanged its old lamp for a new, but it has not found the oil, which the new vessel needs, to lighten the darkness withal.

In the opinion of so highly qualified an authority as Prince Ito, "the sentiments of foreign educated Young China are hopelessly out of touch with the masses." But while there has been alienation from the ideals of the East, there has been no real approach to the ideals of the West.

Education at Harvard or Oxford may imbue the Chinese student with ideas and social tendencies, apparently antagonistic to those of the patriarchal system of his native land; but they do not, and cannot, create in him (as some would have us believe) the Anglo-Saxon outlook on life, the standards of conduct and the beliefs which are the results of centuries of our process of civilisation and structural character. Under his top dressing of Western learning, the Chinese remains true to type, instinctively detached from the practical and scientific attitude, contemplatively philosophical, with the fatalistic philosophy of the prophet Job, concerned rather with the causes than the results of things. Your barrister at Lincoln's Inn, after ten years of cosmopolitan experience in London or Washington, will revert in six months to the ancestral type of morals and manners; the spectacle is so common, even in the case of exceptionally assimilative men like Wu Ting-fang, or the late Marquis Tseng, that it evokes little or no comment amongst Europeans in China.

Notably from the point of view of financial honesty, which, as I have already mentioned, is of cardinal importance if the regeneration of the country is to be undertaken by other means than by mock constitutions, the results of Western education are most disappointing.

The opinion is widely held amongst European residents and traders that the section of Young China which has received its education in Foreign Mission schools displays no more honesty than the rest.

What is the conclusion to be drawn from these facts? It is that not only in order to obtain adequate security for the bond-holders—in whom I am not in any way personally interested, for I shall certainly not be one of them—but also in the interests of the Chinese people, it is essential, before any loan is contracted, to insist on a strict supervision of the expenditure of the loan funds. That Young China, partly on genuine patriotic grounds and also possibly in some cases on grounds which are less worthy of respect and sympathy, should resent the exercise of this supervision, is natural enough, but it can scarcely be doubted that unless it be exercised a large portion of the money advanced by European capitalists will be wasted, and that no really effective step forward will be taken in the solution of the economic problem which constitutes the main Chinese difficulty. The very rudimentary ideas entertained by the Chinese themselves in the matter of applying funds to productive works is sufficiently illustrated by the episode mentioned by Mr. Bland, where he tells us that "the Szechuan Railway Company directors made provision for the building of their line by the appointment of station-masters"; while the fact that but a short time ago 1400 German machine guns, costing £500 apiece, which had never been used or paid for, were lying at Shanghai, indicates the manner in which it is not only possible but highly probable that the loan funds under exclusively Chinese supervision would be frittered away on unproductive objects.

Those, indeed, who have had some practical experience of financial administration in Eastern countries may well entertain some doubts as to whether supervision which only embraces the expenditure, and does not apply to the revenue, will be sufficient to meet all the requirements of the case. The results so far attained by the more limited scheme of supervision do not appear to have been satisfactory. Herr Rump was appointed auditor to the German section of the Tientsin-P'ukou Railway, but Mr. Bland tells us that "the auditorship on this railway has proved worse than useless as a preventive of official peculation." On the other hand, the system of collecting the revenue is in the highest degree defective. It violates flagrantly a principle which, from the days of Adam Smith downwards, has always been regarded as the corner-stone of any sound financial administration. "For every tael officially accounted for by the provincial authorities," Mr. Bland says, in words which recall to my mind the Egyptian fiscal system under the régime of Ismail Pasha, "at least five are actually collected from the taxpayers."

It is, therefore, earnestly to be hoped that the diplomatists and capitalists of Europe will—both in the interests of the investing public and in those of the Chinese people—stand firm and insist on adequate financial control as a preliminary and essential condition to the advance of funds.

As to whether the recently established Republic is destined to last or whether it will prove a mere ephemeral episode in the life-history of China, there seems to be much divergence of opinion among those authorities who are most qualified to speak on the subject. Mr. Bland's views on this point are, however, quite clear. He thinks that Confucianism, and all the political and social habits of thought which are the outcome of Confucianism, have "become ingrained in every fibre of the national life," and that they constitute the "fundamental cause of the longevity of China's social structure and of the innate strength of her civilisation." He refuses to believe that Young China, which is imbued with "a doctrinaire spirit of political speculation," though it may tinker with the superstructure, will be able seriously to shake the foundations of this hoary edifice. He has watched the opinions and activities in every province from the beginning of the present revolution, and he "is compelled to the conviction that salvation from this quarter is impossible." He thinks that although in Canton and the Kuang Provinces, which are the most intellectually advanced portions of China, a system of popular representation may be introduced with some hope of beneficial results,

... as regards the rest of China, as every educated Chinese knows (unless, like Sun Yat-Sen, he has been brought up abroad), the idea of rapidly transforming the masses of the population into an intelligent electorate, and of making a Chinese Parliament the expression of their collective political vitality, is a vain dream, possible only for those who ignore the inherent character of the Chinese people.

There is, however, one consideration set forth by Mr. Bland, which may possibly prove, at all events for a time, the salvation, while it assuredly connotes the condemnation of the present system of government, and that is that the Chinese Republic may continue to exist by abrogating all republican principles. According to Mr. Bland this "gran rifiuto" has already been made. "The actual government of China," he says, "contains none of the elements of genuine Republicanism, but is merely the old despotism, the old Mandarinate, under new names." "The inauguration of the Republican idea of constitutional Government in China," he says in another passage, "can only mean, in the present state of the people, continual transference of an illegal despotism from one group of political adventurers to another, the pretence of popular representation serving merely to increase and perpetuate instability."

It would require a far greater knowledge of Chinese affairs than any to which I can pretend to express either unqualified adherence to or dissent from Mr. Bland's views. But it is clear that his diagnosis of the past is based on a very thorough acquaintance with the facts, while, on *a priori* grounds, his prognosis of the future is calculated to commend itself to those of general experience who have studied Oriental character and are acquainted with Oriental history.

VII
THE CAPITULATIONS IN EGYPT

During the six years which have elapsed since I left Cairo I have, for various reasons on which it is unnecessary to dwell, carefully abstained from taking any part in whatever discussions have arisen on current Egyptian affairs. If I now depart from the reticence which I have hitherto observed it is because there appears at all events some slight prospect that the main reform which is required to render the government and administration of Egypt efficient will be seriously considered. As so frequently happens in political affairs, a casual incident has directed public attention to the need of reform. A short time ago a Russian subject was, at the request of the Consular authorities, arrested by the Egyptian police and handed over to them for deportation to Russia. I am not familiar with the details of the case, neither, for the purposes of my present argument, is any knowledge of those details required. The nature of the offence of which this man, Adamovitch by name, was accused, as also the question of whether he was guilty or innocent of that offence, are altogether beside the point. The legal obligation of the Egyptian Government to comply with the request that the man should be handed over to the Russian Consular authorities would have been precisely the same if he had been accused of no offence at all. The result, however, has been to touch one of the most tender points in the English political conscience. It has become clear that a country which is not, indeed, British territory, but which is held by a British garrison, and in which British influence is predominant, affords no safe asylum for a political refugee. Without in any way wishing to underrate the importance of this consideration, I think it necessary to point out that this is only one out of the many anomalies which might be indicated in the working of that most perplexing political creation entitled the Egyptian Government and administration. Many instances might, in fact, be cited which, albeit they are less calculated to attract public attention in this country, afford even stronger ground for holding that the time has come for reforming the system hitherto known as that of the Capitulations.

Before attempting to deal with this question I may perhaps be pardoned if, at the risk of appearing egotistical, I indulge in a very short chapter of autobiography. My own action in Egypt has formed the subject of frequent comment in this country; neither, assuredly, in spite of occasional blame, have I any reason to complain of the measure of praise—often, I fear, somewhat unmerited praise—which has been accorded to me. But I may perhaps be allowed to say what, in my own opinion, are the main objects achieved during my twenty-four-years' tenure of office. Those achievements are four in number, and let me add that they were not the results of a hand-to-mouth conduct of affairs in which the direction afforded to political events was constantly shifted, but of a deliberate plan persistently pursued with only such temporary deviations and delays as the circumstances of the time rendered inevitable.

In the first place, the tension with the French Government, which lasted for twenty-one years and which might at any moment have become very serious, was never allowed to go beyond a certain point. In spite of a good deal of provocation, a policy of conciliation was persistently adopted, with the result that the conclusion of the Anglo-French Agreement of 1904 became eventually possible. It is on this particular feature of my Egyptian career that personally I look back with far greater pride and pleasure than any other, all the more so because, although it has, comparatively speaking, attracted little public attention, it was, in reality, by far the most difficult and responsible part of my task.

In the second place, bankruptcy was averted and the finances of the country placed on a sound footing.

In the third place, by the relief of taxation and other reforms which remedied any really substantial grievances, the ground was cut away from under the feet of the demagogues whom it was easy to foresee would spring into existence as education advanced.

In the fourth place, the Soudan, which had to be abandoned in 1884-85, was eventually recovered.

These, I say, are the things which were done. Let me now state what was not done. Although, of course, the number of Egyptians employed in the service of the Government was largely increased, and although the charges which have occasionally been made that education was unduly neglected admit of easy refutation, it is none the less true that little, if any, progress was made in the direction of conferring autonomy on Egypt. The reasons why so little progress was made in this direction were twofold.

In the first place, it would have been premature even to think of the question until the long struggle against bankruptcy had been fought and won, and also until, by the conclusion of the Anglo-French Agreement in 1904, the acute international tension which heretofore existed had been relaxed.

In the second place, the idea of what constituted autonomy entertained by those Egyptians who were most in a position to make their voices heard, as also by some of their English sympathisers, differed widely from that entertained by myself and others who were well acquainted with the circumstances of the country, and on whom the responsibility of devising and executing any plan for granting autonomy would naturally devolve. We were, in fact, the poles asunder. The Egyptian idea was that the native Egyptians should rule Egypt. They therefore urged that greatly increased powers should be given to the Legislative Council and Assembly originally instituted by Lord Dufferin. The counter-idea was not based on any alleged incapacity of the Egyptians to govern themselves—a point which, for the purposes of my present argument, it is unnecessary to discuss. Neither was it based on any disinclination gradually to extend the powers of Egyptians in dealing with purely native Egyptian questions. I, and others who shared my views, considered that those who cried "Egypt for the Egyptians" on the house-tops had gone off on an entirely wrong scent because, even had they attained their ends, nothing approaching to Egyptian autonomy would have been realised. The Capitulations would still have barred the way to all important legislation and to the removal of those defects in the administration of which the Egyptians most complained. When the prominent part played by resident Europeans in the political and social life of Egypt is considered, it is indeed little short of ridiculous to speak of Egyptian autonomy if at the same time a system is preserved under which no important law can be made applicable to an Englishman, a Frenchman, or a German, without its detailed provisions having received the consent, not only of the King of England, the President of the French Republic, and the German Emperor, but also that of the President of the United States, the King of Denmark, and every other ruling Potentate in Europe. We therefore held that the only possible method by which the evils of extreme personal government could be averted, and by which the country could be provided with a workable legislative machine, was to include in the term "Egyptians" all the dwellers in Egypt, and to devise some plan by which the European and Egyptian elements of society would be fused together to such an extent at all events as to render them capable of cooperating in legislative effort. It may perhaps be hoped that by taking a first step in this direction some more thorough fusion may possibly follow in the future.

As I have already mentioned, it would have been premature to deal with this question prior to 1904, for any serious modification of the régime of the Capitulations could not be considered as within the domain of practical politics so long as all the Powers, and more especially France and England, were pulling different ways. But directly that agreement was signed I resolved to take the question up, all the more so because what was then known as the Secret Agreement, but which has since that time been published, contained the following very important clause:

In the event of their (His Britannic Majesty's Government) considering it desirable to introduce in Egypt reforms tending to assimilate the Egyptian legislative system to that in force in other civilised countries, the Government of the French Republic will not refuse to entertain any such proposals, on the understanding that His Britannic Majesty's Government will agree to entertain the suggestions that the Government of the French Republic may have to make to them with a view of introducing similar reforms in Morocco.

I was under no delusion as to the formidable nature of the obstacles which stood in the way of reform. Moreover, I held very strongly that even if it had been possible, by diplomatic negotiations with the other Powers, to come to some arrangement which would be binding on the Europeans resident in Egypt, and to force it on them without their consent being obtained, it was most undesirable to adopt anything approaching to this procedure. The European colonists in Egypt, although of course numerically far inferior to the native population, represent a large portion of the wealth, and a still larger portion of the intelligence and energy in the country. Moreover, although the word "privilege" always rather grates on the ear in this democratic age, it is none the less true that in the past the misgovernment of Egypt has afforded excellent reasons why even those Europeans who are most favourably disposed towards native aspirations should demur to any sacrifice of their capitulary rights. My view, therefore, was that the Europeans should not be coerced but persuaded. It had to be proved to them that, under the changed condition of affairs, the Capitulations were not only unnecessary but absolutely detrimental to their own interests. Personally, I was very fully convinced of the truth of this statement, neither was it difficult to convince those who, being behind the scenes of government, were in a position to judge of the extent to which the Capitulations clogged progress in many very important directions. But it was more difficult to convince the general public, many of whom entertained very erroneous ideas as to the extent and nature of the proposed reforms, and could see nothing but the fact that it was intended to deprive them of certain privileges which they then possessed. It cannot be too distinctly understood that there never was—neither do I suppose there is now—the smallest intention of "abolishing the Capitulations," if by that term is meant a complete abrogation of all those safeguards against arbitrary proceedings on the part of the Government which the Capitulations are intended to prevent. Capitulations or no Capitulations, the European charged with a criminal offence must be tried either by European judges or an European jury. All matters connected with the personal status of any European must be judged by the laws in force in his own country. Adequate safeguards must be contrived to guard against any abuse of power on the part of the police. Whatever reforms are introduced into the Mixed Tribunals must be confined to comparatively minor points, and must not touch fundamental principles. In fact, the Capitulations have not to be abolished, but to be modified. An eminent French jurist, M. Gabriel Louis Jaray, in discussing the Egyptian situation a few years ago, wrote:

On peut considérer comme admis qu'une simple occupation ou un protectorat de fait, reconnu par les Puissances Européennes, suffit pour mettre à néant les Capitulations, quand la réorganisation du pays est suffisante pour donner aux Européens pleine garantie de bonne juridiction.

I contend that the reorganisation of Egypt is now sufficiently advanced to admit of the guarantees for the good administration of justice, which M. Jaray very rightly claimed, being afforded to all Europeans without having recourse to the clumsy methods of the Capitulations in their present form.

In the last two reports which I wrote before I left Egypt I developed these and some cognate arguments at considerable length. But from the first moment of taking up the question I never thought that it would fall to my lot to bring the campaign against the Capitulations to a conclusion. The question was eminently one as to which it was undesirable to force the pace. Time was required in order to let public opinion mature. I therefore contented myself with indicating the defects of the present system and the general direction which reform should take, leaving it to those younger than myself to carry on the work when advancing years obliged me to retire. I may add that the manner in which my proposals were received and discussed by the European public in Egypt afforded good reason for supposing that the obstacles to be overcome before any serious reforms could be effected, though formidable, were by no means insuperable. After my departure in 1907, events occurred which rendered it impossible that the subject should at once come under the consideration of the Government, but in 1911 Lord Kitchener was able to report that the legislative powers of the Court of Appeal sitting at Alexandria had been somewhat increased. Sir Malcolm M'Ilwraith, the Judicial Adviser of the Egyptian Government, in commenting on this change, says:

The new scheme, while assuredly a progressive step, and in notable advance of the previous state of affairs ... can hardly be regarded, in its ensemble, as more than a temporary makeshift, and a more or less satisfactory palliative of the legislative impotence under which the Government has suffered for so long.

It is most earnestly to be hoped that the question will now be taken up seriously with a view to more drastic reform than any which has as yet been effected.

There is one, and only one, method by which the evils of the existing system can be made to disappear. The British Government should request the other Powers of Europe to vest in them the legislative power which each now exercises separately. Simultaneously with this request, a legislative Chamber should be created in Egypt for enacting laws to which Europeans will be amenable.

There is, of course, one essential preliminary to the execution of this programme. It is that the Powers of Europe, as also the European residents in Egypt, should have thorough confidence in the intentions of the British Government, by which I mean confidence in the duration of the occupation, and also confidence in the manner in which the affairs of the country will be administered.

As regards the first point, there is certainly no cause for doubt. Under the Anglo-French Agreement of 1904 the French Government specifically declared that "they will not obstruct the action of government in Egypt by asking that a limit of time be fixed for the British occupation, or in any other manner." Moreover, one of the last acts that I performed before I left Egypt in 1907 was to communicate to the British Chamber of Commerce at Alexandria a letter from Sir Edward Grey in which I was authorised to state that His Majesty's Government "recognise that the maintenance and development of such reforms as have hitherto been effected in Egypt depend upon the British occupation. This consideration will apply with equal strength to any changes effected in the régime of the Capitulations. His Majesty's Government, therefore, wish it to be understood that there is no reason for allowing the prospect of any modifications in that régime to be prejudiced by the existence of any doubt as to the continuance of the British occupation of the country." It is, of course, conceivable that in some remote future the British garrison may be withdrawn from Egypt. If any fear is entertained on this ground it may easily be calmed by an arrangement with the Powers that in the event of the British Government wishing to withdraw their troops, they would previously enter into communications with the various Powers of Europe with a view to re-establishing whatever safeguards they might think necessary in the interests of their countrymen.

As regards the second point, that is to say, confidence in the manner in which the administration of the country is conducted, I need only say that, so far as I am able to judge, Lord Kitchener's administration, although one of his measures—the Five Feddan law—has, not unnaturally, been subjected to a good deal of hostile criticism, has inspired the fullest confidence in the minds of the whole of the population of Egypt, whether European or native. I cannot doubt that, when the time arrives for Lord Kitchener, in his turn, to retire, no brusque or radical change will be allowed to take place in the general principles under which he is now administering the country.

The rights and duties of any such Chamber as that which I propose, its composition, its mode of election or nomination, the degree of control to be exercised over it by the Egyptian or British Governments, are, of course, all points which require very careful consideration, and which admit of solution in a great variety of ways. In my report for the year 1906 I put forward certain suggestions in connection with each of these subjects, but I do not doubt that, as the result of further consideration and discussion, my proposals admit of improvement. I need not now dwell on these details, important though they be. I wish, however, to allude to one point which involves a question of principle. I trust that no endeavour will for the present be made to create one Chamber, composed of both Europeans and Egyptians, with power to legislate for all the inhabitants of Egypt. I am strongly convinced that, under the present condition of society in Egypt, any such attempt must end in complete failure. It is, I believe, quite impossible to devise any plan for an united Chamber which would satisfy the very natural aspirations of the Egyptians, and at the same time provide for the Europeans adequate guarantees that their own legitimate rights would be properly safeguarded. I am fully aware of the theoretical objections which may be urged against trying the novel experiment of creating two Chambers in the same country, each of which would deal with separate classes of the community, but I submit that, in the special circumstances of the case, those objections must be set aside, and that one more anomaly should, for the time being at all events, be added to the many strange institutions which exist in the "Land of Paradox." Whether at some probably remote future period it will be possible to create a Chamber in which Europeans and Egyptians will sit side by side will depend very largely on the conduct of the Egyptians themselves. If they follow the advice of those who do not flatter them, but who, however little they may recognise the fact, are in reality their best friends—if, in a word, they act in such a manner as to inspire the European residents of Egypt with confidence in their judgment and absence of class or religious prejudice, it may be that this consummation will eventually be reached. If, on the other hand, they allow themselves to be guided by the class of men who have of late years occasionally posed as their representatives, the prospect of any complete legislative amalgamation will become not merely gloomy but practically hopeless. The true Egyptian patriot is not the man who by his conduct and language stimulates racial animosity in the pursuit of an ideal which can never be realised, but rather one who recognises the true facts of the political situation. Now, the dominating fact of that situation is that Egypt can never become autonomous in the sense in which that word is understood by the Egyptian nationalists. It is, and will always remain, a cosmopolitan country. The real future of Egypt, therefore, lies not in the direction of a narrow nationalism, which will only embrace native Egyptians, nor in that of any endeavour to convert Egypt into a British possession on the model of India or Ceylon, but rather in that of an enlarged cosmopolitanism, which, whilst discarding all the obstructive fetters of the cumbersome old international system, will tend to amalgamate all the inhabitants of the Nile Valley and enable them all alike to share in the government of their native or adopted country.

For the rest, the various points of detail to which I have alluded above present difficulties which are by no means insuperable, if—as I trust may be the case—the various parties concerned approach the subject with a real desire to arrive at some practical solutions. The same may be said as regards almost all the points to which Europeans resident in Egypt attach special importance, such, for instance, as the composition of criminal courts for trying Europeans, the regulation of domiciliary visits by the police, and cognate issues. In all these cases it is by no means difficult to devise methods for preserving all that is really worth keeping in the present system, and at the same time discarding those portions which seriously hinder the progress of the country. There is, however, one important point of detail which, I must admit, presents considerable practical difficulties. It is certain that the services of some of the European judges of the Mixed Tribunals might be utilised in constituting the new Chamber. Their presence would be of great use, and it is highly probable that they will in practice become the real working men of any Chamber which may be created. But apart from the objection in principle to confiding the making as also the administration of the law wholly to the same individuals, it is to be observed that, in order to create a really representative body, it would be essential that other Europeans—merchants, bankers, landowners, and professional men—should be seated in the Chamber. Almost all the Europeans resident in Europe are busy men, and the question will arise whether those whose assistance would, on general grounds, be of special value, are prepared to sacrifice the time required for paying adequate attention to their legislative duties. I can only say that I hope that sufficient public spirit is to be found amongst the many highly qualified European residents in Egypt of divers nationalities to enable this question to be answered in the affirmative.

It is, of course, impossible within the space allotted to me to deal fully on the present occasion with all the aspects of this very difficult and complicated question. I can only attempt to direct attention to the main issue, and that issue, I repeat, is how to devise some plan which shall take the place of the present Egyptian system of legislation by diplomacy. The late Lord Salisbury once epigrammatically described that system to me by saying that it was like the *liberum veto* of the old Polish Diet, "without being able to have recourse to the alternative of striking off the head of any recalcitrant voter." It is high time that such a system should be swept away and some other adopted which will be more in harmony with the actual facts of the Egyptian situation. If, as I trust may be the case, Lord Kitchener is able to devise and to carry into execution some plan which will rescue Egypt from its present legislative Slough of Despond, he will have deserved well, not only of his country, but also of all those Egyptian interests, whether native or European, which are committed to his charge.

"THE SPECTATOR"

VIII
DISRAELI
"The Spectator," November 1912

No one who has lived much in the East can, in reading Mr. Monypenny's volumes, fail to be struck with the fact that Disraeli was a thorough Oriental. The taste for tawdry finery, the habit of enveloping in mystery matters as to which there was nothing to conceal, the love of intrigue, the tenacity of purpose—though this is perhaps more a Jewish than an invariably Oriental characteristic—the luxuriance of the imaginative faculties, the strong addiction to plausible generalities set forth in florid language, the passionate outbursts of grief expressed at times in words so artificial as to leave a doubt in the Anglo-Saxon mind as to whether the sentiments can be genuine, the spasmodic eruption of real kindness of heart into a character steeped in cynicism, the excess of flattery accorded at one time to Peel for purely personal objects contrasted with the excess of vituperation poured forth on O'Connell for purposes of advertisement, and the total absence of any moral principle as a guide of life—all these features, in a character which is perhaps not quite so complex as is often supposed, hail from the East. What is not Eastern is his unconventionality, his undaunted moral courage, and his ready conception of novel political ideas—often specious ideas, resting on no very solid foundation, but always attractive, and always capable of being defended by glittering plausibilities. He was certainly a man of genius, and he used that genius to found a political school based on extreme self-seeking opportunism. In this respect he cannot be acquitted of the charge of having contributed towards the degradation of English political life.

Mr. Monypenny's first volume deals with Disraeli's immature youth. In the second, the story of the period (1837-46) during which Disraeli rose to power is admirably told, and a most interesting story it is.

Whatever views one may adopt of Disraeli's character and career, it is impossible not to be fascinated in watching the moral and intellectual development of this very remarkable man, whose conduct throughout life, far from being wayward and erratic, as has at times been somewhat superficially supposed, was in reality in the highest degree methodical, being directed with unflagging persistency to one end, the gratification of his own ambition—an ambition, it should always be remembered, which, albeit it was honourable, inasmuch as it was directed to no ignoble ends, was wholly personal. If ever there was a man to whom Milton's well-known lines could fitly be applied it was Disraeli. He scorned delights. He lived laborious days. In his youth he eschewed pleasures which generally attract others whose ambition only soars to a lower plane. In the most intimate relations of life he subordinated all private inclinations to the main object he had in view. He avowedly married, in the first instance, for money, although at a later stage his wife was able to afford herself the consolation, and to pay him the graceful compliment of obliterating the sordid reproach by declaring that "if he had the chance again he would marry her for love"—a statement confirmed by his passionate, albeit somewhat histrionic love-letters. The desire of fame, which may easily degenerate into a mere craving for notoriety, was unquestionably the spur which in his case raised his "clear spirit." So early as 1833, on being asked upon what principles he was going to stand at a forthcoming election, he replied, "On my head." He cared, in fact, little for principles of any kind, provided the goal of his ambition could be reached. Throughout his career his main object was to rule his countrymen, and that object he attained by the adoption of methods which, whether they be regarded as tortuous or straightforward, morally justifiable or worthy of condemnation, were of a surety eminently successful.

The interest in Mr. Monypenny's work is enormously enhanced by the personality of his hero. In dealing with the careers of other English statesmen—for instance, with Cromwell, Chatham, or Gladstone—we do, indeed, glance—and more than glance—at the personality of the man, but our mature judgment is, or at all events should be, formed mainly on his measures. We inquire what was their ultimate result, and what effect they produced? We ask ourselves what degree of foresight the statesman displayed. Did he rightly gauge the true nature of the political, economic, or social forces with which he had to deal, or did he mistake the signs of the times and allow himself to be lured away by some ephemeral will-o'-the-wisp in the pursuit of objects of secondary or even fallacious importance? It is necessary to ask these questions in dealing with the career of Disraeli, but this mental process is, in his case, obscured to a very high degree by the absorbing personality of the man. The individual fills the whole canvas almost to the extent of excluding all other objects from view.

No tale of fiction is, indeed, more strange than that which tells how this nimble-witted alien adventurer, with his poetic temperament, his weird Eastern imagination and excessive Western cynicism, his elastic mind which he himself described as "revolutionary," and his apparently wayward but in reality carefully regulated unconventionality, succeeded, in spite of every initial disadvantage of race, birth, manners, and habits of thought, in dominating a proud aristocracy and using its members as so many pawns on the chess-board which he had arranged to suit his own purposes. Thrust into a society which was steeped in conventionality, he enforced attention to his will by a studied neglect of everything that was conventional. Dealing with a class who honoured tradition, he startled the members of that class by shattering all the traditions which they had been taught to revere, and by endeavouring, with the help of specious arguments which many of them only half understood, to substitute others of an entirely novel character in their place. Following much on the lines of those religious reformers who have at times sought to revive the early discipline and practices of the Church, he endeavoured to destroy the Toryism of his day by invoking the shade of a semi-mythical Toryism of the past. Bolingbroke was the model to be followed, Shelburne was the tutelary genius of Pitt, and Charles I. was made to pose as "a virtuous and able monarch," who was "the holocaust of direct taxation." Never, he declared, "did man lay down his heroic life for so great a cause, the cause of the Church and the cause of the Poor." Aspiring to rise to power through the agency of Conservatives, whose narrow-minded conventional conservatism he despised, and to whose defects he was keenly alive, he wisely judged that it was a necessity, if his programme were to be executed, that the association of political power with landed possessions should be the sheet-anchor of his system; and, strong in the support afforded by that material bond of sympathy, he did not hesitate to ridicule the foibles of those "patricians"—to use his own somewhat stilted expression—who, whilst they sneered at his apparent eccentricities, despised their own chosen mouthpiece, and occasionally writhed under his yoke, were none the less so fascinated by the powerful will and keen intellect which held them captive that they blindly followed his lead, even to the verge of being duped.

From earliest youth to green old age his confidence in his own powers was never shaken. He persistently acted up to the sentiment—slightly paraphrased from Terence—which he had characteristically adopted as his family motto, *Forti nihil difficile*; neither could there be any question as to the genuine nature either of his strength or his courage, albeit hostile critics might seek to confound the latter quality with sheer impudence. He abhorred the commonplace, and it is notably this abhorrence which gives a vivid, albeit somewhat meretricious sparkle to his personality. For although truth is generally dull, and although probably most of the reforms and changes which have really benefited mankind partake largely of the commonplace, the attraction of unconventionality and sensationalism cannot be denied. Disraeli made English politics interesting, just as Ismail Pasha gave at one time a spurious interest to the politics of Egypt. No one could tell what would be the next step taken by the juggler in Cairo or by that meteoric statesman in London whom John Bright once called "the great wizard of Buckinghamshire." When Disraeli disappeared from the stage, the atmosphere may have become clearer, and possibly more healthy for the body politic in the aggregate, but the level of interest fell, whilst the barometer of dulness rose.

If the saying generally attributed to Buffon that "the style is the man," is correct, an examination of Disraeli's style ought to give a true insight into his character. There can be no question of the readiness of his wit or of his superabundant power of sarcasm. Besides the classic instances which have almost passed into proverbs, others, less well known, are recorded in these pages. The statement that "from the Chancellor of the Exchequer to an Undersecretary of State is a descent from the sublime to the ridiculous" is very witty. The well-known description of Lord Derby as "the Rupert of debate" is both witty and felicitous, whilst the sarcasm in the context, which is less well known, is both witty and biting. The noble lord, Disraeli said, was like Prince Rupert, because "his charge was resistless, but when he returned from the pursuit he always found his camp in the possession of the enemy."

A favourite subject of Disraeli's sarcasm in his campaign against Peel was that the latter habitually borrowed the ideas of others. "His (Peel's) life," he said, "has been a great appropriation clause. He is a burglar of others' intellect.... From the days of the Conqueror to the termination of the last reign there is no statesman who has committed political petty larceny on so great a scale."

In a happy and inimitable metaphor he likened Sir Robert Peel's action in throwing over Protection to that of the Sultan's admiral who, during the campaign against Mehemet Ali, after preparing a vast armament which left the Dardanelles hallowed by the blessings of "all the muftis of the Empire," discovered when he got to sea that he had "an objection to war," steered at once into the enemy's port, and then explained that "the only reason he had for accepting the command was that he might terminate the contest by betraying his master."

Other utterances of a similar nature abound, as, for instance, when he spoke of Lord Melbourne as "sauntering over the destinies of a nation, and lounging away the glories of an Empire," or when he likened those Tories who followed Sir Robert Peel to the Saxons converted by Charlemagne. "The old chronicler informs us they were converted in battalions and baptized in platoons."

Warned by the fiasco of his first speech in the House of Commons, Disraeli for some while afterwards exercised a wise parsimony in the display of his wit. He discovered that "the House will not allow a man to be a wit and an orator unless they have the credit of finding it out." But when he had once established his position and gained the ear of the House, he gave a free rein to his prodigious powers of satire, which he used to the full in his attacks on Peel. In point of fact, vituperation and sarcasm were his chief weapons of offence. He spoke of Mr. Roebuck as a "meagre-minded rebel," and called Campbell, who was afterwards Lord Chancellor, "a shrewd, coarse, manœuvring Pict," a "base-born Scotchman," and a "booing, fawning, jobbing progeny of haggis and cockaleekie." When he ceased to be witty, sarcastic, or vituperative, he became turgid. Nothing could be more witty than when, in allusion to Peel's borrowing the ideas of others, he spoke of his fiscal project as "Popkins's Plan," but when, having once made this hit, which naturally elicited "peals of laughter from all parts of the House," he proceeded further, he at once lapsed into cheap rhetoric.

"Is England," he said, "to be governed, and is England to be convulsed, by Popkins's plan? Will he go to the country with it? Will he go with it to that ancient and famous England that once was governed by statesmen—by Burleighs and by Walsinghams; by Bolingbrokes and by Walpoles; by a Chatham and a Canning—will he go to it with this fantastic scheming of some presumptuous pedant? I won't believe it. I have that confidence in the common sense, I will say the common spirit of our countrymen, that I believe they will not long endure this huckstering tyranny of the Treasury Bench—these political pedlars that bought their party in the cheapest market and sold us in the dearest."

So also on one occasion when in a characteristically fanciful flight he said that Canning ruled the House of Commons "as a man rules a high-bred steed, as Alexander ruled Bucephalus," and when some member of the House indulged in a very legitimate laugh, he turned on him at once and said, "I thank that honourable gentleman for his laugh. The pulse of the national heart does not beat as high as once it did. I know the temper of this House is not as spirited and brave as it was, nor am I surprised, when the vulture rules where once the eagle reigned." From the days of Horace downwards it has been permitted to actors and orators to pass rapidly from the comic to the tumid strain. But in this case the language was so bombastic and so utterly out of proportion to the occasion which called it forth that a critic of style will hardly acquit the orator of the charge of turgidity. Mr. Monypenny recognises that "in spite of Disraeli's strong grasp of fact, his keen sense of the ridiculous, and his intolerance of cant, he never could quite distinguish between the genuine and the counterfeit either in language or sentiment."

Much has at times been said and written of the solecisms for which Disraeli was famous. They came naturally to him. In his early youth he told his sister that the Danube was an "uncouth stream," because "its bed is far too considerable for its volume." At the same time there can be little doubt that his practice of indulging in carefully prepared solecisms, which became more daring as he advanced in power, was part of a deliberate and perfectly legitimate plan, conceived with the object of arresting the attention and stimulating the interest of his audience.

I have so far only dealt with Disraeli's main object in life, and with the methods by which he endeavoured to attain that object. The important question remains to be considered of whether, as many supposed and still suppose, Disraeli was a mere political charlatan, or whether, as others hold, he was a far-seeing statesman and profound thinker, who read the signs of the times more clearly than his contemporaries, and who was the early apostle of a political creed which his countrymen will do well to adopt and develop.

It is necessary here to say a word or two about Disraeli's biographer. The charm of Mr. Monypenny's style, the lucidity of his narrative, the thorough grasp which he manifestly secured of the forces in movement during the period which his history embraces, and the deep regret that all must feel that his promising career was prematurely cut short by the hand of death, should not blind us to the fact that, in spite of a manifest attempt to write judicially, he must be regarded as an apologist for Disraeli. In respect, indeed, to one point—which, however, is, in my opinion, one of great importance—he threw up the case for his client. The facts of this case are very clear.

When Peel formed his Ministry in 1841, no place was offered to Disraeli. It can be no matter for surprise that he was deeply mortified. His exclusion does not appear to have been due to any personal feeling of animosity entertained by Peel. On the contrary, Peel's relations with Disraeli had up to that time been of a very friendly character. Possibly something may be attributed to that lack of imagination which, at a much later period, Disraeli thought was the main defect of Sir Robert Peel's character, and which may have rendered him incapable of conceiving that a young man, differing so totally not only from himself but from all other contemporaneous politicians in deportment and demeanour, could ever aspire to be a political factor of supreme importance. The explanation given by Peel himself that, as is usual with Prime Ministers similarly situated, he was wholly unable to meet all the just claims made upon him, was unquestionably true, but it is more than probable that the episode related by Mr. Monypenny had something to do with Disraeli's exclusion. Peel, it appears, was inclined to consider Disraeli eligible for office, but Stanley (subsequently Lord Derby), who was a typical representative of that "patrician" class whom Disraeli courted and eventually dominated, stated "in his usual vehement way" that "if that scoundrel were taken in, he would not remain himself." However that may be, two facts are abundantly clear. One is that, in the agony of disappointment, Disraeli threw himself at Peel's feet and implored, in terms which were almost abject, that some official place should be found for him. "I appeal," he said, in a letter dated September 5, 1841, "to that justice and that magnanimity which I feel are your characteristics, to save me from an intolerable humiliation." The other fact is that, speaking to his constituents in 1844, he said: "I never asked Sir Robert Peel for a place," and further that, speaking in the House of Commons in 1846, he repeated this statement even more categorically. He assured the House that "nothing of the kind ever occurred," and he added that "it was totally foreign to his nature to make an application for any place." He was evidently not believed. "The impression in the House," Mr. Monypenny says, "was that Disraeli had better have remained silent."

Mr. Monypenny admits the facts, and does not attempt to defend Disraeli's conduct, but he passes over this very singular episode, which is highly illustrative of the character of the man, somewhat lightly, merely remarking that though Disraeli "must pay the full penalty," at the same time "it is for the politician who is without sin in the matter of veracity to cast the first stone."

I hardly think that this consolatory Biblical reflection disposes of the matter. Politicians, as also diplomatists, are often obliged to give evasive answers to inconvenient questions, but it is not possible for any man, when dealing with a point of primary importance, deliberately to make and to repeat a statement so absolutely untrue as that made by Disraeli on the occasion in question without

47

undermining any confidence which might otherwise be entertained in his general sincerity and rectitude of purpose. A man convicted of deliberate falsehood cannot expect to be believed when he pleads that his public conduct is wholly dictated by public motives. Now all the circumstantial evidence goes to show that from 1841 onwards Disraeli's conduct, culminating in his violent attacks on Peel in 1845-46, was the result of personal resentment due to his exclusion from office in 1841, and that these attacks would never have been made had he been able to climb the ladder of advancement by other means. His proved want of veracity confirms the impression derived from this evidence.

Peel's own opinion on the subject may be gathered from a letter which he wrote to Sir James Graham on December 22, 1843. Disraeli had the assurance to solicit a place for his brother from Sir James Graham. The request met with a flat refusal. Peel's comment on the incident was: "He (Disraeli) asked me for office himself, and I was not surprised that, being refused, he became independent and a patriot."

So far, therefore, as the individual is concerned, the episode on which I have dwelt above appears to me to be a very important factor in estimating not merely Disraeli's moral worth, but also the degree of value to be attached to his opinions. The question of whether Disraeli was or was not a political charlatan remains, however, to be considered.

That Disraeli was a political adventurer is abundantly clear. So was Napoleon, between whose mentality and that of Disraeli a somewhat close analogy exists. Both subordinated their public conduct to the furtherance of their personal aims. It is quite permissible to argue that, as a political adventurer, Disraeli did an incalculable amount of harm in so far as he tainted the sincerity of public life both in his own person and, posthumously, by becoming the progenitor of a school of adventurers who adopted his methods. But it is quite possible to be a self-seeking adventurer without being a charlatan. A careful consideration of Disraeli's opinions and actions leads me to the conclusion that only on a very superficial view of his career can the latter epithet be applied to him. It must, I think, be admitted that his ideas, even although we may disagree with them, were not those of a charlatan, but of a statesman. They cannot be brushed aside as trivial. They deserve serious consideration. Moreover, he had a very remarkable power of penetrating to the core of any question which he treated, coupled with an aptitude for wide generalisation which is rare amongst Englishmen, and which he probably derived from his foreign ancestors. An instance in point is his epigrammatic statement that "In England, where society was strong, they tolerated a weak Government, but in Ireland, where society was weak, the policy should be to have the Government strong." Mr. Monypenny is quite justified in saying: "The significance of the Irish question cannot be exhausted in a formula, but in that single sentence there is more of wisdom and enlightenment than in many thousands of the dreary pages of Irish debate that are buried in the volumes of Hansard."

More than this. In one very important respect he was half a century in advance of his contemporaries. With true political instinct he fell upon what was unquestionably the weakest point in the armour of the so-called Manchester School of politicians. He saw that whilst material civilisation in England was advancing with rapid strides, there was "no proportionate advance in our moral civilisation." "In the hurry-skurry of money-making, men-making, and machine-making," the moral side of national life was being unduly neglected. He was able with justifiable pride to say: "Long before what is called the 'condition of the people question' was discussed in the House of Commons, I had employed my pen on the subject. I had long been aware that there was something rotten in the core of our social system. I had seen that while immense fortunes were accumulating, while wealth was increasing to a superabundance, and while Great Britain was cited throughout Europe as the most prosperous nation in the world, the working classes, the creators of wealth, were steeped in the most abject poverty and gradually sinking into the deepest degradation." The generation of 1912 cannot dub as a charlatan the man who could speak thus in 1844. For in truth, more especially during the last five years, we have been suffering from a failure to recognise betimes the truth of this foreseeing statesman's admonition. Having for years neglected social reform, we have recently tried to make up for lost time by the hurried adoption of a number of measures, often faulty in principle and ill-considered in detail, which seek to obtain by frenzied haste those advantages which can only be secured by the strenuous and persistent application of sound principles embodied in deliberate and well-conceived legislative enactments.

Disraeli, therefore, saw the rock ahead, but how did he endeavour to steer the ship clear of the rock? It is in dealing with this aspect of the case that the view of the statesman dwindles away and is supplanted by that of the self-seeking party manager. His fundamental idea was that "we had altogether outgrown, not the spirit, but the organisation of our institutions." The manner in which he proposed to reorganise our institutions was practically to render the middle classes politically powerless. His scheme, constituting the germ which, at a later period, blossomed into the Tory democracy, was developed as early as 1840 in a letter addressed to Mr. Charles Attwood, who was at that time a popular leader. "I entirely agree with you," he said, "that an union between the Conservative Party and the Radical masses offers the only means by which we can preserve the Empire. Their interests are identical; united they form the nation; and their division has only permitted a miserable minority, under the specious name of the People, to assail all right of property and person."

Mr. Monypenny, if I understand rightly, is generally in sympathy with Disraeli's project, and appears to think that it might have been practicable to carry it into effect. He condemns Peel's counter-idea of substituting a middle-class Toryism for that which then existed as "almost a contradiction in terms." I am unable to concur in this view. I see no contradiction, either real or apparent, in Peel's counter-project, and I hold that events have proved that the premises on which Disraeli based his conclusion were entirely false, for his political descendants, while still pursuing his main aim, viz. to ensure a closer association of the Conservative Party and the masses, have been forced by circumstances into an endeavour to effect that union by means not merely different from but antagonistic to those which Disraeli himself contemplated.

It all depends on what Disraeli meant when he spoke of "Conservatism," and on what Mr. Monypenny meant when he spoke of "Toryism." It may readily be conceded that a "middle-class Toryism," in the sense in which Disraeli would have understood the expression, was "a contradiction in terms," for the bed-rock on which his Toryism was based was that it should find its main strength in the possessors of land. The creation of such a Toryism is a conceivable political programme. In France it was created by the division of property consequent on the Revolution. Thiers said truly enough that in the cottage of every French peasant owning an acre of land would be found a musket ready to be used in the defence of property. In fact, the five million peasant proprietors now existing in France represent an eminently conservative class. But, so far as I know, there is not a trace to be found in any of Disraeli's utterances that he wished to widen the basis of agricultural conservatism by creating a peasant proprietary class. He wished, above all things, to maintain the territorial magnates in the full possession of their properties. When he spoke of a "union between the Conservative Party and the Radical masses" he meant a union between the "patricians" and the working men, and the answer to this somewhat fantastic project is that given by Juvenal 1800 years ago:

Quis enim iam non intelligat artes Patricias?

"Who in our days is not up to the dodges of the patricians?"

The programme was foredoomed to failure, and the failure has been complete. Modern Conservatives can appeal to the middle classes, who—in spite of what Mr. Monypenny says—are their natural allies. They can also appeal to the working classes by educating them and by showing them that Socialism is diametrically contrary to their own interests. But, although they may gain some barren and ephemeral electoral advantages, they cannot hope to advance the cause of rational conservative progress either by alienating the one class or by sailing under false colours before the other. They cannot advantageously masquerade in Radical clothes. There was a profound truth in Lord Goschen's view upon the conduct of Disraeli when, in strict accordance with the principles he enunciated in the 'forties, he forced his reluctant followers to pass a Reform Bill far more Radical than that proposed by the Whigs. "That measure," Lord Goschen said, "might have increased the number of Conservatives, but it had, nevertheless, in his belief, weakened real Conservatism." Many of Disraeli's political descendants seem to care little for Conservatism, but they are prepared to advocate Socialist or quasi-Socialist doctrines in order to increase the number of nominal Conservatives. This, therefore, has been the ultimate result of the gospel of which Disraeli was the chief apostle. It does no credit to his political foresight. He altogether failed to see the consequences which would result from the adoption of his political principles. He hoped that the Radical masses, whom he sought to conciliate, would look to the "patricians" as their guides. They have done nothing of the sort, but a very distinct tendency has been created amongst the "patricians" to allow themselves to be guided by the Radical masses.

I cannot terminate these remarks without saying a word or two about Disraeli's great antagonist, Peel. It appears to me that Mr. Monypenny scarcely does justice to that very eminent man. His main accusation against Peel is that he committed his country "apparently past recall" to an industrial line of growth, and that he sacrificed rural England "to a one-sided and exaggerated industrial development which has done so much to change the English character and the English outlook."

I think that this charge admits of being answered, but I will not now attempt to answer it fully. This much, however, I may say. Mr. Monypenny, if I understand rightly, admits that the transition from agriculture to manufactures was, if not desirable, at all events inevitable, but he holds that this transition should have been gradual. This is practically the same view as that held by the earlier German and American economists, who—whilst condemning Protection in theory—advocated it as a temporary measure which would eventually lead up to Free Trade. The answer is that, in those countries which adopted this policy, the Protection has, in the face of vested interests, been permanent, whilst, although the movement in favour of Free Trade has never entirely died out, and may, indeed, be said recently to have shown signs of increasing vigour, the obstacles to the realisation of the ideas entertained by economists of the type of List have not yet been removed, and are still very formidable. That the plunge made by Sir Robert Peel has been accompanied by some disadvantages may be admitted, but Free Traders may be pardoned for thinking that, if he had not had the courage to make that plunge, the enormous counter-advantages which have resulted from his policy would never have accrued.

As regards Peel's character, it was twice sketched by Disraeli himself. The first occasion was in 1839. The picture he drew at that time was highly complimentary, but as Disraeli was then a loyal supporter of Peel it may perhaps be discarded on the plea advanced by Voltaire that "we can confidently believe only the evil which a party writer tells of his own side and the good which he recognises in his opponents." The second occasion was after Peel's death. It is given by Mr. Monypenny in ii. 306-308, and is too long to quote. Disraeli on this occasion made some few—probably sound—minor criticisms on Peel's style, manner, and disposition. But he manifestly wrote with a strong desire to do justice to his old antagonist's fine qualities. He concluded with a remark which, in the mouth of a Parliamentarian, may probably be considered the highest praise, namely, that Peel was "the greatest Member of Parliament that ever lived." I cannot but think that even those who reject Peel's economic principles may accord to him higher praise than this. They may admit that Peel attained a very high degree of moral elevation when, at the dictate of duty, he separated himself from all—or the greater part—of his former friends, and had the courage, when honestly convinced by Cobden's arguments, to act upon his convictions. Peel's final utterance on this subject was not only one of the most pathetic, but also one of the finest—because one of the most deeply sincere—speeches ever made in Parliament.

I may conclude these remarks by some recollections of a personal character. My father, who died in 1848, was a Peelite and an intimate friend of Sir Robert Peel, who was frequently his guest at Cromer. I used, therefore, in my childhood to hear a good deal of the subjects treated in Mr. Monypenny's brilliant volumes. I well remember—I think it must have been in 1847—being present on one occasion when a relative of my own, who was a broad-acred Nottinghamshire squire, thumped the table and declared his opinion that "Sir Robert Peel ought to be hanged on the highest tree in England." Since that time I have heard a good many statesmen accused of ruining their country, but, so far as my recollection serves me, the denunciations launched against John Bright, Gladstone, and even the present Chancellor of the Exchequer, may be considered as sweetly reasonable by comparison with the language employed about Sir Robert Peel by those who were opposed to his policy.

I was only once brought into personal communication with Disraeli. Happening to call on my old friend, Lord Rowton, in the summer of 1879, when I was about to return to Egypt as Controller-General, he expressed a wish that I should see Lord Beaconsfield, as he then was. The interview was very short; neither has anything Lord Beaconsfield said about Egyptian affairs remained in my memory. But I remember that he appeared much interested to learn whether "there were many pelicans on the banks of the Nile."

The late Sir Mountstuart Grant-Duff was a repository of numerous very amusing *Beaconsfieldiana*.

IX

RUSSIAN ROMANCE

"The Spectator," March 15, 1913

De Vogüé's well-known book, *Le Roman Russe*, was published so long ago as 1886. It is still well worth reading. In the first place, the literary style is altogether admirable. It is the perfection of

French prose, and to read the best French prose is always an intellectual treat. In the second place, the author displays in a marked degree that power of wide generalisation which distinguishes the best French writers. Then, again, M. de Vogüé writes with a very thorough knowledge of his subject. He resided for long in Russia. He spoke Russian, and had an intimate acquaintance with Russian literature. He endeavoured to identify himself with Russian aspirations, and, being himself a man of poetic and imaginative temperament, he was able to sympathise with the highly emotional side of the Slav character, whilst, at the same time, he never lost sight of the fact that he was the representative of a civilisation which is superior to that of Russia. He admires the eruptions of that volcanic genius Dostoïevsky, but, with true European instinct, charges him with a want of "mesure"—the Greek Sophrosyne—which he defines as "l'art d'assujettir ses pensées." Moreover, he at times brings a dose of vivacious French wit to temper the gloom of Russian realism. Thus, when he speaks of the Russian writers of romance, who, from 1830 to 1840, "eurent le privilège de faire pleurer les jeunes filles russes," he observes in thorough man-of-the-world fashion, "il faut toujours que quelqu'un fasse pleurer les jeunes filles, mais le génie n'y est pas nécessaire."

When Taine had finished his great history of the Revolution, he sent it forth to the world with the remark that the only general conclusion at which a profound study of the facts had enabled him to arrive was that the true comprehension, and therefore, *a fortiori*, the government of human beings, and especially of Frenchmen, was an extremely difficult matter. Those who have lived longest in the East are the first to testify to the fact that, to the Western mind, the Oriental habit of thought is well-nigh incomprehensible. The European may do his best to understand, but he cannot cast off his love of symmetry any more than he can change his skin, and unless he can become asymmetrical he can never hope to attune his reason in perfect accordance to the Oriental key. Similarly, it is impossible to rise from a perusal of De Vogüé's book without a strong feeling of the incomprehensibility of the Russians.

What, in fact, are these puzzling Russians? They are certainly not Europeans. They possess none of the mental equipoise of the Teutons, neither do they appear to possess that logical faculty which, in spite of many wayward outbursts of passion, generally enables the Latin races in the end to cast off idealism when it tends to lapse altogether from sanity; or perhaps it would be more correct to say that, having by association acquired some portion of that Western faculty, the Russians misapply it. They seem to be impelled by a variety of causes—such as climatic and economic influences, a long course of misgovernment, Byzantinism in religion, and an inherited leaning to Oriental mysticism—to distort their reasoning powers, and far from using them, as was the case with the pre-eminently sane Greek genius, to temper the excesses of the imagination, to employ them rather as an oestrus to lash the imaginative faculties to a state verging on madness.

If the Russians are not Europeans, neither are they thorough Asiatics. It may well be, as De Vogüé says, that they have preserved the idiom and even the features of their original Aryan ancestors to a greater extent than has been the case with other Aryan nations who finally settled farther West, and that this is a fact of which many Russians boast. But, for all that, they have been inoculated with far too strong a dose of Western culture, religion, and habits of thought to display the apathy or submit to the fatalism which characterises the conduct of the true Eastern.

If, therefore, the Russians are neither Europeans nor Asiatics, what are they? Manifestly their geographical position and other attendant circumstances have, from an ethnological point of view, rendered them a hybrid race, whose national development will display the most startling anomalies and contradictions, in which the theory and practice derived from the original Oriental stock will be constantly struggling for mastery with an Occidental aftergrowth. From the earliest days there have been two types of Russian reformers, viz. on the one hand, those who wished that the country should be developed on Eastern lines, and, on the other, those who looked to Western civilisation for guidance. De Vogüé says that from the accession of Peter the Great to the death of the Emperor Nicolas—that is to say, for a period of a hundred and fifty years—the government of Russia may be likened to a ship, of which the captain and the principal officers were persistently endeavouring to steer towards the West, while at the same time the whole of the crew were trimming the sails in order to catch any breeze which would bear the vessel Eastward. It can be no matter for surprise that this strange medley should have produced results which are bewildering even to Russians themselves and well-nigh incomprehensible to foreigners. One of their poets has said:

On ne comprend pas la Russie avec la raison, On ne peut que croire à la Russie.

One of the most singular incidents of Russian development on which De Vogüé has fastened, and which induced him to write this book, has been the predominant influence exercised on Russian thought and action by novels. Writers of romance have indeed at times exercised no inconsiderable amount of influence elsewhere than in Russia. Mrs. Beecher Stowe's epoch-making novel, *Uncle Tom's Cabin*, certainly contributed towards the abolition of slavery in the United States. Dickens gave a powerful impetus to the reform of our law-courts and our Poor Law. Moreover, even in free England, political writers have at times resorted to allegory in order to promulgate their ideas. Swift's Brobdingnagians and Lilliputians furnish a case in point. In France, Voltaire called fictitious Chinamen, Bulgarians, and Avars into existence in order to satirise the proceedings of his own countrymen. But the effect produced by these writings may be classed as trivial compared to that exercised by the great writers of Russian romance. In the works of men like Tourguenef and Dostoïevsky the Russian people appear to have recognised, for the first time, that their real condition was truthfully depicted, and that their inchoate aspirations had found sympathetic expression. "Dans le roman, et là seulement," De Vogüé says, "on trouvera l'histoire de Russie depuis un demi-siècle."

Such being the case, it becomes of interest to form a correct judgment on the character and careers of the men whom the Russians have very generally regarded as the true interpreters of their domestic facts, and whom large numbers of them have accepted as their political pilots.

The first point to be noted about them is that they are all, for the most part, ultra-realists; but apparently we may search their writings in vain for the cheerfulness which at times illumines the pages of their English, or the light-hearted vivacity which sparkles in the pages of their French counterparts. In Dostoïevsky's powerfully written *Crime and Punishment* all is gloom and horror; the hero of the tale is a madman and a murderer. To a foreigner these authors seem to present the picture of a society oppressed with an all-pervading sense of the misery of existence, and with the impossibility of finding any means by which that misery can be alleviated. In many instances, their lives—and still more their deaths—were as sad and depressing as their thoughts. Several of their most noted authors died violent deaths. At thirty-seven years of age the poet Pouchkine was killed in a duel, Lermontof met the same fate at the age of twenty-six. Griboïédof was assassinated at the age of thirty-four. But the most tragic history is that of Dostoïevsky, albeit he lived to a green old age, and eventually died a natural death. In 1849, he was connected with some political society, but he does not appear, even at that time, to have been a violent politician. Nevertheless, he and his companions, after being kept for several months in close confinement, were condemned to death. They were brought to the place of execution, but at the last moment, when the soldiers were about to fire, their sentences were commuted to exile. Dostoïevsky remained for some years in Siberia, but was eventually allowed to return to Russia. The inhuman cruelty to which he had been subject naturally dominated his mind and inspired his pen for the remainder of his days.

De Vogüé deals almost exclusively with the writings of Pouchkine, Gogol, Dostoïevsky, Tourguenef, who was the inventor of the word Nihilism, and the mystic Tolstoy, who was the principal apostle of the doctrine. All these, with the possible exception of Tourguenef, had one characteristic in common. Their intellects were in a state of unstable equilibrium. As poets, they could excite the enthusiasm of the masses, but as political guides they were mere Jack-o'-Lanterns, leading to the deadly swamp of despair. Dostoïevsky was in some respects the most interesting and also the most typical of the group. De Vogüé met him in his old age, and the account he gives of his appearance is most graphic. His history could be read in his face.

On y lisait mieux que dans le livre, les souvenirs de la maison des morts, les longues habitudes d'effroi, de méfiance et de martyre. Les paupières, les lèvres, toutes les fibres de cette face tremblaient de tics nerveux. Quand il s'animait de colère sur une idée, on eût juré qu'on avait déjà vu cette tête sur les banes d'une cour criminelle, ou parmi les vagabonds qui mendient aux portes des prisons. A d'autres moments, elle avait la mansuétude triste des vieux saints sur les images slavonnes.

And here is what De Vogüé says of the writings of this semi-lunatic man of genius:

Psychologue incomparable, dès qu'il étudie des âmes noires ou blessées, dramaturge habile, mais borné aux scènes d'effroi et de pitié.... Selon qu'on est plus touché par tel ou tel excès de son talent, on peut l'appeler avec justice un philosophe, un apôtre, un aliéné, le consolateur des affligés ou le bourreau des esprits tranquilles, le Jérémie de bagne ou le Shakespeare de la maison des fous; toutes ces appellations seront méritées; prise isolément, aucune ne sera suffisante.

There is manifestly much which is deeply interesting, and also much which is really lovable in the Russian national character. It must, however, be singularly mournful and unpleasant to pass through life burdened with the reflection that it would have been better not to have been born, albeit such sentiments are not altogether inconsistent with the power of deriving a certain amount of enjoyment from living. It was that pleasure-loving old cynic, Madame du Deffand, who said: "Il n'y a qu'un seul malheur, celui d'être né." Nevertheless, the avowed joyousness bred by the laughing tides and purple skies of Greece is certainly more conducive to human happiness, though at times even Greeks, such as Theognis and Palladas, lapsed into a morbid pessimism comparable to that of Tolstoy. Metrodorus, however, more fully represented the true Greek spirit when he sang, "All things are good in life" (πάντα γὰρ ἐσθλὰ βίῳ). The Roman pagan, Juvenal, gave a fairly satisfactory answer to the question, "Nil ergo optabunt homines?" whilst the Christian holds out hopes of that compensation in the next world for the afflictions of the present, which the sombre and despondent Russian philosopher, determined that we shall not find enjoyment in either world, denies to his morose and grief-stricken followers.

X

THE WRITING OF HISTORY
"The Spectator," April 26, 1913

What are the purposes of history, and in what spirit should it be written? Such, in effect, are the questions which Mr. Gooch propounds in this very interesting volume. He wisely abstains from giving any dogmatic answers to these questions, but in a work which shows manifest signs of great erudition and far-reaching research he ranges over the whole field of European and American literature, and gives us a very complete summary both of how, as a matter of fact, history has been written, and of the spirit in which the leading historians of the nineteenth century have approached their task.

Mr. Bryce, himself one of the most eminent of modern historians, recently laid down the main principle which, in his opinion, should guide his fellow-craftsmen. "Truth," he said, "and truth only is our aim." The maxim is one which would probably be unreservedly accepted in theory by the most ardent propagandist who has ever used history as a vehicle for the dissemination of his own views on political, economic, or social questions. For so fallible is human nature that the proclivities of the individual can rarely be entirely submerged by the judicial impartiality of the historian. It is impossible to peruse Mr. Gooch's work without being struck by the fact that, amongst the greatest writers of history, bias—often unconscious bias—has been the rule, and the total absence of preconceived opinions the exception. Generally speaking, the subjective spirit has prevailed amongst historians in all ages. The danger of following the scent of analogies—not infrequently somewhat strained analogies—between the present and the past is comparatively less imminent in cases where some huge upheaval, such as the French Revolution, has inaugurated an entirely new epoch, accompanied by the introduction of fresh ideals and habits of thought. It is, as Macaulay has somewhere observed, a more serious stumbling-block in the path of a writer who deals with the history of a country like England, which has through long centuries preserved its historical continuity. Hallam and Macaulay viewed history through Whig, and Alison through Tory spectacles. Neither has the remoteness of the events described proved any adequate safeguard against the introduction of bias born of contemporary circumstances. Mitford, who composed his history of Greece during the stormy times of the French Revolution, thought it compatible with his duty as an historian to strike a blow at Whigs and Jacobins. Grote's sympathy with the democracy of Athens was unquestionably to some extent the outcome of the views which he entertained of events passing under his own eyes at Westminster. Mommsen, by inaugurating the publication of the Corpus of Latin Inscriptions, has earned the eternal gratitude of scholarly posterity, but Mr. Gooch very truly remarks that his historical work is tainted with the "strident partisanship" of a keen politician and journalist. Truth, as the old Greek adage says, is indeed the fellow-citizen of the gods; but if the standard of historical truth be rated too high, and if the authority of all who have not strictly complied with that standard is to be discarded on the ground that they stand convicted of partiality, we should be left with little to instruct subsequent ages beyond the dry records of men such as the laborious, the useful, though somewhat over-credulous Clinton, or the learned but arid Marquardt, whose "massive scholarship" Mr. Gooch dismisses somewhat summarily in a single line. Such writers are not historians, but rather compilers of records, upon the foundations of which others can build history.

Under the process we have assumed, Droysen, Sybel, and Treitschke would have to be cast down from their pedestals. They were the political schoolmasters of Germany during a period of profound national discouragement. They used history in order to stir their countrymen to action, but "if the supreme aim of history is to discover truth and to interpret the movement of humanity, they have no claim to a place in the first class." Patriotism, as the Portuguese historian, Herculano da Carvalho, said, is "a bad counsellor for historians"; albeit, few have had the courage to discard patriotic considerations altogether, as was the case with the Swiss Kopp, who wrote a history of his country "from which Gessler and Tell disappeared," and in which "the familiar anecdotes of Austrian tyranny and cruelty were dismissed as legends."

Philosophic historians, who have endeavoured to bend facts into conformity with some special theory of their own, would fare little better than those who have been ardent politicians. Sainte-Beuve, after reading Guizot's sweeping and lofty generalisations, declared that they were far too logical to be true, and forthwith "took down from his shelves a volume of De Retz to remind him how history was really made." Second-or third-rate historians, such as Lamartine, who, according to Dumas, "raised history to the level of the novel," or the vitriolic Lanfrey, who was a mere pamphleteer, would, of course, be consigned—and very rightly consigned—to utter oblivion. The notorious inaccuracy of Thiers and the avowed hero-worship of Masson alike preclude their admissibility into the select circle of trustworthy and veracious historians. It is even questionable whether one of the most objectively minded of French writers, the illustrious Taine, would gain admission. His work, he himself declared, "was nothing but pure or applied psychology," and psychology is apt to clash with the facts of history. Scherer described Taine, somewhat unjustly, as "a pessimist in a passion," whilst the critical and conscientious Aulard declared that his work was "virtually useless for the purposes of history." Mr. Gooch classes Sorel's work as "incomparably higher" than that of Taine. Montalembert is an extreme case of a French historian who adopted thoroughly unsound historical methods. Clearly, as Mr. Gooch says, "the author of the famous battle-cry, 'We are the sons of the Crusades, and we will never yield to the sons of Voltaire,' was not the man for objective study."

The fate of some of the most distinguished American and British historians would be even more calamitous than that of their Continental brethren. If the touchstone of impartiality were applied, Prescott might perhaps pass unscathed through the trial. But few will deny that Motley wrote his very attractive histories at a white heat of Republican and anti-Catholic fervour. He, as also Bancroft, are classed by Mr. Gooch amongst those who "made their histories the vehicles of political and religious propaganda." Washington Irving's claim to rank in the first class of historians may be dismissed on other grounds. "He had no taste for research," and merely presented to the world "a poet's appreciation" of historical events.

But perhaps the two greatest sinners against the code of frigid impartiality were Froude and Carlyle. Both were intensely convinced of the truth of the gospel which they preached, and both were careless of detail if they could strain the facts of history to support their doctrines. The apotheosis of the strong man formed no part of Carlyle's original philosophy. In 1830, he wrote: "Which was the greatest benefactor, he who gained the battles of Cannae and Trasimene or the nameless poor who first hammered out for himself an iron spade?" He condemned Scott's historical writings: "Strange," he said, "that a man should think he was writing the history of a nation while he is describing the amours of a wanton young woman and a sulky booby blown up with gunpowder." After having slighted biography in this characteristically Carlylese utterance, he straightway set to work, with splendid inconsistency, to base his philosophy of history mainly on the biographies of men of the type of Cromwell and Frederic.

The invective levelled against Froude by Freeman is now generally recognised as exaggerated and unjust, but it would certainly appear, as Mr. Gooch says, that Froude "never realised that the main duty of the historian is neither eulogy nor criticism, but interpretation of the complex processes and conflicting ideals which have built up the chequered life of humanity."

Yet when all is said that can be said on the necessity of insisting on historical veracity, it has to be borne in mind that inaccuracy is not the only pitfall which lies in the path of the expounder of truth. History is not written merely for students and scholars. It ought to instruct and enlighten the statesman. It should quicken the intelligence of the masses. Whilst any tendency to distort facts, or to sway public opinion by sensational writing of questionable veracity, cannot be too strongly condemned, it is none the less true that it requires not merely a touch of literary genius, but also a lively and receptive imagination to tell a perfectly truthful tale in such a manner as to arrest the attention, to excite the wayward imagination and to guide the thoughts of the vast majority of those who will scan the finished work of the historian. It is here that some of the best writers of history have failed, Gardiner has written what is probably the best, and is certainly the most dispassionate and impartial history of the Stuart period. "With one exception," Mr. Gooch says, "Gardiner possessed all the tools of his craft—an accurate mind, perfect impartiality, insight into character, sympathy with ideas different from his own and from one another. The exception was style. Had he possessed this talisman his noble work would have been a popular classic. His pages are wholly lacking in grace and distinction." The result is that Gardiner's really fine work has proved an ineffectual instrument for historical education. The majority of readers will continue to turn to the brilliant if relatively partial pages of Macaulay.

The case of Freeman, though different from that of Gardiner, for his style, though lacking in grace and flexibility was vigorous, may serve as another illustration of the same thesis. Freeman was a keen politician, but he would never have for a moment entertained the thought of departing by one iota from strict historical truth in order to further any political cause in which he was interested. Mr. Gooch says, "He regarded history as not only primarily, but almost exclusively, a record of political events. Past politics, he used to say, were present history." Why is it, therefore, that his works are little read, and that they have exercised but slight influence on the opinions of the mass of his countrymen? The answer is supplied by Mr. Gooch. Freeman ignored organic evolution. "The world of ideas had no existence for him.... No less philosophic historian has ever lived." For one man who, with effort, has toiled through Freeman's ponderous but severely accurate Norman and Sicilian histories, there are probably a hundred whose imagination has been fired by Carlyle's rhapsody on the French Revolution, or who have pored with interested delight over Froude's account of the death of Cranmer.

Much the same may be said of Creighton's intrinsically valuable but somewhat colourless work. "He had no theories," Mr. Gooch says, "no philosophy of history, no wish to prove or disprove anything." He took historical facts as they came, and recorded them. "When events are tedious," he wrote, "we must be tedious."

The most meritorious, as also the most popular historians are probably those of the didactic school. Of these, Seeley and Acton are notable instances. Seeley always endeavoured to establish some principle which would capture the attention of the student and might be of interest to the statesman. He held that "history faded into mere literature when it lost sight of its relation to practical politics." Acton, who brought his encyclopaedic learning to bear on the defence of liberty in all its forms, "believed that historical study was not merely the basis of all real insight into the present, but a school of virtue and a guide to life."

Limitations of space preclude any adequate treatment of the illuminating work done by Ranke, whom Mr. Gooch regards as the nearest approximation the world has yet known to the "ideal historian"; by Lecky, who was driven by the Home Rule conflict from the ranks of historians into those of politicians; by Milman, whose style, in the opinion of Macaulay, was wanting in grace and colour, but who was distinguished for his "soundness of judgment and inexorable love of truth"; by Otfried Müller, Bérard, Gilbert Murray, and numerous other classical scholars of divers nationalities; by Fustel de Coulanges, the greatest of nineteenth-century mediaevalists; by Mahan, whose writings have exercised a marked influence on current politics, and who is thus an instance of "an historian who has helped to make history as well as to record it," and by a host of others.

At the close of his book Mr. Gooch very truly points out that "the scope of history has gradually widened till it has come to include every aspect of the life of humanity." Many of the social and economic subjects of which the historian has now to treat are of an extremely controversial character. However high may be the ideal of truth, which will be entertained, it would appear that the various forms in which the facts of history may be stated, as also the conclusions to be drawn from these facts, will tend to divergence rather than to uniformity of treatment. It is not, therefore, probable that the partisan historian—or, at all events, the historian who will be accused of partisanship—will altogether disappear from literature. Neither, on the whole, is his disappearance to be desired, for it would almost certainly connote the composition of somewhat vapid and colourless histories.

The verdicts which Mr. Gooch passes on the historians whose writings he briefly summarises are eminently judicious, though it cannot be expected that in all cases they will command universal assent. In a work which ranges over so wide a field it is scarcely possible that some slips should not have occurred. We may indicate one of these, which it would be as well to correct in the event of any future editions being published. On p. 435 the authorship of *Fieramosca* and *Nicolo dei Lapi*, which were written by Azeglio, is erroneously attributed to Cesare Balbo.

XI
THE GREEK ANTHOLOGY

"The Spectator," May 10, 1913
Shelley, himself a translator of one of the best known of the epigrams of the Anthology, has borne emphatic testimony to the difficulties of translation. "It were as wise," he said, "to cast a violet into a crucible that you might discover the formal principle of its colour and odour, as seek to transfuse from one language into another the creations of a poet."

The task of rendering Greek into English verse is in some respects specially difficult. In the first place, the translator has to deal with a language remarkable for its unity and fluency, qualities which, according to Curtius (*History of Greece*, i. 18), are the result of the "delicately conceived law, according to which all Greek words must end in vowels, or such consonants as give rise to no harshness when followed by others, viz. *n*, *r*, and *s*." Then, again, the translator must struggle with the difficulties arising from the fact that the Greeks regarded condensation in speech as a fine art. Demetrius, or whoever was the author of *De Elocutione*, said: "The first grace of style is that which results from compression." The use of an inflected language of course enabled the Greeks to carry this art to a far higher degree of perfection than can be attained by any modern Europeans. Jebb, for instance, takes twelve words—"Well hath he spoken for one who giveth heed not to fall"—to express a sentiment which Sophocles (*Œd. Tyr.* 616) is able to compress into four—καλῶς ἔλεξεν εὐλαβουμένῳ πεσεῖν. Moreover, albeit under the stress of metrical and linguistic necessity the translator must generally indulge in paraphrase, let him beware lest in doing so he sacrifices that quality in which the Greeks excelled, to wit, simplicity. Nietzsche said, with great truth, "Die Griechen sind, wie das Genie, einfach; deshalb sind sie die unsterblichen Lehrer." Further, the translator has at times so to manipulate his material as to incorporate into his verse epithets and figures of speech of surpassing grace and expressiveness, which do not readily admit of transfiguration into any modern language; such, for instance, as the "much-wooed white-armed Maiden Muse" (πολυμνήστη λευκώλενε παρθένε Μοῦσα) of Empedocles; the "long countless Time" (μακρὸς κἀναρίθμητος Χρόνος), or "babbling Echo" (ἀθυρόστομος Ἀχώ) of Sophocles; the "son, the subject of many prayers" (πολυεύχετος υἱός) and countless other expressions of the Homeric Hymns; the "blooming Love with his pinions of gold" (ὁ δ' ἀμφιθαλής Ἔρος χρυσόπτερος ἡνίας) of Aristophanes; "the eagle, messenger of wide-ruling Zeus, the lord of Thunder" (αἰετός, εὐρυάνακτος ἄγγελος Ζηνὸς ἐρισφαράγου) of Bacchylides; or mighty Pindar's "snowy Etna nursing the whole year's length her frozen snow" (νιφόεσς' Αἴτνα πανετες χιόνος ὀξείας τιθήνα).

In no branch of Greek literature are these difficulties more conspicuous than in the Anthology, yet it is the Anthology that has from time immemorial notably attracted the attention of translators. It is indeed true that the compositions of Agathias, Palladas, Paulus Silentiarius, and the rest of the poetic tribe who "like the dun nightingale" were "insatiate of song" (οἷά τις ξουθὰ ἀκόρεστος βοᾶς ... ἀηδών), must, comparatively speaking, rank low amongst the priceless legacies which Greece bequeathed to a grateful posterity. A considerable number of the writers whose works are comprised in the Anthology lived during the Alexandrian age. The artificiality of French society before the French Revolution developed a taste for shallow versifying. Somewhat similar symptoms characterised the decadent society of Alexandria, albeit there were occasions when a nobler note was struck, as in the splendid hymn of Cleanthes, written in the early part of the second century B.C. Generally speaking, however, Professor Mahaffy's criticism of the literature of this period (*Greek Life and Thought*, p. 264) holds good. "We feel in most of these poems that it is no real lover languishing for his mistress, but a pedant posing before a critical public. If ever poet was consoled by his muse, it was he; he was far prouder if Alexandria applauded the grace of his epigram than if it whispered the success of his suit." How have these manifest defects been condoned? Why is it that, in spite of much that is artificial and commonplace, the poetry of the Anthology still exercises, and will continue to exercise, an undying charm alike over the student, the moralist, and the man of the world? The reasons are not far to seek. In the first place, no productions of the Greek genius conform more wholly to the Aristotelian canon that poetry should be an imitation of the universal. Few of the poems in the Anthology depict any ephemeral phase or fashion of opinion, like the Euphuism of the sixteenth century. All appeal to emotions which endure for all time, and which, it has been aptly said, are the true raw material of poetry. The patriot can still feel his blood stirred by the ringing verse of Simonides. The moralist can ponder over the vanity of human wishes, which is portrayed in endless varieties of form, and which, even when the writer most exults in the worship of youth (πολυήρατος ἥβη) or extols the philosophy of Epicurus, is always tinged with a shade of profound melancholy, inasmuch as every poet bids us bear in mind, to use the beautiful metaphor of Keats, that the hand of Joy is "ever on his lips bidding adieu," and that the "wave of death"—the κοινὸν κῦμ' Αΐδα of Pindar—persistently dogs the steps of all mankind. The curious in literature will find in the Anthology much apparent confirmation of the saying of Terence that nothing is ever said that has not been said before. He will note that not only did the gloomy Palladas say that he came naked into the world, and that naked he will depart, but that he forestalled Shakespeare in describing the world as a stage (σκηνὴ πᾶς ὁ βίος καὶ παίγνιον), whilst Philostratus, Meleager, and Agathias implored their respective mistresses to drink to them only with their eyes and to leave a kiss within the cup. The man of the world will give Agathias credit for keen powers of observation when he notes that the Greek poet said that gambling was a test of character (κύβος ἀγγέλλει βένθος ἐχεφροσύης), whilst if for a moment he would step outside the immediate choir of the recognised Anthologists, he may smile when he reads that Menander thought it all very well to "know oneself," but that it was in practice far more useful to know other people (χρησιμώτερον γὰρ ἦν τὸ γνῶθι τοὺς ἄλλουσ).

Then, again, the pungent brevity of such of the poetry of the Anthology as is epigrammatic is highly attractive. Much has at times been said as to what constitutes an epigram, but the case for brevity has probably never been better stated than by a witty Frenchwoman of the eighteenth century. Madame de Boufflers wrote:

Il faut dire en deux mots Ce qu'on veut dire; Les longs propos Sont sots.

In this respect, indeed, French can probably compete more successfully than any other modern language with Greek. Democritus (410 B.C.) wrote, ὁ κόσμος σκηνή, ὁ βίος πάραδος· ἦλθες, εἶδες, ἀπῆλθες. The French version of the same idea is in no way inferior to the Greek:

On entre, on crie, Et c'est la vie! On crie, on sort, Et c'est la mort!

Lastly, although much of the sentiment expressed in the Anthology is artificial, and although the language is at times offensive to modern ears, the writers almost invariably exhibit that leading quality of the Greek genius on which the late Professor Butcher was wont to insist so strongly—its virile sanity.

For these reasons the literary world may cordially welcome a further addition to the abundant literature which already exists on the subject of the Anthology. The principle adopted by Dr. Grundy is unquestionably sound. He recognises that great Homer sometimes nods, that even men of real poetic genius are not always at their best, and that mere versifiers can at times, by a happy inspiration, embody an idea in language superior to the general level of their poetic compositions. English literature of the seventeenth and eighteenth centuries abounds in cases in point. Lovelace, Montrose, and even, it may almost be said, Wither and Herrick, live mainly in public estimation owing to the composition of a small number of exquisitely felicitous verses which have raised them for ever to thrones amongst the immortals. Dr. Grundy, therefore, has very wisely ranged over the whole wide field of Anthology translators, and has culled a flower here and a flower there. His method in making his selections is as unimpeachable as his principle. He has discarded all predilections based on the authority of names or on other considerations, and has simply chosen those translations which he himself likes best.

Dr. Grundy, in his preface, expresses a hope that he will be pardoned for "the human weakness" of having in many cases preferred his own translations to those of others. That pardon will be readily extended to him, for although in a brief review of this nature it is impossible to quote his compositions at any length, it is certainly true that some at least of his translations are probably better than any that have yet been attempted. Dr. Grundy says in his preface that he "has abided in most instances as closely as possible to the literal translations of the originals." That is the principle on which all, or nearly all, translators have proceeded, but the qualifying phrase—"as closely as possible"—has admitted of wide divergence in their practice. In some cases, indeed, it is possible to combine strict adherence to the original text with graceful language and harmonious metre in the translation, but in a large number of instances the translator has to sacrifice one language or the other. He has to choose between being blamed by the purist who will not admit of any expansion in the ideas of the original writer, or being accused of turning the King's English to base uses by the employment of doubtful rhythm or cacophonous expressions. Is it necessary to decide between these two rival schools and to condemn one of them? Assuredly not. Both have their merits. An instance in point is the exquisite "Rosa Rosarum" of Dionysius, which runs thus:

Ἡ τὰ ῥόδα, ῥοδόεσσαν ἔχεις χάριν· ἀλλὰ τί πωλεῖς, σαυτήν, ἢ τὰ ῥόδα, ἠέ συναμφότερα;

Mr. Pott, in his *Greek Love Songs and Epigrams*, adopted the triolet metre, which is singularly suitable to the subject, in dealing with this epigram, and gracefully translated thus:

Which roses do you offer me, Those on your cheeks, or those beside you? Since both are passing fair to see, Which roses do you offer me? To give me both would you agree, Or must I choose, and so divide you? Which roses do you offer me, Those on your cheeks or those beside you?

Here the two lines of the original are expanded into eight lines in the translation, and some fresh matter is introduced. Dr. Grundy imposes more severe limitations on his muse. His translation, which is more literal, but at the same time singularly felicitous, is as follows:

Hail, thou who hast the roses, thou hast the rose's grace! But sellest thou the roses, or e'en thine own fair face?

Any one of literary taste will find it difficult to decide which of these versions to prefer, and will impartially welcome both.

It cannot, however, be doubted that strict adherence to Dr. Grundy's principle occasionally leads to results which are open to criticism from the point of view of English style. A case in point is his translation of Plato's epitaph on a shipwrecked sailor:

Ναυηγοῦ τάφος εἰμί· ὁ δ' ἀντίον ἐστὶ γεωργοῦ· ὡς ἁλὶ καὶ γαίῃ ξυνὸς ὕπεστ' Ἀίδης.

Dr. Grundy's translation, which is as follows, adheres closely to the original text, but somewhat grates on the English ear:

A sailor's tomb am I; o'er there a yokel's tomb there be; For Hades lies below the earth as well as 'neath the sea.

Another instance is the translation of the epigram of Nicarchus on The Lifeboat, in which the inexorable necessities of finding a rhyme to "e'en Almighty Zeus" has compelled the translator to resort to the colloquial and somewhat graceless phrase "in fact, the very deuce."

But criticisms such as these may be levelled against well-nigh all translators. They merely constitute a reason for holding that Shelley was not far wrong in the opinion quoted above. Few translators have, indeed, been able to work up to the standard of William Cory's well-known version of Callimachus's epitaph on Heraclitus, which Dr. Grundy rightly remarks is "one of the most beautiful in our language," or to Dr. Symonds's translation of the epitaph on Proté, which "is perhaps the finest extant version in English of any of the verses from the Anthology." But many have contributed in a minor degree to render these exquisite products of the Greek genius available to English readers, and amongst them Dr. Grundy may fairly claim to occupy a distinguished place. He says in his preface, with great truth, that the poets of the Anthology are never wearisome. Neither is Dr. Grundy.

XII

LORD MILNER AND PARTY

"The Spectator," May 24, 1913

The preface which Lord Milner has written to his volume of speeches constitutes not merely a general statement of his political views, but is also in reality a chapter of autobiography extending over the past sixteen years. If, as is to be feared, it does not help much towards the immediate solution of the various problems which are treated, it is, none the less, a very interesting record of the mental processes undergone by an eminent politician, who combines in a high degree the qualities of a man of action and those of a political thinker. We are presented with the picture of a man of high intellectual gifts, great moral courage, and unquestionable honesty of purpose, who has a gospel to preach to his fellow countrymen—the gospel of Imperialism, or, in other words, the methods which should be adopted to consolidate and to maintain the integrity of the British Empire. In his missionary efforts on behalf of his special creed Lord Milner has found that he has been well-nigh throttled by the ligatures of the party system—a system which he spurns and loathes, but from which he has found by experience that he could by no means free himself. As a practical politician he had to recognise that, in order to gain the ear of the public on the subjects for which he cares, he was obliged to do some "vigorous swashbuckling in the field of party politics" in connection with other subjects in which he is relatively less interested. He resigned himself, albeit reluctantly, to his fate, holding apparently not only that the end justified the means, but also that without the adoption of those means there could not be the smallest prospect of the end being attained. The difficulty in which Lord Milner has found himself is probably felt more keenly by those who, like himself, have been behind the scenes of government, and have thus been able fully to realise the difficulties of dealing with public questions on their own merits to the exclusion of all considerations based on party advantages or disadvantages, than by others who have had no such experience. Nevertheless, the dilemma must in one form or another have presented itself to every thinking man who is not wholly carried away by prejudice. Most thinking men, however, unless they are prepared to pass their political lives in a state of dreamy idealism, come rapidly to the conclusion that to seek for any thoroughly satisfactory practical solution of this dilemma is as fruitless as to search for the philosopher's stone. They see that the party system is the natural outcome of the system of representative government, that it of necessity connotes a certain amount of party discipline, and that if that discipline be altogether shattered, political chaos would ensue. They, therefore, join that party with which, on the whole, they are most in agreement, and they do so knowing full well that they will almost certainly at times be associated with measures which do not fully command their sympathies. What is it that makes such men, for instance, as Lord Morley and Mr. Arthur Balfour not merely strong political partisans, but also stern party disciplinarians? It would be absurd to suppose that they consider a monopoly of political wisdom to be possessed by the party to which each belongs, or that they fail to see that every public question presents at least two sides. The inference is that, recognising the necessity of association with others, they are prepared to waive all minor objections in order to advance the main lines of the policy to which each respectively adheres.

The plan which has always commended itself to those who see clearly the evils of the party system, but fail to realise the even greater evils to which its non-existence would open the door, has been to combine in one administration a number of men possessed of sufficient patriotism and disinterestedness to work together for the common good, in spite of the fact that they differ widely, if not on the objects to be attained, at all events on the methods of attaining them. Experience has shown that this plan is wholly impracticable. It does not take sufficient account of the fact that, as the immortal Mr. Squeers or some other of Dickens's characters said, there is a great deal of human nature in man, and that one of man's most cherished characteristics—notably if he is an Englishman—is combativeness. In the early days of the party system even so hardened and positive a parliamentarian as Walpole thought that effect might be given to some such project, but when it came to the actual formation of a hybrid Ministry, Mr. Grant Robertson, the historian of the Hanoverian period, says that it "vanished into thin air," and that, as Pulteney remarked about the celebrated Sinking Fund plan, the "proposal to make England patriotic, pure and independent of Crown and Ministerial corruption, ended in some little thing for curing the itch." Neither have somewhat similar attempts which have been made since Walpole's time succeeded in abating the rancour of party strife. Moreover, it cannot be said that the attempt to treat female suffrage as a non-party question has so far yielded any very satisfactory or encouraging results.

Lord Milner, however, does not live in Utopia. He does not look forward to the possibility of abolishing the party system. "It is not," he says, "a new party that is wanted." But he thinks—and he is unquestionably right in thinking—"that the number of men profoundly interested in public affairs, and anxious to discharge their full duty of citizens who are in revolt against the rigidity and insincerity of our present party system, is very considerable and steadily increasing." He wishes people in this category to be organised with a view to encouraging a national as opposed to a party spirit, and he holds that "with a little organisation they could play the umpire between the two parties and make the unscrupulous pursuit of mere party advantage an unprofitable game."

The idea is not novel, but it is certainly statesmanlike. The general principle which Lord Milner advocates will probably commend itself to thousands of his countrymen, and most of all to those whose education and experience are a warrant for the value of their political opinions. But how far is the scheme practicable? The answer to this question is that there is one essential preliminary condition necessary to bring it within the domain of practical politics; that condition is that a sufficient number of leading politicians should be thoroughly imbued with the virtue of compromise. They must erase the word "thorough" from their political vocabulary. Each must recognise that whilst, to use Lord Milner's expression, he himself holds firmly to a "creed" on some special question, he will have to co-operate with others who hold with equally sincere conviction to a more or less antagonistic creed, and that this co-operation cannot be secured by mere assertion and still less by vituperation, but only by calm discussion and mutual concessions. Marie Antoinette, who was very courageous and very unwise, said during the most acute crisis of the Revolution, "Better to die than allow ourselves to be saved by Lafayette and the Constitutionalists." That is an example of the party spirit *in extremis*, and when it is adopted it is that spirit which causes the shipwreck of many a scheme which might, with more moderation and conciliation, be brought safely into port. In order to carry out Lord Milner's plan any such spirit must be wholly cast aside. Politicians—and none more than many of those with whom Lord Milner is associated—must act on the principle which Shakespeare puts into the mouth of Henry V.:

There is some soul of goodness in things evil Would men observingly distil it out.

They must be prepared to recognise that, whatever be their personal convictions, there may be some "soul of goodness" in views diametrically opposed to their own, and, moreover, they must not be scared by what Emerson called that "hobgoblin of little minds"—the charge of inconsistency.

It cannot be said that just at present the omens are very favourable in the direction of indicating any widespread prevalence amongst active politicians of the spirit of compromise. The reception given to Lord Curzon's very reasonable proposal that army affairs should be treated as a non-party question is apparently scouted by Radical politicians. Neither does there appear to be the least disposition to accept the statesmanlike suggestion that in order to avoid the risk of civil war in Ulster, with its almost inevitable consequence, viz. that the loyalty of the army will be strained to the utmost, the Home Rule Bill should not be submitted to the King for his assent until after another general election. On the other hand, the "Die-hard" spirit, which led to the disastrous rejection of the Budget of 1909, and was with difficulty prevented from rejecting the Parliament Bill, is still prevalent amongst many Unionists, whilst although a somewhat greater latitudinarian spirit prevails than heretofore, the influence of extreme Unionist politicians is still sufficiently powerful to prevent full acceptance of the fact that the only sound and wise Conservative principle is to neglect minor differences of opinion and to rally together all who are generally favourable to the Conservative cause.

Moreover, it must be admitted that Lord Milner is asking a great deal of party politicians. He points out, in connection with his special "creed," that the object of Mr. Chamberlain's original proposal was "undoubtedly laudable. It was prompted by motives of Imperial patriotism." There are probably few people who would be inclined to challenge the accuracy of this statement. He alludes to the unquestionable fact that it is well for every community from time to time to review the traditional foundations of its policy, and he holds that, if the controversy which Mr. Chamberlain evoked "had been conducted on anything like rational lines, the result, whether favourable or unfavourable to the proposals themselves, might have been of great public advantage." All these fair hopes, Lord Milner thinks, were wrecked by the spirit of party. "The new issue raised by Mr. Chamberlain was sucked into the vortex of our local party struggle." Lord Milner, therefore, wishes to lift Imperialism out of the party bog and to treat the subject on broad national lines.

Here, again, the proposal is undoubtedly statesmanlike, but is it practicable? There can, it is to be feared, be but one answer to that question. For the time being, at all events, Lord Milner's proposal is quite impracticable. Whatever be the merits or demerits of the proposals initiated by Mr. Chamberlain, one thing appears tolerably manifest, and that is that so long as Tariff Reform and Imperial policy are intimately connected together there is not, so far as can at present be judged, the most remote chance of Imperialism emerging from the arena of party strife. It is true, and is, moreover, a subject for national congratulation, that there has been of late years a steady growth of Imperialist ideas. The day is probably past for ever when Ministers, whether Liberal or Conservative, could speak of the colonies as a burden, and look forward with equanimity, if not with actual pleasure, to their complete severance from the Mother country. Few, if any, pronounced anti-Imperialists exist, but a wide difference of opinion prevails as to the method for giving effect to an Imperial policy. These differences do not depend solely, as is often erroneously supposed, on a rigid adherence by Free Traders to what are now called Cobdenite principles. There are many Free Traders who would be disposed to make a considerable sacrifice of their opinions on economic principles, if they thought that the policy proposed by Mr. Chamberlain would really achieve the object he unquestionably had in view, viz. that of tightening the bonds between the Mother country and the colonies. But that is what they deny. They rely mainly on a common ancestry, common traditions, a common language, and a common religion to cement those bonds; and, moreover, they hold, to quote the words of an able article published two years ago in the *Round Table*: "The chief reason for the sentiment of Imperial unity is the conscious or unconscious belief of the people of the Empire in their own political system.... There is in the British Empire a unity which it is often difficult to discern amid the conflict of racial nationalities, provincial politics, and geographical differences. It is a unity which is based upon the conviction amongst the British self-governing communities that the political system of the Empire is indispensable to their own progress, and that to allow it to collapse would be fatal alike to their happiness and their self-respect." They therefore demur to granting special economic concessions which—unless, indeed, a policy of perfect Free Trade throughout the Empire could be adopted—they think, whatever might be the immediate result, would eventually cause endless friction and tend to weaken rather than strengthen the Imperial connection.

Further, it is to be observed that whatever exacerbation has been caused by party exaggeration and misrepresentation, it is more than doubtful whether Lord Milner's special accusation against the party system can be made good, for it must be remembered that Mr. Chamberlain's original programme was strongly opposed by many who, on mere party grounds, were earnestly desirous to accord it a hearty welcome. Rather would it be true to say that, looking back on past events, it is amazing that any one of political experience could have imagined for one moment that a proposal which touched the opinions and interests of almost every individual in the United Kingdom, and which was wholly at variance with the views heretofore held by Mr. Chamberlain himself, could have been kept outside the whirlpool of party politics. "A great statesman," it has been truly said, "must have two qualities; the first is prudence, the second imprudence." Cavour has often been held up as the example of an eminent man who combined, in his own person, these apparently paradoxical qualities. Accepting the aphorism as true, it has to be applied with the corollary that the main point is to know when to allow imprudence to predominate over prudence. It is difficult to resist the conclusion that when Mr. Chamberlain launched his programme, which Lord Milner admits "burst like a bombshell in the camp of his friends," he overweighted the balance on the imprudent side. The heat with which the controversy has been conducted, and which Lord Milner very rightly deplores, must be attributed mainly to this cause rather than to any inherent and, to a great extent, unavoidable defects in the party system.

But in spite of all these difficulties and objections, Lord Milner and those who hold with him may take heart of grace in so far as their campaign against the extravagances of the party system is concerned. It may well be that no special organisation will enable the non-party partisans to occupy the position of umpires, but the steady pressure of public opinion and the stern exposure of the abuses of the party system will probably in time mitigate existing evils, and will possibly in some degree purge other issues, besides those connected with foreign affairs, from the rancour of the party spirit. As a contribution to this end Lord Milner's utterances are to be heartily welcomed.

XIII
THE FRENCH IN ALGERIA
"The Spectator," May 31, 1913

In the very interesting account which Mrs. Devereux Roy has given of the present condition of Algeria, she says that France "is now about to embark upon a radical change of policy in regard to her African colonies." If it be thought presumptuous for a foreigner who has no local knowledge of Algerian affairs to make certain suggestions as to the direction which those changes might profitably assume, an apology must be found in Mrs. Roy's very true remark that England "can no more afford to be indifferent to the relations of France with her Moslem subjects than she can disregard the trend of our policy in Egypt and India." It is, indeed, manifest that somewhat drastic reforms of a liberal character will have to be undertaken in Algeria. The French Government have adopted the only policy which is worthy of a civilised nation. They have educated the Algerians, albeit Mrs. Roy tells us that grants for educational purposes have been doled out "with a very sparing hand." They must bear the consequences of the generous policy which they have pursued. They must recognise, as Macaulay said years ago, that it is impossible to impart knowledge without stimulating ambition. Reforms are, therefore, imposed by the necessities of the situation.

These reforms may be classified under three heads, namely, fiscal, judicial, and political. The order in which changes under each head should be undertaken would appear to be a matter of vital importance. If responsible French statesmen make a mistake in this matter—if, to use the language of proverbial philosophy, they put the cart before the horse—they may not improbably lay the seeds of very great trouble for their countrymen in the future. Prince Bismarck once said: "Mistakes committed in statesmanship are not always punished at once, but they always do harm in the end. The logic of history is a more exact and a more exacting accountant than is the strictest national auditing department."

It should never be forgotten that, however much local circumstances may differ, there are certain broad features which always exist wherever the European—be he French, English, German, or of any other nationality—is brought in contact with the Oriental—be he Algerian, Indian, or Egyptian. When the former once steps outside the influence acquired by the power of the sword, and seeks for any common ground of understanding with the subject race, he finds that he is, by the elementary facts of the case, debarred from using all those moral influences which, in more homogeneous countries, bind society together. These are a common religion, a common language, common traditions, and—save in very rare instances—intermarriage and really intimate social relations. What therefore remains? Practically nothing but the bond of material interest, tempered by as much sympathy as it is possible in the difficult circumstances of the case to bring into play. But on this poor material—for it must be admitted that it is poor material—experience has shown that a wise statesmanship can build a political edifice, not indeed on such assured foundations as prevail in more homogeneous societies, but nevertheless of a character which will give some solid guarantees of stability, and which will, in any case, minimise the risk that the sword, which the European would fain leave in the scabbard, shall be constantly flaunted before the eyes both of the subject and the governing races, the latter of whom, on grounds alike of policy and humanity, deprecate its use save in cases of extreme necessity.

In the long course of our history many mistakes have been made in dealing with subject races, and the line of conduct pursued at various times has often been very erratic. Nevertheless, it would be true to say that, broadly speaking, British policy has been persistently directed towards an endeavour to strengthen political bonds through the medium of attention to material interests. The recent history of Egypt is a case in point.

No one who was well acquainted with the facts could at any time have thought that it would be possible to create in the minds of the Egyptians a feeling of devotion towards England which might in some degree take the place of patriotism. Neither, in spite of the relatively higher degree of social elasticity possessed by the French, is it at all probable that any such feeling towards France will be created in Algeria. But it was thought that by careful attention to the material interests of the people it might eventually be possible to bring into existence a conservative class who, albeit animated by no great love for their foreign rulers, would be sufficiently contented to prevent their becoming easily the prey either of the Nationalist demagogue, who was sure sooner or later to spring into existence, or that of some barbarous religious fanatic, such as the Mahdi, or, finally, that of some wily politician, such as the Sultan Abdul Hamid who would, for his own purposes, fan the flame of religious and racial hatred. For many years after the British occupation of Egypt began, the efforts of the British administrators in that country were unceasingly directed towards the attainment of that object. The methods adopted, which it should be observed were in the main carried out before any large sums were spent on education, were the relief of taxation, the abolition of fiscal inequality and of the *corvée*, the improvement of irrigation, and last, but not least, a variety of measures having for their object the maintenance of a peasant proprietary class. The results which have been attained fully justify the adoption of this policy, which has probably never been fully understood on the Continent of Europe, even if—which is very doubtful—it has been understood in England. What, in fact, has happened in Egypt? Nationalists have enjoyed an excess of licence in a free press. The Sultan has preached pan-Islamism. The usual Oriental intrigue has been rife. British politicians and a section of the British press, being very imperfectly informed as to the situation, have occasionally dealt with Egyptian affairs in a manner which, to say the least, was indiscreet. But all has been of no avail. In spite of some outward appearances to the contrary, the whole Nationalist movement in Egypt has been a mere splutter on the surface. It never extended deep down in the social ranks. More than this. When a very well-intentioned but rather rash attempt was made to advance too rapidly in a liberal direction, the inevitable reaction, which was to have been foreseen, took place. Not merely Europeans but also Egyptians cried out loudly for a halt, and, with the appointment of Lord Kitchener, they got what they wanted. The case would have been very different if the Nationalist, the religious fanatic, or the scheming politician, in dealing with some controversial point or incident of ephemeral interest, had been able to appeal to a mass of deep-seated discontent due to general causes and to the existence of substantial grievances. In that case the Nationalist movement would have been less artificial. It would have extended not merely to the surface but to the core of society. It would have possessed a real rather than, as has been shown to be the case, a spurious vitality. The recent history of Egypt, therefore, is merely an illustration of the general lesson taught by universal history. That lesson is that the best, and indeed the only, way to combat successfully the proceedings of the demagogue or the agitator is to limit his field of action by the removal of any real grievances which, if still existent, he would be able to use as a lever to awaken the blind wrath of Demos.

How far can principles somewhat analogous to these be applied in Algeria?

In the first place, it is abundantly clear that, from many points of view, the French Government have successfully carried out the policy of ministering to the material wants of the native population. Public works of great utility have been constructed. Means of locomotion have been improved. Modern agricultural methods have been introduced. Famine has been rendered impossible. Mutual benefit societies have been established. The creation of economic habits has been encouraged. In all these matters the French have certainly nothing to learn from us. Possibly, indeed, we may have something to learn from them. Nevertheless, when it is asked whether the French Government is likely to reap the political fruits which it might have been hoped would be the result of their efforts, whether they are in a fair way towards creating a conservative spirit which would be adverse to any radical change, and whether, in reliance on that spirit, they are in a position to move boldly forward in the direction of that liberal reform, the demand for which has naturally sprung into existence from their educational policy, it is at once clear that they are heavily weighted by the policy originated some seventy years ago by Marshal Bugeaud, under which the interests of the native population were made subservient to those of the colonists, numbering about three-quarters of a million, of whom, Mrs. Roy tells us, less than one-half are of French origin. It may have been wise and necessary to initiate that policy. It may be wise and necessary to continue it with certain modifications. But it is obvious that the adoption of Marshal Bugeaud's plan has necessarily led to the creation of substantial grievances, which are important alike from the point of view of sentiment and from that of material interests. It appears now that there is some probability that this policy will be modified in at least one very important respect, namely, by the removal of the fiscal inequality which at present exists between the natives and the colonists. The former are at present heavily taxed; the latter pay relatively very little. It may be suggested that it would be worth the while of the French Government to consider whether this change should not occupy the first place in the programme of reform. The present system is obviously indefensible on general grounds, whilst its continuance, until its abolition results from the strong native pressure which will certainly ensue after the adoption of any drastic measure of political reform, would appear to be undesirable. It would probably be wise and statesmanlike not to await this pressure, but to let the concession be the spontaneous act of the French Government and nation rather than give the appearance of its having been wrung reluctantly from France by the insistence of the native population and its representatives.

Next, there is the question of judicial reform. Mrs. Roy tells us that, under what is called the *Code de l'Indigénat*, "a native can be arrested and imprisoned practically without trial at the will of the *administrateur* for his district." It would require full local knowledge to treat this question adequately, but it would obviously be desirable that the French Government should go as far as possible in the direction of providing that all judicial matters should be settled by judicial officers who would be independent of the executive and, for the most part, irremovable. Some local friction between the executive and the judicial authorities is probably to be expected. That cannot be helped. It might perhaps be mitigated by a very careful choice of the officials in each case.

In the third place, there is the question of political reform. M. Philippe Millet, who has published an interesting article on this subject in the April number of *The Nineteenth Century*, is of course quite right in saying that political reform is the "key to every other change." Once give the natives of Algeria effective political strength, and the reforms will be forced upon the Government. But, as has been already stated, it would perhaps be wiser and more statesmanlike that these changes should be conceded spontaneously by the French Government, and that then, after a reasonable interval, the bulk of the political reforms should follow.

A distinction, however, has to be made between the various representative institutions which already exist. The *Conseil Supérieur* and the *Délégations Financières* have very extensive powers, including that of rejecting or modifying the Budget. At present these bodies may be said, for all practical purposes, to be merely representative of the colonists. It would certainly appear wise eventually to allow the natives both a larger numerical strength on the *Conseil* and on the *Délégations*, and also, by rearranging the franchise, to endeavour to secure a more real representation of native interests. It must, however, be borne in mind that the difficulties of securing any real representation of the best interests in the country will almost certainly be very great, if not altogether insuperable. In all probability the loquacious, semi-educated native, who has in him the makings of an agitator, will, under any system, naturally float to the top, whilst the really representative man will sink to the bottom. It would perhaps, therefore, be as well not to move in too great a hurry in this matter, and, when any move is made, that the advance should be of a very cautious and tentative nature.

The *Conseils Généraux*, which are provincial and municipal bodies, stand on a very different footing. Here it may be safe to move forward in the path of reform with greater boldness and with less delay. But whatever is done it will probably be found that real progress in the direction of self-government will depend more on the attitude of the French officials who are associated with the Councils than on any system which can be devised on paper. It may be assumed that the French officials in Algeria present the usual characteristics of their class, that is to say, that they are courageous, intelligent, zealous, and thoroughly honest. Also it may probably be assumed that they are somewhat inelastic, somewhat unduly wedded to bureaucratic ideas, and more especially that they are possessed with the very natural idea that the main end and object of their lives is to secure the efficiency of the administration. Now if self-government is to be a success, they will have to modify to some extent their ideas as to the supreme necessity of efficiency. That is to say, they will have to recognise that it is politically wiser to put up with an imperfect reform carried with native consent, rather than to insist on some more perfect measure executed in the teeth of strong—albeit often unreasonable—native opposition. English experience has shown that this is a very hard lesson for officials to learn. Nevertheless, the task of inculcating general principles of this nature is not altogether impossible. It depends mainly on the impulse which is given from above. To entrust the execution of a policy of reform in Algeria to a man of ultra-bureaucratic tendencies, who is hostile to reform of any kind, would, of course, be to court failure. On the other hand, to select an extreme radical visionary, who will probably not recognise the difference between East and West, would be scarcely less disastrous. What, in fact, is required is a man of somewhat exceptional qualities. He must be strong—that is to say, he must impress the natives with the conviction that, albeit an advocate of liberal ideas, he is firmly resolved to consent to nothing which is likely to be detrimental to the true interests of France. He must also be sufficiently strong to keep his own officials in hand and to make them conform to his policy, whilst at the same time he must be sufficiently tactful to win their confidence and to prevent their being banded together against him. The latter is a point of very special importance, for in a country like Algeria no government, however powerful, will be able to carry out a really beneficial programme of reform if the organised strength of the bureaucracy— backed up, as would probably be the case, by the whole of the European unofficial community—is thrown into bitter and irreconcilable opposition. The task, it may be repeated, is a difficult one. Nevertheless, amongst the many men of very high ability in the French service there must assuredly be some who would be able to undertake it with a fair chance of success.

One further remark on this very interesting subject may be made. M. Millet, in the article to which allusion has already been made, says, "The Algerian natives will look more and more to France as their natural protector against the colonists." It will, it is to be hoped, not be thought over-presumptuous to sound a note of warning against trusting too much to this argument. That for the present the natives should look to France rather than to the colonists is natural enough. It is manifestly their interest to do so. But it may be doubted whether they will be "more and more" inspired by such sentiments as time goes on. There is an Arabic proverb to the effect that "all Christians are of one tribe." That is the spirit which in reality inspires the whole Moslem world. It is illustrated by the author of that very remarkable work, *Turkey in Europe*, in an amusing apologue. Let once some semi-religious, semi-patriotic leader arise, who will play skilfully on the passions of the masses, and it will be somewhat surprising if the distinction which now exists will long survive. All Frenchmen, those in France equally with those in Algeria, will then, it may confidently be expected, be speedily confounded in one general anathema.

XIV

THE OTTOMAN EMPIRE

"The Spectator," June 14, 1913

Although proverbial philosophy warns us never to prophesy unless we know, experience has shown that political prophets have often made singularly correct forecasts of the future. Lord Chesterfield, and at a much earlier period Marshal Vauban, foretold the French Revolution, whilst the impending ruin of the Ottoman Empire has formed the theme of numerous prophecies made by close observers of contemporaneous events from the days of Horace Walpole downwards. "It is of no use," Napoleon wrote to the Directory, "to try to maintain the Turkish Empire; we shall witness its fall in our time." During the War of Greek Independence the Duke of Wellington believed that the end of Turkey was at hand. Where the prophets have for the most part failed is not so much in making a mistaken estimate of the effects likely to be produced by the causes which they saw were acting on the body politic, as in not allowing sufficient time for the operation of those causes. Political evolution in its early stages is generally very slow. It is only after long internal travail that it moves with vertiginous rapidity. De Tocqueville cast a remarkably accurate horoscope of the course which would be run by the Second Empire, but it took some seventeen years to bring about results which he thought would be accomplished in a much shorter period. It has been reserved for the present generation to witness the fulfilment of prophecy in the case of European Turkey. The blindness displayed by Turkish statesmen to the lessons taught by history, their complete sterility in the domain of political thought, and their inability to adapt themselves and the institutions of their country to the growing requirements of the age, might almost lead an historical student to suppose that they were bent on committing political suicide. The combined diplomatists of Europe, Lord

Salisbury sorrowfully remarked in 1877, "all tried to save Turkey," but she scorned salvation and persisted in a course of action which could lead to but one result. That result has now been attained. The dismemberment of European Turkey, begun so long ago as the Peace of Karlovitz in 1699, is now almost complete. "Modern history," Lord Acton said, "begins under the stress of the Ottoman conquest." Whatever troubles the future may have in store, Europe has at last thrown off the Ottoman incubus. A new chapter in modern history has thus been opened. Henceforth, if Ottoman power is to survive at all, it must be in Asia, albeit the conflicting jealousies of the European Powers allow for the time being the maintenance of an Asiatic outpost on European soil.

It is as yet too early to expect any complete or philosophic account of this stupendous occurrence, which the future historian will rank with the unification first of Italy and later of Germany, as one of the most epoch-making events of the later nineteenth and early twentieth centuries. Notably, there are two subjects which require much further elucidation before the final verdict of contemporaries or posterity can be passed upon them. In the first place, the causes which have led to the military humiliation of a race which, whatever may be its defects, has been noted in history for its martial virility, require to be differentiated. Was the collapse of the Turkish army due merely to incapacity and mismanagement on the part of the commanders, aided by the corruption which has eaten like a canker into the whole Ottoman system of government and administration? Or must the causes be sought deeper, and, if so, was it the palsy of an unbridled and malevolent despotism which in itself produced the result, or did the sudden downfall of the despot, by the removal of a time-honoured, if unworthy, symbol of government, abstract the corner-stone from the tottering political edifice, and thus, by disarranging the whole administrative gear of the Empire at a critical moment, render the catastrophe inevitable? Further information is required before a matured opinion on this point, which possesses more than a mere academic importance, can be formed.

There is yet another subject which, if only from a biographical point of view, is of great interest. Two untoward circumstances have caused Turkish domination in Europe to survive, and to resist the pressure of the civilisation by which it was surrounded, but which seemed at one time doomed to thunder ineffectually at its gates. One was excessive jealousy—in Solomon's words, "as cruel as the grave"—amongst European States, which would not permit of any political advantage being gained by a rival nation. The other, and, as subsequent events proved, more potent consideration, was the fratricidal jealousy which the populations of the Balkan Peninsula mutually entertained towards each other. The maintenance and encouragement of mutual suspicions was, in either case, sedulously fostered by Turkish Sultans, the last of whom, more especially, acted throughout his inglorious career in the firm belief that mere mediaeval diplomatic trickery could be made to take the place of statesmanship. He must have chuckled when he joyously put his hand to the firman creating a Bulgarian Exarch, who was forthwith excommunicated by the Greek Patriarch, with the result, as Mr. Miller tells us, that "peasants killed each other in the name of contending ecclesiastical establishments."

In the early days of the last century the poet Rhigas, who was to Greece what Arndt was to Germany and Rouget de Lisle to Revolutionary France, appealed to all Balkan Christians to rise on behalf of the liberties of Greece. But the hour had not yet come for any such unity to be cemented. At that time, and for many years afterwards, Europe was scarcely conscious of the fact that there existed "a long-forgotten, silent nationality" which, after a lapse of nearly five centuries, would again spring into existence and bear a leading part in the liberation of the Balkan populations. But the rise of Bulgaria, far from bringing unity in its wake, appeared at first only to exacerbate not merely the mercurial Greek, proud of the intellectual and political primacy which he had heretofore enjoyed, but also the brother Slav, with whom differences arose which necessitated an appeal to the arbitrament of arms.

Although the thunder of the guns of Kirk Kilisse and Lüle Burgas proclaimed to Europe, in the words of the English Prime Minister, that "the map of Eastern Europe had to be recast," it is none the less true that the cause of the Turk was doomed from the moment when Balkan discord ceased, and when the Greek, the Bulgarian, the Serb, and the Montenegrin agreed to sink their differences and to act together against the common enemy. Who was it who accomplished this miracle? Mr. Miller says, "the authorship of this marvellous work, hitherto the despair of statesmen, is uncertain, but it has been ascribed chiefly to M. Venezélos." All, therefore, that can now be said is that it was the brain, or possibly brains, of some master-workers which gave liberty to the Balkan populations as surely as it was the brain of Cavour which united Italy.

Although these and possibly other points will, without doubt, eventually receive more ample treatment at the hands of some future historian, Mr. Miller has performed a most useful service in affording a guide by the aid of which the historical student can find his way through the labyrinthine maze of Balkan politics. He begins his story about the time when Napoleon had appeared like a comet in the political firmament, and by his erratic movements had caused all the statesmen of Europe to diverge temporarily from their normal and conventional orbits, one result being that the British Admiral Duckworth wandered in a somewhat aimless fashion through the Dardanelles to Constantinople, and had very little idea of what to do when he got there. Mr. Miller reminds us of events of great importance in their day, but now almost wholly forgotten: of how the ancient Republic of Ragusa, which had existed for eleven centuries and which had earned the title of the "South Slavonic Athens," was crushed out of existence under the iron heel of Marmont, who forthwith proceeded to make some good roads and to vaccinate the Dalmatians; of how Napoleon tried to partition the Balkans, but found, with all his political and administrative genius, that he was face to face with an "insoluble problem"; of how that rough man of genius, Mahmoud II., hanged the Greek Patriarch from the gate of his palace, but between the interludes of massacres and executions, brought his "energy and indomitable force of will" to bear on the introduction of reforms; of how the Venetian Count Capo d'Istria, who was eventually assassinated, produced a local revolt by a well-intentioned attempt to amend the primitive ethics of the Mainote Greeks—a tale which is not without its warning if ever the time comes for dealing with a cognate question amongst the wild tribes of Albania; and of how, amidst the ever-shifting vicissitudes of Eastern politics, the Tsar of Russia, who had heretofore posed as the "protector" of Roumans and Serbs against their sovereign, sent his fleet to the Bosphorus in 1833 in order to "protect" the sovereign against his rebellious vassal, Mehemet Ali, and exacted a reward for his services in the shape of the leonine arrangement signed at Hunkiar-Iskelesi. And so Mr. Miller carries us on from massacre to massacre, from murder to murder, and from one bewildering treaty to another, all of which, however, present this feature of uniformity, that the Turk, signing of his own free will, but with an unwilling mind—ἐκὼν ἀέκοντί γε θυμῷ—made on each occasion either some new concession to the ever-rising tide of Christian demand, or ratified the loss of a province which had been forcibly torn from his flank. Finally, we get to the period when the tragedy connected with the name of Queen Draga acted like an electric shock on Europe, and when the accession of King Peter, "who had translated Mill *On Liberty*," to the blood-stained Servian throne, revealed to an astonished world that the processes of Byzantinism survived to the present day. Five years later followed the assumption by Prince Ferdinand of the title of "Tsar of the Bulgarians," and it then only required the occurrence of some opportunity and the appearance on the scene of some Balkan Cavour to bring the struggle of centuries to the final issue of a death-grapple between the followers of aggressive Christianity and those of stagnant Islamism.

The whole tale is at once dramatic and dreary, dramatic because it is occasionally illumined by acts of real heroism, such as the gallant defence of Plevna by Ghazi Osman, a graphic account of which was written by an adventurous young Englishman (Mr. W.V. Herbert) who served in the Turkish army, or again as the conduct of the Cretan Abbot Máneses who, in 1866, rather than surrender to the Turks, "put a match to the powder-magazine, thus uniting defenders and assailants in one common hecatomb." It is dreary because the mind turns with horror and disgust from the endless record of government by massacre, in which, it is to be observed, the crime of bloodguiltiness can by no means be laid exclusively at the door of the dominant race, whilst Mr. Miller's sombre but perfectly true remark that "assassination or abdication, execution or exile, has been the normal fate of Balkan rulers," throws a lurid light on the whole state of Balkan society.

But how does the work of diplomacy, and especially of British diplomacy, stand revealed by the light of the history of the past century? The point is one of importance, all the more so because there is a tendency on the part of some British politicians to mistrust diplomatists, to think that, either from incapacity or design, they serve as agents to stimulate war rather than as peace-makers, and to hold that a more minute interference by the House of Commons in the details of diplomatic negotiations would be useful and beneficial. It would be impossible within the limits of an ordinary newspaper article to deal adequately with this question. This much, however, may be said—that, even taking the most unfavourable view of the results achieved by diplomacy, there is nothing whatever in Mr. Miller's history to engender the belief that better results would have been obtained by shifting the responsibility to a greater degree from the shoulders of the executive to those of Parliament. The evidence indeed rather points to an opposite conclusion. For instance, Mr. Miller informs us that inopportune action taken in England was one of the causes which contributed to the outbreak of hostilities between Greece and Turkey in 1897. "An address from a hundred British members of Parliament encouraged the masses, ignorant of the true condition of British politics, to count upon the help of Great Britain."

It is, however, quite true that a moralist, if he were so minded, might in Mr. Miller's pages find abundant material for a series of homilies on the vanity of human wishes, and especially of diplomatic human wishes. But would he on that account be right in pronouncing a wholesale condemnation of diplomacy? Assuredly not. Rather, the conclusion to be drawn from a review of past history is that a small number of very well-informed and experienced diplomatists showed remarkable foresight in perceiving the future drift of events. So early as 1837 Lord Palmerston supported Milosh Obrenovitch II., the ruler of Servia, against Turkey, as he had "come to the conclusion that to strengthen the small Christian States of the Near East was the true policy of both Turkey and Great Britain." Similar views were held at a later period by Sir William White, and were eventually adopted by the Government of Lord Beaconsfield. An equal amount of foresight was displayed by some Russian diplomatists. In Lord Morley's *Life of Gladstone* (vol. i. p. 479) a very remarkable letter is given, which was addressed to the Emperor Nicholas by Baron Brunnow, just before the outbreak of the Crimean War, in which he advocated peace on the ground that "war would not turn to Russian advantage.... The Ottoman Empire may be transformed into independent States, which for us will only become either burdensome clients or hostile neighbours." It may be that, as is now very generally thought, the Crimean War was a mistake, and that, in the classic words of Lord Salisbury, we "put our money on the wrong horse." But it is none the less true that had it not been for the Crimean War and the policy subsequently adopted by Lord Beaconsfield's government, the independence of the Balkan States would never have been achieved, and the Russians would now be in possession of Constantinople. It is quite permissible to argue that, had they been left unopposed, British interests would not have suffered; but even supposing this very debatable proposition to be true, it must be regarded, from an historical point of view, as at best an *ex post facto* argument. British diplomacy has to represent British public opinion, and during almost the whole period of which Mr. Miller's history treats, a cardinal article of British political faith was that, in the interests of Great Britain, Constantinople should not be allowed to fall into Russian hands. The occupation of Egypt in 1882 without doubt introduced a new and very important element into the discussion. The most serious as also the least excusable mistake in British Near-Eastern policy of recent years has been the occupation of Cyprus, which burthened us with a perfectly useless possession, and inflicted a serious blow on our prestige. Sir Edward Grey's recent diplomatic success is in a large measure due to the fact that all the Powers concerned were convinced of British disinterestedness.

XV
WELLINGTONIANA
"The Spectator," June 21, 1913
In dealing with Lady Shelley's sprightly and discursive comments upon the current events of her day, we have to transport ourselves back into a society which, though not very remote in point of time, has now so completely passed away that it is difficult fully to realise its feelings, opinions, and aspirations. It was a time when a learned divine, writing in the *Church and State Gazette*, had proved entirely to his own satisfaction, and apparently also to that of Lady Shelley, that a "remarkable fulfilment of that hitherto incomprehensible prophecy in the Revelations" had taken place, inasmuch as Napoleon Bonaparte was most assuredly "the seventh head of the Beast." It was a time when Londoners rode in the Green Park instead of Rotten Row, and when, in spite of the admiration expressed for the talents of that rising young politician, Mr. Robert Peel, it was impossible to deny that "his birth ran strongly against him"—a consideration which elicited from Lady Shelley the profound remark that it is "strange to search into the recesses of the human mind."

Lady Shelley herself seems to have been rather a *femme incomprise*. She had lived much on the Continent, and appreciated the greater deference paid to a charming and accomplished woman in Viennese and Parisian society, compared with the boorishness of Englishmen who would not "waste their time" in paying pretty compliments to ladies which "could be repaid by a smile." She records her impressions in French, a language in which she was thoroughly proficient. "Je sais," she says, "qu'en Angleterre il ne faut pas s'attendre à cultiver son esprit; qu'il faut, pour être contente à Londres, se résoudre à se plaire avec la médiocrité; à entendre tous les jours répéter les mêmes banalités et à s'abaisser autant qu'on le peut au niveau des femmelettes avec lesquelles l'on vit, et qui, pour plaire, affectent plus de frivolité qu'elles n'ont réellement. Le plaisir de causer nous est défendu." Nevertheless, however much she may have mentally appreciated the solitude of a crowd, she determined to adapt herself to her social surroundings. "C'est un sacrifice," she says, "que je fais à mon Dieu et à mon devoir comme Anglaise." Impelled, therefore, alike by piety and patriotism, she cast aside all ideas of leading an eremitic life, plunged into the vortex of the social world, and mixed with all the great men and women of the day. Of these the most notable was the Duke of Wellington.

Lady Shelley certainly possessed one quality which eminently fitted her to play the part of Boswell to the Duke. The worship of her hero was without the least mixture of alloy. She had a pheasant, which the Duke had killed, stuffed, and "added to other souvenirs which ornamented her dressing-room"; and she records, with manifest pride, that "amongst her other treasures" was a chair on which he sat upon the first occasion of his dining with her husband and herself in 1814. It was well to have that pheasant stuffed, for apparently the Duke, like his great antagonist, did not shoot many pheasants. He was not only "a very wild shot," but also a very bad shot. Napoleon, Mr. Oman tells us, on one occasion "lodged some pellets in Masséna's left eye while letting fly at a pheasant," and then without the least hesitation accused "the faithful Berthier" of having fired the shot, an accusation which was at once confirmed by the mendacious but courtierlike victim of the accident. Wellington also, Lady Shelley records, "after wounding a retriever early in the day and later on peppering the keeper's gaiters, inadvertently sprinkled the bare arms of an old woman who chanced to be washing clothes at her cottage window." Lady Shelley, who "was attracted by her screams," promptly told the widow that "it ought to be the proudest moment of her life. She had had the distinction of being shot by the great Duke of Wellington," but the eminently practical instinct of the great Duke at once whispered to him that something more than the moral satisfaction to be derived from this reflection was required, so he very wisely "slipped a golden coin into her trembling hand."

For many years Lady Shelley lived on very friendly and intimate terms with the Duke, who appears to have confided to her many things about which he would perhaps have acted more wisely if he had held his tongue. When he went on an important diplomatic mission to Paris in 1822, she requested him to buy her a blouse—a commission which he faithfully executed. All went well until 1848. Then a terrific explosion occurred. It is no longer "My dearest Lady! Mind you bring the blouse! Ever yours most affectionately, Wellington," but "My dear Lady Shelley," who is addressed by "Her Ladyship's most obedient humble servant, Wellington," and soundly rated for her conduct. The reason for this abrupt and volcanic change was that owing to an indiscretion on the part of Lady Shelley a very important letter about the defenceless state of the country, which the Duke had addressed to Sir John Burgoyne, then the head of the Engineer Department at the Horse Guards, got into the newspapers. The Duke's wrath boiled over, and was expressed in terms which, albeit the reproaches were just, showed but little chivalrous consideration towards a peccant but very contrite woman. He told her that he "had much to do besides defending himself from the consequences of the meddling gossip of the ladies of modern times," and he asked indignantly, "What do Sir John Burgoyne and his family and your Ladyship and others—talking of old friendship—say to the share which each of you have had in this transaction, which, in my opinion, is disgraceful to the times in which we live?" What Sir John Burgoyne and his family might very reasonably have said in answer to this formidable interrogatory is that, although no one can defend the conduct of Delilah, it was certainly most unwise of Samson to trust her with his secret. It is consolatory to know that, under the influence of Sir John Shelley's tact and good-humour, a treaty of peace was eventually concluded. Sir John happened to meet the Duke at a party. "'Good-evening, Duke,' said Sir John, in his most winning manner. 'Do you know, it has been said, by some one who must have been present, that the cackling of geese once saved Rome. I have been thinking that perhaps the cackling of my old Goose may yet save England!' This wholly unexpected sally proved too much for the Duke, who burst out into a hearty laugh. 'By G——d, Shelley!' said he, 'you are right: give me your honest hand.'" The Duke then returned to Apsley House and "penned a playful letter to Lady Shelley."

It is not to be expected that much of real historical interest can be extracted from a Diary of this sort. It may, however, be noted that when the *Bellerophon* reached the English coast "it was only by coercion that the Ministers prevented George IV. from receiving Bonaparte. The King wanted to hold him as a captive." Moreover, Brougham, who was in a position to know, said, "There can be little doubt that if Bonaparte had got to London, the Whig Opposition were ready to use him as their trump card to overturn the Government."

The main interest in the book, however, lies in the light which it throws on the Duke's inner life and in the characteristic *obiter dicta* which he occasionally let fall. Of these, none is more characteristic than the remark he made on meeting his former love, Miss Catherine Pakenham, after an absence of eight years in India. He wrote to her, making a proposal of marriage, but Miss Pakenham told him "that before any engagement was made he must see her again; as she had grown old, had lost all her good looks, and was a very different person to the girl he had loved in former years." The story, which has been frequently repeated, that Miss Pakenham was marked with the smallpox, is untrue, but, without doubt, during the Duke's absence, she had a good deal changed. The Duke himself certainly thought so, for, on first meeting her again, he whispered to his brother, "She has grown d——d ugly, by Jove!" Nevertheless he married her, being moved to do so, not apparently from any very deep feelings of affection, but because his leading passion was a profound regard for truth and loyalty which led him to admire and appreciate the straightforwardness of Miss Pakenham's conduct. Lady Shelley exultingly exclaims, "Well might she be proud and happy, and glory in such a husband." That the Duchess was proud of her husband is certain. Whether she was altogether happy is more doubtful.

One of the stock anecdotes about the Duke of Wellington is that when on one occasion some one asked him whether he was surprised at Waterloo, he replied, "No. I was not surprised then, but I am now." We are indebted to Lady Shelley for letting us know what the Duke really thought on this much-debated question. In a letter written to her on March 22, 1820, he stated, with his usual downright common sense, all that there is to be said on this subject. "Supposing I *was* surprised; I won the battle; and what could you have had more, even if I had not been surprised?"

It is known on the authority of his niece, Lady Burghersh, that the Duke "never read poetry," but his "real love of music," to which Lady Shelley alludes, will perhaps come as a surprise to many. Mr. Fortescue, however, has told us that in his youth the Duke learnt to play the violin, and that he only abandoned it, when he was about thirty years old, "because he judged it unseemly or perhaps ill-sounding for a General to be a fiddler." The Duke is not the only great soldier who has been a musical performer. Marshal St. Cyr used to play the violin "in the quiet moments of a campaign," and Sir Hope Grant was a very fair performer on the violoncello.

It was characteristic of the Duke to keep the fact of his being about to fight a duel with Lord Winchelsea carefully concealed from all his friends. When it was over, he walked into Lady Shelley's room while she was at breakfast and said, "Well, what do you think of a gentleman who has been fighting a duel?"

It appears that during the last years of his life the Duke's great companion-in-arms, Blücher, was subject to some strange hallucinations. The following affords a fitting counterpart to those "fears of the brave" which Pope attributed to the dying Marlborough. On March 17, 1819, Lady Shelley made the following entry in her diary:

We laughed at poor Blücher's strange hallucination, which, though ludicrous, is very sad. He fancies himself with child by a Frenchman; and deplores that such an event should have happened to him in his old age! He does not so much mind being with child, but cannot reconcile himself to the thought that he—of all people in the world—should be destined to give birth to a *Frenchman*! On every other subject Blücher is said to be quite rational. This peculiar form of madness shows the bent of his mind; so that while we laugh our hearts reproach us. The Duke of Wellington assures me that he knows this to be a fact.

Finally, attention may be drawn to a singular and interesting letter from Sir Walter Scott to Shelley, giving some advice which it may be presumed the young poet did not take to heart. He was "cautioned against enthusiasm, which, while it argued an excellent disposition and a feeling heart, requires to be watched and restrained, though not repressed."

XVI
BURMA
"The Spectator," June 28, 1913

The early history of the British connection with Burma presents all the features uniformly to be found in the growth of British Imperialism. These are, first, reluctance to move, coupled with fear of the results of expansion, ending finally with a cession to the irresistible tendency to expand; secondly, vagueness of purpose as to what should be done with a new and somewhat unwelcome acquisition; thirdly, a tardy recognition of its value, with the result that what was first an inclination to make the best of a bad job only gradually transforms itself into a feeling of satisfaction and congratulation that, after all, the unconscious founders of the British Empire, here as elsewhere, blundered more or less unawares into the adoption of a sound and far-seeing Imperial policy.

In 1825, Lord Amherst, in one of those "fits of absence" which the dictum of Sir John Seeley has rendered famous, took possession of some of the maritime provinces of Burma, and in doing so lost three thousand one hundred and fifteen men, of whom only a hundred and fifty were killed in action. Then the customary fit of doubt and despondency supervened. It was not until four years after the conclusion of peace that a British Resident was sent to the Court of Ava in the vain hope that he would be able to negotiate the retrocession of the province of Tenasserim, as "the Directors of the East India Company looked upon this territory as of no value to them." For a quarter of a century peace was preserved, for there ruled at Ava a prince "who was too clear-sighted to attempt again to measure arms with the British troops." Anon he was succeeded by a new king—the Pagàn Prince— "who cared for nothing but mains of cocks, games, and other infantile amusements," and who, after the manner of Oriental despots, inaugurated his reign by putting to death his two brothers and all their households. "There were several hundreds of them." It is not surprising that under a ruler addicted to such practices the British sailors who frequented the Burmese ports should have been subjected to maltreatment. Their complaints reached the ears of the iron-fisted and acquisitive Lord Dalhousie, who himself went to Rangoon in 1852, and forthwith "decided on the immediate attack of Prome and Pegu." M. Dautremer speaks in flattering terms of "the tenacity and persistence of purpose which make the strength and glory of British policy." He might truthfully have added another characteristic feature which that policy at times displays, to wit, sluggishness. It was not until sixteen years after Lord Dalhousie's annexation of Lower Burma that the English bethought themselves of improving their newly acquired province by the construction of a railway, and it was not till 1877 that the first line from Rangoon to Prome—a distance of only one hundred and sixty-one miles—was opened. During all this time King Mindon ruled in native Burma. He "gave abundant alms to monks," and, moreover, which was perhaps more to the purpose, he was wise enough to maintain relations with Great Britain which were "quite cordial." Eventually the Nemesis which appears to attend on all semi-civilised and moribund States when they are brought in contact with a vigorous and aggressive civilisation appeared in the person of the "Sapaya-lat," the "middle princess," who induced her feeble husband, King Thibaw, to carry out massacres on a scale which, even in Burma, had been heretofore unprecedented. Then the British on the other side of the frontier began to murmur and "to consider whether it was possible to endure a neighbour who was so cruel and so unpopular." All doubts as to whether the limits of endurance had or had not been reached were removed when the impecunious and spendthrift king not only imposed a very unjust fine of some £150,000 on the Bombay-Burma Trading Corporation, but also had the extreme folly to "throw himself into the arms of France"—a scheme which was at once communicated by M. Jules Ferry to Lord Lyons, the British Ambassador in Paris. Then war with Burma was declared, and after some tedious operations, which involved the sacrifice of many valuable lives, and which extended over three years, the country was "completely pacified" by 1889, and Lord Dufferin added the title of "Ava" to the Marquisate which was conferred on him.

In 1852, when Lord Dalhousie annexed Lower Burma, Rangoon was "merely a fishing village." It is now a flourishing commercial town of some 300,000 inhabitants. In 1910-11 the imports into Burmese ports, including coast trade, amounted to £13,600,000. The exports, in spite of a duty on rice which is of a nature rather to shock orthodox economists, were nearly £23,000,000 in value. The revenue in 1910 was about £7,391,000, of which about £2,590,000 was on Imperial and the balance on local account. Burma is in the happy position of being in a normal state of surplus, and is thus able to contribute annually a sum of about £2,500,000 to the Indian exchequer, a sum which those who are specially interested in Burmese prosperity regard as excessive, whilst it is apparently regarded as inadequate by some of those who look only to the interests of the Indian taxpayers.

The account which M. Dautremer, who was for long French Consul at Rangoon, has given of the present condition of Burma is preceded by an introduction from the pen of Sir George Scott, who can speak with unquestionable authority on Burmese affairs. It is clear that neither author has allowed himself in any way to be biassed by national proclivities, for whilst the Frenchman compares British and French administrative methods in a manner which is very much to the detriment of the latter, the Englishman, on the other hand, launches the most fiery denunciations against those of his countrymen who are responsible for Indian policy. Their want of enterprise is characterised by the appalling polysyllabic adjective "hebetudinous," which it is perhaps as well to explain means obtuse or dull, and they are told that they "are infected with the Babu spirit, and cannot see beyond their immediate horizon."

M. Dautremer thinks that it is somewhat narrow-minded of the Englishman to inflict on himself the torture of wearing cloth or flannel clothes in order that he may not be taken for a *chi-chi* or half-caste, who very wisely dresses in white. He expostulates against the social tyranny which obliges him to pay visits between twelve and two "in such a climate and with such a temperature," and he gently satirises the isolation of the different layers of English society—civilian, military, and subordinate services—in words which call to mind the striking account given by the immortal Mr.

Jingle of the dockyard society of Chatham and Rochester. It is, however, consolatory to learn that all classes combined in giving a hearty welcome to the genial and sympathetic Frenchman who was living in their midst. Save on these minor points, M. Dautremer has, for the most part, nothing but praise to accord. He thinks that "all the British administrative officers in Burma are well-educated and capable men, who know the country of which they are put in charge, and are fluent in the language." He writhes under the highly centralised and bureaucratic system adopted by his own countrymen. He commends the English practice under which "the Home Government never interferes in the management of internal affairs," and it is earnestly to be hoped that the commendation is deserved, albeit of late years there have occasionally been some ominous signs of a tendency to govern India rather too much in detail from London. Speaking of the rapid development of Burmese trade, M. Dautremer says, in words which are manifestly intended to convey a criticism of his own Government, "This is an example of the use of colonies to a nation which knows how to put a proper value on them and to profit by them."

The warm appreciation which M. Dautremer displays of the best parts of the English administrative system enhances his claims for respectful attention whenever he indulges in criticism. He finds two rather weak points in the administration. In the first place, he attributes the large falling-off in the export of teak, *inter alia*, to "the increase in Government duties and the much more rigid rules for extraction," and he adds that the Government, which is itself a large dealer in timber, has "by its action created a monopoly which has raised prices to the highest possible limit." The subject is one which would appear to require attention. The primary business of any Government is not to trade but to administer, and, as invariably happens, the violation of a sound economic principle of this sort is certain sooner or later to carry its own punishment with it. In the second place, the Forest Department, which is of very special importance in Burma, is a good deal crippled by the "want of energy and want of industry which are unfortunately common in the subordinate grades. The reason for this state of things is to be found in the fact that the pay and prospects are not good enough to attract really capable men." In many quarters, notably in Central Africa, British Treasury officials have yet to learn that, from every point of view, it is quite as great a mistake to employ underpaid administrative agents as it would be for an employer of labour to proceed on the principle that low wages necessarily connote cheap production.

Sir George Scott in his introduction strikes a very different note from that sounded by M. Dautremer. He alleges that the wealthy province of Burma, which M. Dautremer tells us is not unseldom called "the milch-cow of India," is starved, that its financial policy has been directed by "cautious, nothing-venture, mole-horizon people," who have hid their talent in a napkin; that "everything seems expressly designed to drive out the capital" of which the country stands so much in need; that not nearly enough has been done in the way of expenditure on public works, notably on roads and railways, and that when these latter have been constructed, they have sometimes been in the wrong directions. He cavils at M. Dautremer's description of Burma as "a model possession," and holds that "as a matter of bitter fact, the administrative view is that of the parish beadle, and the enterprise that of the country-carrier with a light cart instead of a motor-van."

It would require greater local knowledge than any possessed by the writer of the present article either to endorse or to reject these formidable accusations, although it may be said that the violence of Sir George Scott's invective is not very convincing, but rather raises a strong suspicion that he has overstated his case. Nothing is more difficult, either for a private individual or for a State financier, than to decide the question of when to be bold and when cautious in the matter of capital outlay. It is quite possible to push to an extreme the commonplace, albeit attractive, argument that large expenditure will be amply remunerative, or even if not directly remunerative, highly beneficial "in the long run." Although this plea is often—indeed, perhaps generally—valid, it is none the less true that the run which is foreshadowed is at times so long as to make the taxpayer, who has to bear the present cost, gasp for breath before the promised goal is reached. Pericles, by laying out huge sums on the public buildings of Athens, earned the undying gratitude of artistic posterity. Whether his action was in the true interests of his Athenian contemporaries is perhaps rather more doubtful. The recent history of Argentina is an instance of a country in which, as subsequent events have proved, the plea for lavish capital expenditure was perfectly justifiable, but in which, nevertheless, the over-haste shown in incurring heavy liabilities led to much temporary inconvenience and even disaster. But on the whole it may be said that where all the general conditions are favourable, and point conclusively to the possibility and probability of fairly rapid economic development, a bold financial policy may and should be adopted, even although it may not be easy to prove beforehand by very exact calculations that any special project under consideration will be directly remunerative.

Egyptian finance is a case in point. At a time when the country was in the throes of bankruptcy, a fresh loan of £1,000,000 was, to the dismay of the conventional financiers, contracted, the proceeds of which were spent on irrigation works. So also the construction of the Assouan dam, which cost nearly double the sum originally estimated, was taken in hand at a moment when a liability of a wholly unknown amount on account of the war in the Soudan was hanging over the head of the Egyptian Treasury. In both of these cases subsequent events amply justified the financial audacity which had been shown. In the case of Burma there appears to be no doubt as to the wealth of the province or its capacity for further development. In view of all the circumstances of the case the amount of twelve millions, which is apparently all that has been spent on railway construction since 1869, would certainly appear to be rather a niggardly sum. In spite, therefore, of the very unnecessary warmth with which Sir George Scott has urged his views, it is to be hoped that his plea for the adoption of a somewhat bolder financial policy in the direction of expenditure on railways, and still more on feeder roads, will receive from the India Office, with whom the matter really rests, the attention which it would certainly appear to deserve. The case of public buildings, of which Burma apparently stands much in need, is different. They cannot, strictly speaking, be said to be remunerative, and should almost, if not quite, invariably be paid for out of revenue.

XVII
A PSEUDO-HERO OF THE REVOLUTION
"The Spectator," July 5, 1913

If it be a fact, as Carlyle said, that "History is the essence of innumerable biographies," it is very necessary that the biographies from which that essence is extracted should be true. It was probably a profound want of confidence in the accuracy of biographical writing that led Horace Walpole to beg for "anything but history, for history must be false." Modern industry and research, ferreting in the less frequented bypaths of history, have exposed many fictions, and have often led to some strikingly paradoxical conclusions. They have substituted for Cambronne's apocryphal saying at Waterloo the blunt sarcasm of the Duke of Wellington that there were a number of ladies at Brussels who were termed "la vieille garde," and of whom it was said "elles ne meurent pas et se rendent toujours." They have led one eminent historian to apologise for the polygamous tendencies of Henry VIII.; another to advance the startling proposition that the "amazing" but, as the world has heretofore held, infamous Emperor Heliogabalus was a great religious reformer, who was in advance of his times; a third to present Lucrezia Borgia to the world as a much-maligned and very virtuous woman; and a fourth to tell us that the "ever pusillanimous" Barère, as he is called by M. Louis Madelin, was "persistently vilified and deliberately misunderstood." Biographical research has, moreover, destroyed many picturesque legends, with some of which posterity cannot part without a pang of regret. We are reluctant to believe that William Tell was a mythological marksman and Gessler a wholly impossible bailiff. Nevertheless the inexorable laws of evidence demand that this sacrifice should be made on the altar of historical truth. M. Gastine has now ruthlessly quashed out another picturesque legend. Tallien—the "bristly, fox-haired" Tallien of Carlyle's historical rhapsody—and La Cabarrus—the fair Spanish Proserpine whom, "Pluto-like, he gathered at Bordeaux"—have so far floated down the tide of history as individuals who, like Byron's Corsair, were

Linked with one virtue and a thousand crimes.

Of the crimes there could, indeed, never have been any doubt, but posterity took but little heed of them, for they were amply condoned by the single virtue. That virtue was, indeed, of a transcendent character, for it was nothing less than the delivery of the French nation from the Dahomey-like rule of that Robespierre who deluged France in blood, and who, albeit in Fouché's words he was "terribly sincere," at the same time "never in his life cared for any one but himself and never forgave an offence." Moreover, the act of delivery was associated with an episode eminently calculated to appeal to human sentiment and sympathy. It was thought that the love of a fair woman whose life was endangered had nerved the lover and the patriot to perform an heroic act at the imminent risk of his own life. Hence the hero became "Le Lion Amoureux," and the heroine was canonised as "Notre Dame de Thermidor."

M. Gastine has now torn this legend to shreds. Under his pitiless analysis of the facts, nothing is left but the story of a contemptible adventurer, who was "a robber, a murderer, and a poltroon," mated to a grasping, heartless courtesan. Both were alike infamous. The ignoble careers of both from the cradle to the grave do not, in reality, present a single redeeming feature.

Madame Tallien was the daughter of François Cabarrus, a wealthy Spaniard who was the banker of the Spanish Court. The great influence which she unquestionably exerted over her contemporaries was wholly due to her astounding physical beauty. Her intellectual equipment was meagre in the extreme. At one period of her life she courted the society of Madame de Staël and other intellectuals, but Princess Hélène Ligne said of her that she "had more jargon than wit." As regards her physical attractions, however, no dissentient voice has ever been raised. "Her beauty," the Duchess d'Abrantès says in her memoirs, "of which the sculptors of antiquity give us but an incomplete idea, had a charm not met with in the types of Greece and Rome." Every man who approached her appears to have become her victim. Lacretelle, who himself worshipped at her shrine, says, "She appeared to most of us as the Spirit of Clemency incarnate in the loveliest of human forms." At a very early age she married a young French nobleman, the Marquis de Fontenay, from whom she was speedily divorced. It is not known for what offence she was arrested and imprisoned. Probably the mere fact that she was a marquise was sufficient to entangle her in the meshes of the revolutionary net. It is certain, however, that whilst lying under sentence of death in the prison at Bordeaux she attracted the attention of Tallien, the son of the Marquis of Bercy's butler and *ci-devant* lawyer's clerk, who had blossomed into "a Terrorist of the first water." He obtained her release and she became his mistress. She took advantage of the equivocal but influential position which she had attained to engage in a vile traffic. She and her paramour amassed a huge fortune by accepting money from the unfortunate prisoners who were threatened with the fate which she had so narrowly escaped, and to which she was again to be exposed. The venal lenity shown by Tallien to aristocrats rendered him an object of suspicion, whilst the marked tendency displayed by Robespierre to mistrust and, finally, to immolate his coadjutors was an ominous indication of the probable course of future events. Robespierre had already destroyed Vergniaud by means of Hébert, Hébert by means of Danton, and Danton by means of Billaud. As a preliminary step to the destruction of Tallien, he caused his mistress to be arrested, probably with a view to seeing what evidence against her paramour could be extracted before she was herself guillotined.

From this point in the narrative history is merged into legend. The legend would have us believe that on the 7th Thermidor the "Citoyenne Fontenay" sent a dagger to the "Citoyen Tallien," accompanied by a letter in which she said that she had dreamt that Robespierre was no more, and that the gates of her prison had been flung open. "Alas!" she added, "thanks to your signal cowardice there will soon be no one left in France capable of bringing such a dream to pass." Tallien besought Robespierre to show mercy, but "the Incorruptible was inflexible." Then the "Lion Amoureux" roared, being, as the legend relates, stricken to the heart at the appalling danger to which his beloved mistress was exposed or, as his detractors put the case, being in deadly fear that the untoward revelations of the Citoyenne might cost him his own head. The next act in this Aeschylean drama is described by the believers in the legend in the following words: "Tallien drew Theresia's dagger from his breast and flashed it in the sunlight as though to nerve himself for the desperate business that confronted him. 'This,' he cried passionately, 'will be my final argument,' and looking about him to make sure he was alone he raised the blade to his lips and kissed it."

The result, it is alleged, was that Tallien provoked the episode of the 9th Thermidor (July 22, 1794). The few faltering sentences which Robespierre wished to utter were never spoken. He was "choked by the blood of Danton," and hurried off to the guillotine which awaited him on the morrow.

History, which in this instance is not legendary, relates that on the death of the tyrant a wild shout of exultation was raised by the joyous people who had for so long wandered in the Valley of the Shadow of Death. To whom, they asked, did they owe their liberty? What was more natural than to assume that it was to the brave Tallien and to the loving woman who armed him to strike a blow for the freedom of France? Tallien and his mistress became, therefore, the idols of the French people. The Chancellor Pasquier relates their appearance at a theatre:

The enthusiasm and the applause were indescribable. The occupants of the boxes, the people in the pit, men and women alike, stood up on their chairs to look at him. It seemed as though they would never weary of gazing at him. He was young, rather good-looking, and his manner was calm and serene. Madame Tallien was at his side and shared his triumph. In her case also everything had been forgiven and forgotten. Similar scenes were enacted all through the autumn of that year. Never was any service, however great, rewarded by gratitude so lively and so touching.

It would be impossible within the limits of the present article to summarise the arguments by which M. Gastine seeks to destroy this myth. Allusion may, however, be made to two points of special importance. The first is that neither Tallien nor the lovely Spaniard languishing in the dungeon of La Force had much to do with the episode of the 9th Thermidor. "Tallien was a mere super, a mere puppet that had to be galvanised into action up to the very last." The man who really organised the movement and persuaded his coadjutors that they were engaged in a life and death struggle with Robespierre was he who, as every reader of revolutionary history knows, was busily engaged in pulling the strings behind the scenes during the whole of this chaotic period. It was the man whose iron nerve and subtle brain enabled him, in spite of a secular course of betrayals, to keep his head on his shoulders, and finally to escape the clutches of Napoleon, who, as Lord Rosebery tells us, always deeply regretted that he had not had him "hanged or shot." It was Fouché.

In the second place, there is conclusive evidence to show that, to use the ordinary slang expression of the present day, the celebrated dagger letter was "faked." When Robespierre fell, Tallien never gave a thought to his mistress. He still trembled for his own life. "His sole aim was to make away with Robespierre's papers." It was only on the 12th Thermidor—that is to say, two days after Robespierre's mangled head had been sheared off by the guillotine—that, noting the trend of public opinion, and appreciating the capital which might be made out of the current myth, he hurried off to La Force and there concocted with his mistress the famous letter which he, of course, antedated.

The subsequent careers of Tallien and his wife—for he married La Cabarrus in December 1794— are merely characterised by a number of unedifying details. The hero of this sordid tale passed through many vicissitudes. He went with Napoleon to Egypt. He was, on his return voyage, taken prisoner by an English cruiser. On his arrival in London he was well received by Fox and the Whigs—a fact which cannot be said to redound much to the credit either of the Whig party or its leader. He gambled on the Stock Exchange, and at one time "blossomed out as a dealer in soap, candles, and cotton bonnets." After passing through an unhonoured old age, he died in great poverty in 1820. The heroine became intimate with Josephine during Napoleon's absence in Egypt, was subsequently divorced from Tallien, and later, after passing through a phase when she was the mistress of the banker Ouvrard, married the Prince of Caraman-Chimay. Her conduct during the latter years of her life appears to have been irreproachable. She died in 1835.

XVIII

THE FUTURE OF THE CLASSICS
"The Spectator," July 5, 1913

There was a time, not so very long ago, when the humanists enjoyed a practical monopoly in the domain of English education, and, by doing so, exercised a considerable, perhaps even a predominant, influence not only over the social life but also over the policy, both external and internal, adopted by their countrymen. Like most monopolists, they showed a marked tendency to abuse the advantages of their position. Science was relegated to a position of humiliating inferiority, and had to content itself with picking up whatever crumbs were, with a lordly and at times almost contemptuous tolerance, allowed to fall from the humanistic table. Bossuet once defined a heretic as "celui qui a une opinion" (αἵρεσις). A somewhat similar attitude was at one time adopted to those who were inclined to doubt whether a knowledge of Latin and Greek could be considered the Alpha and Omega of a sound education. The calm judgment of that great humanist, Professor Jebb, led him to the conclusion that the claims of the humanities have been at times defended by pleas which were exaggerated and paradoxical—using this latter term in the sense of arguments which contain an element of truth, but of truth which has been distorted—and that in an age remarkable beyond all previous ages for scientific research and discoveries, that nation must necessarily lag behind which, in the well-known words uttered by Gibbon at a time when science was still in swaddling-clothes, fears that the "finer feelings" are destroyed if the mind becomes "hardened by the habit of rigid demonstration." All this has now been changed. Professor Huxley did not live in vain. His mantle fell on the shoulders of many other doughty champions who shared his views. Science no longer slinks modestly in educational bypaths, but occupies the high road, and, to say the least, marches abreast of her humanistic sister. Yet the scientists are not yet content. Their souls are athirst for further victories. A high authority on education, himself a classical scholar, has recently told us that, although the English boy "as he emerges from the crucible of the public school laboratory" may be a fairly good agent for dealing with the "lower or more submissive races in the wilds of Africa or in the plains of India," elsewhere—notably in Canada—he is "a conspicuous failure"; that one of the principal reasons why he is a failure is that "the influence of the humanists still reigns over us"; and that "the future destiny of the Empire is wrapt up in the immediate reform of England's educational system." In the course of that reform, which it is proposed should be of a very drastic character, some half-hearted efforts may conceivably be made to effect the salvage of whatever will remain of the humanistic wreck, but the real motto of the reformers will almost certainly be Utilitarianism, writ large. The humanists, therefore, are placed on their defence. It may be that the walls of their entrenchment, which have already been a good deal battered, will fall down altogether, and that the garrison will be asked to submit to a capitulation which will be almost unconditional.

In the midst of the din of battle which may already be heard, and which will probably ere long become louder, it seems very desirable that the voices of those who are neither profound scholars nor accomplished scientists nor educational experts should be heard. These—and there are many such—ask, What is the end which we should seek to attain? Can science alone be trusted to prevent education becoming, in the words of that sturdy old pagan, Thomas Love Peacock, a "means for giving a fixed direction to stupidity"? The answer they, or many of them, give to these questions is that the main end of education is to teach people to think, and that they are not prepared to play false to their own intellects to such an extent as to believe that the national power of thinking will not be impaired if it is deprived of the teaching of the most thoughtful nation which the world has ever known. That nation is Greece. These classes, therefore, lift up their hands in supplication to scientists, educational experts, and parliamentarians—yea, even to soulless wire-pullers who would perhaps willingly cast Homer and Sophocles to the dogs in order to win a contested election—and with one voice cry: We recognise the need of reform; we wish to march with the times; we are no enemies to science; but in the midst of your utilitarian ideas, we implore you, in the name both of learning and common sense, to devise some scheme which will still enable the humanities to act as some check on the growing materialism of the age; otherwise the last stage of the educated youth of this country will be worse than the first; remember what Lucretius—on the bold assumption that wire-pullers ever read Lucretius—said, "Hic Acherusia stultorum denique vita"; above all things, let there be no panic legislation—and panic is a danger to which democracies and even, Pindar has told us, "the sons of the gods," are greatly exposed; in taking any new departure let us, therefore, very carefully and deliberately consider how we can best preserve all that is good in our existing system.

Whatever temporary effect appeals of this sort may produce, it is certain that the ultimate result must depend very greatly on the extent to which a real interest in classical literature can be kept alive in the minds of the rising and of future generations. How can this object best be achieved? The question is one of vital importance.

The writer of the present article would be the last to attempt to raise a cheap laugh at the expense of that laborious and, as it may appear to some, almost useless erudition which, for instance, led Professor Hermann to write four books on the particle ἄν and to indite a learned dissertation on αὐτός. The combination of industry and enthusiasm displayed in efforts such as these has not been wasted. The spirit which inspired them has materially contributed to the real stock of valuable knowledge which the world possesses. None the less it must be admitted that something more than mere erudition is required to conjure away the perils which the humanities now have to face. It is necessary to quicken the interest of the rising generation, to show them that it is not only historically true to say, with Lessing, that "with Greece the morning broke," but that it is equally true to maintain that in what may, relatively speaking, be called the midday splendour of learning, we cannot dispense with the guiding light of the early morn; that Greek literature, in Professor Gilbert Murray's words, is "an embodiment of the progressive spirit, an expression of the struggle of the human soul towards freedom and ennoblement"; and that our young men and women will be, both morally and intellectually, the poorer if they listen to the insidious and deceptive voice of an exaggerated materialism which whispers that amidst the hum of modern machinery and the heated wrangles incident to the perplexing problems which arise as the world grows older, the knowledge of a language and a literature which have survived two thousand eight hundred storm-tossed years is "of no practical use."

It is this interest which the works of a man like the late Dr. Verrall serve to stimulate. He was eminently fitted for the task. On the principle which Dr. Johnson mocked by saying that "who drives fat oxen should himself be fat," it may be said that an advocate of humanistic learning should himself be human in the true and Terentian meaning of that somewhat ambiguous word. This is what Verrall was. All who knew him speak of his lovable character, and others who were in this respect less favoured can judge of the genuineness of his human sympathies by applying two well-nigh infallible tests. He loved children, and he was imbued with what Professor Mackail very appropriately calls in his commemorative address "a delightful love of nonsense." His kindly and genial humour sparkles, indeed, in every line he wrote. Moreover, whether he was right or wrong in the highly unconventional views which he at times expressed, his scorn for literary orthodoxy was in itself very attractive. Whenever he found what he called a "boggle"—that is to say an incident or a phrase in respect to which, he was dissatisfied with the conventional explanation—"he could not rest until he had made an effort to get to the bottom of it." He treated old subjects with an originality which rejuvenated them, and decked them again with the charm of novelty. He bade us, with a copy of Martial in our hands, accompany him to the Coliseum and be, in imagination, one of the sixty thousand spectators who thronged to behold the strange Africans, Sarmatians, and others who are gathered together from the four quarters of the Roman world to take part in the Saturnalia. He asked us to watch with Propertius whilst the slumbers of his Cynthia were disturbed by dreams that she was flying from one of her all too numerous lovers. Under his treatment, Mr. Cornford says, the most commonplace passages in classical literature "began to glow with passion and to flash with wit." His main literary achievement is thus recorded on the tablet erected to his memory at Trinity College: "Euripidis famam vindicavit." He threw himself with ardour into the discussion on the merits and demerits of the Greek tragedian which has been going on ever since it was originally started by Aristophanes, and he may at least be said to have shown that what French Boileau said of his own poetry applies with equal force to the Greek—"Mon vers, bien ou mal, dit toujours quelque chose." In the process of rehabilitating Euripides, Verrall threw out brilliantly original ideas in every direction. Take, for instance, his treatment of the *Ion*. Every one who has dabbled in Greek literature knows that Euripides was a free-thinker, albeit in his old age he did lip-service to the current theology of the day, and told the Athenians that they should not "apply sophistry," or, in other words rationalise, about the gods. Every one also has rather marvelled at the somewhat lame and impotent conclusion of the play when Athene—herself in reality one of the most infamous of the Olympian deities—is brought on the stage to save the prestige of the oracle at Delphi and to explain away the altogether disreputable behaviour of the no less infamous Apollo. But no one before Verrall had thought of coupling together the free-thinking and the episode in the play. This is what Verrall did. Ion sees that the oracle can lie, and, therefore, "Delphi is plainly discredited as a fountain of truth." The explanation is, of course, somewhat conjectural. Homer, who was certainly not a free-thinker, made his deities sufficiently ridiculous, and, at times, altogether odious. Mr. Lang says with truth: "When Homer touches on the less lovable humours of women—on the nagging shrew, the light o' love, the rather bitter virgin—he selects his examples from the divine society of the gods." But whether the very plausible conjectures made by Verrall as to the real purpose of Euripides in his treatment of the oracle in *Ion*, or, to quote another instance, his explanation of the phantom in *Helen*, be right or wrong, no one can deny that what he wrote is alive with interest. On this point, the testimony of his pupils, albeit in some respects contradictory, is conclusive. One of them (Mr. Marsh) says: "I was usually convinced by everything," whilst another (Mr. J.R.M. Butler) says: "I don't think we believed very much what he said; he always said he was as likely to be wrong as right. But he made all classics so gloriously new and living. He made us criticise by standards of common sense, and presume that the tragedians were not fools and that they did mean something. They were not to be taken as antiques privileged to use conventions that would be nonsense in any one else."

Classical learning will not be kept alive for long by forcing young men with perhaps a taste for science or the integral calculus to apply themselves to the study of Aristotle or Sophocles. The real hope for the humanities in the future lies in the teaching of such men as Butcher, Verrall, Gilbert Murray, Dill, Bevan, Livingstone, Zimmern, and, it may fortunately be said, many others, who can make the literature of the ancient world and the personalities of its inhabitants live in the eyes of the present generation.

XIX
AN INDIAN IDEALIST
"The Spectator," July 12, 1913

Amidst the jumble of political shibboleths, mainly drawn from the vocabulary of extreme Radical sentimentalists, which Mr. Mallik supplies to his readers in rich abundance, two may be selected which give the keynote to his opinions. The first, which is inscribed on the title-page, is St. Paul's statement to the Athenians that all nations of men are of one blood. The second, which occurs towards the close of his work, is that "sane Imperialism is political Idealism." Both statements are paradoxical. Both contain a germ of truth. In both cases an extreme application of the principle involved would lead to dire consequences. The first aphorism leads us to the unquestionably sound conclusion that Newton, equally with a pygmy from the forests of Central Africa, was a human being. It does not take us much further. The second aphorism bids us remember that the statesman who is incapable of conceiving and attempting to realise an ideal is a mere empiricist, but it omits to mention that if this same statesman, in pursuit of his ideal, neglects all his facts and allows himself to become an inhabitant of a political Cloud Cuckoo-land, he will certainly ruin his own reputation, and may not improbably inflict very great injury upon the country and people which form the subject of his crude experiments. On the whole, if we are to apply that proverbial philosophy which is so dear to the mind of all Europeanised Easterns to the solution of political problems, it will perhaps be as well to bear constantly in mind the excellent Sanskrit maxim which, amidst a collection of wise saws, Mr. Mallik quotes in his final chapter, "A wise man thinks of both *pro* and *con*."

Starting with a basis of somewhat extreme idealism, it is not surprising that Mr. Mallik has developed not only into an ardent Indian nationalist, but also into an advanced Indian Radical. As to the latter characteristic, he manifestly does not like the upper classes of his own country. They are, in fact, as bad or even worse than English peers. They are "like the 'idle rich' elsewhere; they squander annually in luxuries and frivolities huge sums of money, besides hoarding up jewels, gold and silver of immense value." Occasionally, they pose as "upholders of the Government." "Even so they do not conceal their fangs. When small measures of conciliation have in recent times been proposed, the 'Peers' in India have not been slow to proclaim through their organs that the Government were rousing their suspicion."

Turning, however, to the relations between Europe and Asia, Mr. Mallik says that it is often asserted that the two continents "cannot understand each other—that Asia is a mystery to Europe, and must always remain so." Most people who have considered this subject have so far thought that the main reason why Europeans find it difficult to understand Asia is because, in some matters, Asia is difficult to understand. They have, therefore, been deeply grateful to men like the late Sir Alfred Lyall, who have endeavoured with marked ability and sympathy to explain the mystery to them. But Mr. Mallik now explains to us that no such gratitude is due, for the reason why Asia is so often misunderstood is not on account of any difficulties attendant on comprehension, but because those who have paid special attention to the subject are "persons whose nature or training or self-interest leads them not to wish the understanding to take place." Whether Mr. Mallik has done much to lighten the prevailing darkness and to explain the East to the West is perhaps somewhat doubtful, but it is quite certain that he has done his utmost to explain to those of his countrymen who are conversant with the English language the attitude which, in his opinion, they should adopt towards Westerns and Western civilisation. In one of the sweeping generalities in which his work abounds, Mr. Mallik says with great truth, that "however manners may differ ... nothing is gained by nursing a feeling of animosity." It is to be regretted that Mr. Mallik has not himself acted on the wise principle which he here enunciates. He has, however, not done so. Under the familiar garb of a friend who indulges in an excess of candour he has made a number of observations which, whether true or false, are eminently calculated to inflame that racial animosity which it is the duty of every well-wisher of India to endeavour by every means in his power to allay. He makes a lengthy and elaborate comparison between East and West, in which every plague-spot in European civilisation is carefully catalogued. Every ulcer in Western life is probed. Every possible sore in the connection between the European and Asiatic is made to rankle. On the other hand, with the cries of the Christians massacred at Adana still ringing in our ears, Mr. Mallik, forgetful apparently of the fact that the Turk is an Asian, tells us that "Asia, typical of the East, looks upon all races and creeds with absolute impartiality," and, further, that "gentleness and consideration are the peculiar characteristics of the East, as overbearing and rudeness, miscalled independence, and not unfrequently deserving to be called insolence, are products of the West."

But it is the word Imperialism which more especially excites Mr. Mallik's wrath. In the first place, he altogether denies the existence of an "imperial race," being convinced of its non-existence by the strangely inconclusive argument that "if a race is made by nature imperial, every member of that race must be imperial too and equally able to rule." In the second place, he points out that the results which flow from the Imperial idea are in all respects deplorable. The East had "always believed that mankind could be made saints and philosophers," but the West, represented by Imperialism, stepped in and "shattered its belief." The West, as shown by the deference now paid to Japan, "values the bloodthirsty propensities much more than humane activities." "The expressed desire of the Imperialist is to let darkness flourish in order that he may personally benefit by it.... Empire and Imperialism mean the triumph of retrograde notions and the infliction of insult and suffering on three hundred millions of human beings." It is this Imperial policy which has led to the most gross injustice being inflicted on every class of the community in India. As regards the civil services, "the policy of fat pay, ease, perquisites, and praise are the share of the European officers, and hard work and blame that of the Indian rank and file." It is the same in the army. "In frontier wars the Indian troops have had to bear the brunt of the fighting, the European portion being 'held in reserve' and coming up at the end to receive all the glory of victory and the consequent rewards." It is sometimes said that the masses in India trust Englishmen more than their own countrymen. That this statement is erroneous is clearly proved by "the absence of interest of the rulers themselves in the moral and material advancement of the poorer classes." Not content with uttering this prodigious falsehood, Mr. Mallik adds a further and fouler calumny. He alludes to the rudeness at times displayed by Englishmen towards the natives of India—a feature in Indian social life which every right-thinking Englishman will be prepared to condemn as strongly as Mr. Mallik. But, not content with indicating the evil, Mr. Mallik alleges that any special act of insolence perpetrated by an Indian official meets with the warm approval of the Government. Promotion, he says, is "usual in such cases." Again, Mr. Mallik's dislike and distrust of Moslems crops up whenever he alludes to them. Nevertheless, he does not hesitate to denounce that Government whose presence alone prevents an outbreak of sectarian strife for "sedulously fomenting" religious animosities with a view to arresting the Nationalist movement. Similarly, the constitution of the Universities has been changed with a view to rendering the youth of India "stupid and servile" instead of "clever and patriotic."

Moreover, whilst India, under the sway of Imperialism, is "drifting to its doom," Mr. Mallik seems to fear that a somewhat similar fate awaits England. He observes many symptoms of decay to which, for the most part, Englishmen are blind. He greatly fears that "the liberties of the people are not safe when the Tory Party continues in power for a long period." Neither is the prospect of Liberal ascendancy much less gloomy. Liberals are becoming "Easternised." They are getting "more and more leavened by reaction imported from India." It really looks as if "English Liberalism might soon sink to a pious tradition." In the meanwhile, Mr. Mallik, with true Eastern proclivities, warmly admires that portion of the English system which Englishmen generally tolerate as a necessary evil, but of which they are by no means proud. Most thinking men in this country resent the idea of Indian interests being made a shuttlecock in the strife of party. Not so Mr. Mallik. He shudders at the idea of Indian affairs being considered exclusively on their own merits. "If it is no party's duty to champion the cause of any part of the Empire, that part must be made over to Satan, or retained, like a convict settlement, for the breeding of 'Imperial' ideas." He is himself quite prepared to adopt an ultra-partisan attitude. In spite of his evident dislike to the nomination of any Englishman to take part in the administration of India, he warmly applauds the appointment of "a young and able official" to the Viceroy's Council, because he was "associated with a great Liberal Minister of the Crown."

It is not quite clear what, beyond a manifestation of that sympathy which his own writings are so well calculated to alienate, Mr. Mallik really wants. He thinks that there is "perhaps some truth" in the assertion that the "Aryans of India are not yet fit for self-government," and he says that "wise Indians do not claim at once the political institutions that Europeans have gained by a long course of struggle and training, the value of which in advancing happiness is not yet always perceptible in Europe." On the other hand, he appears to be of opinion that the somewhat sweeping reforms recently inaugurated by Lord Morley and Lord Minto do not go far enough. The only practical proposals he makes are, first, that the old *punchayet* system in every village should be revived, and that a consultative assembly should be created, whose functions "should be wholly social and religious, political topics being out of its jurisdiction." He adds—and there need be no hesitation in cordially accepting his view on this point—that the "plan would have to be carefully thought out" before it is adopted.

The problem of how to govern India is very difficult, and is unquestionably becoming more and more so every year. Although many of the slanders uttered by Mr. Mallik are very contemptible, it is useless to ignore the fact that they are believed not only by a large number of the educated youth of India, of which he may perhaps to some extent be considered a type, but also by many of their English sympathisers. Moreover, in spite of much culpable misstatement and exaggeration, Mr. Mallik may have occasionally blundered unawares into making some observations which are deserving of some slight consideration on their own merits. The only wise course for English statesmen to adopt is to possess their souls in patience, to continue to govern India in the best interests of its inhabitants, and to avoid on the one hand the extreme of repressive measures, and on the other hand the equally dangerous extreme of premature and drastic reform in the fundamental institutions of the country. In the meanwhile, it may be noted that literature such as Mr. Mallik's book can do no good, and may do much harm.

XX
THE FISCAL QUESTION IN INDIA
"The Spectator," July 19, 1913

Sir Roper Lethbridge says that his object in writing the book which he has recently published (*The Indian Offer of Imperial Preference*) is to provoke discussion, but "not to lay down any dogma." It is related that a certain clergyman, after he had preached a sermon, said to Lord Melbourne, who had been one of his congregation, "I tried not to be tedious," to which Lord Melbourne replied, "You were." Sir Roper Lethbridge may have tried not to dogmatise, but his efforts in this direction have certainly not been crowned with success. On the contrary, although dealing with a subject which bristles with points of a highly controversial nature, he states his conclusions with an assurance which is little short of oracular. Heedless of the woful fate which has attended many of the fiscal seers who have preceded him, he does not hesitate to pronounce the most confident prophecies upon a subject as to which experience has proved that prophecy is eminently hazardous, viz. the economic effect likely to be produced by drastic changes in the fiscal system. Moreover, his pages are disfigured by a good deal of commonplace invective about "the shibboleths of an obsolete Cobdenism," the "worship of the fetish of Cobdenism," and "the bigotry of the Cobden Club," as to whom the stale fallacy is repeated that they "consider the well-being of the 'poor foreigner'" rather than "our own commercial interests." Language of this sort can only serve to irritate. It cannot convince. Sir Roper Lethbridge appears to forget that, apart from those who, on general party grounds, are little inclined to listen to the gospel which he has to preach, there are a large number of Unionists who are to a greater extent open to conviction, and who, if their conversion can be effected, are, in the interests of the cause which he advocates, well worth convincing. These blemishes—for blemishes they unquestionably are—should not, however, blind us to the fact that Sir Roper Lethbridge deals with a subject of very great importance and also of very great difficulty. It is most desirable that it should be discussed. Sir Fleetwood Wilson, in the very statesmanlike speech delivered in the Indian Legislative Council last March, indicated the spirit in which the discussion should take place. "The subject," he said, "is one which in the public interest calls for consideration, not recrimination." It would be Utopian to suppose that it can be kept altogether outside the arena of party strife, but those who are not uncompromising partisans, and who also strongly deprecate Indian questions being made the shuttlecock of party interests, can at all events endeavour to approach the question with an open mind and to treat it dispassionately and exclusively on its own merits.

The main issue involved may be broadly stated in the following terms. Up to the present time the fiscal policy of the Indian Government has been based on Free Trade principles. Customs duties are collected for revenue purposes. A general 5 per cent *ad valorem* duty is imposed on imports. Cotton goods pay a duty of 3½ per cent. An excise duty of a similar amount is imposed on cotton woven at Indian mills. A duty of three annas a maund is paid on exported rice. Sir Roper Lethbridge and those who concur with him now propose that this system should undergo a radical change. The main features of their proposal, if the writer of the present article understands them correctly, seem to be that the duty on cotton goods imported from the United Kingdom, as also the corresponding excise duty levied in India, should be altogether abolished; that the duties raised on goods—apparently of all descriptions—imported into India from non-British ports should be raised; that a preference should be accorded in British ports to Indian tea, coffee, sugar, tobacco, etc.; and that an export duty should be levied at Indian ports on certain products, notably on jute and lac. This new duty would not, however, be levied on goods sent to the United Kingdom.

There does not appear to be any absolute necessity for dealing with this question at once, but Sir Roper Lethbridge is quite justified in calling attention to it, for it is not only conceivable, but even probable, that at no very remote period the Government of India will have to deal with a problem which, it may readily be admitted, will tax their statesmanship to the very utmost. It is no exaggeration to say that since the Crown took over the direct management of Indian affairs no issue of greater magnitude has been raised. Moreover, although Lord Crewe had an easy task in showing that in some respects the difficulties attendant on any solution would be enhanced rather than diminished if the fiscal policy of the British Government in the United Kingdom underwent a radical change, it is none the less true that those difficulties will remain of a very formidable character even if no such change is effected.

It is essential to bear in mind that the difficulties which beset this question are not solely fiscal, but also political. This feature is almost invariably characteristic of Oriental finance, and nowhere is it more prominent than in India. The writer of the present article can speak with some special knowledge of the circumstances attendant on the great Free Trade measures introduced in India under the auspices of Lord Ripon. He can state very confidently that, although Lord Ripon and all the leading members of his Government were convinced Free Traders, it was the political to a far greater extent than the fiscal arguments which led them to the conclusion that the Indian Customs barriers should be abolished. They foresaw that the rival commercial interests of India and Lancashire would cause a rankling and persistent sore which might do infinite political harm. They wished, therefore, to apply a timely remedy, and it cannot be doubted that, so long as it lasted, the remedy was effective. In most respects the fiscal policy adopted then and that now advocated by Sir Roper Lethbridge and his coadjutors are the poles asunder. Nevertheless, in one respect they coincide. Sir Roper Lethbridge places in the forefront of his proposals the abolition both of the import duty on cotton goods and the corresponding excise duty levied in India. He is unquestionably right. That is an ideal which both Free Traders and Protectionists may very reasonably seek to attain. It is, in fact, the only really satisfactory solution of the main point at issue. The difficulty is to realise this ideal without doing more than an equivalent amount of injury to Indian interests in other directions.

The chief arguments by which Sir Roper Lethbridge defends the special proposals which he advances are three in number. They are (1) that the nascent industries of India require protection; (2) that it is necessary to raise more revenue, and that the suggestions now made afford an unobjectionable method for achieving this object; and (3) that the economic facts connected with India afford special facilities for the adoption of a policy of retaliation.

From a purely economic point of view the first of these three pleas is singularly inconclusive. It was refuted by Sir Fleetwood Wilson, whom both Mr. Austen Chamberlain, in the introduction which he has written to Sir Roper Lethbridge's book, and Sir Roper Lethbridge himself seem to regard, on grounds which are apparently somewhat insufficient, as a partial convert to their views. It may be said without exaggeration that if any country in the world is likely to benefit by the adoption of Free Trade principles that country is India. Industries cannot, as Sir Fleetwood Wilson very truly said, be "encouraged" by means of a protective tariff without raising home prices. Without going over all the well-trodden ground on this subject, which must be familiar to all who have taken part in the fiscal controversy, and without, moreover, denying that nascent industries have in some countries been successfully encouraged by the adoption of a protective system, it will be sufficient to say that, looking at all the economic facts existent in India, the period of partial transition from agriculture to industries, during which the process of encouragement will have to be maintained, will almost certainly last much longer than even in America or Germany, and that during the whole of that lengthy period the mass of the population, who are very poor and who are engaged in agricultural pursuits, will not benefit from the protection, although they will at the same time suffer grievously from the rise in prices.

The main importance of this argument, however, is not to be derived from its economic value, but rather from the important political fact that it is one which finds favour with a large and influential body of Indian opinion. Sir Roper Lethbridge claims that the leaders of Indian thought are almost to a man Protectionists, and in his work he gives, as an example of their views, the very able speech delivered by Sir Gangadhar Chitnavis in the Calcutta Legislative Council last March. He is probably right; neither is anything to be gained by ignoring the gravity of the situation which is thus created. Whether the Indian Protectionists be right or wrong as to the fiscal policy which is best adapted to Indian interests, there is no denying the fact that with Protection flourishing in the self-governing colonies, with the recent enlargement of the scope and functions of representative institutions in India, and with the grievance created by the sacrifice of the opium revenue on the altar of British vicarious philanthropy, it is a serious matter for the British Government to assert their own views if those views run diametrically counter to the wishes expressed by the only representatives of Indian opinion who are in a position to make their voices heard. Nevertheless, there are two limitations on the extent to which concessions can or ought to be made to Indian opinion. The first is based on the necessities of English internal politics. It cannot be doubted that although Sir Gangadhar Chitnavis and those who agree with him may perhaps be willing, as a *pis aller*, to accept Sir Roper Lethbridge's preferential plan, what they really want is not Preference but Protection against England, and this they cannot have, because, in Sir Roper Lethbridge's words, "no British Government that offered India Protection against Lancashire would live for a week." The second limitation is based on less egotistical and, therefore, nobler grounds. In spite of recent concessions, India is still, politically speaking, *in statu pupillari*, neither do the concessions recently made in the direction of granting self-governing institutions dispense the British Government from the duty of looking to the interests of the masses, who are at present very inadequately represented. It must be remembered that in India, perhaps even more than elsewhere, the voice of the consumer is hushed, whilst that of the producer is loud and strident.

The second of Sir Roper Lethbridge's arguments is based on the alleged necessity of raising more revenue. He, as also Sir Gangadhar Chitnavis, take it for granted that this necessity has already arisen. It would be essential, before taking any practical steps to give effect to the proposals now under discussion, to ascertain beyond any manner of doubt whether this statement is correct, and also, if correct, what alternatives exist to the plan proposed by Sir Roper Lethbridge. Sir Fleetwood Wilson carefully abstained from pledging himself to the accuracy of Sir Gangadhar Chitnavis's view on this point. "There is," he said, "much room for the development of India's other resources, and it has yet to be shown that there is no room for further economies in our administration." In the meanwhile, it would tend to the elucidation of the subject if Sir Roper Lethbridge and those who agree with him would lay before the world a carefully prepared and detailed estimate of the financial results which they consider would accrue from the adoption of their proposals. We are told, for instance, that raw jute to the value of £13,000,000 is exported annually from Bengal, of which only £3,000,000 worth is worked up in Great Britain, and that "a moderate duty" on this article would produce two millions a year. The prospect of obtaining a revenue of £2,000,000 in the manner proposed by Sir Roper Lethbridge appears at first sight somewhat illusory. In the first place, the tax would, on the basis of Sir Roper Lethbridge's figures, amount to 20 per cent, which can scarcely be called "moderate." In the second place, unless an equivalent export duty were imposed at British ports it would appear probable that the process of re-export for the benefit of "the lucky artisans of foreign protected nations" would not merely continue unchecked, but would even be encouraged, for those artisans would certainly not be supplied direct from India with the duty-laden raw material, but would draw their supplies from the jute sent to the ports of the United Kingdom, which would have paid no duty. Is it, moreover, quite certain that a duty such as that proposed by Sir Roper Lethbridge would be insufficient, as he alleges, "to bring in any competing fibres in the world"? These and other cognate points manifestly require further elucidation.

The third argument adduced by Sir Roper Lethbridge is based on the allegation that India is in a specially favourable position to adopt a policy of retaliation. It is unnecessary to go into the general arguments for and against retaliatory duties. They have been exhausted in the very remarkable and frigidly impartial book written on this subject by Professor Dietzel. It will be sufficient to say that here Sir Roper Lethbridge is on stronger ground. The main argument against retaliation in the United Kingdom is that foreign nations, by stopping our supplies of raw material, could check our manufactures. We are, therefore, in a singularly unfavourable position for engaging in a tariff war. The case of India is wholly different. Foreign nations cannot, it is alleged, dispense with the raw material which India supplies. There is, therefore, a good *prima facie* case for supposing that India has relatively little to fear from retaliation on their part.

It would be impossible within the limits of the present article to deal fully with all the aspects of this vitally important question. Attention may, however, be drawn to the very weighty remarks of Sir Fleetwood Wilson when he speaks of "the great alteration which a tariff war in India would effect in the balance of our trade, in the arrangements that now exist for the payment of our external debt, and in the whole of our exchange policy. This aspect of the question is one of extraordinary complexity, as well as of no small speculation." On the whole, although the proposals made by Sir Roper Lethbridge and his associates deserve full and fair consideration, it is most earnestly to be hoped that party leaders in this country will insist on their elaboration in full detail, and will then study every aspect of the question with the utmost care before giving even a qualified pledge to afford them support. The situation is already sufficiently difficult and complicated. It is not improbable that the difficulties and complications, far from being mitigated, would be increased by the pursuit into the economic wilderness of the *ignis fatuus* involved in the idea that it is possible for a nation to impose a tax on itself and then make the inhabitants of other countries pay the whole or the greater part of it.

XXI

ROME AND MUNICIPAL GOVERNMENT

"The Spectator," July 19, 1913

In spite of the obvious danger of establishing doubtful analogies and of making insufficient allowance for differences, the history of Imperial Rome can never cease to be of more than academic interest to the statesmen and politicians of Imperial England. Rome bequeathed to us much that is of inestimable value, both in the way of precept and example. She also bequeathed to us a word of ill omen—the word "Imperialism." The attempt to embody the broad outlines of a policy in a single word or phrase has at times exercised great influence in deciding the fate of nations. M. Vandal says with truth, "Nul ne comprendra la Révolution s'il ne tient compte de l'extraordinaire empire exercé à cette époque par les mots et les formules." Imperialism, though infinitely preferable to its quasi-synonym Caesarism, is, in fact, a term which, although not absolutely incorrect, is at the same time, by reason of its historical associations, misleading when applied to the mild and beneficent hegemony exercised by the rulers and people of England over their scattered transmarine dominions. It affords a convenient peg on which hostile critics, such as Mr. Mallik, whose work was reviewed last week in these columns, as also those ultra-cosmopolitan Englishmen who are the friends of every country but their own, may hang partisan homilies dwelling on the brutality of conquest and on all the harsh features of alien rule, whilst they leave sedulously in the background that aspect of the case which Polybius, parodying a famous saying of Themistocles, embodied in a phrase which he attributes to the Greeks after they had been absorbed into the Roman Empire, "If we had not been quickly ruined, we should not have been saved." This pessimistic aspect of Imperialism has certainly to some extent an historical basis. It is founded on the procedure generally believed to have been adopted in the process by which Rome acquired the dominion of the world. The careful attention given of late years to the study of inscriptions, and generally the results obtained by the co-operation established between historians and those who have more especially studied other branches of science, such as archaeology, epigraphy, and numismatics, have, however, now enabled us to approach the question of Roman expansion with far greater advantages than those possessed by writers even so late as the days of Mommsen. We are able to reply with a greater degree of confidence than at any previous period to the question of how far Roman policy was really associated with those principles and practices which many are accustomed to designate as Imperial. The valuable and erudite work which Mr. Reid has now given to the world comes opportunely to remind us of a very obvious and commonplace consideration. It is that although Roman expansion not only began, but was far advanced during the days of the Republic, Roman Imperialism did not exist before the creation of Roman Emperors, and did not in any considerable degree develop the vices generally, and sometimes rightly, attributed to the system until some while after Republican had given way to Imperial sway. "The residuary impression of the ancient world," Mr. Reid says in his preface, "left by a classical education comprises commonly the idea that the Romans ran, so to speak, a sort of political steam-roller over the ancient world. This has a semblance of truth for the period of decline, but none for the earlier days."

The fundamental idea which ran through the whole of Roman policy during the earliest, which was also the wisest and most statesmanlike stage of expansion, was not any desire to ensure the detailed and direct government of a number of outlying districts from one all-powerful centre, but rather to adopt every possible means calculated to maintain local autonomy, and to minimise the interference of the central authority. Herself originally a city-state, Rome aspired to become the predominant partner in a federation of municipalities, to which autonomy was granted even to the extent of waiving that prerogative which has generally been considered the distinctive mark of sovereignty, viz. the right of coinage. Broadly speaking, the only conditions imposed were very similar to those now forming the basis of the relations between the British Government and the Native States of India. These were (1) that the various commonwealths should keep the peace between each other; and (2) that their foreign policy should be dictated by Rome. It is often tacitly assumed, Mr. Reid says, that "in dealing with conquered peoples, the Romans were animated from the first by a passion for immediate domination and for grinding uniformity." This idea is not merely false; it is the very reverse of the truth. The most distinctive feature of Roman rule during the early period of expansion was its marvellous elasticity and pliability. Everywhere local customs were scrupulously respected. Everywhere the maintenance of whatever autonomous institutions existed at the time of conquest was secured. Everywhere the allies were treated with what the Greeks termed ἐπιμέλεια, which may be rendered into English by the word "consideration." Nowhere was the fatal mistake made of endeavouring to stamp out by force a local language or dialect, whilst until the Romans were brought into contact with the stubborn monotheism of the Jews, the easy-going pantheistic ideas current in the ancient world readily obviated the occurrence of any serious difficulties based on religious belief or ritual.

That this system produced results which were, from a political point of view, eminently satisfactory cannot for a moment be doubted. Mr. Reid says—and it were well that those who are interested in the cause of British Imperial Federation should note the remark—"In history the lightest bonds have often proved to be the strongest." The loosely compacted alliance of the Italic states withstood all the efforts of Hannibal to rend it asunder. The Roman system, in fact, created a double patriotism, that which attached itself to the locality, and that which broadened out into devotion to the metropolis. Neither was the one allegiance destructive of the other. When Ennius made his famous boast he did not mean that he spurned Rudiae and that he would for the future look exclusively to Rome as his mother-country, but rather that both the smaller and the larger patriotism would continue to exist side by side. "English local life," it has been truly said, "was the source and safeguard of English liberty." It may be said with equal truth that the notion of constituting self-governing town communities as the basis of Empire, which, Mr. Reid tells us, "was deeply ingrained in the Roman consciousness," stood Rome in good stead during some of the most stormy periods of her history. The process of voluntary Romanisation was so speedy that the natives of any province which, to use the Roman expression, had been but recently "pacated," became in a very short time loyal and zealous Roman subjects, and rarely if ever took advantage of distress elsewhere to vindicate their independence by seeking to cast off the light shackles which had been imposed on them.

"So long as municipal liberty maintained its vigour, the empire flourished." This is the fundamental fact to be borne in mind in dealing with the history of Roman expansion. Mr. Reid then takes us, step by step and province by province, through the pitiful history of subsequent deterioration and decay. After the Hannibalic war, Roman hegemony in Italy began to pass into domination. A policy of unwise exclusion applied to the federated states and cities, coupled with the assertion of irritating privileges on behalf of Roman citizens, led to the cataclysm of the Great Social War, at the close of which burgess rights were reluctantly conceded to all Italic communities who had not joined the rebels. Then followed the era of the great Julius, who probably—though of this we cannot be quite certain—wished to create a "world-state" with Rome as its head; Augustus, to whose genius and administrative ability tardy justice is now being done, and who, albeit he continued the policy of his uncle, possibly leant rather more to the idea, realised eighteen centuries later by Cavour, of a united Italy; Adrian, who aimed above all things at the consolidation of the Empire; and many others. Consolidation in whatsoever form almost necessarily connoted the insistence on some degree of uniformity, and "when the Emperors pressed uniformity upon the imperial system, it rapidly went to pieces." Finally, we get to the stage of Imperial penury and extravagance, accompanied by centralisation *in extremis*, when "hordes of official locusts, military and civil," were let loose on the land, and the tax-gatherers destroyed the main sources of the public revenues, with the result that the tax-payers were utterly ruined. The municipal system possessed wonderful vitality, and displayed remarkable aptitude for offering a passive resistance to the attacks directed against it. It survived longer than might have been expected. But when it became clear that the only function which the *curiales* were expected to perform was to emulate the Danaides by pouring gold into the bottomless cask of the Imperial Treasury, they naturally rejected the dubious honours conferred on them, and fled either to be the companions of the monks in the desert or elsewhere so as to be safe from the crushing load of Imperial distinction. Mr. Hodgkin and others have pointed out that the diversion of local funds to the Imperial Exchequer was one of the proximate causes which led to the downfall of the empire. Whilst the municipal system lasted, it produced admirable results. Dealing with Northern Africa, whose progress was eventually arrested by the withering hand of Islam, Mr. Reid speaks of "the contrast between the Roman civilisation and the culture which exists in the same regions to-day; flourishing cities, villages, and farms abounded in districts which are now sterile and deserted."

Apart from the special causes to which Mr. Reid and other historians have alluded, and, apart, moreover, from the intentions—often the very wise intentions—of individual Emperors, the municipal system, and with it the principle that local affairs should be dealt with locally, was almost bound to founder directly the force of circumstances strengthened the hands of the central authority at Rome. The battle between centralisation and decentralisation still continues. Every one who has been engaged in it knows that, whatever be the system adopted, the spirit in which it is carried out counts for even more than the system itself. Once place a firm, self-confident man with the centralising spirit strong within him at the head of affairs, and he will often, without any apparent change, go far to shatter any system, however carefully it may have been devised, to encourage decentralisation. Such a man was Napoleon. Every conceivable subject bearing on the government of his fellow-men was, as M. Taine says, "classified and docketed" in his ultra-methodical brain. It is useless to ask a man of this sort to decentralise. He cannot do so, not always by reason of a deliberate wish to grasp at absolute power, but because he sees so clearly what he thinks should be done that he cannot tolerate the local ineptitude, as he considers it, that leads to the rejection of his views. Thus, whilst Napoleon said to Count Chaptal, "Ce n'est pas des Tuileries qu'on peut diriger une armée," at the same time, as a matter of fact, he never ceased to interfere with the action of his generals employed at a distance, with results which, especially in Spain, were generally disastrous to French arms. Another general cause which militates against decentralisation is the inevitable tendency of any disputant who is dissatisfied with a decision given locally to seek redress at the hands of the central authority. St. Paul appealed to Caesar. A discontented Rajah will appeal to the Secretary of State for India. It is certain that in these cases, unless the appellate authority acts with the greatest circumspection, a risk will be incurred of giving a severe blow to the fundamental principles of decentralisation. It is no very hazardous conjecture to assume that many of the Roman Emperors were, like Napoleon, constitutionally disposed to centralise, and that the greater their ability the more likely was this disposition to dominate their minds. Thus Tacitus, speaking of Tiberius, says, "He never relaxed from the cares of government, but derived relief from his occupations." A man of this temperament is a born centraliser. However much his reason or his statesmanship may hold him in check, he will probably sooner or later yield to the temptation of stretching his own authority to such an extent as materially to weaken that of his distant and subordinate agents.

Considerations of space preclude the possibility of dwelling any further on the many points of interest suggested by Mr. Reid's instructive work. This much, however, may be said, that whilst British Imperialism is not exposed to many of the dangers which proved fatal to Imperial Rome, there is one principle adopted by the early founders of the Roman Empire which is fraught with enduring political wisdom, and which may be applied as well now as it was nineteen centuries ago. That principle is the preference shown to diversity over uniformity of system. Sir Alfred Lyall, whose receptive intellect was impregnated with modern applications of ancient precedents, said, "We ought to acknowledge that we cannot impose a uniform type of civilisation." Let us beware that we do not violate this very sound principle by too eager a disposition to transport institutions, whose natural habitat is Westminster, to Calcutta or Cairo.

XXII
A ROYAL PHILOSOPHER
"The Spectator," August 2, 1913

Those who are inclined to take a gloomy view of the future on the subject of the survival of the humanities in this country may derive some consolation from two considerations. One is that there is not the smallest sign either of relaxation in the quantity or deterioration in the quality of the humanistic literature turned out from our seats of learning. Year by year, indeed, both the interest in classical studies and the standard of scholarship appear to rise to a higher level. The other is that the mere fact that humanistic works are supplied shows that there must be a demand for them, and that there exists amongst the general public a number of readers outside the ranks of scholars, properly so called, who are anxious and willing to acquaint themselves with whatever new lights assiduous research can throw on the sayings and doings of the ancient world. Archaeology, epigraphy, and numismatics are year by year opening out new fields for inquiry, and affording fresh material for the reconstruction of history. More especially much light has of late been thrown on that chaotic period which lies between the death of the Macedonian conqueror and the final assertion of Roman domination. Professor Mahaffy has dealt with the Ptolemies, and Mr. Bevan with the Seleucids. A welcome complement to these instructive works is now furnished by Mr. Tarn's comprehensive treatment of an important chapter in the history of the Antigonids. It is surely the irony of posthumous fame that whereas every schoolboy knows something about Pyrrhus—how he fought the Romans with elephants, and eventually met a somewhat ignoble death from the hand of an old Argive woman who dropped a tile on his head—but few outside the ranks of historical students probably know anything of his great rival and relative, Antigonus Gonatas, the son of Demetrius the Besieger. Yet there can in reality be no manner of doubt as to which of these two careers should more excite the interest of posterity. Pyrrhus made a great stir in the world whilst he lived. "He thought it," Plutarch says—we quote from Dryden's translation—"a nauseous course of life not to be doing mischief to others or receiving some from them." But he was in reality an unlettered soldier of fortune, probably very much of the same type as some of Napoleon's rougher marshals, such as Augereau or Masséna. His manners were those of the camp, and his statesmanship that of the barrack-room. He blundered in everything he undertook except in the actual management of troops on the field of battle. "Not a common soldier in his army," Mr. Tarn says, "could have managed things as badly as the brilliant Pyrrhus." Antigonus was a man of a very different type. "He was the one monarch before Marcus Aurelius whom philosophy could definitely claim as her own." But in forming an estimate of his character it is necessary to bear constantly in mind the many different constructions which in the course of ages have been placed on the term "philosophy." Antigonus, albeit a disciple of Zeno, the most unpractical idealist of his age, was himself eminently practical. He indulged in no such hallucinations as those which cost the Egyptian Akhnaton his Syrian kingdom. As a thinker he moved on a distinctly lower plane than Marcus Aurelius. Perhaps of all the characters of antiquity he most resembles Julian, whose career as a man of action wrung from the Christian Prudentius the fine epitaph, "Perfidus ille Deo, quamvis non perfidus orbi." These early Greek philosophers were, in fact, a strange set of men. They were not always engaged in the study of philosophy. They occasionally, whilst pursuing knowledge and wisdom, indulged in practices of singular unwisdom or of very dubious morality. Thus the eminent historian Hieronymus endeavoured to establish what we should now call a "corner" in the bitumen which floated on the surface of the Dead Sea, and which was largely used for purposes of embalming in Egypt; but his efforts were completely frustrated by the Arabs who were interested in the local trade. The philosopher Lycon, besides displaying an excessive love for the pleasures of the table, was a noted wrestler, boxer, and tennis-player. Antigonus himself, in spite of his love of learning, vied with his great predecessors, Philip and Alexander, in his addiction to the wine-cup. When, by a somewhat unworthy stratagem, he had tricked the widowed queen Nikaia out of the possession of the Acrocorinthian citadel, which was, politically speaking, the apple of his eye, he celebrated the occasion by getting exceedingly drunk, and went "reeling through Corinth at the head of a drunken rout, a garland on his head and a wine-cup in his hand." Antigonus was, in fact, not so much what we should call a philosopher as a man of action with literary tastes, standing thus in marked contrast to Pyrrhus, who "cared as little for knowledge or culture as did any baron of the Dark Ages." When he was engaged in a difficult negotiation with Ptolemy Philadelphus he allowed himself to be mollified by a quotation from Homer, who, as Plato said, was "the educator of Hellas." Although not himself an original thinker, he encouraged thought in others. He surrounded himself with men of learning, and even received at his court the yellow-robed envoys of Asoka, the far-distant ruler and religious reformer of India. Moreover, in spite of his wholly practical turn of mind, Antigonus learnt something from his philosophic friends; notably, he imbibed somewhat of the Stoic sense of duty. "Do you not understand," he said to his son, who had misused some of his subjects, "that *our* kingship is a noble servitude?" Nevertheless, throughout his career, the sentiments of the man of action strongly predominated over those of the man of thought. He treated all shams with a truly Carlylean hatred and contempt. Moreover, one trait in his character strongly indicates the pride of the masterful man of action who scorns all adventitious advantages and claims to stand or fall by his own merits. Napoleon, whilst the members of his family were putting forth ignoble claims to noble birth, said that his patent of nobility dated from the battle of Montenotte. Antigonus, albeit he came of a royal stock, laid aside all ancestral claims to the throne of Macedonia. He aspired to be king because of his kingly qualities. He wished his people to apply to him the words which Tiberius used of a distinguished Roman of humble birth: "Curtius Rufinus videtur mihi ex se natus" (*Ann.* xi. 21). He succeeded in his attempt. He won the hearts of his people, and although he failed in his endeavour to govern the whole of Greece through the agency of subservient "tyrants," he accomplished the main object which through good and evil fortune he pursued with dogged tenacity throughout the whole of his chequered career. He lived and died King of Macedonia.

The world-politics of this period are almost as confused as the relationships which were the outcome of the matrimonial alliances contracted by the principal actors on the world's stage. How bewildering these alliances were may be judged from what Mr. Tarn says of Stratonice, the daughter of Antiochus I., who married Demetrius, the son of Antigonus: "Stratonice was her husband's first cousin and also his aunt, her mother-in-law's half-sister and also her niece, her father-in-law's niece, her own mother's granddaughter-in-law, and perhaps other things which the curious may work out." Mr. Tarn has unravelled the tangled political web with singular lucidity. Here it must be sufficient to say that, after the death of Pyrrhus, a conflict between Macedonia and Egypt, which stood at the head of an anti-Macedonian coalition of which Athens, Epirus, and Sparta were the principal members, became inevitable. The rivalry between the two States led to the Chremonidean war—so called because in 266 the Athenian Chremonides moved the declaration of war against Antigonus. The result of the war was that on land Antigonus remained the complete master of the situation.

With true political instinct, however, he recognised the truth of that maxim which history teaches from the days of Aegospotami to those of Trafalgar, viz. that the execution of an imperial policy is impossible without the command of the sea. This command had been secured by his predecessors, but had fallen to Egypt after the fine fleet created by Demetrius the Besieger had been shattered in 280 by Ptolemy Keraunos with the help of the navy which had been created by Lysimachus. Antigonus decided to regain the power which had been lost. His efforts were at first frustrated by the wily and wealthy Egyptian monarch, who knew the power of gold. "Egypt neither moved a man nor launched a ship, but Antigonus found himself brought up short, his friends gone, his fleet paralysed." Then death came unexpectedly to his aid and removed his principal enemies. His great opponent, the masterful Arsinoë, who had engineered the Chremonidean war, was already dead, and, in Mr. Tarn's words, "comfortably deified." Other important deaths now followed in rapid succession. Alexander of Corinth, Antiochus, and Ptolemy all passed away. "The imposing edifice reared by Ptolemy's diplomacy suddenly collapsed like the card-house of a little child." Antigonus was not the man to neglect the opportunity thus afforded to him. Though now advanced in years, he reorganised his navy and made an alliance with Rhodes, with the result that "the sea power of Egypt went down, never to rise again." Then he triumphantly dedicated his flagship to the Delian Apollo. The possession of Delos had always been one of the main objects of his ambition. It did more than symbolise the rule of the seas. It definitely brought within the sphere of Macedonian influence one of the greatest centres of Greek religious thought.

The rest of the story may be read in Mr. Tarn's graphic pages. He relates how Antigonus incurred the undying enmity of Aratus of Sicyon, one of those Greek democrats who held "that the very worst democracy was infinitely better than the very best 'tyranny'—a conventional view which neglects the uncomfortable fact that the tyranny of a democracy can be the worst in the world." He lost Corinth, which he never endeavoured to regain. His system of governing the Peloponnesus through the agency of subservient "tyrants" utterly collapsed. "It is," Mr. Tarn says, "a strange case of historical justice. As regards Macedonia, Antigonus had followed throughout a sound and just idea of government, and all that he did for Macedonia prospered. But in the Peloponnese, though he found himself there from necessity rather than from choice, he had employed an unjustifiable system; he lived long enough to see it collapse."

The main interest to the present generation of the career of this remarkable man consists in the fact that it is illustrative of the belief that a man of action can also be a man of letters. As it was in the days of the Antigonids, so it is now. Napier says that there is no instance on record of a successful general who was not also a well-read man. General Wolfe, the hero of Quebec, on being asked how he came to adopt a certain tactical combination which proved eminently successful at Louisbourg, said, "I had it from Xenophon." Havelock "loved Homer and took pattern by Thucydides," and, according to Mr. Forrest, adopted tactics at the battle of Cawnpore which he had learnt from a close study of "Old Frederick's" dispositions at Leuthen. There is no greater delusion than to suppose that study weakens the arm of the practical politician, administrator, or soldier. On the contrary it fortifies it. Lord Wolseley, himself a very distinguished man of action, speaking to the students of the Royal Military Academy of Sir Frederick Maurice, who possessed an inherited literary talent, said that he was "a fine example of the combination of study and practice. He is not only the ablest student of war we have, but is also the bravest man I have ever seen under fire"; and on another occasion he wrote: "It is often said that dull soldiers make the best fighters, because they do not think of danger. Now, Maurice is one of the very few men I know who, if I told him to run his head against a stone wall, would do so without question. His is also the quickest and keenest intellect I have met in my service."

XXIII
ANCIENT ART AND RITUAL
"The Spectator," August 9, 1913

Any new work written by Miss Jane Harrison is sure to be eagerly welcomed by all who take an interest in classical study or in anthropology. The conclusions at which she arrives are invariably based on profound study and assiduous research. Her generalisations are always bold, and at times strikingly original. Moreover, it is impossible for any lover of the classics, albeit he may move on a somewhat lower plane of erudition, not to sympathise with the erudite enthusiasm of an author who expresses "great delight" in discovering that Aristotle traced the origin of the Greek drama to the Dithyramb—that puzzling and "ox-driving" Dithyramb, of which Müller said that "it was vain to seek an etymology," but whose meaning has been very lucidly explained by Miss Harrison herself—and whose "heart stands still" in noting that "by a piece of luck" Plutarch gives the Dionysiac hymn which the women of Elis addressed to the "noble Bull."

It is probable that the first feeling excited in the mind of an ordinary reader, when he is asked to accept some of the conclusions at which modern students of anthropology and comparative religion have arrived, is one of scepticism. Miss Harrison is evidently alive to the existence of this feeling, for in dealing with the ritualistic significance of the Panathenaic frieze she bids her readers not to "suspect they are being juggled with," or to think that she has any wish to strain an argument with a view to "bolstering up her own art and ritual theory." It can, indeed, be no matter for surprise that such suspicions should be aroused. When, for instance, an educated man hears that the Israelites worshipped a golden calf, or that the owl and the peacock were respectively sacred to Juno and Minerva, he can readily understand what is meant. But when he is told that an Australian Emu man, strutting about in the feathers of that bird, does not think that he is imitating an Emu, but that in very fact he is an Emu, it must be admitted that his intellect, or it may be his imagination, is subjected to a somewhat severe strain. Similarly, he may at first sight find some difficulty in believing that any strict relationship can be established between the Anthesteria and Bouphonia of the cultured Athenians and the idolatrous veneration paid by the hairy and hyperborean Ainos to a sacred bear, who is at first pampered and then sacrificed, or the ritualistic tug-of-war performed by the Esquimaux, in which one side, personifying ducks, represents Summer, whilst the other, personifying ptarmigans, represents Winter. Although this scepticism is not only very natural, but even commendable, it is certain that the science of modern anthropology, in which we may reflect with legitimate pride that England has taken the lead, rests on very solid foundations. Indeed, its foundations are in some respects even better assured than those of some other sciences, such, for instance, as craniology, whose conclusions would appear at first sight to be capable of more precise demonstration, but which, in spite of this fair appearance, has as yet yielded results which are somewhat disappointing. At the birth of every science it is necessary to postulate something. The postulates that the anthropologist demands rival in simplicity those formulated by Euclid. He merely asks us to accept as facts that the main object of every living creature is to go on living, that he cannot attain this object without being supplied with food, and that, in the case of man, his supply of food must necessarily be obtained from the earth, the forest, the sea, or the river. On the basis of these elementary facts, the anthropologist then asks us to accept the conclusion that the main beliefs and acts of primitive man are intimately, and indeed almost solely, connected with his food supply; and having first, by a deductive process of reasoning, established a high degree of probability that this conclusion is correct, he proceeds to confirm its accuracy by reasoning inductively and showing that a similarity, too marked to be the result of mere accident or coincidence, exists in the practices which primitive man has adopted, throughout the world, and which can only be explained on the assumption that by methods, differing indeed in detail but substantially the same in principle, endeavours have been, and still are being, made to secure an identical object, viz. to obtain food and thus to sustain life. The various methods adopted both in the past and the present are invariably associated in one form or another with the invocation of magical influences. The primitive savage, Miss Harrison says, "is a man of action." He does not pray. He acts. If he wishes for sun or wind or rain, "he summons his tribe, and dances a sun dance or a wind dance or a rain dance." If he wants bear's flesh to eat, he does not pray to his god for strength to outwit or to master the bear, but he rehearses his hunt in a bear dance. If he notices that two things occur one after the other, his untrained intellect at once jumps to the conclusion that one is the cause and the other the effect. Thus in Australia—a specially fertile field for anthropological research, which has recently been explored with great thoroughness and intelligence by Messrs. Spencer and Gillen—the cry of the plover is frequently heard before rain falls. Therefore, when the natives wish for rain they sing a rain song in which the cry of that bird is faithfully imitated.

Before alluding to the special point which Miss Harrison deals with in *Ancient Art and Ritual*, it will be as well to glance at the views which she sets forth in her previous illuminating treatise entitled *Themis*. The former is in reality a continuation of the latter work. The view heretofore generally entertained as regards the anthropomorphic gods of Greece has been that the conception of the deity preceded the adoption of the ritual. Moreover, one school of anthropologists ably represented by Professor Ridgeway, has maintained that the phenomena of vegetation spirits, totemism, etc., rose from primary elements, notably from the belief in the existence of the soul after the death of the body. Miss Harrison and those who agree with her hold that this view involves an anthropological heresy. She deprecates the use of the word "anthropomorphic," which she describes as clumsy and too narrow. She prefers the expression ἀνθρωποφυής used by Herodotus (i. 131), signifying "of human growth." She points out that the anthropomorphism of the Greeks was preceded by theriomorphism and phytomorphism, that the ritual was "prior to the God," that so long as man was engaged in a hand-to-hand struggle for bare existence his sole care was to obtain food, and that during this stage of his existence his religious observances took almost exclusively the form of magical inducements to the earth to renew that fertility which, by the periodicity of the seasons, was at times temporarily suspended. It was only at a later period, when the struggle for existence had become less arduous, that the belief in the efficacy of magical rites decayed, and that in matters of religion the primitive Greeks "shifted from a nature-god to a human-nature god."

In her more recent work Miss Harrison reverts to this theme, and subsequently carries us one step further. She maintains that the original conception of the Greek drama was in no way spectacular. The Athenians went to the theatre as we go to church. They did not attend to see players act, but to take part in certain ritualistic things done (*dromena*). The priests of Dionysos Eleuthereus, of Apollo Daphnephoros, and of other deities attended in solemn state to assist in the performance of the rites. With that keen sense of humour which enlivens all her pages, and which made her speak in her *Themis* of the august father of gods and men as "an automatically explosive thunderstorm," Miss Harrison says, "It is as though at His Majesty's the front row of stalls was occupied by the whole bench of bishops, with the Archbishop of Canterbury enthroned in the central stall." The actual *dromenon* performed was of the same nature as that which in more modern times has induced villagers to make Jacks-in-the-Green and to dance round maypoles. It was always connected with the recurrence of the seasons and with the death and resurrection of vegetation. In fact, the whole ritual clustered round the idea represented at a later period in the well-known and very beautiful lines of Moschus in the *Lament for Bion*, which may be freely translated thus:

Ah me! The mallows, anise, and each flower That withers at the blast of winter's breath Await the vernal, renovating hour And joyously awake from feignèd death.

The idea which impelled these ancient Greeks to perform ritualistic *dromena* on their orchestras, which took the place of what we should call the stage, is not yet dead. Miss Harrison quotes from Mr. Lawson's work on modern Greek folklore, which is a perfect mine of knowledge on the subject of the survival of ancient religious customs in modern Greece, the story of an old woman in Euboea who was asked on Easter Eve why village society was in a state of gloom and despondency, and who replied: "Of course, I am anxious; for if Christ does not rise to-morrow, we shall have no corn this year."

It was during the fifth century that the *dromenon* and the Dionysiac Dithyramb passed to some extent away and were merged into the drama. "Homer came to Athens, and out of Homeric stories playwrights began to make their plots." The chief agent in effecting this important change was the so-called "tyrant" Pisistratus, who was probably a free-thinker and "cared little for magic and ancestral ghosts," but who for political reasons wished to transport the Dionysia from the country to the town. "Now," Miss Harrison says, "to bring Homer to Athens was like opening the eyes of the blind." Independently of the inevitable growth of scepticism which was the natural result of increased knowledge and more acute powers of observation, it is no very hazardous conjecture to assume that the quick-witted and pleasure-loving Athenians welcomed the relief afforded to the dreary monotony of the ancient *dromena* by the introduction of the more lively episodes drawn from the heroic sagas. "Without destroying the old, Pisistratus contrived to introduce the new, to add to the old plot of Summer and Winter the life-stories of heroes, and thereby arose the drama."

Having established her case so far, Miss Harrison makes what she herself terms "a great leap." She passes from the thing *done*, whether *dromenon* or drama, to the thing *made*. She holds that as it was the god who arose from the rite, similarly it was the ritual connected with the worship of the god which gave birth to his representation in sculpture. Art, she says, is not, as is commonly supposed, the "handmaid of religion." "She springs straight out of the rite, and her first outward leap is the image of the god." Miss Harrison gives two examples to substantiate her contention. In the first place, she states at some length arguments of irrefutable validity to show that the Panathenaic frieze, which originally surrounded the Parthenon, represents a great ritual procession, and she adds, "Practically the whole of the reliefs that remain to us from the archaic period, and a very large proportion of those of later date, when they do not represent heroic mythology, are ritual reliefs, 'votive' reliefs, as we call them; that is, prayers or praises translated into stone."

Miss Harrison's second example is eminently calculated to give a shock to the conventional ideas generally entertained, for, as she herself says, if there is a statue in the world which apparently represents "art for art's sake" it is that of the Apollo Belvedere. Much discussion has taken place as to what Apollo is supposed to be doing in this famous statue. "There is only one answer. We do not know." Miss Harrison, however, thinks that as he is poised on tiptoe he may be in the act of taking flight from the earth. Eventually, after discussing the matter at some little length, she appears to come to the audacious conclusion which, in spite of its hardy irreverence, may very probably be true, that as Apollo was, after all, only an early Jack-in-the-Green, he has been artistically represented in marble by some sculptor of genius in that capacity.

Finally, before leaving this very interesting and instructive work, it may be noted that Miss Harrison quotes a remarkable passage from Athenaeus (xiv. 26), which certainly affords strong confirmation of her view that in the eyes of ancient authors there was an intimate connection between art and dancing, and therefore, inasmuch as dancing was ritualistic, between art and ritual. "The statues of the craftsmen of old times," Athenaeus says, "are the relics of ancient dancing."

It is greatly to be hoped that Miss Harrison will continue the study of this subject, and that she will eventually give to the world the results of her further inquiries.

XXIV

PORTUGUESE SLAVERY

"The Spectator," August 16, 23, 30, 1913

It is impossible to read the White Paper recently published on the subject of slavery in the West African dominions of Portugal without coming to the conclusion that the discussion has been allowed to degenerate into a rather unseemly wrangle between the Foreign Office officials and the Anti-Slavery Society. There is always a considerable risk that this will happen when enthusiasts and officials are brought into contact with each other. On the one hand, the enthusiasts in any great cause are rather prone to let their emotions dominate their reason, to generalise on somewhat imperfect data, and occasionally to fall unwittingly into making statements of fact which, if not altogether incorrect, are exaggerated or partial. On the other hand, there is a disposition on the part of officials to push to an excess Sir Arthur Helps's dictum that most of the evils of the world arise from inaccuracy, and to surround all enthusiasts with one general atmosphere of profound mistrust. An old official may perhaps be allowed to say, without giving offence, that, quite apart from the nobility and moral worth of the issue at stake, it is, from the point of view of mere worldly wisdom, a very great error to adopt this latter attitude. There are enthusiasts and enthusiasts. It is probably quite useless for an anti-suffragist or a supporter of vivisection to endeavour to meet half-way a militant suffragist or a whole-hearted anti-vivisectionist. In these cases the line of cleavage is too marked to admit of compromise, and still less of co-operation. But the case is very different if the matter under discussion is the suppression of slavery. Here it may readily be admitted that both the enthusiasts and the officials, although they may differ in opinion as to the methods which should be adopted, are honestly striving to attain the same objects. The Anti-Slavery Society, and those who habitually work with them, have performed work of which their countrymen are very justly proud. But they are not infallible. It is quite right that the accuracy of any statements which they make should be carefully tested by whatever means exist for testing them. For instance, when the Society of Friends say that they are in possession of "first-hand information" to show that "atrocities" are being committed in the Portuguese dominions, the Foreign Office is obviously justified in asking them to state on what evidence this formidable accusation is founded, and when it appears that they cannot produce "exactly the kind of evidence as to 'atrocities' which would strengthen your (*i.e.* the British Government's) hands in any protest made by you to the Portuguese Government," it is not unnatural that the officials should be somewhat hardened in their belief that humanitarian testimony has to be accepted with caution. It would obviously be much wiser for the humanitarians to recognise that incorrect statements, or sweeping generalisations which are incapable of proof, do their cause more harm than good.

The fact that erroneous statements are frequently made in controversial matters, and that the data on which generalisations are based are often imperfect, should not, however, beget the error of attaching undue importance to matters of this sort, and thus failing to see the wood by reason of the trees. What object, for instance, is to be gained by addressing to the Anti-Slavery Society a remonstrance because they only quote a portion and not the whole of a conversation between Sir Edward Grey and the Portuguese Minister (M. de Bocage) when, on reference to the account of that conversation, it would appear that the passages omitted were not very material to the point under discussion? Again, considering that the manner in which the so-called "contracts" with slaves are concluded is notorious, is it not rather begging the question and falling back on a legal quibble to say that there would "be no reason for insisting on the repatriation (of a British subject) if he were working under a contract which could not be shown to be illegal"? Can it be expected, moreover, that Sir Eyre Crowe's contention that the slaves "are now legally free" should carry much conviction when it is abundantly clear from the testimony of all independent and also official witnesses that this legal freedom does not constitute freedom in the sense in which we generally employ the term, but that it has, in fact, up to the present time been little more than an euphemism for slavery?

Every allowance should, of course, be made for the embarrassing position in which the present Government of Portugal, from no fault of its own, is placed. The fact, however, remains that at this moment the criticisms of those who are interested in the cause of anti-slavery are not solely directed against the Portuguese Government. They also demur to the attitude taken up by the British Government. It is, indeed, impossible to read the papers presented to Parliament without feeling that the Archbishop of Canterbury was justified in saying, during a recent debate in the House of Lords, that the Foreign Office and its subordinates have shown some excess of zeal in apologising for the Portuguese. After all, it should not be forgotten that the voice of civilised humanity calls loudly on the Portuguese Government and nation to purge themselves, and that speedily, of a very heinous offence against civilisation, namely, that of placing their black fellow-creatures much on the same footing as the oxen that plough their fields and the horses which draw their carts, in order that the white man may acquire wealth. It is only fair to remember that at no very remote period of their history the Anglo-Saxon race were also guilty of this offence; but the facts that one branch of that race purged itself of crime by the expenditure of huge sums of money, and that the other branch shed its best blood in order to ensure the black man's freedom, give them a moral right, based on very substantial title-deeds, to plead the cause of freedom. Neither should it be forgotten that, whatever mistakes those interested in the Anti-Slavery cause may make in dealing with points of detail, they are right on the chief issue—right, that is to say, not merely in intention, but also on the main fact, viz. that virtual slavery still exists in the Portuguese dominions. Any one who has had practical experience of dealing with these matters, and can read between the lines of the official correspondence, cannot fail to see that if the Foreign Office authorities, instead of dwelling with somewhat unnecessary insistence on controversial points and only half-accepting the realities of the situation, had candidly admitted the main facts and had confined themselves to a discussion of the means available for arriving at the object which they, in common with the Anti-Slavery Society, wished to attain, much useless recrimination might have been avoided and the interests of the cause would, to a far greater extent, have been served.

The writer of the present article has had a good deal to do with the Anti-Slavery and other similar societies, such, for instance, as that which, until recently, dealt with the affairs of the Congo. He has not always agreed with their proposals, but, being in thorough sympathy with the objects which they wished to attain, he was fortunately able to establish the mutual confidence which that bond of sympathy connoted. He can, moreover, from his own experience, testify to the fact that, although there may occasionally be exceptions, the humanitarians generally, however enthusiastic, are by no means unreasonable. On the contrary, if once they are thoroughly convinced that the officials are honestly and energetically striving to do their best to remove the abuses of which they complain, they are quite prepared to make due allowance for practical difficulties, and to abstain from causing unnecessary and hurtful embarrassment. They are not open to the suspicion which often attaches itself to Parliamentarians who take up some special cause, viz. that they may be seeking to acquire personal notoriety or to gain some party advantage. The righteousness and disinterestedness of their motives cannot be doubted. The question of the abolition of slavery in the Soudan presented many and great difficulties, which might easily have formed the subject of acrimonious correspondence and of agitation in Parliament and in the press. Any such agitation would very probably have led to the adoption of measures whose value would have been illusory rather than real, and which might well have endangered both public security and the economic welfare of the country. The main reason why no such agitation took place was that a mutual feeling of confidence was established. Sir Reginald Wingate and his very able staff of officials were left to deal with the matter after their own fashion. The result has been that, without the adoption of any very sensational measures calculated to attract public attention, it may be said, with truth, that for all practical purposes slavery has quietly disappeared from the Soudan. But if once this confidence is conspicuous by its absence, a state of more or less latent warfare between the humanitarians and the official world, such as that revealed in the papers recently laid before Parliament, is almost certain to be created, with the results that the public interests suffer, that rather heated arguments and counter-arguments are bandied about in the columns of the newspapers, and that the differences of opinion on minor points between those who ought to be allies tend to obscure the main issue, and preclude that co-operation which should be secured, and which in itself would be no slight earnest of success.

Stress has been laid on this point because of its practical importance, and also in the hope that, in connection with this question, it may be found possible ere long to establish better relations between the Foreign Office officials and the Anti-Slavery Society than those which apparently exist at present. There ought to be no great difficulty in effecting an improvement in those relations, for it cannot for one moment be doubted that both sides are honestly endeavouring to perform what they consider to be their duty according to their respective lights.

Turning now to the consideration of the question on its own merits, it is obvious that, before discussing any remedies, it is essential to arrive at a correct diagnosis of the disease. Is the trade in slaves still carried on, and does slavery still exist in the Portuguese dominions? The two points deserve separate treatment, for although slavery is bad, the slave trade is infinitely worse.

It is not denied that until very recently the trade in slaves between the mainland and the Portuguese islands was carried on upon an extensive scale. The Anti-Slavery Society state that within the last twenty-five years sixty-three thousand slaves, constituting "a human cargo worth something over £2,500,000," have been shipped to the islands. Moreover, it appears that, as was to be expected, this trade was, and perhaps to a certain extent still is, in the hands of individuals who constitute the dregs of society, and who, it may confidently be assumed, have not allowed their operations to be hampered by any kind of moral or humane scruples. Colonel Freire d'Andrade informed Sir Arthur Hardinge that "many of the Portuguese slave-traders at Angola had been convicts sentenced to transportation," who had been allowed to settle in the colony. "It was from among these old convicts or ex-convict settlers and their half-caste progeny that the slave-trading element, denounced by the Belgian Government, was largely recruited; they at least were its most direct agents." Since the accession to power of the Republican Government in Portugal the trade in slaves has been absolutely prohibited. No Government which professes to follow the dictates of civilisation, and especially of Liberalism, could indeed tolerate for a day the continuance of such a practice. The question which remains for consideration is whether the efforts of the Portuguese Government, in the sincerity of which there can be no doubt, have been successful or the reverse. Has the cessation of the traffic been real and complete or, as the Anti-Slavery Society appear disposed to think, only partial and "nominal"? On this point the evidence is somewhat conflicting. On the one hand, M. Ramaix, writing on behalf of the Belgian Government on May 1, 1912, says, "It is well known that the slave trade is still carried on to a certain extent in the neighbourhood of the sources of the Zambesi and Kasai, in a region which extends over the frontiers of the Congo, Angola, and North-Western Rhodesia," and on June 8, 1912, Baron Lalaing, the Belgian Minister in London, said, "At the instigation of the traders the population living on the two slopes of the watershed, from Lake Dilolo to the meridian of Kayoyo, are actively engaged in smuggling, arms traffic, and slave trade." On the other hand, Mr. Wallace, writing from Livingstone, in Northern Rhodesia, on June 25, 1912, says that "active slave-trading does not now exist along our borders." On December 6 of the same year he confirmed this statement, but added, "occasional cases may occur, for the status of slave exists, but they cannot be many." Looking to all the circumstances of the case—to the great extent and, in some cases, to the remoteness of the Portuguese dominions, the ruthless character of the slave-traders, the pecuniary inducements which exist for engaging in a very lucrative traffic, the helplessness of the slaves themselves, and the fact that traffic in slaves is apparently a common inter-tribal practice in Central Africa, it would be unreasonable to expect that the Portuguese Government should be able at once to put a complete stop to these infamous proceedings. It may well be that, in spite of every effort, the slave trade may still linger on for a while. All that can be reasonably expected is that the Portuguese authorities should do their utmost to stop it. That they are doing a good deal cannot be doubted, but it is somewhat of a shock to read (*Africa*, No. 2 of 1912, p. 59) that Senhor Vasconcellos rather prided himself on the fact that certain "Europeans who were found guilty of acts of slave traffic" had merely been "immediately expelled from the region," and were "not allowed to return to the colonies." Surely, considering the nature of the offence, a punishment of this sort errs somewhat on the side of leniency. Had these men been residing in Egypt or the Soudan they would have been condemned to penal servitude for a term of years. It is more satisfactory to learn, on the authority of Colonel Freire d'Andrade, that the convicts to whom allusion has already been made are "no longer permitted to roam at large about the colony, but are, save a very few who are allowed to live outside on giving a security, kept in the forts of Loanda."

91

Further, it would appear that until recently the officials who registered the "serviçaes," or native contract labourers, had a direct pecuniary interest in the matter, and were "thus exposed to the temptation of not scrutinising too closely the genuineness of the contracts themselves, or the extent to which they were understood and accepted by savage or semi-savage contracting parties." In other words, the Portuguese officials employed in registration, far from having any inducements offered to them to protect the labourers, were strongly tempted to engage in what, brushing aside official euphemism, may with greater accuracy be termed the slave trade pure and simple. It seems that this practice is now to be altered. The registration fees are no longer to go into the pockets of the registering officials, but are to be paid into the Provincial Treasury. The change is unquestionably for the better. But it is impossible in this connection not to be struck by the somewhat curious standard of official discipline and morality which appears to exist in the Portuguese service. Colonel Freire d'Andrade told Sir Arthur Hardinge that "he knew of one case where £1,000 had been made over a single contract for 'serviçaes' in this way by a local official who had winked, in this connection, at some dishonest or, at least, highly doubtful transactions, and who had been censured and obliged to refund the money." As in the case of the Europeans found guilty of engaging in the slave trade, the punishment awarded appears to be somewhat disproportionate to the gravity of the offence. One would have thought that peculation of this description would have been visited at least with dismissal, if not with a short sojourn in the Loanda gaol.

Colonel Freire d'Andrade further states that "the Lisbon Colonial Office had sent out very stringent orders to the Governor-General of Angola to put a stop once and for all to these slavery operations. New military outposts had now been created near the northern and eastern frontiers of the province." It is to be hoped that these orders will be obeyed, and that they will prove effectual to attain the object in view.

On the whole, in spite of some features in the case which would appear to justify friendly criticism, it would seem that the Portuguese Government are really endeavouring to suppress the trade in slaves. All that the British Government can do is to afford them whatever assistance is possible in British territory, and to encourage them in bold and strenuous action against the influential opposition whose enmity has necessarily been evoked.

Turning now to the question of whether slavery—as distinct from the slave trade—still exists in Portuguese West Africa, it is to be observed that it is essential to inquire thoroughly into this question for the reason already given, viz. that before considering what remedies should be applied it is very necessary that the true nature of the evil should be recognised. On this point there is a direct conflict of opinion. The Anti-Slavery Society maintain that the present system of contract labourers ('serviçaes') is merely another name for slavery, and as one proof of the wide discrepancy between theory and practice they point to the fact that whereas there can be no manner of doubt that undisguised slavery existed until only recently, it was nominally abolished by law so long ago as 1876. On the other hand, to quote the words of Mr. Smallbones, the British Consul at Loanda, the Portuguese Government, whose views on this matter appear to have been received with a certain amount of qualified acceptance by the British Foreign Office, "consistently deny" the existence of a state of slavery.

The whole controversy really hangs on what is meant by the word "slavery." In this, as in so many cases, it is easier to say what the thing is not than to embrace in one short sentence an accurate and sufficiently wide explanation of what it is. *Definitio est negatio.* De Brunetière said that, after fifty years of discussion, it was impossible to define romanticism. Half a century or more ago, a talented German writer (Hackländer) wrote a book entitled *European Slave-life*, in which he attempted to show that, without knowing it, we were all slaves one of another, and, in fact, that the artisan working in a cotton factory or the sempstress employed in a milliner's shop was as truly in a state of slavery as the negro who at that time was working in the fields of Georgia or Carolina. In a sense, of course, it may be said that every one who works for his living, from a Cabinet Minister to a crossing-sweeper, is a slave, for he has to conform to certain rules, and unless he works he will be deprived of many advantages which he wishes to acquire, and may even be reduced to a state of starvation. But speculations of this sort may be left to the philosopher and the sociologist. They have little interest for the practical politician. Sir Edward Grey endeavoured, for the purposes of the subject now under discussion, to define slavery. "Voluntary engagement," he said, "is not slavery, but forcible engagement is slavery." The definition is correct as far as it goes, but it is incomplete, for it fails to answer the question on which a great part of this Portuguese controversy hangs, viz. what do the words "voluntary" and "forcible" mean? The truth is that it is quite unnecessary, in dealing with this subject, to wander off into a field strewn with dialectical subtleties. It may not be possible to define slavery with the same mathematical precision which Euclid gave to his definitions of a straight line or a point, but every man of ordinary common sense knows the difference between slavery and freedom in the usual acceptation of those terms. He knows well enough that however much want or the force of circumstances may oblige an Englishman, a Frenchman, or a German to accept hard conditions in fixing the price at which he is prepared to sell his labour or his services, none of these individuals is, in reality, a slave; and he has only to inquire very cursorily into the subject to satisfy himself that the relations between employer and employed in Portuguese West Africa differ widely from those which exist in any European country, and are in fact far more akin to what, in the general acceptance of the word, is termed slavery.

Broadly speaking, it may be said that the contention that the present system of contract labour is merely slavery in disguise rests on three pleas, viz. (1) that even if, as was often the case, the contract labourers now actually serving were not forcibly recruited, they were very frequently wholly unaware of the true nature of the engagements which they had taken, or of the conditions under which they would be called upon to serve; (2) that not only are they unable to terminate their contracts if they find they have been deceived, but that even on the termination of those contracts they are not free to leave their employers; and (3) that, even when nominal freedom is conceded, they cannot take advantage of it, for the reason that the employers or their Government have virtually by their own acts created a state of things which only leaves the slaves to choose between the alternative of continuing in a state of servitude or undergoing extreme suffering, ending not improbably in death. It is submitted that, if these three propositions can be proved, it is mere juggling with words to maintain that no state of slavery exists.

As regards the first point, it is to be observed that when the superior intelligence and education of the recruiting agents are contrasted with the complete savagery and ignorance of the individuals recruited, there is obviously a strong presumption that in numberless cases the latter have been cozened into making contracts, the nature of which they did not in the least understand, and this presumption may almost be said to harden into certainty when the fact, to which allusion has already been made, is remembered, that the Portuguese officials engaged in the registration of contract labourers had until very recently a direct pecuniary interest in augmenting the number of labourers. Further, Mr. Smallbones, writing on September 26, 1912, alludes to a letter signed "Carlos de Silva," which appeared in a local paper termed the *Independente*. M. de Silva says that the "serviçaes" engaged in Novo Redondo "all answered the interpreter's question whether they were willing to go to San Thomé with a decided 'No,' which was translated by the interpreter as signifying their utmost willingness to be embarked." If this statement is correct, it is in itself almost sufficient to satisfy the most severe condemnation of the whole system heretofore adopted. It is, indeed, impossible to read the evidence adduced in the White Paper without coming to the conclusion that, whatever may be the case at present, the system of recruiting in the past has not differed materially from the slave trade. If this be the case, it is clear that, in spite of any legal technicalities to the contrary, the great majority of labourers now serving under contract in the islands should, for all purposes of repatriation and the acquisition of freedom, be placed on a precisely similar footing to those whose contracts have expired. There can be no moral justification whatever for taking advantage of the engagements into which they may have entered to keep them in what is practically a condition of servitude.

Recently, certain improvements appeared to have been made in the system of recruiting. Mr. Smallbones states his "impression that the present Governor-General will do all in his power to put the recruiting of native labour on a sound footing." Moreover, that some change has taken place, and that the labourers are alive to the fact that they have certain rights, would appear evident from the fact that Vice-Consul Fussell, writing from Lobito on September 15, 1912, reports that "the authorities appear unable to oblige natives to contract themselves." It is not, however, clear that all the changes are in the right direction. Formerly, M. Carlos de Silva says, "There was at least a slight guarantee that 'serviçaes' were not shipped against their wishes in the fact that they had to contract in the presence of a curator in this (*i.e.* the Angola) colony." Now this guarantee has been removed. The contracts may be made in San Thomé before the local guardian, and Mr. Smallbones, although he is, without doubt, quite right in thinking that "the best guarantee against abuses will lie in the choice of the recruiting officials, and the way in which their operations are controlled," adds the somewhat ominous remark that the object of the change has been to "override the refusal of a curator in Angola to contract certain 'serviçaes' should the Governor-General consider that refusal unreasonable or inexpedient." Sir Edward Grey very naturally drew attention to this point. "It is obvious," he wrote to Sir Arthur Hardinge, "that a labourer once in San Thomé can be much more easily coerced into accepting his lot than if the contract is publicly made in Angola before he leaves the mainland." It cannot be said that the answer he received from M. Texeira Gomes was altogether complete or satisfactory. All the latter would say was that Colonel Wyllie, who had lately returned from San Thomé, had never heard of any case of a labourer signing a contract after he had arrived in the island.

All, therefore, that can at present be said on this branch of the question is that the evils of the recruiting system which has been so far adopted are abundantly clear, that the Portuguese Government is endeavouring to improve that system, but that it would as yet be premature to pronounce any opinion on the results which are likely to be obtained.

The next point to be considered is the position of the contract labourer on the expiry of his contract. That position is very strikingly illustrated by an incident which Mr. Smallbones relates in a despatch dated September 23, 1912. It appears that towards the end of last August the Governor-General visited an important plantation on which seven hundred labourers are employed. The contracts of these men had expired. They asked to be allowed to leave the plantation. They were not permitted to do so. "Thirteen soldiers were sent from Loanda to intimidate them, and they returned to work." They were then forced to recontract. Mr. Smallbones very rightly pointed out to the Governor-General the illegality of this proceeding. "His Excellency," he says, "admitted my contention, but remarked that in the present state of the labour supply such scrupulous observance of the regulations would entail the entire stoppage of a large plantation, for which he could not be responsible." Mr. Smallbones adds the following comment: "I have ventured to relate this incident, because it shows the difficulties of the situation. The plantation on which it occurred is very well managed, and the labourers are very well treated there. Yet it has failed to make the conditions of labour attractive to the natives. And as long as the Government are unable to force a supply of labour according to the regulations, they will have to tolerate or even practise irregularities in order to safeguard the property and interests of the employers."

There need be no hesitation in recognising "the difficulties of the situation." They are unquestionably very real. But how does the incident related by Mr. Smallbones bear on the contention of the Portuguese Government that no state of slavery exists? In truth, it shatters to fragments the whole of their argument. As has been already mentioned, Sir Edward Grey defined "forcible engagement" as "slavery." Can it be for one moment contended that the engagement of these seven hundred men was voluntary and not forcible? Obviously not. Therefore slavery still exists, or at all events existed so late as August 1912.

The third point to be considered is whether the liberated slave is practically able to take advantage of the freedom which has been conferred on him. Assuredly, he cannot do so. Consider what the position of these men is. They, or their parents before them, have in numerous instances been forcibly removed from their homes, which often lie at a great distance from the spot where they are liberated. They are apparently asked to contribute out of their wages to a repatriation fund. Why should they do so? They were, in a great many, probably in a majority of cases, expatriated either against their will or without really understanding what they were doing. Why should they pay for repatriation? The responsibility of the Portuguese does not end when the men have been paid their wages and are set free. Neither can it be for one moment admitted that that responsibility is limited, as the Governor-General would appear to maintain in a Memorandum communicated to Mr. Smallbones on October 25, 1912, merely to seeing that repatriated slaves disembarked on the mainland "shall be protected against the effects of the change of climate, and principally against themselves." No one will expect the Portuguese Government to perform the impossible, but it is clear that, unless the institution of slavery itself is considered justifiable, the slaves have a right to be placed by the Portuguese Government and nation in precisely the same position as they would have occupied had they never been led into slavery. Apart from the impossibility, it may, on several grounds, be undesirable to seek to attain this ideal, but that is no reason why the validity of the moral claim should not be recognised. In many cases it is abundantly clear that to speak of a slave liberated at San Thomé being really a free man in the sense in which that word is generally understood, is merely an abuse of terms. The only freedom he possesses is that created for him by his employers. It consists of being able to wander aimlessly about the African mainland at the imminent risk of starvation, or of being robbed of whatever miserable pittance may have been served out to him. For these reasons it is maintained that the starting-point for any further discussion on this question is that the plea that slavery no longer exists in the West African dominions of Portugal is altogether untenable. It still exists, though under another name. There remains the question of how its existence can be terminated.

The writer of the present article would be the last to underrate the enormous practical difficulties to be encountered in dealing effectively with this question. His own experience in cognate matters enables him in some degree to recognise the nature of those difficulties. When the *corvée* system was abolished in Egypt, the question which really confronted the Government of that country was how the whole of a very backward population, the vast majority of whom had for centuries been in reality, though not nominally, slaves, could be made to understand that, although they would not be flogged if they did not clear out the mud from the canals on which the irrigation of their fields depended, they would run an imminent risk of starvation unless they voluntarily accepted payment for performing that service. The difficulties were enhanced owing to the facts that the country was in a state of quasi-bankruptcy, and the political situation was in the highest degree complicated and bewildering. Nevertheless, after a period of transition, which, it must be admitted, was somewhat agonising, the problem was solved, but it was only thoroughly solved after a struggle which lasted for some years. It is a vivid recollection of the arduous nature of that struggle that induces the writer of the present article so far to plead the cause of the Portuguese Government as to urge that, if once it can be fully established that they are moving steadily but strenuously in the right direction, no excessive amount of impatience should be shown if the results obtained do not immediately answer all the expectations of those who wish to witness the complete abolition of the hateful system under which the cultivation of cocoa in the West African Islands has hitherto been conducted. The financial interests involved are important, and deserve a certain, albeit a limited, amount of consideration. There need be no hesitation whatever in pressing for the adoption of measures which may result in diminishing the profits of the cocoa proprietors and possibly increasing the price paid by the consumers of cocoa. Indeed, there would be nothing unreasonable in arguing that the output of cocoa, worth £2,000,000 a year, had much better be lost to the world altogether rather than that the life of the present vicious system should be prolonged. But even if it were desirable—which is probably not the case—it is certainly impossible to take all the thirty thousand men now employed in the islands and suddenly transport them elsewhere. It would be Utopian to expect that the Portuguese Government, in the face of the vehement opposition which they would certainly have to encounter, would consent to the adoption of any such heroic measure. As practical men we must, whilst acknowledging the highly regrettable nature of the facts, accept them as they stand. Slight importance can, indeed, be attached to the argument put forward by one of the British Consular authorities, that "the native lives under far better conditions in San Thomé than in his own country." It is somewhat too much akin to the plea advanced by ardent fox-hunters that the fox enjoys the sport of being hunted. Neither, although it is satisfactory to learn that the slaves are now generally well treated, does this fact in itself constitute any justification for slavery. The system must disappear, and the main question is to devise some other less objectionable system to take its place.

There are two radical solutions of this problem. One is to abandon cocoa-growing altogether, at all events in the island of Principe, a part of which is infected with sleeping-sickness, and to start the industry afresh elsewhere. The other is to substitute free for slave labour in the islands themselves. Both plans are discussed in Lieutenant-Colonel Wyllie's very able report addressed to the Foreign Office on December 8, 1912. This report is, indeed, one of the most valuable contributions to the literature on this subject which have yet appeared. Colonel Wyllie has evidently gone thoroughly into the matter, and, moreover, appears to realise the fact, which all experience teaches, that slavery is as indefensible from an economic as it is from a moral point of view. Free labour, when it can be obtained, is far less expensive than slave labour.

Colonel Wyllie suggests that the Principe planters should abandon their present plantations and receive "free grants of land in the fertile and populous colony of Portuguese Guinea, the soil of which is reported by all competent authorities to be better suited to cacao-growing than even that of San Thomé itself, and certainly far superior to that of Principe. Guinea has from time to time supplied labour to these islands, so that the besetting trouble of the latter is nonexistent there." He adds: "I am decidedly of opinion that some such scheme as this is the only cure for the blight that has fallen on the island of Principe." It would require greater local knowledge than any to which the writer of the present article can pretend to discuss the merits of this proposal, but at first sight it would certainly appear to deserve full and careful consideration.

But as regards San Thomé, which is by far the larger and more important of the two islands, it would appear that the importation of free labour is not only the best, but, indeed, the only really possible solution of the whole problem. It may be suggested that, without by any means neglecting other points, such as the repatriation of men now serving, the efforts both of the Portuguese Government and of all others interested in the question should be mainly centred on this issue.

95

Something has been already done in this direction, Mr. Harris, writing in the *Contemporary Review* of May 1912, said: "Mozambique labour was tried in 1908, and this experiment is proving, for the time, so successful, that many planters look to the East rather than West Africa for their future supply. All available evidence appears to prove that Cabinda, Cape Verde, and Mozambique labour is, so far as contract labour goes, fairly recruited and honestly treated as 'free labour.'" It is an encouraging sign that a Portuguese Company has been formed whose object is "to recruit free, paid labourers, natives of the provinces of Angola, Mozambique, Cape Verde, and Guinea." Moreover, the following passage from Colonel Wyllie's report deserves very special attention:

"Several San Thomé planters," he says, "realising the advantage of having a more intelligent and industrious labourer than the Angolan, have signed contracts with an English Company trading in Liberia for the supply of labour from Cape Palmas and its hinterland, on terms to which no exception can be taken from any point of view. Two, if not by now three, batches of Liberians have arrived at San Thomé and have been placed on estates for work. The Company has posted an English agent there to act as curador to the men, banking their money, arranging their home remittances, and mediating in any disputes arising between them and their employers. The system works wonderfully well, giving satisfaction both to the masters and to the men, the latter being as pleased with their treatment as the former are with their physique and intelligence. There is every prospect of the arrangement being developed to the extent of enabling Angolan labour to be permanently dispensed with, and possibly superseding Mozambique importations as well."

Colonel Wyllie then goes on to say: "The company and its agents complain of the many obstacles they have had to overcome in the form of hostility and intrigue on the part of interested parties. Systematic attempts have been made in Liberia to intimidate the gangs from going to San Thomé by tales of cruelty practised by the Portuguese in the islands." More especially it would appear that the "missionaries" have been advising the Liberians not to accept the offers made to them. It is not altogether surprising that they should do so, for the Portuguese have acquired an evil reputation which it will take time to efface. To an outside observer it would appear that an admirable opportunity is here afforded for the Portuguese Government and the Anti-Slavery Society, who are in close relation with many of the missionaries, to co-operate in the attainment of a common object. Why should not the Portuguese authorities invite some agents of the Anti-Slavery Society to visit the islands and place before them evidence which will enable them conscientiously to guarantee proper treatment to the Liberian labourers, and why, when they are once convinced, should not those agents, far from discouraging, encourage Liberians, and perhaps others, to go to San Thomé? If this miracle could be effected—and with real good-will on both sides it ought to be possible to effect it—a very great step in advance would have been taken to solve this difficult problem. But in order to realise such an ideal, mutual confidence would have to be established. When the affairs of the Congo were under discussion the Belgian air was thick with rumours that British humanitarianism was a mere cloak to hide the greed of British merchants. Similar ideas are, it would appear, now afloat at Lisbon. When men's pockets are touched they are apt to become extremely suspicious of humanitarian intentions. Mr. Wingfield, writing on August 17, 1912, said that the Portuguese Government was not "convinced of the disinterestedness of all those who criticise them," and he intimated that there were schemes on foot on the part of British subjects to acquire "roças" in the islands "at very low prices." It ought not to be difficult to convince the Portuguese authorities that the agents employed by the Anti-Slavery Society are in no way connected with any such projects. On the other hand, it would be necessary that those agents should be very carefully chosen, that besides being humanitarians they should have some knowledge of business, and that they should enter upon their inquiry in a spirit of fairness, and not with any preconceived intention to push to an extreme any suspicions they may entertain of Portuguese acts and intentions. It is suggested that the adoption of some such mode of proceeding as is here indicated is worthy of consideration. The Foreign Office might very properly act as an intermediary to bring the two parties together.

Finally, before leaving this branch of the subject, it is to be observed that the difficulty of obtaining free labour has occurred elsewhere than in the Portuguese possessions. It has generally admitted, at all events, of a partial solution if the labourers are well treated and adequately paid. Portuguese experience points to a similar conclusion. Mr. Smallbones, writing on September 23, 1912, quotes the report of the manager of the Lobito railway, in which the latter, after stating that he has had no difficulty in obtaining all the labour he has required, adds, "I attribute the facility in obtaining so large a supply of labour, relatively cheaply, to the good food we supply them with, and chiefly to the regularity with which payments in cash are effected, and also to the justice with which they are treated."

The question of repatriation remains to be treated. It must, of course, be remembered that repatriation is an act of justice to the men already enslaved, but that, by itself, it does little or nothing towards solving the main difficulties of the slavery problem. Mr. Wingfield, writing to Sir Edward Grey on August 24, 1912, relates a conversation he had had with Senhor Vasconcellos. "His Excellency first observed that they were generally subjected to severe criticism in England, and said to be fostering slavery because they did not at once repatriate all natives who had served the term of their original contracts. Now they were blamed for the misfortunes which resulted from their endeavour to act as England was always suggesting that they should act!" His Excellency made what Parliamentarians would call a good debating point, but the complaint is obviously more specious than real, for what people in England expect is not merely that the slaves should, if they wish it, be repatriated, but that the repatriation should be conducted under reasonably humane conditions. For the purposes of the present argument it is needless to inquire whether the ghastly story adopted by the Anti-Slavery Society on the strength of a statement in a Portuguese newspaper, but denied by the Portuguese Government, that the corpses of fifty repatriated men who had died of starvation were at one time to be seen lying about in the outskirts of Benguella, be true or false. Independently of this incident, all the evidence goes to show that Colonel Wyllie is saying no more than the truth when he writes: "To repatriate, *i.e.* to dump on the African mainland without previous arrangement for his reception, protection, or safe conduct over his further route, an Angolan or hinterland 'serviçal' who has spent years of his life in San Thomé, is not merely to sentence him to death, but to execute that sentence with the shortest possible delay." It is against this system that those interested in the subject in England protested. The Portuguese Government appear now to have recognised the justice of their protests, for they have recently adopted a plan somewhat similar to that initiated by the late Lord Salisbury for dealing with immigrant coolies from India. By an Order in Council dated October 17, 1912, it has been provided that repatriated "serviçaes" should receive a grant of land and should be set up, free of charge, with agricultural implements and seeds. This is certainly a step in the right direction. It is as yet too early to say how far the plan will succeed, but if it is honestly carried out it ought to go far towards solving the repatriation question. Mr. Smallbones would appear justified in claiming that it "should be given a fair trial before more heroic measures are applied." The repatriation fund, which appears, to say the least, to have been very badly administered, ought, without difficulty, to be able to meet the expenses which the adoption of this plan will entail.

XXV
ENGLAND AND ISLAM
"The Spectator," August 23, 1913

Amidst the many important remarks made by Sir Edward Grey in his recent Parliamentary statement on the affairs of the Balkan Peninsula, none deserve greater attention than those which dealt with the duties and responsibilities of England towards Mohammedans in general. It was, indeed, high time that some clear and authoritative declaration of principle on this important subject should be made by a Minister of the Crown. We are constantly being reminded that King George V. is the greatest Mohammedan ruler in the world, that some seventy millions of his subjects in India are Moslems, and that the inhabitants of Egypt are also, for the most part, followers of the Prophet of Arabia. It is not infrequently maintained that it is a duty incumbent on Great Britain to defend the interests and to secure the welfare of Moslems all over the world because a very large number of their co-religionists are British subjects and reside in British territory. It is not at all surprising that this claim should be advanced, but it is manifestly one which cannot be admitted without very great and important qualifications. Moreover, it is one which, from a European point of view, represents a somewhat belated order of ideas. It is true that community of religion constitutes the main bond of union between Russia and the population of the Balkan Peninsula, but apart from the fact that no such community of religious thought exists between Christian England and Moslem or Hindu India, it is to be noted that, generally speaking, the tie of a common creed, which played so important a part in European politics and diplomacy during the sixteenth and seventeenth centuries, has now been greatly weakened, even if it has not disappeared altogether. It has been supplanted almost everywhere by the bond of nationality. No practical politician would now argue that, if the Protestants of Holland or Sweden had any special causes for complaint, a direct responsibility rested on their co-religionists in Germany or England to see that those grievances were redressed. No Roman Catholic nation would now advance a claim to interfere in the affairs of Ireland on the ground that the majority of the population of that country are Roman Catholics.

This transformation of political thought and action has not yet taken place in the East. It may be, as some competent observers are disposed to think, that the principle of nationality is gaining ground in Eastern countries, but it has certainly not as yet taken firm root. The bond which holds Moslem societies together is still religious rather than patriotic. Its binding strength has been greatly enhanced by two circumstances. One is that Mecca is to the Moslem far more than Jerusalem is to the Christian or to the Jew. From Delhi to Zanzibar, from Constantinople to Java, every devout Moslem turns when he prays to what Mr. Stanley Lane-Poole aptly calls the "cradle of his creed." The other circumstance is that, although, as Mr. Hughes has said, "we have not seen a single work of authority, nor met with a single man of learning who has ever attempted to prove that the Sultans of Turkey are rightful Caliphs," at the same time the spiritual authority usurped by Selim I. is generally recognised throughout Islam, with the result not only that unity of thought has been engendered amongst Moslems, but also that religion has to a great extent been incorporated into politics, and identified with the maintenance of a special form of government in a portion of the Moslem world.

The growth of the principle of nationality in those eastern countries which are under western dominion might not inconceivably raise political issues of considerable magnitude, but in the discussions which have from time to time taken place on this subject the inconveniences and even danger caused by the universality of a non-national bond based on community of religion have perhaps been somewhat unduly neglected. These inconveniences have, however, always existed. That the policy which led to the Crimean War and generally the prolonged tension which existed between England and Russia were due to the British connection with India is universally recognised. It would be difficult to differentiate the causes of that tension, and to say how far it was, on the one hand, due to purely strategical considerations, or, on the other hand, to a desire to meet the wishes and satisfy the aspirations of the many millions of Moslems who are British subjects. Since, however, the general diplomatic relations between England and Russia have, fortunately for both countries, been placed on a footing of more assured confidence and friendship than any which have existed for a long time past, strategical considerations have greatly diminished in importance. The natural result has been that the alternative plea for regarding Near Eastern affairs from the point of view of Indian interests has acquired greater prominence. Those who have been closely in touch with the affairs of the Near East, and have watched the gradual decay of Turkey, have for some while past foreseen that the time was inevitably approaching when British statesmen and the British nation would be forced by the necessities of the situation to give a definite answer to the question how far their diplomatic action in Europe would have to be governed by the alleged obligation to conciliate Moslem opinion in India. That question received, to a certain limited extent, a practical answer when Bulgaria declared war on Turkey and when not a voice was raised in this country to urge that the policy which dictated the Crimean War should be rehabilitated.

The answer, however, is not yet complete. England is now apparently expected by many Moslems to separate herself from the Concert of Europe, and not impossibly to imperil the peace of the world, in order that the Turks should continue in occupation of Adrianople. The secretary of the Punjab Moslem League has informed us through the medium of the press that unless this is done the efforts of the extreme Indian Nationalists to secure the sympathies of Mohammedans in India "will meet with growing success."

It was in reality to this challenge that Sir Edward Grey replied. His answer was decisive, and left no manner of doubt as to the policy which the British Government intends to pursue. It will almost certainly meet with well-nigh universal approval in this country. After explaining that the racial sentiments and religious feelings of Moslem subjects of the Crown would be respected and have full scope, that British policy would never be one of intolerance or wanton and unprovoked aggression against a Mohammedan Power, and that the British Government would never join in any outrage on Mohammedan feelings and sentiments in any part of the world, Sir Edward Grey added, "We cannot undertake the duty of protecting Mohammedan Powers outside the British dominions from the consequences of their own action.... To suppose that we can undertake the protection of and are bound to regulate our European policy so as to side with a Mussulman Power when that Mussulman Power rejects the advice given to it, that is not a claim we can admit."

These are wise words, and it is greatly to be hoped that not only the Moslems of Turkey, but also those inhabiting other countries, will read, mark, learn, and inwardly digest them. Notably, the Moslems of India should recognise that, with the collapse of Turkish power in Europe, a new order of things has arisen, that the change which the attitude of England towards Turkey has undergone is the necessary consequence of that collapse, and that it does not in the smallest degree connote unfriendliness to Islam. In fact, they must now endeavour to separate Islamism from politics. With the single exception of the occupation of Cyprus, which, as Lord Goschen very truly said at the time, "prevented British Ambassadors from showing 'clean hands' to the Sultan in proof of the unselfishness of British action," the policy of England in the Near East has been actuated, ever since the close of the Napoleonic wars, by a sincere and wholly disinterested desire to save Turkish statesmen from the consequences of their own folly. In this cause no effort has been spared, even to the shedding of the best blood of England. All has been in vain. History does not relate a more striking instance of the truth of the old Latin saying that self-deception is the first step on the road to ruin. Advice tendered in the best interests of the Ottoman Empire has been persistently rejected. The Turks, who have always been strangers in Europe, have shown conspicuous inability to comply with the elementary requirements of European civilisation, and have at last failed to maintain that military efficiency which has, from the days when they crossed the Bosphorus, been the sole mainstay of their power and position. It is, as Sir Edward Grey pointed out, unreasonable to expect that we should now save them from the consequences of their own action. Whether Moslems all over the world will or should still continue to regard the Sultan of Turkey as their spiritual head is a matter on which it would be presumptuous for a Christian to offer any opinion, but however this may be, Indian Moslems would do well to recognise the fact that circumstances, and not the hostility of Great Britain or of any other foreign Power, have materially altered the position of the Sultan in so far as the world of politics and diplomacy is concerned. Whether the statesman in whose hands the destinies of Turkey now lie at once abandon Adrianople, or whether they continue to remain there for a time with the certainty that they will be sowing the seeds of further bloodshed in the near future, one thing is certain. It is that the days of Turkey as an European Power are numbered. Asia must henceforth be her sphere of action.

That these truths should be unpalatable to Indian Moslems is but natural; neither is it possible to withhold some sympathy from them in the distress which they must now feel at the partial wreck of the most important Moslem State which the world has yet seen. But facts, however distasteful, have to be faced, and it would be truly deplorable if the non-recognition of those facts should lead our Moslem fellow-subjects in India to resent the action of the British Government and to adopt a line of conduct from which they have nothing to gain and everything to lose. But whatever that line of conduct may be, the duty of the British Government and nation is clear. Their European policy, whilst allowing all due weight to Indian interests and sentiment, must in the main be guided by general considerations based on the necessities of civilised progress throughout the world, and on the interests and welfare of the British Empire as a whole. The idea that that policy should be diverted from its course in order to subserve the cause of a single Moslem Power which has rejected British advice is, as Sir Edward Grey very rightly remarked, wholly inadmissible.

XXVI
SOME INDIAN PROBLEMS
"The Spectator," August 30, 1913

In spite of the optimism at times displayed in dealing with Indian affairs, which may be justified on grounds which are often, to say the least, plausible, it is impossible to ignore the fact that the general condition of India gives cause for serious reflection, if not for grave anxiety. We are told on all sides that the East is rapidly awakening from its torpid slumbers—even to the extent of forgetting that characteristically Oriental habit of thought embodied in the Arabic proverb, "Slowness is from God, hurry from the Devil." If this be so, we must expect that, year by year, problems of ever-increasing complexity will arise which will tax to the utmost the statesmanship of those Western nations who are most brought in contact with Eastern peoples. In these circumstances, it is specially desirable that the different points of view from which Indian questions may be regarded should be laid before the British public by representatives of various schools of thought. But a short time ago a very able Socialist member of Parliament (Mr. Ramsay MacDonald) gave to the world the impressions he had derived whilst he was "careering over the plains of Rajputana," and paying hurried visits to other parts of India. His views, although manifestly in some degree the result of preconceived opinions, and somewhat tainted with the dogmatism which is characteristic of the political school of thought to which he belongs, exhibit at the same time habits of acute observation and powers of rapid—sometimes unduly rapid—generalisation. Neither are they, on the whole, so prejudiced as might have been expected from the antecedents and political connections of the author. More recently we have had in a work written by Mr. Mallik, which was lately reviewed in these columns, a striking specimen of one of those pernicious by-products which are the natural and unavoidable outcome of Eastern and Western contact. We have now to deal with a work of a very different type. Many of the very difficult problems which Mr. Mitra discusses in his interesting series of *Anglo-Indian Studies* open up a wide field for differences of opinion, but whatever views may be entertained about them, all must recognise not only that no kind of exception can be taken to the general spirit in which Mr. Mitra approaches Indian subjects, but also that his observations are the result of deep reflection, and of an honest endeavour to improve rather than exacerbate racial relations. His remarks are, therefore, well worthy of consideration.

Mr. Mitra shows a perfectly legitimate pride in the past history of his country. He tells us how Hindu international lawyers anticipated Grotius by some thirty centuries, how the Mahabharata embodies many of the principles adopted by the Hague Conference, how India preceded Europe in her knowledge of all the arts and sciences, even including that of medicine, and how "Hindu drama was in its heyday before the theatres of England, France, or Spain could be said to exist." But Mr. Mitra's ardent patriotism does not blind him to the realities of the present situation. A very intelligent Frenchman, M. Paul Boell, who visited India a few years ago, came to the conclusion that the real Indian question was not whether the English were justified in staying in the country, but whether they could find any moral justification for withdrawing from it. Mr. Mitra arrives at much the same conclusion as M. Boell. "If the English were to withdraw from India to-morrow," he says, "I fear that, notwithstanding all the peace precepts of our Mahabharata, and in spite of the stupendous philosophy and so-called fatalism of the Hindus, our Maharajahs would speedily be at each other's throats, as they were before the *pax Britannica* was established there." Moreover, he asserts a principle of vital importance, which is but too often ignored by his countrymen, and even at times by those who sympathise with them in England. "Education and knowledge," he says, "can be pumped into the student, but there is no royal road for instruction in 'capacity of management.' A Clive, with inferior education, may be a better manager of men or of an industrial concern than the most learned student." In other words, character rather than intellect is the foundation not only of national but also of individual greatness—a profound truth which is brought home every day to those who are engaged in the actual management of public affairs, especially in the East. Mr. Mitra, moreover, makes various praiseworthy efforts to dispel certain illusions frequently nourished by some of his countrymen, and to diminish the width of the religious gulf which separates the rulers from the ruled. He quotes with approval Sir Rajendra Mookerjee's complete, albeit facile, exposure of the fallacy, dear to the hearts of many Indian press writers and platform speakers, that Indian interests suffer by the introduction of British capital into India. "It is wise," Sir Rajendra said, "to allow British capitalists to interest themselves in our industries and thus take an active part in their development." He prefers to dwell on the points of similarity which unite rather than on the differences which separate Hinduism and Christianity. "The two religions," he says, "have so much in common when one gets down to essentials that it seems to me this ought to furnish a great bond of sympathy between the two peoples," and he urges that "every attempt should be made to utilise the Hindu University to remove the spirit of segregation which unquestionably exists between the Christian Government in India and its Hindu subjects, and thus pave the way to harmonious co-operation between the Aryan rulers and the ruled in India."

It will be as well, however, to turn from these points to what Mr. Mitra considers the shortcomings of the British Government. He is not sparing in his criticisms. He freely admits that British statesmen have devoted their energies to improving the conditions of the masses, but he adds, and it must be sorrowfully admitted that he is justified in adding, "Material advantages set forth in dry statistics have never made a nation enthusiastically loyal to the Government." He urges that, especially in dealing with a population the vast majority of which is illiterate, "it is the *human element* that counts most in Imperialism, far more than the dry bones of political economy." In an interesting chapter of his book entitled *British Statesmanship and Indian Psychology*, he asks the very pertinent question, "What does loyalty mean to the Indian, whether Moslem or Hindu?" The answer which he gives to this question is that when the idea of loyalty is brought before the native of India, "it comes in most cases with a jerk, and quickly disappears." The reason for its disappearance is that no bond of fellowship has been established between the rulers and the ruled, that the native of India is not made to feel that "he has any real part in England's greatness," that the influence and high position of the native Princes receive inadequate recognition, and that no scope is offered to the military ambition of the citizens of the Indian Empire. "Under the Crescent, the Hindu has been Commander of a Brigade; under the Union Jack, even after a century, he sees no likelihood of rising as high as a little subaltern."

There is, of course, nothing very new in all this. It has been pointed out over and over again by all who have considered Indian or Egyptian problems seriously that the creation of some sort of rather spurious patriotism when all the elements out of which patriotism naturally grows are wanting, is rather like searching for the philosopher's stone. At the same time, when so sympathetic a critic as Mr. Mitra bids us study the "psychological traits" of Indian character, it is certainly worth while to inquire whether all that is possible has been done in the way of evoking sentiments of loyalty based on considerations which lie outside the domain of material advantage. The most imaginative British statesman of recent years has been Lord Beaconsfield. Himself a quasi-Oriental, he grasped the idea that it would be possible to appeal to the imagination of other Orientals. The laughter which was to some extent provoked when, at his suggestion, Queen Victoria assumed the title of Empress of India has now died away, and it is generally recognised, even by those who are not on other grounds disposed to indulge in any exaggerated worship of the primrose, that in this respect Lord Beaconsfield performed an act dictated by true statesmanship. He appealed to those personal and monarchical sentiments which, to a far greater extent than democratic ideas, dominate the minds of Easterns. The somewhat lavish expenditure incurred in connection with the King's recent visit to India may be justified on similar grounds. Following generally the same order of ideas, Mr. Mitra has some further suggestions to make. The question of opening some field to the very natural aspirations of the martial races and classes of India presents, indeed, very great practical difficulties which it would be impossible to discuss adequately on the present occasion. All that can be said is that, although the well-intentioned efforts so far made to solve this thorny problem do not appear to have met with all the success they deserve, it is one which should earnestly engage the attention of the Government in the hope that some practical and unobjectionable solution may eventually be found. Mr. Mitra, however, draws attention to other cognate points which would certainly appear to merit attention. "The first thing," he says, "necessary to rouse Indian sentiment is to give India a flag of her own." He points out that Canada, Australia, South Africa, and some of the West Indian islands have flags of their own, and he asks why, without in any way serving as a symbol of separation, India should not be similarly treated? Then, again, he remarks—and it would be well if some of our Parliamentarians took careful note of the observation—that "British statesmen, in their zeal for introducing their democratic system of government into India, forget that India is pre-eminently an aristocratic land." This appreciation of the Indian situation formed the basis of the political system favoured by no less an authority than Sir Henry Lawrence, and stood in marked contrast to that advocated by his no less distinguished brother, Lord Lawrence. Mr. Mitra, therefore, suggests that a certain number of ruling princes or their heirs-apparent should be allowed to sit in a reformed House of Lords. "Canada," Lord Meath said some years ago, "is already represented in the House of Lords," and he pertinently asked, "Why should not India also have her peers in that assembly?" The particular proposal made by Mr. Mitra in this connection may possibly be open to some objections, but the general principle which he advocates, as also the suggestion that a special flag should be devised for India, would certainly appear to be well worthy of consideration.

It is interesting to turn to the view entertained by Mr. Mitra on the recent transfer of the seat of Government from Calcutta to Delhi. He manifestly does not regard that transfer with any degree of favour. Moreover, he thinks that from the point of view of the stability of British rule, a great mistake has been made. Delhi, he says, has "for centuries symbolised Moslem-Hindu collective sentiment." He assumes that it is the object of British statesmanship to prevent any union between Moslems and Hindus, and that the recent transfer will go far to cement that union. "In transferring the capital to the old centre of Indian Imperialism, England has, in a flash, aroused memories to a degree that thousands of demagogues and agitators would not have done in a century." He holds, therefore, that the action of British statesmen in this respect may not improbably "produce the reverse of the result they intended." The question of whether it was or was not wise to transfer the seat of Government to Delhi is one on which differences of opinion may well exist, but Mr. Mitra is in error in supposing that either the British nation collectively or British statesmen individually have ever proceeded so far on the *divide et impera* principle as to endeavour in their own interests to foster and perpetuate racial and religious animosities. On the contrary, although they have accepted as a fact that those animosities exist, and although they have at times been obliged to interfere with a view to preventing one race or religion infringing the rights and liberties of others, they have persistently done their best to allay discord and sectarian strife. In spite of Mr. Mitra's obvious and honourable attempts to preserve an attitude of judicial impartiality, it is conceivable that in this instance he may, as a Hindu, have allowed himself to be unconsciously influenced by fear that, in transferring the capital to a Moslem centre, the British Government has, in his own words, "placed itself more within the sway of Moslem influence than the authorities would care to admit."

Mr. Mitra alludes to several important points of detail, such, for instance, as the proposal to establish a port at Cochin, which he fears "may be allowed to perish in the coils of official routine," and the suggestion made by Sir Rajendra Mookerjee that by a reduction of railway freights from the mines in the Central Provinces to the port the trade in manganese might be encouraged. It is to be hoped that these and some other similar points will receive due attention from the Indian authorities. Sufficient has been said to justify the opinion that Mr. Mitra's thoughtful work is a valuable contribution to Indian literature, and will well repay perusal by all who are interested in the solution of existing Indian problems.

XXVII
THE NAPOLEON OF TAINE
"The Spectator" September 13, 1913

It has happened to most of the great actors on the world's stage that their posthumous fame has undergone many vicissitudes. *Laudatur ab his, culpatur ab illis.* They have at times been eulogised or depreciated by partisan historians who have searched eagerly the records of the past with a view to eliciting facts and arguments to support the political views they have severally entertained as regards the present. Even when no such incentive has existed, the temptation to adopt a novel view of some celebrated man or woman whose character and career have floated down the tide of history cast in a conventional mould has occasionally proved highly attractive from a mere literary point of view. The process of whitewashing the bad characters of history may almost be said to have established itself as a fashion.

A similar fate has attended the historians who have recorded the deeds of the world's principal actors. A few cases, of which perhaps Ranke is the most conspicuous, may indeed be cited of historical writers whose reputations are built on foundations so solid and so impervious to attack as to defy criticism. But it has more usually happened, as in the case of Macaulay, that eminent historians have passed through various phases of repute. The accuracy of their facts, the justice of their conclusions, their powers of correct generalisation, and the merits or demerits of their literary style have all been brought into court, with the result that attention has often been to a great extent diverted from history to the personality of the historians, and that the verdict pronounced has varied according to the special qualities the display of which were for the time being uppermost in the public mind.

No recent writer of history has experienced these vicissitudes to a greater extent than the illustrious author of *Les Origines de la France contemporaine.* That Taine should evoke the enthusiasm of any particular school of politicians, and still less the partisans of any particular régime in France, was from the very outset obviously impossible. When we read his account of the *ancien régime* we think we are listening to the voice of a calm but convinced republican or constitutionalist. When we note his scathing exposure of the criminal folly and ineptitude of the Jacobins we remain momentarily under the impression that we are being guided by a writer imbued with strong conservative or even monarchical sympathies. The iconoclast both of the revolutionary and of the Napoleonic legends chills alike the heart of the worshippers at either shrine. A writer who announces in the preface of his work that the only conclusion at which he is able to arrive, after a profound study of the most interesting and stormy period of modern history, is that the government of human beings is an extremely difficult task, will look in vain for sympathy from all who have adopted any special theory as to the best way in which that task should be accomplished. Yet, in spite of Taine's political nihilism, it would be a grave error to suppose that he has no general principle to enounce, or no plan of government to propound. Such is far from being the case. Though no politician, he was a profoundly analytical psychologist. M. Le Bon, in his brilliant treatise on the psychological laws which govern national development, says, "Dans toutes manifestations de la vie d'une nation, nous retrouvons toujours l'âme immuable de la race tissant son propre destin." The commonplace method of stating the same proposition is to say that every nation gets the government it deserves. This, in fact, is the gospel which Taine had to preach. He thought, in Lady Blennerhassett's words, that it was "the underlying characteristics of a people; and not their franchise, which determines their Constitution."

After having enjoyed for long a high reputation amongst non-partisan students of revolutionary history, Taine's claim to rank as an historian of the first order has of late been vigorously assailed by a school of writers, of whom M. Aulard is probably the best known and the most distinguished. They impugn his authority, and even go so far as to maintain that his historical testimony is of little or no value. How far is this view justified? The question is one of real interest to the historical student, whatsoever may be his nationality, and it is, perhaps, for more than one reason, of special interest to Englishmen. In the first place, Taine's method of writing history is eminently calculated to commend itself to English readers. His mind was eminently objective. He avoided those brilliant and often somewhat specious *a priori* generalisations in which even the best French authors are at times prone to indulge. His process of reasoning was strictly inductive. He only drew conclusions when he had laid an elaborate foundation of facts on which they could be based. The spirit in which he wrote was more Teutonic than Latin. Again, in the absence of any really complete English history of the French Revolution—for Carlyle's rhapsody, in spite of its unquestionable merits, can scarcely be held to supply the want—most Englishmen have been accustomed to think that, with De Tocqueville and Taine as their guides, they would be able to secure an adequate grasp both of the history of the revolutionary period and of the main political lessons which that history tends to inculcate.

In a very interesting essay published in Lady Blennerhassett's recent work, entitled *Sidelights*, which has been admirably translated into English by Mrs. Gülcher, she deals with the subject now under discussion. No one could be more fitted to cope with the task. Lady Blennerhassett's previous contributions to literature, her encyclopaedic knowledge of historical facts, and her thorough grasp of the main political, religious, and economic considerations which moved the hearts and influenced the actions of men during the revolutionary convulsion give her a claim, which none will dare to dispute, to speak with authority on this subject. Those who have heretofore looked for guidance to Taine will, therefore, rejoice to note that she is able to vindicate his reputation as an historian. "The six volumes of the *Origines*," she says, "are, like other human works, not free from errors and exaggerations, but in all essentials their author has proved himself right, and his singular merit remains."

As the most suitable illustration of Taine's historical methods Lady Blennerhassett selects his study of Napoleon. That, she thinks, is "the severest test of the author's skill." Taine did not, like Fournier and others, attempt to write a history of Napoleonic facts. The strategical and tactical genius which enabled Napoleon to sweep across Europe and to crush Austria and Prussia on the fields of Austerlitz and Jena had no attraction for him. He wrote a history of ideas. True to his own psychological habit of thought, he endeavoured to "reconstruct the figure of Napoleon on psychological and physiological lines." The justification of this method is to be found in the fact, the truth of which cannot be gainsaid, that a right estimate of the character of Napoleon affords one of the principal keys to the true comprehension of European history for a period of some twenty stirring years. History, Lord Acton said, "is often made by energetic men steadfastly following ideas, mostly wrong, that determine events." Napoleon is a case in point. "The man in Napoleon explains his work." But what were the ideas of this remarkable man, and were those ideas "mostly wrong"?

His main idea was certainly to satisfy his personal ambition. "Ma maîtresse," he said, "c'est le pouvoir," and in 1811, when, although he knew it not, his star was about to wane, he said to the Bavarian General Wrede, "In three years I shall be master of the universe." He was not deterred by any love of country, for it should never be forgotten that, as Lady Blennerhassett says, "this French Caesar was not a Frenchman." Whatever patriotic feelings moved in his breast were not French but Corsican. He never even thoroughly mastered the French language, and his mother spoke not only bad French, but bad Italian. Her natural language, Masson tells us, was the Corsican *patois*. In order to gratify his ambition, all considerations based on morality were cast to the winds. "I am not like any other man," he told Madame de Rémusat; "the laws of morality and decorum do not apply to me." Acting on this principle he did not hesitate to plunge the world into a series of wars. *Saevit toto Mars impius orbe.*

The other fundamental idea which dominated the whole of Napoleon's conduct was based on Voltaire's cynical dictum, "Quand les hommes s'attroupent, leurs oreilles s'allongent." He was a total disbeliever in the wisdom or intelligence of corporate bodies. Therefore, as he told Sir Henry Keating at St. Helena, "It is necessary always to talk of liberty, equality, justice, and disinterestedness, and never to grant any liberty whatever." Low as was his opinion of human intelligence, his estimate of human honesty was still lower. Mr. Lecky, speaking of Napoleon's relations with Madame de Staël, says: "A perfectly honest man was the only kind of man he could never understand. Such a man perplexed and baffled his calculations, acting on them as the sign of the cross acts on the machinations of a demon." In his callow youth he had coquetted with ultra-Liberal ideas. He had even written an essay in which he expressed warm admiration for Algernon

Sidney as an "enemy to monarchies, princes, and nobles," and added that "there are few kings who have not deserved to be dethroned." These ideas soon vanished. He became the incarnation of ruthless but highly intelligent despotism. The reputation acquired at Marengo gave him the authority which was necessary as a preliminary to decisive action, and albeit, if all accounts are true, he lost his head at the most important crisis of his career and owed success to the firmness of that Sieyès whom he scornfully called an "idéologue" and a "faiseur de constitutions," nevertheless on the 18th Brumaire he was able to make captive a tired nation which pined for peace, and little recked that it was handing over its destinies to the most ardent devotee of the god of war that the world has ever known.

Once seated firmly in his saddle Napoleon proceeded to centralise the whole French administration, and to establish a régime as despotic as that of any of the hereditary monarchs who had preceded him. But it was a despotism of a very different type from theirs. Theirs was stupid, and excited the jealousy and hatred of almost every class. His was intelligent and appealed both to the imagination and to the material interests of every individual Frenchman. Theirs was based on privilege; his on absolute equality. "About Napoleon's throne," Lady Blennerhassett says, "were gathered Girondists and Jacobins, Royalists and Thermidorians, Plebeians and the one-time Knights of the Holy Ghost, Roman Catholics and Voltaireans. Kitchen lads became marshals; Drouet, the postmaster of Varennes, became Under-Secretary of State; Fouché, the torturer and wholesale murderer, a duke; the Suabian candidate for the Lutheran Ministry, Reinhard, was appointed an Imperial Ambassador; Murat, son of an innkeeper, a king."

Death, it has been truly said, is the real measure of greatness. What now remains of the stupendous fabric erected by Napoleon? "Of the work of the Conqueror," Lady Blennerhassett says, "not one stone remains upon another." As regards the internal reconstruction of France, the case is very different. All inquirers are agreed that Napoleon's work endures. Taine said that "the machinery of the year VIII." still remains. Mr. Fisher, in his work on *Napoleonic Statesmanship*, says that Napoleon "created a bureaucracy more competent, active, and enlightened than any which Europe had seen." Mr. Bodley bears similar testimony. "The whole centralised administration of France, which, in its stability, has survived every political crisis, was the creation of Napoleon and the keystone of his fabric."

Napoleon's administrative creations may, indeed, be criticised from many points of view. Notably, it may be said that, if he did not initiate, he stimulated that excessive "fonctionnarisme" which is often regarded as the main defect of the French system. But his creations were adapted to the special character and genius of the nation over which he ruled. His main title-deed to enduring fame is that, for good or evil, he constructed an edifice which, in its main features, has lasted to this day, which shows no signs of decay, and which has exercised a predominant influence on the administration and judicial systems of neighbouring countries. Neither the system itself nor the history of its creation can be thoroughly understood without a correct appreciation of the character and political creed of its founder. It is this consideration which affords an ample justification of the special method adopted by Taine in dealing with the history of the Napoleonic period.

Nothing illustrates Napoleon's character more clearly than the numerous *ana* which may be culled from the pages of Madame de Rémusat, Masson, Beugnot, Rœderer, and others. Of these, some are reproduced by Lady Blennerhassett. The writer of the present article was informed on good authority of the following Napoleonic anecdote. It is related that Napoleon ordered from Bréguet, the famous Paris watchmaker, a watch for his brother Joseph, who was at the time King of Spain. The back was of blue enamel decorated with the letter J in diamonds. In 1813 Napoleon was present at a military parade when a messenger arrived bearing a brief despatch, in which it was stated that the French army had been completely defeated at Vittoria. It was manifest that Spain was lost. Always severely practical, all that Napoleon did, after glancing at the despatch, was to turn to his secretary and say, "Write to Bréguet and tell him that I shall not want that watch." It is believed that the watch was eventually bought by the Duke of Wellington.

XXVIII

SONGS, PATRIOTIC AND NATIONAL

"The Spectator," September 13, 1913

All historians are agreed that contemporary ballads and broadsheets constitute a priceless storehouse from which to draw a picture of the society existing at the period whose history they seek to relate. Some of those which have survived to become generally known to later ages show such poverty of imagination and such total absence of literary merit as to evoke the surprise of posterity at the ephemeral success which they unquestionably achieved. An instance in point is the celebrated poem "Lillibullero," or, as it is sometimes written, "Lilli Burlero." Here is the final stanza of the pitiful doggerel with which Wharton boasted that he had "sung a king out of three kingdoms":

There was an old prophecy found in a bog: Ireland shall be ruled by an ass and a dog; And now this prophecy is come to pass, For Talbot's the dog, and James is the ass. Lillibullero, Bullen-a-la.

Doggerel as this was, it survived the special occasion for which it was written. When Queen Anne's reign was well advanced balladmongers were singing:

So God bless the Queen and the House of Hanover, And never may Pope or Pretender come over. Lillibullero, Bullen-a-la.

If the song is still remembered by other than historical students, it is probably more because Uncle Toby, when he was hard pressed in argument, "had accustomed himself, in such attacks, to whistle Lillibullero," than for any other reason.

But whether it be doggerel or dignified verse, popular poetry almost invariably possesses one great merit. When we read the outpourings of the seventeenth and eighteenth century poets to the innumerable Julias, Sacharissas, and Celias whom they celebrated in verse, we cannot but feel that we are often in contact with a display of spurious passion which is the outcome of the head rather than of the heart. Thus Johnson tells us that Prior's Chloe "was probably sometimes ideal, but the woman with whom he cohabited was a despicable drab of the lowest species." The case of popular and patriotic poetry is very different. It is wholly devoid of affectation. Whatever be its literary merits or demerits, it always represents some genuine and usually deep-rooted conviction. It enables us to gauge the national aspirations of the day, and to estimate the character of the nation whose yearnings found expression in song. The following lines—written by Bishop Still, the reputed author of "Gammer Gurton's Needle"—very faithfully represent the feelings excited in England at the time of the Spanish Armada:

We will not change our Credo For Pope, nor boke, nor bell; And yf the Devil come himself We'll hounde him back to hell.

The fiery Protestant spirit which is breathed forth in these lines found its counterpart in Germany. Luther, at a somewhat earlier period, wrote:

Erhalt uns, Herr, bei deinem Wort, Und steur des Papsts und Türken Mord.

Take again the case of French Revolutionary poetry. The noble, as also the ignoble, sides of that vast upheaval were alike represented in the current popular poetry of the day. Posterity has no difficulty in understanding why the whole French nation was thrilled by Rouget de Lisle's famous song, to whose lofty strains the young conscripts rushed to the frontier in order to hurl back the invaders of their country. On the other hand, the ferocity of the period found expression in such lines as:

Ah! ça ira, ça ira, ça ira! Les aristocrates à la lanterne,

which was composed by one Ladré, a street singer, or in the savage "Carmagnole," a name originally applied to a peasant costume worn in the Piedmontese town of Carmagnola, and afterwards adopted by the Maenads and Bacchanals, who sang and danced in frenzied joy over the judicial murder of poor "Monsieur et Madame Véto."

The light-hearted and characteristically Latin buoyancy of the French nation, which they have inherited from the days of that fifth-century Gaulish bishop (Salvianus) who said that the Roman world was laughing when it died ("moritur et ridet"), and which has stood them in good stead in many an arduous trial, is also fully represented in their national poetry. No other people, after such a crushing defeat as that incurred at Pavia, would have been convulsed with laughter over the innumerable stanzas which have immortalised their slain commander, M. de la Palisse:

Il mourut le vendredi, Le dernier jour de son âge; S'il fut mort le samedi, Il eût vécu davantage.

The inchoate national aspirations, as also the grave and resolute patriotism of the Germans, found interpreters of genius in the persons of Arndt and Körner, the latter of whom laid down his life for the people whom he loved so well. During the Napoleonic period all their compositions, many of which will live so long as the German language lasts, strike the same note—the determination of Germans to be free:

Lasst klingen, was nur klingen kann, Die Trommeln und die Flöten! Wir wollen heute Mann für Mann Mit Blut das Eisen röten. Mit Henkerblut, Französenblut— O süsser Tag der Rache! Das klinget allen Deutschen gut, Das ist die grosse Sache.

Some six decades later, when Arndt's famous question "Was ist das deutsche Vaterland?" was about to receive a practical answer, the German soldier marched to the frontier to the inspiriting strains of "Die Wacht am Rhein."

No more characteristic national poetry was ever written than that evoked by the civil war which raged in America some fifty years ago. Those who, like the present writer, were witnesses on the spot of some portion of that great struggle, are never likely to forget the different impressions left on their minds by the poetry respectively of the North and of the South. The pathetic song of the Southerners, "Maryland, my Maryland," which was composed by Mr. T.R. Randall, appeared, even whilst the contest was still undecided, to embody the plaintive wail of a doomed cause, and stood in strong contrast to the aggressive and almost rollicking vigour of "John Brown's Body" and "The Union for ever, Hurrah, boys, Hurrah!"

Even a nation so little distinguished in literature as the Ottoman Turks is able, under the stress of genuine patriotism, to embody its hopes and aspirations in stirring verse. The following, which was written during the last Russo-Turkish war, suffers in translation. Its rhythm and heroic, albeit savage, vigour may perhaps even be appreciated by those who are not familiar with the language in which it is written:

Achalum sanjaklari! Ghechelim Balkanlari! Allah! Allah! deyerek, Dushman kanin' ichelim! Padishahmiz chok yasha! Ghazi Osman chok yasha!

Let us now turn to Italy and Greece, the nations from which modern Europe inherits most of its ideas, and which have furnished the greater part of the models in which those ideas are expressed, whether in prose or in verse.

Although lines from Virgil, who may almost be said to have created Roman Imperialism, have been found scribbled on the walls of Pompeii, it is probable that in his day no popular poetry, in the sense in which we should understand the word, existed. But there is something extremely pathetic—more especially in the days when the Empire was hastening to its ruin—in the feeling, little short of adoration, which the Latin poets showed to the city of Rome, and in the overweening confidence which they evinced in the stability of Roman rule. This feeling runs through the whole of Latin literature from the days of Ovid and Virgil to the fifth-century Rutilius, who was the last of the classic poets. Virgil speaks of Rome as "the mistress of the world" (maxima rerum Roma). Claudian deified Rome, "O numen amicum et legum genetrix," and Rutilius wrote:

Exaudi, regina tui pulcherrima mundi, Inter sidereos Roma recepta polos, Exaudi, genetrix hominum, genetrixque deorum, Non procul a caelo per tua templa sumus.

Modern Italians have made ample amends for any lack of purely popular poetry which may have prevailed in the days of their ancestors. It would, indeed, have been strange if the enthusiasm for liberty which arose in the ranks of a highly gifted and emotional nation such as the Italians had not found expression in song. When the proper time came, Giusti, Carducci, Mameli, Gordigiani, and scores of others voiced the patriotic sentiments of their countrymen. They all dwelt on the theme embodied in the stirring Garibaldian hymn:

Va fuori d'Italia! Va fuori, o stranier!

It will suffice to quote, as an example of the rest, one stanza from an "Inno di Guerra" chosen at random from a collection of popular poetry published at Turin in 1863:

Coraggio ... All' armi, all' armi, O fanti e cavalieri, Snudiamo ardenti e fieri, Snudiam l'invito acciar! Dall' Umbria mesto e oppresso Ci chiama il pio fratello, Rispondasi all' appello, Corriamo a guerreggiar!

The cramping isolation of the city-states of ancient Greece arrested the growth of Hellenic nationalism, and therefore precluded the birth of any genuinely nationalist poetry. But it only required the occasion to arise in order to give birth to patriotic song. Such an occasion was furnished when, under the pressing danger of Asiatic invasion, some degree of Hellenic unity and cohesion was temporarily achieved. Then the tuneful Simonides recorded the raising of an altar to "Zeus, the free man's god, a fair token of freedom for Hellas."

In more modern times the long struggle for Greek independence produced a crop of poets who, if they could not emulate the dignity and linguistic elegance of their predecessors, were none the less able to express their national aspirations in rugged but withal very tuneful verse which went straight to the hearts of their countrymen. The Klephtic ballads played a very important part in rousing the Greek spirit during the Graeco-Turkish war at the beginning of the last century. The fine ode of the Zantiote Solomos has been adopted as the national anthem, whilst the poetry of another Ionian, Aristotle Valaorites, and of numerous others glows with genuine and perfervid patriotism. But perhaps the greatest nationalist poet that modern Greece has produced was Rhigas Pheraios, who, as proto-martyr in the Greek cause, was executed by the Turks in 1798, with the prophecy on his dying lips that he had "sown a rich seed, and that the hour was coming when his country would reap its glorious fruits." His Greek Marseillaise (Δεύτε παῖδες τῶν Ἑλλήνων) is known to Englishmen through Byron's translation, "Sons of the Greeks, arise, etc." But the glorious lilt and swing of his *Polemisterion*, though probably familiar to every child in Greece, is less known in this country. The lines,

καλλίτερα μιᾶς ὥρας ἐλευθέρη ζωή, παρὰ σαράντα χρόνων σκλαβιὰ καὶ φυλακή,

recall to the mind Tennyson's

Better fifty years of Europe than a cycle of Cathay.

XXIX

SONGS, NAVAL AND MILITARY

"The Spectator," September 20, 1913

A British Aeschylus, were such a person conceivable, might very fitly tell his countrymen, in the words addressed to Prometheus some twenty-three centuries ago, that they would find no friend more staunch than Oceanus:

οὐ γὰρ ποτ' ἐρεῖς ὡς Ὠκεανοῦ φίλος ἐστὶ βεβαιότερός σοι.

In truth, the whole national life of England is summed up in the fine lines of Swinburne:

All our past comes wailing in the wind, And all our future thunders in the sea.

The natural instincts of a maritime nation are brought out in strong relief throughout the whole of English literature, from its very birth down to the present day. The author of "The Lay of Beowulf," whoever he may have been, rivalled Homer in the awe-stricken epithets he applied to the "immense stream of ocean murmuring with foam" (*Il.* xviii. 402). "Then," he wrote, "most like a bird, the foamy-necked floater went wind-driven over the sea-wave; ... the sea-timber thundered; the wind over the billows did not hinder the wave-floater in her course; the sea-goer put forth; forth over the flood floated she, foamy-necked, over the sea-streams, with wreathed prow until they could make out the cliffs of the Goths."

Although the claim of Alfred the Great to be the founder of the British navy is now generally rejected by historians, it is certain that from the very earliest times the need of dominating the sea was present in the minds of Englishmen, and that this feeling gained in strength as the centuries rolled on and the value of sea-power became more and more apparent. In a poem entitled "The Libel of English Policy," which is believed to have been written about the year 1436, the following lines occur:

Kepe then the see abought in specialle, Whiche of England is the rounde walle; As thoughe England were lykened to a cité. And the walle enviroun were the see. Kepe then the see, that is the walle of England, And then is England kepte by Goddes sonde.

A long succession of poets dwelt on the same theme. Waller—presumably during a Royalist phase of his chequered career—addressed the King in lines which forestalled the very modern political idea that a powerful British navy is not only necessary for the security of England, but also affords a guarantee for the peace of all the world:

Where'er thy navy spreads her canvas wings Homage to thee, and peace to all, she brings.

Thomson's "Rule, Britannia," was not composed till 1740, but before that time the heroism displayed both by the navy collectively and by individual sailors was frequently celebrated in popular verse. The death of Admiral Benbow, who continued to give orders after his leg had been carried off by a chain-shot at the battle of Carthagena in 1702, is recorded in the lines:

While the surgeon dressed his wounds Thus he said, thus he said, While the surgeon dressed his wounds thus he said: "Let my cradle now in haste On the quarter-deck be placed, That my enemies I may face Till I'm dead, till I'm dead."

But it was more especially the long struggle with Napoleon that led to an outburst of naval poetry. It is to the national feelings current during this period that we owe such songs as "The Bay of Biscay, O," by Andrew Cherry; "Hearts of Oak," by David Garrick; "The Saucy Arethusa," by Prince Hoare; "A Wet Sheet and a Flowing Sea," by Allan Cunningham; "Ye Mariners of England," by Thomas Campbell, and a host of others. Amongst this nautical choir, Charles Dibdin, who was born in 1745, stands pre-eminent. Sir Cyprian Bridge, in his introduction to Mr. Stone's collection of *Sea Songs*, tells us that it is doubtful whether Dibdin's songs "were ever very popular on the forecastle." The really popular songs, he thinks, were of a much more simple type, and were termed

"Fore-bitters," from the fact that the man who sang them took his place on the fore-bitts, "a stout construction of timber near the foremast, through which many of the principal ropes were led." However this may be, there cannot be the smallest doubt that Dibdin's songs exercised a very powerful effect on landsmen, and contributed greatly to foster national pride in the navy and popular sympathy with sailors. It was presumably a cordial recognition of this fact that led Pitt to grant him a pension. It would, indeed, be difficult to conceive poetry more calculated to make the chord of national sentiment vibrate responsively than "Tom Bowling" or that well-known song in which Dibdin depicted at once the high sense of duty and the rough, albeit affectionate, love-making of "Poor Jack":

I said to our Poll, for, d'ye see, she would cry, When last we made anchor for sea, What argufies sniv'ling and piping your eye? Why, what a damn'd fool you must be! . . . . . As for me in all weathers, all times, tides and ends, Nought's a trouble from duty that springs, For my heart is my Poll's, and my rhino my friend's, And as for my life it's the King's; Even when my time comes, ne'er believe me so soft As for grief to be taken aback, For the same little cherub that sits up aloft Will look out a good berth for poor Jack!

Pride in the navy and its commanders is breathed forth in the following eulogy of Admiral Jervis (Lord St. Vincent):

You've heard, I s'pose, the people talk Of Benbow and Boscawen, Of Anson, Pocock, Vernon, Hawke, And many more then going; All pretty lads, and brave, and rum, That seed much noble service; But, Lord, their merit's all a hum, Compared to Admiral Jervis!

"Tom Tough" is an example of the same spirit:

I've sailed with gallant Howe, I've sailed with noble Jervis, And in valiant Duncan's fleet I've sung yo, heave ho! Yet more ye shall be knowing, I was cox'n to Boscawen, And even with brave Hawke have I nobly faced the foe.

Perfervid patriotism and ardent loyalty find expression in the following swinging lines:

Some drank our Queen, and some our land, Our glorious land of freedom; Some that our tars might never stand For heroes brave to lead 'em! That beauty in distress might find Such friends as ne'er would fail her; But the standing toast that pleased the most Was—the wind that blows, the ship that goes, And the lass that loves the sailor!

The whole-hearted Gallophobia which prevailed at the period, but which did not preclude generous admiration for a gallant foe, finds, of course, adequate expression in most of the songs of the period. Thus an unknown author, who, it is believed, lived at the commencement rather than at the close of the eighteenth century, wrote:

Stick stout to orders, messmates, We'll plunder, burn, and sink, Then, France, have at your first-rates, For Britons never shrink: We'll rummage all we fancy, We'll bring them in by scores, And Moll and Kate and Nancy Shall roll in louis-d'ors.

It was long before this spirit died out. Twenty-two years after the battle of Waterloo, when, on the occasion of the coronation of Queen Victoria, Marshal Soult visited England and it was suggested that the Duke of Wellington should propose the health of the French army at a public dinner, he replied: "D—— 'em. I'll have nothing to do with them but beat them."

Inspiriting songs, such as "When Johnny comes marching home" and "The British Grenadiers," which, Mr. Stone informs us, "cannot be older than 1678, when the Grenadier Company was formed, and not later than 1714, when hand-grenades were discontinued," abundantly testify to the fact that the British soldier has also not lacked poets to vaunt his prowess. Many of the military songs have served as a distinct stimulus to recruiting, and possibly some of them were written with that express object in view. Sir Ian Hamilton, in his preface to Mr. Stone's collection of *War Songs*, says, "The Royal Fusiliers are the heroes of a modern but inspiriting song, 'Fighting with the 7th Royal Fusiliers.' It was composed in the early 'nineties, and produced such an overwhelming rush of recruits that the authorities could easily, had they so chosen, have raised several additional battalions." The writer of the present article remembers in his childhood to have learnt the following lines from his old nurse, who was the widow of a corporal in the army employed in the recruiting service:

'Twas in the merry month of May, When bees from flower to flower do hum, And soldiers through the town march gay, And villagers flock to the sound of the drum. Young Roger swore he'd leave his plough, His team and tillage all begun; Of country life he'd had enow, He'd leave it all and follow the drum.

The British military has perhaps been somewhat less happily inspired than the naval muse. Nevertheless the army can boast of some good poetry. "Why, soldiers, why?" the authorship of which is sometimes erroneously attributed to Wolfe, is a fine song, and the following lines written by an unknown author after the crushing blow inflicted on Lord Galway's force at Almanza, in 1707, display that absence of discouragement after defeat which is perhaps one of the most severe tests by which the discipline and spirit of an army can be tried:

Let no brave soldier be dismayed For losing of a battle; We have more forces coming on Will make Jack Frenchman rattle.

Abundant evidence might be adduced to show that the British soldier is amenable to poetic influences. Sir Adam Fergusson, writing to Sir Walter Scott on August 31, 1811, said that the canto of the *Lady of the Lake* describing the stag hunt "was the favourite among the rough sons of the fighting Third Division," and Professor Courthope in his *History of English Poetry* quotes the following passage from Lockhart's *Life of Scott*:

When the *Lady of the Lake* first reached Sir Adam Fergusson, he was posted with his company on a point of ground exposed to the enemy's artillery; somewhere no doubt on the lines of Torres Vedras. The men were ordered to lie prostrate on the ground; while they kept that attitude, the Captain, kneeling at their head, read aloud the description of the battle in Canto VI., and the listening soldiers only interrupted him by a joyous huzza whenever the French shot struck the bank close above them.

Finally, before leaving this subject, it may be noted that amidst the verse, sometimes pathetic and sometimes rollicking, which appealed more especially to the naval and military temperament, there occasionally cropped up a political allusion which is very indicative of the state of popular feeling at the time the songs were composed. Thus the following, from a song entitled "A cruising we will go," shows the unpopularity of the war waged against the United States in 1812:

Be Britain to herself but true, To France defiance hurled; Give peace, America, with you, And war with all the world.

The sixteenth-century Spaniards embodied a somewhat similar maxim of State policy as applied to England in the following distich, the principle of which was, however, flagrantly violated by that fervent Catholic, Philip II.:

Con todo el mundo guerra Y paz con Inglaterra.

Lightning Source UK Ltd.
Milton Keynes UK
UKOW06f1831180416

272514UK00011B/160/P